JACKIE ROSE

was born and raised in Mo[illegible] now lives with her husband, [illegible] and dog. After cutting her teeth in the publishing world editing a travel magazine, she decided to devote herself to writing full-time. *Slim Chance* is her debut novel.

When she's not looking herself up on the Internet, Jackie likes to spend her time sleeping, shopping and musing about the meaning of it all. She's also currently hard at work on her second book.

For Dan, my one and only love

SLIM CHANCE

JACKIE ROSE

First edition July 2003

SLIM CHANCE

A Red Dress Ink novel

ISBN 0-373-25031-2

Visit Red Dress Ink at www.reddressink.com

Printed in U.S.A.

ACKNOWLEDGMENTS

Thanks to…
Robyn Berman, for lighting a fire under me and keeping it burning. Sam Bell, my devoted editor, for all your help and encouragement, every step of the way. Rachel Pritzker, for being the absolute polar opposite of the mother-in-law in this book. Nelu Wolfensohn, for that whole roof over our heads thing. Riana Levy, Tara Cogan, Wendy Cooper, Kathy De Koven and Ilana Kronick, for being the very paragons of friendship, if not always virtue. Lorne Scharf, photo expert, for the back-cover shot. Rose and Issie Lipkus, for your endless smiles and support. Natalie Rosenhek—aka "Bubba"—for baby-sitting with a passion. Shoel Rosenhek, for getting me started with all those trips to the library. Jordy, for sending news of the world home from New York, London and beyond. Sarah, lover of ideas and pursuer of wisdom, for everything, always. Sandy Lipkus, for being the best teacher I ever had.

And, of course, Abigail,
for helping with revisions from the inside.

1

If you've ever puked at work, it has probably been for one of two reasons—either you're desperately, uncontrollably ill with some type of stomach flu or food poisoning, in which case you're just glad to have made it to the bathroom on time and don't really care if anyone hears you throwing your guts up, or else you're sick in the sort of way you'd prefer to keep to yourself (i.e., violently hung over; just discovered you're pregnant; fired, and so on). That afternoon, as I stared down into the bowl in the unforgiving light of the ladies' room on the third-floor offices of Kendra White Cosmetics, The Second-Largest Direct-Selling Makeup Company In America, I realized that this situation definitely falls into the latter category, the sort of barfing where you pray for privacy while processing the certain knowledge that your entire life as you know it is about to change.

I can't believe I said yes.

Until that moment, thanks to a healthy aversion to mayonnaise and an inherited ability to hold my liquor, I'd never suffered the indignity of being sick in public. Now, though, a gaggle of thick-stockinged co-workers fretted outside the stall door, gossipful glee disguised as concern. They'd seen me bolt for the bathroom. Now they waited for completion.

Please, just let me not puke.

But it was no use. My eyes filled with water, my knees hit the floor and the bowl became my whole world. In my day-to-day life at Kendra White, I make a concerted effort not to put my ass anywhere *near* these toilets. Now, my face was inside one.

An eternity passed, during which time I pretended I was in the Ally McBeal Unisex, so sterile, so sleek, so much *fun*…not at all like this abysmal pit, where ladies' unmentionables are strewn all over the wet floor and the garbage can's always overstuffed. *Oh my God, is that a pubic hair on the seat?*

"Are you all right, Evelyn? Do you need someone to hold your hair back?" Pruscilla Cockburn, my boss, wheezed from the other side.

"No, I'm fine," I gagged.

"Well then, get a hold of yourself, dear. It's only nerves! You're going to make a *wonderful* wife. And what a fellow, that Bruce. He's waiting just outside the door, you know. Gosh! Have you ever *seen* such a romantic proposal? Well I know I certainly haven't—not even on *A Wedding Story,* and I've got every one on tape. I mean, can you *imagine?* Asking her at *work?* In front of *everyone…?*"

At this point, it was obvious she'd forgotten all about me, and was simply sharing with the others. What a hag. I had just suffered the worst sort of humiliation imaginable, my love life savagely ripped from the privacy of my own heart and put on display in front of everyone I hate most in the world, and all Pruscilla could think about was what a great story it would make at the coffee cart tomorrow morning. My entire life had just been turned upside down, and all they could think about was how it affected *them.* I turned away from the bowl and saw four pairs of feet, each in worse shoes than the next. Pruscilla's were stuffed like sausages into worn-out red pumps. She always matches her shoes to her outfits—vast swaths of brightly colored fabric that go under the guise of "caftans" and "capes" in plus-size stores. They should be illegal, as far as I'm concerned.

"I'm okay. I'm coming out," I sniffed, opening the door.

I should have seen it coming. Bruce's proposal, I mean, not the puking.

That morning, for some reason, I read my horoscope, which is something I never do, seeing as how I'm usually far too late to read the paper, or even bring it in, mind you. Plus, I hate touching newsprint—it always ends up all over everything, especially my face. Not that I really believe in astrology anyway. Except for maybe the page at the back of *Cosmo,* since it's a magazine, not a newspaper, and because once I used the lucky numbers and won $125 in the lottery. But I suppose that's numerology.

Anyway, that morning, my horoscope was dead-on, although I had no way of knowing it at the time. The first sign that the planets were aligning against me occurred when I actually woke up early. Well, not so much *early* as just not late. And Bruce, dear that he is, made us breakfast. Three-egg cheese and mushroom omelets—*with* the yolks, of course; none of that whites-only shit for us—and coffee. It was unusual for me to lose my dietary resolve so early in the day (that usually doesn't happen until right before lunch), but I knew that since it was Friday anyway, Monday would doubtlessly be a better time to start watching myself. Better not to spoil the weekend, and all the wonderful meals that might have been.

"Evie, you wanna go out for dinner tonight, just us?" Bruce asked, knowing full well we almost always go out Friday nights, just us. He probably thought he was being adorable for asking, but to tell you the truth he was verging on smarmy. Or maybe it was just that he'd already asked me three times. With our busy career-person schedules, Bruce doesn't always see as much of me as he'd like, so I try to keep our weekly date sacred no matter what. That is, unless his mother, Roberta—known as Bertie to those who love her, or at the very least to those who don't despise her, since not too many people can claim more than that—decides that she wants to have us over for watery soup and boiled potatoes, in which case we drop everything and run directly to the Fulbrights' Greenwich, Connecticut compound for a meal that would make dinner with the Royal Family seem like a hoedown.

I was at the very least glad to hear tonight would not be one of those nights. One Friday a month with his mother is quite enough for me, though Bertie would have us over every week if I didn't put my foot down. It's my theory that these so-called family nights are really just an excuse for her to try and turn Bruce against me, since she obviously thinks I'm stopping him from fulfilling his true potential. And who could blame me? Bertie sets the tone with interview-style questions like "Bruce, do you feel that teaching second grade is a challenge for you, intellectually speaking?" (A: "As you know, Mother, it's a school for gifted children, so yes—it *is* a challenge"). Or perhaps a confusing zinger like, "Evelyn, does being Italo-American give you an edge in the mail-order cosmetics industry?" (A: Well, I'm only one half *Italian*-American, Mrs. Fulbright, but no, I don't think it really makes a difference.")

Then we all sit back and enjoy the show while Bruce's wicked WASPy sisters, Brooke, Wendy and, of course, Diana—each lovelier and thinner and perkier-breasted than the next—turn the emasculation of their older brother into a spectator sport, while at the same time taking an obvious mental inventory of every bite I manage to put in my mouth without gagging. By the end of the night, I'm ready to kill, ready to shake his sweet old dad and say "Wake up! They've got you by the balls, man! Get out now, while you've still got a good 20 years left!" But nobody seems to notice any of it except me, and Bruce and I spend the train ride home fighting.

But we'll save all that for next Friday. Tonight, we're free.

"I was thinking Luna," Bruce continued. "I made reservations for nine."

He knows I love it there. Luna is where my parents had their first date, a blind date. It was where they fell in love the second they laid eyes on each other. When I was little, and sad or not feeling well, I begged my mom to tell me the story over and over, and she would always oblige, sparing no details—what she was wearing, the food they ate, how my dad said she looked like Elizabeth Taylor, only with brown eyes and a bigger butt. I tried to imagine them there, sitting next to the steamy window on a dark winter night. Luna was also where they went to eat the night I was conceived. It was the last time they did it before my dad died, although she left that part out until I was a little older.

Bruce and I always save Luna for special occasions, never more than once or twice a year. And walking around Little Italy makes us horny and couple-y feeling, so it's always a guaranteed good time. There's something so nice about prancing around, arm in arm, flaunting our delirious happiness to the droves of miserable Manhattan singletons out hunting in packs, or, even better, those on obviously painful blind dates. It's like we're members of a private club of two, and it reminds me how being a part of something, no matter how troubled or even depressing it may be at times, is usually far superior to being a part of nothing.

"That sounds all right, sweetie," I said, playing along. Our anniversary was coming up—six years. I figured that's what he had in mind.

"Okay, so I'll call you around lunchtime. Will you be in the office or are you planning to go out?" he asked.

"Um, I should be in all day, but I have a meeting around one." In retrospect, I can see now that he was being unusually inquisitive, but since interest in my workday comings and goings wasn't something Bruce normally displays, his clumsy attempts at making sure I'd be there were lost on me.

"Good, good," he said. "Well, have a nice day, then. Call me if you leave work for some reason."

★ ★ ★

So I was wide-awake, full of omelet and full of energy as I stepped out the door on September 24, a glorious autumn morning, and decided to bring the paper to read on the train, despite the fact that I was wearing my new winter-white three-quarter-length trench from Anne Klein (*Marie Claire,* September: "Revamp Your Fall Wardrobe with These 10 Must-Haves"). It's about a 40-minute commute from our Park Slope apartment in Brooklyn to the midtown Manhattan offices of Kendra White. Normally, I use the time to drift in and out of consciousness. Yes, I'm one of those unfortunate sorts you see on the train or bus whose head lolls to one side like an idiot or whose mouth suddenly drops open. At least once a week I miss my stop, usually twice a week.

That morning, though, I read the paper alongside the other commuters like a real Cosmo girl, maneuvering the pages deftly, spilling my grande latte only once. *There's the usual something or other about Afghanistan on the front page... Better turn to the Entertainment section...oooh, it seems Madonna might be considering having another baby, just as I suspected. That's good. She's such a stylish mom... Bla, bla, bla, Leonardo DiCaprio broke his clavicle tripping over his feet outside a hot but unnamed L.A. nightclub... That little cross-eyed boy from Jerry Maguire has a new movie coming out.... Dreadful, I'm sure... Wonder how far off my horoscope will be for today....*

> Virgo *(August 23-September 22)* See the forest for the trees. Focus on partnership, communication, personal advances. Individual close to you confides, "I need you now more than ever." Keep an eye out for details. Work situation may be stressful, but don't lose your head. Taurus plays key role today. Spotlight on domestic situation, home, cooking. Financial prospects good. Be leery of Uranus, planet of sudden changes. Stay cool! This too, shall pass.

Oh for God's sake, that could mean anything—they really do all sound the same. I can see why Morgan thinks horoscopes are for idiots who feel powerless over their own lives. How utterly ridiculous! As if planets could have any effect whatsoever on what's happening down here on Earth. Except for the moon, maybe. Now that's another story. And it's not really a planet anyway. I've heard that since the moon controls the tides, it can also pull all the water in your body around every which way, accounting for things like PMS and unexplained weight gain....

I woke up only one stop too late. By the time I got off the subway, the front of my trench coat was covered in black smudges and coffee, more than enough to ruin my good mood for the day. Ridiculous—white coats are even sillier than white carpet. What the hell was I thinking?

Upstairs, comfortably ensconced in my gray-carpeted cubicle, I worked hard at online solitaire for a good two hours until I realized that I'd forgotten to forward out Pruscilla's memo regarding that afternoon's staff meeting. *Oh God, no one even knows about it, and it's Friday—half of them are probably out to lunch already.*

As one of the legion of marketing assistants at KW, and, more specifically, as Pruscilla's immediate underling, my responsibilities tend to lean more toward the administrative than the intellectual. A great way to put my four-year honors degree in philosophy (with a minor in psychology) to work, although, to be fair, I suppose my career does allow me to hone my existential angst.

After an hour of damage control and an hour and a half of lunch, I managed to round up most everybody in the department and assemble them in the boardroom. It's not like it would matter much who was there, although pretty much everybody was. Pruscilla, Queen of the Universe and Director of Product Marketing for the East Coast, had called the meeting for no reason really, other than that she likes to call meetings from time to time to berate some of us for our laziness and impress others with her uncanny knack for finding typographical errors in promotional materials *after* they've been printed by the tens of thousands. The usual blame-laying and defensiveness followed, and I was getting quite sleepy, until there was a knock at the door.

And then someone walked in. A tall guy with rounded, wire-rimmed glasses and freckles. I stared at him for a few seconds until I realized that I recognized him. It was Bruce. *My* Bruce. Of course, my first thought was that someone had died. My mother? My heart flew up into my throat. His mother? My heart settled back down to its usual position.

"Wh-what are you doing here?" I stammered, already embarrassed. At this point, the ten or twelve women seated around the boardroom table realized with interest that Bruce wasn't a courier. One of them whispered to me, "Isn't he yours? He's got *roses!*"

And he did. A gigantic bouquet of bloody-looking ones. I know red roses are supposed to signify romantic love and all that, but to me they've always seemed a bit on the cheesy side. Orchids—now those make a beautiful bouquet, or maybe lilies... I glanced around the room nervously. All eyes were on Bruce. Awe and jealousy and confusion hung thick in the air. *Oh, Evie—give it a rest! Red roses are beautiful, and you know it! Most of the desperados in here would drop dead with shock and gratitude if they got even a single half-dead rose on Valentine's Day, and here it was, a Friday afternoon in September, and my man was holding at least two dozen....*

"Evelyn..." Bruce got down on one knee on the floor in front of me. Instantly, my cheeks start to burn. In my peripheral vision, I could see open mouths and stunned faces. None more stunned than mine, I'm sure.

"Evelyn, I came here today to tell you that I love you, that the past six years have been the best of my life, that I cannot imagine my world without you...."

Was he really talking to me?

"...From the day we met in the cafeteria at NYU, when we reached for that same pudding, I knew you were special...." Somebody behind me giggled loudly. Panic set in, along with elaborate fantasies of revenge.

I can barely breathe—how can she laugh? She's ruining my moment. I will kill her, whoever she is, I will kill her. I will drill everybody later and find out who laughed. I bet it was Violet from Skincare. She never really liked me, even though I visited her twice in the hos-

pital after she had those polyps removed. It really makes you wonder how some people can be so selfish and intrusive, especially regarding things that don't even concern them. When it comes to their own amusement, jealous people will do just about anything to take the focus and attention away from those who deserve it....

All of a sudden, everybody laughed, shocking me out of my reverie.

"...which is why you finally agreed to let me take you out to dinner, and promised to throw out that hot plate and never try cooking in your dorm room again!"

Oh God, was he still talking? I had no idea what he'd just said. What the hell was the matter with me?

"So all that to say, that if it wasn't for the New York City Fire Department, I might not be kneeling here before you today," Bruce concluded. Everyone laughed again.

Bruce put the roses down on the table beside me and grabbed my hand. "You're my best friend, Evie, and I adore you. I love you more today than I did yesterday, and I will love you more tomorrow than I do today. And that will be true for every day of the rest of my life..."

Tears suddenly filled my eyes. I blinked and they fell onto my lap. It was undeniably the sweetest thing I'd ever heard. But he wasn't finished. Not by a long shot.

"...So I want to know, Evie...will you do me the honor of becoming my wife?" And just like that, he pulled out a little blue velvet box and opened it up. Everyone gasped.

But I didn't even see it. The room started to spin.

For the next few moments, it was like I'd somehow been dropped into someone else's body on the other side of the world, and everyone was speaking a different language. I couldn't make sense of any of it. Where was I? Who was this guy with the glasses in front of me? He needed a haircut, that was for sure. Time stood still.

"Evelyn?" the man said.

"Evelyn?"

And then, just as quickly, it all came thundering back. It was Bruce, the love of my life. Asking me to marry him. I guess I must have been on autopilot or something because I jumped up and someone that sounded an awful lot like me shouted, "Yes! Yes! Of course I will!" He scooped me up in his arms and then the tears really started and I was laughing and crying and I couldn't stop. Everyone burst up out of their chairs and began clapping and cheering. People from outside heard the fuss and came flowing into the boardroom, incredulous that such a spontaneous display of romance and drama could ever invade the unlikely weekday world of Kendra White. And it was all happening to me. Everyone was looking at *me.*

And then I was running from the room.

When I opened the stall door, four blank faces stared at me through overly made-up eyes.

"I'm all right, I'm all right. I just need to freshen up a bit," I sniffled, managing a smile. "I'm just so *excited.* I mean, I guess I'm in shock. I never expected it, well not like this, anyway. I just can't believe it." It was the truth.

"Aw, it's just like being tossed into a tub full of icewater, hon," laughed Cheryl-Anne, who works in Sales Rep Training and looks the part. "You'll get over it soon enough. When my Dickie proposed to me, I just about flipped my wig." Chuckles all around—she really does wear a wig.

"It was New Year's Eve, and I'd had more than one too many," she continued unnecessarily. "I sure do like to have a good time, though, as you ladies already know. Remember the Christmas party of '98? Oh, *Lord*—the buns on that copy boy. Anyway, when Dickie popped the question, the whole world started to spin, and I just fainted dead away. I was sick for two months after that. But I guess it musta had something to do with the morning sickness!" she shrieked and slapped her thigh.

Everyone hooted like it was the funniest thing they'd ever

heard. As if a drunken, unwed pregnant woman falling flat on her face in the middle of Times Square were a legitimate source of amusement. How could they laugh? I'd seen pictures of her children. They were very disturbing.

"I think you're right," I managed in a weak voice. "It must be nerves." *Back to me now, please.*

"I'm sorry, dear," Winnie from Cosmetics said and grabbed my hand. "This is your day and here we are going on and on. You just have a good cry if you need to and don't worry about a thing. You don't have to go back out there before you're good and ready."

I hugged her and nodded. I didn't really know her all that well, but at that moment, it didn't matter. She was sweeter in one instant than my own mother had ever been, and I vowed then and there not to ditch out on the surprise 50th birthday party I knew was planned for her next Thursday night, although I normally try and get out of those types of things. Hell, I might even chip in for the present.

I straightened myself up a bit and faced the mirror.

Pathetic. I looked as bad as the rest of them. Puffy black eyes, puffy white face, puffy alien body. A distorted imprint of Winnie's pink-and-tan face remained on my collar. My wrinkled, camel-colored CK jacket (*Glamour,* March: "15 Work Essentials You Can't Live Without") strained at the chest, buttons silently groaning. The size twelve felt like a size two. *When did this happen to me?*

But Bruce doesn't seem to mind. He's good that way. In fact, he never really says a thing about my weight, even though I've gained about thirty pounds since we met in my junior year. He just listens patiently as I rail on and on about it, fit after fit, diet after diet, year after year. *Feeding me M&M's all the while... Oh God, that's it, isn't it? He must actually like me fat.*

Funny how it had never occurred to me before now. He must be one of those guys who gets off on it (*Marie Claire,* October: "Men Who Like Their Ladies Large"). But should that piss me off or not? I couldn't decide. Was it wonderful that Bruce loved me no matter how I looked, or was he betraying me by fattening me up just to satisfy his own twisted sexual fetish? My heart began pounding again.

Courage, Evie. Pull it together—now is not the time to lose it. Bruce loves you, you love him, and it's all gonna be okay.

Pruscilla caught my gaze in the mirror, sighed and looked over toward the door dramatically. Bruce was waiting outside. *What to do? What to do?*

I loved him. I really did. Besides, I'd said yes. How could I have let myself say yes if I didn't really want to marry him? And if there was only one thing in this world that I knew for sure, it was to trust my instincts. Always listen to your inner voice—I've taken away at least that from years of watching *Oprah* (plus the fact that liquid diets don't work in the long run).

Bruce was the best thing for me. Everybody knows it—Morgan, all my other friends, Mom, my grandmother. Bruce grounds me. He accepts me. He *loves* me. And even though he usually drives me crazy, we're a perfect match. I'd be a fool to let him go.

So there really was only one thing I could do—plan a fabulous wedding. That, and lose about forty pounds.

2

Later that afternoon, Pruscilla Cockburn stood over me dictating her latest memo, shifting the ample burden of her weight from foot to foot. With each lumbering sway, a noxious waft of Kendra White's "Honeysuckle Garden" perfume, discontinued since 1996, assaulted my senses. Through watering eyes, I squinted at my screen.

"Evie, please try and pay attention. I'll start again. Date it for today." Obviously. "And send it out to the usual team—all the Division Managers."

I typed dutifully.

To: Marketing Department Product Division Managers

cc: Teresa Delallo, Fragrances; Alexis Desmond, Cosmetics; Sophie Swartz, Skin Care; Thelma Thorpe, Hair Care; Elaine Scarfield, Health and Fitness.

As per company policy, employee evaluations will take

place during the last two weeks of October. Please schedule meetings for each of your senior team members during this period, and remind them to schedule evaluation meetings with their own staff. Self-evaluation forms and suggestion sheets must be distributed no later than by the end of next week. See me for the proper forms. Please try to keep these meetings short (no more than 30 minutes)...

"Do you think half an hour is long enough?" I interrupted, remembering my evaluation last year. Pruscilla spent the whole meeting extolling the virtues of a serious attitude. If I ever expected to be promoted, she'd said, then I'd have to start buckling down, taking things seriously. She never so much as glanced at my list of grievances ("Nobody else I know has to work between Christmas and New Year's"; "Why can't we have fat-free creamer in the coffee cart?") and helpful suggestions ("Year-end bonuses should be scaled according to company profits and not employee salaries"). In the end, we ran out of time before I even had the chance to plead my case for a raise, which to my mind, is the whole point of these meetings in the first place.

Pruscilla glared at me and continued.

"...and do not engage in endless discussions regarding salary increases. Notify me regarding any employee whom you feel has met the requirements for a raise..."

"That's good," I assured her. "You're definitely right about that. No sense in wasting time."

"I'm not done yet," she said. "I will be out of the office from October 16 to December 1, so all five Product Division Managers will need to see me within the next two weeks to complete their own evaluations. Please make an appointment with me as soon as possible, as my schedule is already quite full. Pruscilla Cockburn, Director of Product Marketing, East Coast Division."

Pruscilla, gone for six weeks? This was the woman who'd notoriously used a personal day to clean out her desk. She hadn't missed a single day of work in the three years I'd been there.

"You're leaving for *six* weeks?" I asked, barely able to contain myself. My mind was reeling with the possibilities. I could come in late, leave early, take long lunches…

*Wait a second…instead of just slacking off, this could be a great professional opportunity, provided I take proper advantage of the situation. After all, there's supposed to be more to work than just getting away with things and looking busy (*Cosmopolitan, *September: "Seven Secrets to Job Security"). And everyone knows that the higher up you climb on the corporate ladder, the less you actually have to do yourself and the more you can delegate to others, not to mention perks like expense accounts and parking spots.*

This was brilliant! Pruscilla would probably entrust me with everything. As chief note-taker at her biweekly brainstorming sessions, I know exactly how her mind works. Once or twice I even had the feeling she'd taken credit for my work. My gift for product names, especially lipstick, has gone completely unappreciated (Prissy Persimmon, Sycophantic Cinnamon—those were mine!) and I also have a way with words, as my contributions to the wildly successful direct-mailing campaign of the Fall of '99 can attest ("Why Buy Foreign Makeup at Department-Store Prices When You Can Have American Quality for Less, Delivered Right to Your Door?"). With her gone, I could make a real name for myself, maybe even get promoted before she gets back….

Pruscilla interrupted with a thoughtful wheeze, "I'm just taking some time off for personal reasons."

"Are you okay?" I asked, trying to sound concerned. I was still pissed off at her for not giving me the afternoon off. True to form, Bruce had to go back to work anyway, but still—it isn't every day a girl gets engaged, and it's not like I was going to get anything done here. I'd spent the last hour staring at my ring and graciously fielding congratulatory visits from co-workers who'd heard about the proposal.

"I'm fine, nothing to worry about," she replied in a singsong voice about an octave higher than normal.

"Well, I certainly hope so. Six weeks is a long time to be away from the office," I continued, trying to play to her insecurities.

"Thelma Thorpe from Haircare will be stepping in to my position *temporarily* to make sure things run smoothly." Shit.

"Are you sure that's necessary? I can handle..."

"Not to put too fine a point on it," she cut in, "but I need somebody I can trust to stay on top of things. As it is there's going to be a lot more for you to do so you'll have to try very hard to stay focussed, Evelyn. Especially since I'm sure you're going to be preoccupied with your engagement for the next little while."

Nice reversal. I had to hand it to her.

"Don't worry about me. I'm up to speed on everything," I said with a wave of the hand. "And you know I'm not one to get distracted easily. But can I call you if I need to after you're gone? I mean, if there's an emergency or something I can't handle?" I *had* to know what she was up to, if she was leaving town or something.

"No...I don't think so," she said. What the hell was that supposed to mean? "At least not for the first month or so. But we'll work out all the details later. For now, why don't you go home early? You've had quite a day!"

Pruscilla smiled beneficently. I looked at my watch. Five-fifteen. Thanks a lot. I grabbed my bag and coat.

"But come in a bit early Monday morning, say around seven-thirty?" She was still smiling. "We'll sit down and have a quick meeting when it's nice and quiet." Then she leaned in for a hug. "Congratulations again, dear."

"Thanks." An invisible cloud of Honeysuckle Garden all but consumed me.

The subway ride home was a long one. As the train lurched forward, my stomach bubbled and my mind raced, playing over the day's events. Sure, my private life had been dragged kicking and screaming through the office like some kind of circus sideshow, but aside from that, I felt quite good. And the rest of the day had passed pleasantly enough.

Most days at work, I tend to keep to myself more or less, especially since there are really only a handful of people there I actually like. All in all, I think I've managed to maintain just the right combination of professional courtesy, friendly water-cooler approachability and social aloofness. That way, after I'm promoted, the respect I'll need will already be in place. Without that, things can get pretty messy—I heard of one girl down in Accounts who, after a promotion, ended up having to fire her daughter's godmother, a woman she'd worked side by side with for years. Eventually, she became so reviled by the underlings that she was forced to quit, and ended up playing the fiddle in the subway for spare change.

But today, anonymity shattered, I decided to make a show of it. At the coffee cart, I let Andrea, a bitter marketing drone who works in Fragrances, grab my hand to get a better look at The Ring. On cue, it sparkled brilliantly under the fluorescent lights. Inspired by her courage, two other girls skulking nearby came in for a peek.

"That's at least a carat and a half, you know," Andrea said. "I thought your boyfriend was a teacher." The girls behind her laughed. It was well known that Andrea had been expecting Phil, her boyfriend of far too many years, to propose during Labor Day weekend on their romantic Caribbean cruise. But Phil, an actuary, had booked during hurricane season to save a few bucks. He ended up spending the rainy days in their cabin with his laptop, while Andrea played bingo and shopped for gold-plated chain by the foot.

"Oh, he *is* a teacher," I replied coyly. "He teaches gifted children at a private school on the Upper East Side. He went there himself, actually."

"Really? Must pay well," she said, releasing my hand and reaching for a Sweet'n Low.

"Not really," I told her, leaving her to wonder about Bruce's mysterious and wealthy family.

So I'd managed to keep it together quite nicely, apart from that little thing in the bathroom. But Bruce was a pretty good sport about it. He always is when it comes to my dramatics. After I came out of the bathroom, there he was, surrounded by five or six women hanging on his every word, and looking remarkably pleased for a guy whose girlfriend had vomited at the thought of marrying him.

"...I wanted it to be old-fashioned and romantic, a real public declaration of my love, you know?" I heard him saying as I walked up behind him. His fan club quickly scattered at the sight of me and my puffy eyes.

"Are you okay?" he asked, stifling a laugh.

"Yeah," I sniffed, and laughed myself.

"You know, if I didn't think you could handle this, I wouldn't have done it."

"You mean ask me to marry you?"

"No, stupid, I mean ask you here at work!"

"Oh," I replied, feeling a bit foolish. Loud shushing sounds came from behind the bathroom door, but Bruce didn't seem to notice. "Of course I can handle it. I guess I just never expected my professional life and my personal life to collide in exactly this way."

"I just wanted it to be something you'd remember forever. Like a story we'll tell our grandkids, you know?"

"Well, good job, then. But I'm pretty sure I would have remembered it no matter what, even if we were, um, I don't know...walking in the park or something," I said, glaring at the crowd of women pretending to be fixing a photocopy machine nearby.

Bruce just laughed and hugged me. His shirt smelled good, and I buried my face deeper.

"But we never go for walks in the park, Evie. If I'd asked you to go for a walk in the park, you wouldn't have wanted to." True. Walks in the park are for old ladies and people without cable.

"You needed this, Evie. *We* needed this. Shake things up a bit, you know?" He held my tear-stained cheeks between his hands and kissed me. Not a long kiss, but it was more than just a peck. And then he looked at me with a face that, in an instant, said, "You silly, silly thing. Don't you know that I'll take care of you? And whatever problems we may have, we'll work them out. These people, this job, the rest of world, none of it matters. What matters is us, so let's forget all this crap and get on with it!"

Yes, let's get on with it. Bruce has a wonderful way of forgiving me no matter what; it's really one of the things I love most about him. So, once again, even though I'd behaved like a complete idiot, he managed to make me believe I was a completely normal person, and not the freak I truly was.

He kissed me again. Whether it was all the crying or the barfing or the seven cups of coffee or the kiss, I felt a little wobbly. I took it to be the kiss—even though it had been a long time since Bruce made me weak in the knees. He looked into my eyes and smiled. It was pretty obvious that he was pleased with himself. I guess he deserved to be.

We'd talked about getting married before. You don't date a guy for six years and not talk about it. But I really, truly didn't expect it to happen any time soon. For us, or for me, rather, it was more of an abstract idea, like "Of course we'll get married one day. Then we'll move out to the suburbs and buy our kid a pony." But this time it was for real. And the more I thought about it on the ride home, the more I saw that it was a great thing. And on top of it all, for what might have been the first time in his life, Bruce had done something completely on his own. Made a real decision, without consulting me, his mother or anybody. He deserved to feel good. And so did I. Something was finally happening in my life, something real. Like I'd been asleep for years, content to play the woman in the gray flannel suit, only now the alarm clock was ringing.

★ ★ ★

The train was pretty crowded, and I hadn't noticed till then but the man sitting on my right was leaning up against me. Out of the corner of my eye I could see that he was clutching a ratty pink Barbie backpack tied up with brown cord. His left knee bounced up and down frenetically as he tapped his heel against the floor. On one foot, he wore a filthy Reebok cross-trainer smeared with what was probably not rust-colored paint. On the other foot, a purple toe with a black nail stuck out of a dirty sock. Disgusting. *I'm so sick of this shit.* His bulging eyes darted from my hand to my chest then back down to my hand. My Ring! He was staring at my Ring!

Normally, in situations like these, which occur not altogether infrequently on the A Train, I get up and move. But today, the sight of this greasy interloper inspired within me the courage to take a stand for all peace-loving female commuters everywhere.

I looked directly at him and cleared my throat. Bruce would have absolutely killed me. The guy looked up suddenly and when his eyes met mine, he let out a shriek so loud that the force of his very bad breath blew my bangs up off my forehead (*In Style,* April: "The New-Fashioned Fringe: Bangs Are Back!"). With a gasp, I jumped back onto the lady beside me. But she was wearing a Walkman and I guess she hadn't heard him yell, so she freaked out and reflexively pushed me forward into the group of stunned passengers. I reached out wildly for the man standing in front of me wearing a black trench coat (as it turns out, a very sensible color for a trench coat). But he just deflected me and used the opportunity to slide into my seat. I landed on my hands and knees on the floor of the car. The crazy guy, whimpering a little, just rocked back and forth, staring at someone else's hands.

By the time I got home, Bruce was already there. I threw down my newspaper-stained, Pruscilla-smelling, mud-smeared, formerly white trench coat and flopped onto the couch and cried again. We decided not to go for dinner, not to call our parents, not to call our friends. We just stayed in and ordered a pizza. It may not sound romantic, but it was. We talked and talked, and by the time we went to bed, I felt like myself again.

I woke up before Bruce the next morning, something which almost never happens. He's the type who claims not to be a morning person, because it's such an unpopular way to be, but who actually gets up on weekends at the exact same time, almost to the minute, that he does during the week. He usually spends Saturday and Sunday mornings on the Internet researching obscure factoids for his students or doing the grocery shopping or reorganizing my closet, while I sleep till noon and then thrash about in bed for a half hour or so complaining about him making noise. Like Bruce, I suppose I have an internal clock, too, it's just that mine must be permanently set on Snooze because I've been working full-time since college and waking up at 7:00 a.m. was as torturous yesterday as it was my first day of work. I think it bugs the crap out of him, my sleeping in—his early-morning antics sure piss *me* off—although he'd never admit it. Let him think I'm lazy. I am.

In that blissful moment of nothingness before I opened my eyes, before true awareness set in, the first thing I remembered was that it was finally Saturday. *Thank God, no work. Maybe I'll just go back to sleep for a bit. Then later I'll go into the city. Yeah. There's that Clinique Gift With Purchase thing on now at Saks...and I need some new pants for work. But I refuse to buy a size 14. Okay, so no clothes shopping till I've dropped 15 pounds, till I'm a 10. Serves me right, after what I ate this week, and last night, that pizza...wait a minute...the pizza...ohmygod...Bruce....*

And it all came flooding back. I turned over and looked at him. He lay on his back, still asleep, his chest rising and falling. Bruce always seems different without his glasses on, like I don't really know him. Still cute, though. He was whistling softly through his nose. *Did I really say yes? Did yesterday really happen? Am I actually going to marry this guy?* My heart began to pound as I replayed the scene at work in my head about 37 times. *God, I can't believe I actually threw up.* With a psychic snort, Bruce turned over and faced the wall.

Just to make sure it was all real, I pulled my left hand out from under the pillow. The room was dark, but there it was, plain as day—The Ring. Turns out it was his grandmother's. Mr. Fulbright had kept it for Bruce since she died, like, twenty years ago. Last night was nice, come to think of it. Bruce told me all about how he'd been planning to propose, and how his dad had been in on the whole thing.

"My grandfather gave her this ring in 1939, the night before he left to fight in the war," Bruce explained as he held my hand. "Six months later, he came back and married her. And nine months after that, my father was born in an air raid shelter during the Blitz." Over the years, the Fulbright Nativity Story has evolved into an epic tale, complete with evil Nazis and valiant R.A.F. pilots fighting to the death in the Battle of Britain, including Bruce's grandfather, shot down three months before little Bruce Jr. came into the world.

I already knew the story, minus the ring detail. Bruce's dad, whose name is also Bruce (Bruce Jr., actually—yes, that makes *my* Bruce, Bruce Fulbright III. God, that better not make me Mrs. Bruce Fulbright III), loves talking about the night he was born. The only time he's ever animated about anything seems to be when he's telling stories about the war and his parents and the horror of butter rations and all that. It was as if being born was the only thing Bruce Sr. had ever done with any style, and it's been all downhill from there.

Poor Mr. Fulbright. With the exception of Bruce, the only respect his family ever shows him is when he's telling his stories, now only once or twice a year, usually on his birthday. His perpetually self-involved daughters know better than to dismiss him on this, and even Bertie tries her hardest to refrain from seeming bored. And while Bruce doesn't quite hang on his dad's every word like he probably did when he was a kid, now he listens intently. I'm sure trying to memorize every word so that one day he can tell his own kids. Make that our kids, I guess.

"An insane woman tried to steal the ring—*this very ring*—off her finger while she was in labor," Bruce continued, almost in a whisper. This was a new twist. Sounds like ole Bruce Jr. was getting a bit carried away.

"Oh, come on," I said, incredulous.

Bruce raised his eyebrows and cocked his head to one side. "I'm just telling you what he told me when he gave it to me."

I looked down at The Ring, imagining a stoic, placenta-splattered Granny Fulbright fending off crazies in the bomb shelter as she simultaneously struggled to birth a child and hang on to the only thing she had left of her dead war-hero husband.

It made me think about my mom and what she must have gone through having me all alone, especially since her parents had disowned her because my dad wasn't Italian, or even Catholic for that matter. But then I wondered if Granny Fulbright would have cruelly refused to let her child go to school in California, even though she'd scored over 1300 on her SATs and had a partial scholarship to UCLA… Oh, no wait…that was *my* mother. And *I* was the one stuck at NYU, pissing distance from the house I grew up in. No, there would be no great collegiate adventure for me. But that's where I met Bruce, so I suppose it had all worked out for the best. If you consider marrying your first real boyfriend the best.

So last night was pretty good. We talked a ton about the wedding, what we wanted and all that. And we really laid our cards on the table. Bruce is as far from a commitmentphobe as is humanly possible in this city (*Glamour,* April: "Is Your Man Afraid To Commit? Take This Test and Find Out!"), so the usual male worry of only being able to have sex with one person for the rest of his life doesn't really seem to concern him. "Evie, I would have asked you two years ago if I thought you were ready," he'd said while massaging my feet.

"How can you ever really be ready for something like this," I mused, but he just looked at me, not understanding at all how marriage isn't the most comfortable or logical step for some people.

No, Bruce's marital stress comes from more of a mama's boy place. He was worried, and rightly so, that his mother was going to give him a hard time about it, especially since his dad didn't even tell her he'd given Bruce his mother's ring.

"Especially since she hates me, you mean," I said.

"She doesn't hate you. She's just a negative person sometimes. And she'll think my dad went behind her back. I think she wanted to give the ring to Brooke, 'cuz she's the eldest daughter or something I guess."

"Oh great. Now Brooke will hate me, too."

"Oh, Evie, don't say that. She won't."

"Yeah right. Then it'll be my fault when she loses it and has another one of her 'spells.'" His sister is a frail, skittish girl with four full-blown nervous breakdowns under her belt and she's barely twenty-four. "She'll probably cry as soon as she sees the ring on my finger."

And that's a scene I can look forward to witnessing in person tomorrow night when we "stop by" to break the good news. Bruce's dad was so excited about the whole thing that he made Bruce promise we'd come as soon as possible.

"I doubt it," Bruce said.

"You just watch—she'll be back in the looney bin by the end of the week," I said, then instantly regretted it. Sometimes, I can go a little too far. It's not that I don't mean what I say, it's just that I know that some thoughts are better left unsaid, especially when it comes to things like people's families or haircuts. I think I get my big mouth from Claire, my grandmother. Only she gets away with murder because she's old, and people seem happy to confuse her brutal honesty with quaint eccentricity.

"Sorry," I mumbled.

"It was a relaxation facility, not a looney bin," Bruce said, peeved. "They didn't strap her down or anything." He knows I know that—he's only told me like a thousand times—but he can't control himself either, sometimes.

Despite my occasional overstepping of boundaries, it's this sort of honest interchange about important things like family that convinces me that Bruce and I may actually have a chance. And in my own defense, there is an upside: There's no point in letting the little things fester into giant, repressed issues when a bit of well-directed hostility can bring stuff out into the open right away. And so we make a point of being very open with each other about everything, although it's not a natural thing for Bruce to be like that. He's much more reserved when it comes to saying what's on his mind, especially if it involves hurting someone's feelings, but I've been helping him to try and get over that a little bit.

It was in this spirit of openness that I admitted to Bruce later in the conversation that the idea of marriage makes me a bit crazy.

"It does? I thought the puking and crying meant you were calm and rational about the whole thing," he laughed.

"I'm glad you can laugh about it already," I told him. "That's a good sign, I'm sure."

"Yeah, well, I hope so. But I think we'll leave that part out when we're telling our grandkids the story."

"Seriously, Bruce. I'm really sorry. I don't know what came over me."

"Don't worry. Have another piece of pizza. And don't be so hard on yourself."

I wanted to tell him that I knew that getting married was the next logical step in our relationship, and that it was definitely the right thing for us. Because we love each other and that's what's important. And not to worry about me—that I was ecstatic and sure and positive and all that sort of thing. But I don't think he wanted to talk about it anymore.

But there I was the next morning, lying in bed in a full sweat, feeling an awful lot like I had the day before in the bathroom. It was almost twenty minutes before my heart stopped thumping and I had psyched myself into a "Marriage is Good" place again.

After mentally planning my nuptial dietary strategy for a good half hour—wavering back and forth between invoking the Member for Life clause in the Weight Watchers contract and developing a simple starvation plan on my own—I was firmly back in the camp of, "I'm getting married and I'm gonna look like a million bucks!" Trying not to ruin Bruce's first attempt at sleeping in in years, I snuck out of the bedroom and into the kitchen and put a pot of coffee on. There were so many people who had no idea what had happened, and it was too cruel to keep them in the dark any longer.

3

First things first. I had to call Morgan—it was outrageous that I'd been engaged for almost *24 hours* and she didn't know.

In high school, Morgan Russell and I were the quintessential loser odd couple—she, tall and freckly and skinny; me, dumpy and short and dark. By the time she came back from Berkeley, though, she was a bombshell. I, on the other hand, have remained vaguely potato-shaped over the years, although my skin has cleared up some. But Morgan is the kind of person who makes you not hate beautiful people. She's just like that—smart, bitchy, funny, but still with enough hang-ups that it just gives you faith. She's definitely no fun to shop with, though, not just because everything looks good on her, but because she hates it. She lets salesgirls dress her, and says things like, "Just give me what that mannequin in the window is wearing, in a size four."

"Hello?" her husky voice whispered on the other end.

"Morgan? Wake up. It's me."

"What time is it? Did I oversleep?"

"No, no. It's almost eleven. I just wanted to talk to you," I said. "What did you do last night?" I asked, not really caring.

"I'm going back to sleep," she said, and hung up.

I called her back.

"What do you want, Evie? I didn't get to bed till seven."

"You're already up, or else you wouldn't have answered the phone."

"Your logic astounds me," she said. I could hear her lighting a cigarette.

"So what did you do?"

"I went out with Billy, remember?"

"Oh, yeah. Did you have fun?" Billy is Morgan's latest fling—thirty-seven years old, an architect, Ivy League, the whole deal. I get the sense that he's a bit less uptight than her usual assortment of asshole Wall-Street types. She met him a few months ago at Lemon Bar, which to me sounds more like a dessert than a suitable place to meet men, but Morgan isn't interested in finding Mr. Right. She gave up on that urban legend a long time ago.

"We met up with some of his college friends. Dreadful bunch. They've all got debating trophies stuck up their asses. It makes you wonder, you know? How a person you like can like people you hate?"

"I thought you didn't like Billy, either," I reminded her. Because of her bad instincts, Morgan had sworn off dating anyone she liked. After college, she had a string of bad luck with men she all thought were The One. The first guy, Tom, turned out to be gay, and was only dating her, he eventually realized, because something about her reminded him of Joan Crawford. Morgan didn't find out her next boyfriend, Ryan, was married until after they'd been together for six months, and Matthew, the last guy, whom she was with for almost three years, was the most damaging of all of them—emotionally unavailable. After him, she decided it was best to stick with guys she was sure *weren't* The One.

"I don't like Billy. Not really, I guess. I mean, he's okay. More fun than his friends, anyway. I think it's because he's from Detroit."

"*Detroit?* How can being from Detroit make somebody fun?"

"He sort of has that sexy working man thing going on," she said sulkily.

"Morgan, he's not exactly blue-collar, he's an *architect* for chrissake," I said. "You're talking like he wears overalls to work."

"He actually did work at GM one summer," she added.

"Oh, well there you go—you don't like his personality or his friends, but he worked on an assembly line for one month and that makes him somehow more noble than the spoiled overachievers you usually date."

"Now you get it!" she laughed. "Evie, it's not that I don't like him, I do—he's just not someone I plan to get all crazy about."

"Just because his friends aren't your thing doesn't mean he's not a nice guy," I said, trying to get back to the point. "I hate Bruce's friends, and look at us."

"I know, but I don't really give a shit about Billy's friends anyway. Come to think of it, I don't really care if he's a nice guy or not. If he can get me to forget about work and take me out for a few drinks and a good meal, and then not want to spend the whole night cuddling, that's all I want. I don't give a good goddamn about anything else right now."

"Are we still talking about Billy?" I asked. "He'd want to cuddle with you if you had leprosy." The guy is so bloody crazy about her that he turned down a better job in Philadelphia to wait around for her scraps of affection. And he *is* a nice guy, no matter how hard she tries to pretend he isn't. I suddenly realized how much fun it would be if Morgan and I were engaged at the same time. If I could get her to see what a good idea marriage is, and if Billy didn't scare her off too soon…

"He told me that he wants me to stop seeing other guys," she sighed. So much for picking out wedding dresses together.

"Gee, what a surprise. What did you say?" I asked, knowing the answer.

"I told him to piss off and then let his best friend do body shots off my stomach."

"Seriously, Morgan."

"I said that he knew what I was all about when we got into this thing, and that I wasn't really willing to date one guy exclusively—take it or leave it."

"But you *have* been dating him exclusively. It's not like you have someone else waiting in the wings," I pointed out, pouring my third cup of coffee.

"I know, but he's definitely not someone I want to get tied down to."

"Why not?" Did she think getting tied down was a bad idea in general? Would she think I was making a bad choice?

Morgan sighed. "Evie, I'm sick of having this conversation with you. Why are you pushing me so hard about this?"

"Bruce asked me to marry him," I blurted out.

Silence.

"And I threw up."

More silence.

"Morgan?"

"We've been talking about Billy for *ten minutes* and *now* you tell me this? What the hell's the matter with you?" she shrieked. "So old Brucie finally got around to it! I knew he would, you know. I knew it! I just had this feeling. I really did. Last week when you were talking about how you wanted to take a leave of absence in June as soon as Bruce finishes school and go trekking through South America for the summer and he just didn't say anything. Aw, I *knew* it! It was either that or he was dumping you!"

I guess she realized then there might be a little more to the story. "You said yes, right?" she asked, in a much smaller voice.

"Of course I said yes. Why didn't you tell me you suspected?" I snapped, relieved. It sounded like she thought it was a good idea. Morgan has always believed that I was meant for monogamy. She doesn't think I have the emotional fortitude to handle dating more than one person. Know thyself, she says.

"Oh, come on. I can't believe the thought hadn't occurred to you. Tell me everything! Did you really throw up?"

"I did," I said proudly, and told her the whole story. She particularly liked the part about me falling down on the train.

"It's incredibly important to me that you think this is okay," I admitted. The truth was, if she didn't think it was a good idea, I'd almost be tempted to call the whole thing off, crazy as that might sound.

"Evie, you don't need me to tell you that. It shouldn't matter what I think, technically anyway. But I love Bruce, and I love you and I love the two of you together. You need each other. He wouldn't know what to do without you. And you're a much better person when you're with him. And since you're not breaking up anytime soon, you might as well tie the knot!"

"That's exactly how I feel about it!" I knew she'd understand. "And I hope you know that this doesn't mean things are going to change. We can still do all the things we planned, like our California road trip. Bruce doesn't have to come."

"You bitch!" Morgan laughed, impressed.

"Well, maybe we can all go together—you, me, Bruce and Billy."

She snorted and said, "As long as they take a separate car."

Morgan really is happy for me, which is good, since she's the only one whose opinion counts. Whenever Bruce and I hit a rough spot, like when he wanted to get a cat, and I said I'd prefer to eat a cat, she knew just what to say to make me feel like I wasn't being a bitch. There's a very fine line between being right and being wrong, and Morgan helps me not to cross onto the wrong side. After all these years, she knows Bruce almost as well as I do, and isn't afraid to point out what a jerk I can be, or how rare it is to find a guy you can trust.

Morgan's a hell of a lot better at getting me to see the errors of my ways than my mom is, especially when Bruce and I are in a fight. Somehow, Mom has a way of getting Bruce to sound like medicine that'll cure what's wrong with me. It just makes me want to go home and flush him down the toilet.

Since I was still a little pissed off at her for last month's whole therapy debacle (*Cosmopolitan,* August: "Does Your Mother Need Help? Tell It To Her Like It Is!"), and lest her reaction have the unanticipated side effect of me changing my mind, I thought I'd spare myself the trauma of a live scene and call her with the good news on speakerphone instead. I like secretly putting her on speaker. Bruce never used to believe me when she said something awful. At first he felt a bit guilty about it, but after he heard all the hideous things she says to me, he could no longer deny the pure entertainment value.

"Oh, Evelyn," she sniffed, "I'm so happy for you." Understatement of the century. She's been dreaming about this moment for twenty-seven years. "I knew he'd get around to it eventually, but I was starting to wonder. It's not like you're getting any younger! Bruce are you there?"

She often has trouble choosing between the high road and the low road.

"Hi, Lilly. I'm here," he said, stifling a laugh.

"Mom, wait till you hear how he proposed," I said.

"Good, Bruce. You did good. So now you'll officially be part of the family!" she said, ignoring me.

"That's why I asked her." Part of Bruce's mission in life is to impress my mom.

"You got yourself a special girl, Bruce," she continued. "You know that. Truth be told, though, *she's* the lucky one. That's what I've been telling her for years. But whether she'll make a good wife or not, who knows?" They both cackled like hyenas.

"Ha, ha," I said. "I'm still here, you know."

"She's going to make a great wife," Bruce said, and squeezed my hand. "I have no doubt about that."

"Well at least with Evie you can be sure there's always gonna be enough to eat around the house!" she finished triumphantly. Bruce knew better than to laugh at this, although it looked like he wanted to.

"Aw, Lilly, you're right. Evie *is* a great cook."

Mom snorted. I don't know which was more absurd to her—the fact that I might be a good cook (which I'm not) or the fact that her witless insult might accidentally have been misconstrued as a compliment.

"I'm pretty sure that's not what she meant," I said. Bruce snickered, and I shot him my meanest "you're gonna get it later" glance.

"I just can't believe it—*my* Evelyn, a married woman," she said sweetly, and sighed. "After all these years...I just...I just..."

"You just *what?*" Enough already.

She somehow managed to compose herself, and continued. "I just never thought I'd be around to witness it." I could just see her there, sitting at the kitchen table in her tiny apartment, her bottom lip trembling for effect with each tearful breath even though there was nobody around to witness it. She was trying to win Bruce back to her side.

"You're really something," I exploded. "Bruce is NOT impressed with this and neither am I. This silliness has got to stop. I mean, do you actually expect me to believe you thought you'd be DEAD before anyone wanted to marry me? Thanks a lot, but I don't *believe* you!"

Bruce shook his head. "Now you've done it," he said under his breath.

"Oh, Evelyn," she sobbed, "being alone in this world is an awful, awful thing, and I wouldn't wish it on my worst enemy. To go through life alone is a curse...a *punishment*. I'm just thankful that at least you won't have to." There was that pesky high road, with a healthy dollop of guilt thrown in for good measure.

I wasn't going to let her see that I felt bad. "Well you don't have to worry about me anymore, Mom. I finally tricked some poor unsuspecting slob into marrying me."

"I'd resent that if it weren't true," Bruce said. I laughed silently.

"Evelyn, dear, please don't joke," she sniffed. "Marriage is a holy institution." So now she was pious.

It just wasn't worth the aggravation. "Jeez, Mom, I never said you should be in an *institution,* I just thought maybe you should go and see someone. I think I've heard more than enough about this whole therapy thing. God, I wish I'd never brought it up." It was either tease her or lose it completely.

"I don't know what I'm going to do with you," she sighed, exasperated. "Bruce loves you so much, Evelyn. And you love him so much." Was that a direct order?

"So?"

"Marriage is a blessed union," she continued. "Your whole lives are opening up before you. And it all starts with a wedding. A wedding! Oh, your grandmother will be so delighted. She'll just flip out. Bruce, you'll be making an old woman very, very happy."

"C'mon, Mom, you're not *that* old," I said.

"Acch, you know what I mean, Evelyn. She really will be so happy to hear the news. Bruce, call her right away. Right now."

Claire, my father's mother, is pretty much the only family I have, aside from Auntie Lucy, Mom's twin sister, who lives in England with her lame husband Roderick. After my dad died, Claire took Mom in for a few years, to help out with me and to get her back on her feet. If she hadn't been around, I don't know how Mom would have survived, especially since her own parents wouldn't have anything to do with her. It's not that I don't understand the impulse to reject my mother; I do, but what a bunch of assholes they must have been to leave a grieving widow out in the cold just because my dad wasn't Catholic. I know she tried to make peace with them a few times; after her mother died, when I was eight, she even brought me over to meet her dad, but he wouldn't open the door. So Claire just kind of became her surrogate parent, united in grief and all that, I guess.

She's the quintessential cool old lady, painting and taking classes and teaching self-defense to other rich old bags on the Upper East Side. My grandmother has also always been the arbiter between Mom and me. If it wasn't for Claire, I probably would have killed her by now, especially after she wouldn't let me go out West to school.

"We'll call her right now," I said.

"A wedding, at last! It's going to be a real celebration," Mom went on, her voice rising. I could hear ice cubes clinking in a glass. "Just like a fairy tale!"

"Let's not get ahead of ourselves," Bruce interjected, sensing danger. We'd already decided that we wanted something very low-key, very elegant. I could just picture the big church wedding of my mother's dreams—our worst nightmare.

"Well, whatever you want. As long as it actually happens, I don't care," she lied. "That you love each other, that you're together, that you've opened your hearts to love—that's the most important thing." This from a woman who's refused to go on a date in almost fifteen years.

Pruscilla worked me to the bone all week, to the point where all I wanted to do when I got home was eat dinner and go to bed. Okay—so that's what I do every night. But this week I'd really planned to go for a jog every day after work and take at least three yoga classes at the Y (*In Style,* May: "Why the Stars Choose Yoga To Stay Fit").

All this to say that I'd been engaged for over a week and had hardly told anybody yet. Not that I have a ton of friends; I prefer to limit my circle to a select few. Aside from Morgan, the only people I ever really hang around with are my roommates from college. Morgan doesn't really like any of them too much. She thinks they're all about getting ahead and giving it. I'd long ago given up on trying to integrate her into the group. Besides, they didn't like her much, either.

When I did finally get around to sharing the good news, not everyone was as enthusiastic as Mom and Morgan. When I told Nicole, who might more aptly be called my arch rival than my friend, all she could manage after a weak "OhmygodI'msohappyforyou" was, "Didn't you just tell me last week that you were ready to move to L.A. with or without him?" It was true, I had said that. But it was only because I'd just found out that day that I didn't get that internship with *The Tonight Show.* It was a load of crap, frankly, because I knew I could write funnier stuff than the drivel they churn out every night. I didn't even tell Bruce about it, but I assumed he'd move out there with me if I did manage to get a job like that.

After letting me know in her own subtle way that she knew that Bruce and I have our problems, all Nicole really wanted was to be reassured that she was going to be a bridesmaid. "Of course you will!" I assured her. She's heavier than I am. Not a lot, but enough.

Annie couldn't get off on Sunday afternoon, so we all agreed to meet her at work. The girl has the voice of an angel but the nose of a toucan, so getting work on Broadway (or even far, far off Broadway) was proving to be a little more of a challenge than her drama teacher had let on. Now she was waitressing at Grinds, an unpopular little café in the East Village. Over coffee and cheesecake (saboteurs, all of them!) the consensus seemed to be that I am a fabulously lucky girl to have found Mr. Right in New York City *before* the age of thirty.

"You really look different," breathed Annie, almost dropping my slice of Double Chocolate Oreo onto my lap. "You're positively glowing."

"Oh, come on," Nicole said, rolling her big brown eyes. "It's not like she lost her virginity—she's just getting married."

"Well, I do feel different. Like all the work we've put into our relationship has finally paid off. My whole *life* seems clearer now," I said matter-of-factly. "Everything's changed. For the first time ever, I can see the years stretching out in front of me and I'm not completely terrified, because I know that Bruce and I will be together forever." Annie's eyes widened at the romance of it all.

Okay, so I may have been laying it on a little thick. But it was hard not to when Nicole was so obviously jealous.

"The only thing different about you will be your ass if you keep eating cheesecake like that. And you're talking like you just won an Oscar. '*And I'd like to thank the Academy for helping me accept the proposal, and to Bruce, for the ring, and to...*'"

"Knock it off, Nic," Kimby snapped. "This is a big deal."

"Yes, *please.* If you girls are going to get into a catfight, at *least* let me get my camera," said Theo with a wave of his hand. Kimby and Theo are from the same sad little town in Iowa. They've been virtually inseparable since senior year of high school, when they tied for Homecoming Queen. They still live together, unable to deal with New York alone, even though Theo is making it big as a photographer and Kimby's tours of the Museum of the Modern Art have garnered much acclaim.

"I don't see you turning any cake down," I pointed out.

"Maybe not," Nicole said with a grin. "But *I'm* not the one who has to look better than I ever have in my entire life by next summer."

"Meow," whispered Theo.

"Well then you can just give me back my ThighMaster, then, since it's just obviously collecting dust at your place," I said. That might have been a bit mean. She'd had it for about two and half years, and very little progress had been made, although this probably wasn't the right moment for pointing that out. I'd already decided that I was going to have to be extra nice to everyone for the next little while (*Martha Stewart Weddings,* Fall: "How To Be a Gracious Bride-To-Be").

Yes, sensitivity to my friends' feelings would be crucial, now more than ever, especially since none of them had ever really managed to hang on to a boyfriend for more than thirty seconds, and in Theo's case, maybe twenty. Nicole, most of all, would be the hardest hit, I predicted, since she hadn't even had a boyfriend, yet alone been laid, since that brief (four-and-a-half-day) dalliance with her anthropology T.A. almost three years ago. And even though Nicole and I usually enjoy trading insults, this certainly wasn't the time to rub my prenuptial bliss in her face.

"Oh, I'm just teasing you, Nic," I said. "Everyone knows that thing doesn't work for shit and that Suzanne Somers had liposuction anyway. Nobody has thighs like that naturally." Nicole smiled wanly and had another bite of pie.

Even if I was the only one with a long-term prospect at this point, I'd spent five years watching them (except Nicole) flit more or less happily from man to man. On occasion, I'd even envied them their freedom. But now it was easy to see how *they* might be envying *me.* I was really going to have to try and be more compassionate.

Kimby took a sip of her grande skinny hazelnut-pumpkin latte and cleared her throat. "Let's change the subject."

"Yes, let's," Theo said, obviously disappointed that things weren't going to get any uglier.

Annie returned from the kitchen with another round. "Fill us in about the plans. I need details!"

"Well, as Nicole so indelicately pointed out, we don't really have that much time to pull this thing together if I want to be a June bride," I said. "And things are already getting dicey."

"You mean with Bruce?" Nicole perked up, hopeful.

"No," I said, glaring at her. "Just with the plans. First off, the date we wanted was Saturday the tenth of June, but it's booked everywhere...."

"Hotels? Churches? What are we talking about?" asked Kimby impatiently.

"My mom wanted a church..."

"Of course," said Annie, a lapsed Catholic herself.

"...but Bruce and I insisted on a hotel or an inn. Thank God Bertie agreed, because they'll pretty much be paying for the whole thing...."

"Uh-oh," said Kimby softly.

"World War Three, anyone?" Theo said. Kimby bowed her blond head and looked at her lap, her narrow shoulders shaking with silent laughter.

"Yeah well, whatever, but she's been on the phone all week

trying to find a place. I don't think it's going to be all that bad, you know. Bertie may be a lot of things, but cheap isn't one of them," I finished defensively.

"Did she know Bruce was going to propose?" Annie asked.

"No..."

"Did she *freak?*" Nicole always wanted the gory details.

"It wasn't as bad as we thought, really. When we told her she seemed totally confused at first, but then she made a big show of it. I think she was in shock, completely overwhelmed. Who could blame her? I'm stealing away her only son."

"That's one way to look at it," Annie said. "But hopefully she sees it as gaining another daughter."

"Not this bitch," said Theo. "But your optimism is refreshing, Annie."

"Well, she did force herself to hug me," I continued. "Bruce doesn't believe me, but I swear it was the first time the woman's ever actually touched me. Can you believe that? I didn't realize it till I felt her bony ribs. She was even crying a bit. I wouldn't say it was exactly *nice,* because I was uncomfortable as all hell, I won't lie to you, but it was...I don't know...almost normal."

I was censoring, but just a bit. The first thing Bertie did when we told her we were getting married was give Bruce's dad The Look, and then she excused herself politely to go see to the roast. I was immediately pissed off for Bruce's sake, but he seemed more amused by it than hurt, thank God. When she came back out of the kitchen a few minutes later, she was crying—that was when she hugged me—but she smelled like onions, and her finger was bleeding.

"I don't think she was really all that surprised," I lied. "Bruce's dad knew about it the whole time, so he was probably acting like a freak for weeks beforehand. I'm sure she knew something was up."

"Yes, but could she really have expected this?" Theo sighed. "Her precious Bruce, heir to the Fulbright Jam and Jelly empire, marrying a sloppy Italian wench from Brooklyn. *Your* mother got the prize in this scenario, my dear. Bruce is like your mother's knight in shining armour—he fixes her toilet, he does her taxes, and he saved you from the shame of spinsterhood. This wedding is the answer to all her prayers. But what do you do for Bertie?"

"What?"

"I mean, what does she get out of you? Out of your relationship with Bruce? Nothing but a headache, I bet. You spare the maid from doing Bruce's laundry, that's about it."

"That's not true," I pointed out. "Bruce does his own laundry. And mine."

"How silly of me. Of course he does. Just remember though, Bertie's got plenty of daughters already, so it's not like she needs our young Martha Stewart over here to accompany her on afternoon shopping dates or to take care of her when she gets old. This is probably a living nightmare for the woman."

I was incensed. "For your information, Theo, Bruce likes doing laundry. And Bertie called me the next night and we talked about what kind of wedding we want. So she's obviously accepting this."

"Don't be naive. She's got a few tricks up her sleeve, yet," he said.

"What about his sisters?" asked Kimby. Bruce's sisters were a source of endless amusement for all who knew of them. Even Morgan listened with bated breath to tales of their tantrums and addictions.

"His sisters were okay about it, I guess. They just sort of nodded and smiled. Except for Brooke..."

"Is that the oldest one?"

"Yes. She's the one who wanted to go to help free Tibet until she found out that it was in Asia."

Everyone nodded, remembering.

"Well, Brooke kind of seemed like she was about to cry at any moment, and she kept staring at The Ring!"

Annie slapped the table. "That jealous bitch!" she said, with an uncharacteristic touch of venom. "She thinks it should be hers."

"Bruce's dad, though—he's the best. He's just so happy for us about this. It's like he has a new reason to live or something...."

Annie just wanted more details. "And what about the dress, and flowers, and..."

"She's only been engaged for a week, for chrissake," Nicole interrupted.

"Actually, I *do* have a few ideas," I said, reaching into my bag. Thankfully, there's an excellent magazine store in the lobby of the Kendra White building, so I'd already amassed quite a stack of reference materials. "*Martha Stewart Weddings, Bridal Guide, In Style Weddings, Bride*—I can't get enough! I *swear,* I'm going to keep them all in business this year!" I said, and put the stack on the table.

Nicole rolled her eyes, but grabbed *Martha Stewart Weddings* before anyone else could. "What a hideous cake," she said of the picture on the cover.

"Oh, please!" shrieked Theo. "It's fabulous! Marzipan is *so* hard to work with. You just don't get it—it's supposed to look like Wedgewood china. You know, you could do something like this, Evie."

"Let's worry about the cake later," I said wisely. "For now, let's turn to the pages I've marked for bridesmaids' dresses. Oh, you're all going to be so gorgeous, I can't wait!"

"Do I get to be a bridesmaid?" Theo clapped his hands. "I'd look precious in that one—I have a flatter stomach than all of you!"

"No, you idiot, you're a groomsman," said Kimby. "And don't kid yourself, dear. My stomach is flatter than yours."

4

The scale doesn't lie—*three bloody weeks and not a single pound gone.* I stared down in horror at the number between my big toes. Even if I held my boobs up—nothing. I've almost completely cut out chocolate, and for what? *Damn.* But I suppose just not gaining any weight could be seen as a relative success. It's been hell at work, after all. Hell. And we've had so many dinners out, with everyone wanting to celebrate and all that. So just getting on the scale right now was pretty brave in the first place, I think.

But now I cannot hide from the painful truth any longer: I officially had forty pounds to lose by August 18, our wedding day. Make that June 18—two months before the wedding, if I wanted to have my alterations done in time. I glanced down at the scale again. *So let's see, that gives me…about nine months. Plenty of time. But what about The Dress? How can I buy The Dress anytime soon in this state? They'll be able to take it in, thank God for that, but I've at least got to be able to go dress shopping without feeling like a cow. That settles it. Starting today, I've got to get serious….*

"Evie?" Bruce was knocking on the door. "I need the bathroom."

"Get away!" I barked, and jumped down off the scale.

"What's the matter?"

"Nothing. I'm not ready yet."

"Are you on that damn scale again? You've been in there for forty-five minutes. I've got to take a shower. I'm gonna be late."

I hid the scale back behind the cabinet. He'd kill me if he saw it out again. I put on my bathrobe, opened the door and swept past him in a fury. "You know, you *could* give me some privacy once in a while," I yelled back at him. But he just slammed the door.

Later, when I was blow-drying my hair, he sat down on the bed beside me. "What?" I asked.

"I'm throwing it out."

"No you're not," I informed him, and turned the dryer back on.

He pulled the plug out of the wall. "Yes I am. I can't go through this again."

"*You* can't? What about me? *I'm* the pork chop…"

"Evie, you're not fat and I'm throwing that scale out. I can see it in your eyes. You're going to get crazy again."

"But what if I promise not to?" I asked sweetly, and plugged the dryer back in. But he grabbed it out of my hand.

"You can't promise something like that. You know what happens to you…"

"What's that supposed to mean?" I knew exactly what he meant, but I kind of like teasing him.

"Have you forgotten the intervention already? You almost lost all of your friends and I seriously considered tossing you into the East River."

Bruce and apparently everyone else in my life labor under the impression that I have some sort of Dr. Jeckyl and Mrs. Hyde thing going on when I'm on a diet. I admit that I might get a little moody (and possibly even abrasive) when deprived of chocolate for too long, but who the hell doesn't?

"If you're referring to that day when you all managed to force me to eat half a cheesecake, of course I haven't forgotten. And my third chin remembers it too, so thanks for nothing."

"But you were so much better after that...." Bruce said wistfully.

"Because I fell off the wagon and my personality's been dulled by a perpetual sugar high ever since."

Bruce shook his head. "I'm not kidding, Evie."

"I know. And I really do promise not to get bitchy this time, but you have to understand—I need to lose some weight. As soon as I do, I'll feel better about myself, and that'll counteract any nastiness you may experience. But I will try to be good. I promise. Just have a little faith in me, okay?"

"It's not you I don't have faith in, it's the evil Mrs. Hyde who worries me."

I threw a pillow at his head and returned to my blow-drying. I knew Bruce was only trying to make sure that things stay under control, but his attitude was starting to grate on my nerves a bit. His stress was contagious, and I wanted no part of it.

It's all to do with his mother, no doubt. Bertie has officially gone into overdrive, and it has been getting progressively uglier with each passing day. The first crisis was finding the perfect location for the wedding. Every hotel, every inn she considers good enough has, of course, been booked solid for decades. After the banquet manager at one upscale hotel in the city (which I hesitate to name because of a pending lawsuit), actually laughed out loud and then hung up on her after she politely inquired about the possibility of reserving a Saturday night this coming June, Bertie called me in near hysterics. "If you were more sensible," she'd spat, "you'd agree to a longer engagement. *Everyone* knows that you need *at least* a year and a half to be able to be able to plan a proper wedding. You can just *forget* about any getting a decent caterer or photographer. Why? WHY? It's ridiculous—it's not like you're *pregnant*."

I remained silent just long enough to let the possibility creep into her consciousness. After a moment or two, I could feel her panic. Poor thing. Better put her out of her misery.

"No, of course I'm not pregnant, but—"

"Well!" she shrieked. "Guess what? You can do it yourselves. Or tell your mother *she* can do it. *I* just can't take it for another second."

"All right. I'll tell her. I'm sure her church up in Bensonhurst is available. I mean, it's not like anyone in the old neighborhood actually gets married anymore. Her priest will be delighted. You know, he mostly does funerals these days. With a few streamers and balloons, the party room downstairs will look almost as nice as the ballroom at the Waldorf. We might have to clean it up a bit, though, because I think they still hold that doggie obedience school there every Tuesday...."

"Evelyn, that's not funny," she interjected.

"I'm serious. We don't want a three-year engagement. Bruce doesn't care about the best of this or that. He'd be happy if we ran off to Vegas and got married there."

She knew I was right. Bruce probably would go for that type of thing. Of course, *I* would never agree to anything that tacky. But she doesn't know that.

"Why can't you just do it a bit later, like next fall? It'll give us more time," she pleaded.

"I suppose, if we absolutely *have* to," I sighed. "But I hope Bruce doesn't get impatient. He almost flipped out when I told him we were looking at well over two hundred people. And they're mostly from your side. My side is less than forty. I just don't want him getting cold feet about a big wedding. Do you?"

She'd already had three arguments with Bruce about various wedding details, and she could tell his patience was wearing thin. Even worse, how could she tell her friends from the gardening club and the children's hospital foundation that her only son had eloped to some Elvis-themed wedding chapel on the Strip? My God, what would Mona Davenport think? Her daughter's wedding last July was at the Plaza....

"Fine, I'll keep trying," she said. "I just want you to appreciate how difficult it's going to be."

"I know you'll find something," I assured her.

At least things would be calming down at work. Friday was Pruscilla's last day, and Thelma Thorpe, her temporary replacement, was rumored to have the spine of a jellyfish. How these people work their way up is anyone's guess. Monday morning, the woman could barely make eye contact, let alone tell me what to do.

"Er, um, just go ahead with what Pruscilla has planned, and I'll check in with you later," she said quietly, avoiding my steely gaze. If you ask me, Thelma's wild shock of yellowy hair certainly doesn't present the right image for the company, especially considering she heads up the Haircare division. She managed a weak smile, and looked down at the floor. Her skin was red and angry, as if she'd just been scrubbed with a nail brush.

"Don't worry," I told her. "I have a copy of Pruscilla's Action Plan. Just call me if you need anything."

"Thanks. And…oh dear…um…you have something in your…your face," she said quickly, backing away.

I pulled out my compact. Oh God—a booger! Plain as day. It had probably been there all morning. That hag Andrea from Fragrances stared me right in the eye and told me it looked like I'd lost weight. No wonder there was so much snickering at the coffee cart. Before I could plan my revenge, Mom called.

"Evie, I have the most wonderful idea. Let's go to Sternfeld's tonight and try on wedding dresses," she said immediately.

Crap, crap, crap! I'm not ready for this yet.

"I don't know, Mom. Isn't it a bit soon?"

"Oh, don't worry about your tummy," she said excitedly. "There's still plenty of time to lose a few pounds before the wedding."

"No, I mean why now? I didn't plan to start looking for another couple of months. The wedding's not until August, and we're only in October. Don't you think it's a bit soon?" I hadn't even had lunch yet and already my waistband was beginning to cut off all circulation to my legs.

"Absolutely not! I've been doing a little research on my own, and I'll have you know that all the new bridal fashions for the summer are out right now, to give enough time for alterations."

"Well, I guess." I suppose it couldn't hurt. Martha Stewart says that the mother-daughter wedding-dress-shopping experience is a memory every woman will look back on fondly over the years, remembering it as one of the most cherished moments of her pre-married life (*Martha Stewart Weddings,* Fall: "12 Timeless Bridal Traditions").

"And Sternfeld's is the biggest bridal store in Brooklyn—maybe even the world!" She sounded like a commercial, so excited she could barely contain herself. "I just know we'll find something for you there. I called—they come in all sizes."

I undid the top button of my pants and breathed out deeply. If she had been beside me right then, it would have been hard not to smack her. "Mom, could you lay off about that, please? It's hard enough knowing I have to lose so much in so little time," I hissed into the phone. "I sure as hell don't need you telling me I need a plus-size wedding dress." Laetitia Farkle peeped over the wall of my cubicle.

"Curiosity killed the cat, dear," I smiled, my hand over the receiver, and shot her one of my nastiest glares.

"Satisfaction brought him back," she whispered, and sunk back down behind the divider.

Idiot. What passes for wit around here would make Oscar Wilde turn over in his grave.

"Evie, I know you'll lose the weight," Mom continued. "And the lady at the store said they can do alterations as you lose. And even if you don't—"

"Mom. *Please!*" I was trying hard to keep my voice down.

"Let me finish. The lady said they have styles that are flattering for every figure."

"I *know* that already. *God!* I refuse to do this with you if you're going to be mean about it. That means no ganging up on me with the saleslady, no insisting I try on something I don't like, no embarrassing me whatsoever. Can you do that?"

"I can't promise anything. All I know is that shopping with you for a wedding dress is like a dream come true for me. Who'd have thought? It's actually happening for you. I wasn't sure it would—" She was starting to sniffle, so I cut it short with a promise to meet her there at five.

Thankfully, Thelma had elected to remain in her own office across the floor instead of moving into Pruscilla's, which meant my cubicle would be free from prying eyes for the next six weeks. So my first order of business on this Pruscilla-free Monday morn was to announce our engagement on seven different wedding Web sites, two of which offered free presents—one bar set and one wine-and-cheese backpack—to any couple who signed up for their online gift registries.

After lunch, I organized my dress folder, which was already overstuffed with pictures ripped out from magazines. I divided them into two piles: Dream Dresses and Just Okay. The Dream pile consisted mostly of Vera Wang ads (*Vogue,* September: "Gown Goddess: Why Society Brides Love Vera Wang"), along with a few runway shots of gaunt models draped in impossibly narrow but undeniably fabulous couture dresses. But I would definitely settle for anything from the Okay stack—delicate little spaghetti-strapped numbers with antique lace trains, strapless corsets encrusted with glittering Austrian crystals and fairy-princess gowns surrounded in yards of billowing white tulle. I'd been doing my research, and knew the importance of giving the saleslady an idea of my taste in order for her to help serve me best (*Bridal Guide,* October: "The Do's and Don'ts of Dress Shopping").

The afternoon flew by, and I snuck out early. On my way past the switchboard, I told the girls to transfer all of Andrea's calls tomorrow to her boss's extension. "She'll be out all day at the Scents and Sensibility trade show, so send everything through to Teresa," I told them. "She's waiting for some important calls, so she didn't want them getting routed to voice mail." Andrea, whose cubicle is tucked away in a back corner, spends at least four hours a day on the phone gossiping with her friends. Once Teresa fields seventeen calls for her by noon, she should start to get the idea. It was a little mean, but so was making fun of a girl's booger. And if it ever came out, well…who am I kidding? I'd be hailed as a hero—everyone hates Andrea.

By the time I met Mom outside Sternfeld's, it had started to rain. We rushed inside and were met by a spindly old saleslady with a lazy eye and thinning hair. She introduced herself as Greta, and looked me up and down as best she could. "Let's take our shoes off, ladies. We wouldn't want to get the carpets dirty with all these white dresses everywhere!"

"Can she see anything?" I whispered to Mom as we chased Greta up a sweeping, pink-carpeted staircase with gold bannisters.

"She was the only one available tonight. I'm sure she's fine."

"I have a gift for helping brides find their dream dress," Greta shouted back, as if she'd heard us. "It's like what they call ESPN. I can tell just by looking at a girl which one she's going to buy! Been working here near fifty years, you know!"

Mom grinned, pleased that we'd stumbled onto such a quaint character. At the top of the stairs, Greta directed us toward some ratty old slippers and a couple of overstuffed but threadbare French-provincial-style chairs.

"Evelyn is very particular about fashion," Mom offered loudly. "She's brought some clippings from magazines so that you can see what she likes."

"I may have a wonky eye, Mrs. Mays, but I can hear you just fine. No need to yell. And I think it's best if we leave the pictures aside, for now. If fifty years has taught me anything, it's that what we like isn't necessarily what looks good on us. Now just you wait here while I see which room's available," she said and darted across the vast expanse of pink carpet and disappeared behind a maze of mirrored dressing rooms.

"Smooth, Mom," I said as we sat down.

"Was I talking loudly?"

"You were yelling. I want to show her my pictures. I don't trust her to choose something for me."

"Be patient, Evelyn. Let's give her a chance. I'm sure she knows her stuff," she said, picking up an alarmingly old copy of something called *Brooklyn Brides.*

I slumped down in my chair and took it all in. All around the room, other pairs of mothers and daughters waited in chairs, whispering to each other and nodding. Some pored through the rows of plastic-wrapped gowns, under the watchful eyes of Gretas of their own. Everyone seemed perfectly coiffed, in their pastel twin sets and pearls. I looked over at Mom. Her damp black hair, dramatically streaked with gray for as long as I can remember, was plastered to her forehead, and she wasn't wearing a stitch of makeup. She was slouching, and her beige cotton blouse—with an I Heart NY embroidered on the front pocket—was missing a button. I could see the elastic waistband of her pants. *Why the hell does she need an elastic waistband? She weighs about 103 pounds.* She looked like she'd made her own clothes. But I have to admit, even I felt a bit out of place in my bright tangerine pantsuit (*Cosmopolitan,* November: "Orange: The New Neutral"). Not only that, but I was definitely the fattest bride-to-be in the whole joint.

Greta interrupted my reverie with a hurried wave. "Come on, let's get you undressed," she said as we walked across the floor into one of the large dressing rooms. "Did you bring a foundation garment or are we going to build something into the dress?"

"Uh, I don't know. Do I really need something like that? I mean, I plan to lose some weight and—"

"Oh, no! You're not one of them, are you? If I've seen it once I've seen it a thousand times," Greta sighed. "We'll get you a smart dress that fits you NOW. Most girls don't lose *half* the weight they plan to, and end up with gowns that need to be taken out later, at quite an expense I might add."

I glared at my mom, who was nodding treasonously in agreement.

"And I'm sure your fiancé thinks you're quite beautiful as you are, or else we wouldn't be here!" she continued. "So now, all I need to know from you is whether you prefer something traditional or a little more modern?"

"Traditional. She likes traditional," Mom said.

"I do not," I snapped. "Something modern, please."

"So you have a seat Mrs. Mays, and Evelyn, you get undressed, and I'll be right back with a girdle and a few dresses."

I don't know which was worse—the fact that my mother had completely betrayed me, that a blind woman was going to choose my wedding gown, or that I was about to put on a public girdle.

"I'm leaving," I said simply, and made for the door.

"Evelyn, there's nothing to be ashamed of. I gave *birth* to you, for heaven's sake. I know every part of you. And I'm sorry if you feel that I've put pressure on you to lose weight. You know I don't mean it, it's just that you have to learn how to control yourself. Besides, God made us in his own image, and He loves each of us, no matter what we may look like on the outside."

Scratch that. The worst part about this was getting naked in front of my mother under fluorescent lights.

"Forget this," I hissed at her. "This is a living nightmare, and you're not helping. You said you wouldn't do this to me. I refuse to even touch anything she brings back. All I wanted was to try on a few dresses that *I* like. But you won't even let me do that! And I didn't come here to be insulted, either."

"Oh, lighten up. You're getting hysterical. Greta didn't mean to insult you." So now it was Greta. "This is supposed to be fun, Evelyn. And who knows? Maybe she knows what she's doing. Did you ever think of that?"

"Mom, *please,*" I whined.

"Nobody's saying we have to buy a dress here. But we did make an appointment, and Greta hasn't done anything but try to help. I'm sorry, but it never hurts to try. If you don't like anything, we'll leave."

Before I could insist we do just that, Greta returned with another old woman in tow, both of them carrying as many dresses as their osteoporotic arms could handle. They hung them up on a rack.

"Thank you, Ingrid. That will be all. Now Evelyn, let's get you into this foundation garment," she said, extending something gray.

"I will not wear that."

"It'll help with your tummy," Greta said, shaking it at me.

"Can't she try the dresses on without it?" my mother asked. Finally.

"Well, I suppose so. But with your bust you're definitely going to need something. I figured you're around a size fourteen or sixteen."

"I am definitely NOT a size sixteen! I'm not even a fourteen!"

"Hush, Evelyn, people will hear you," Mom whispered loudly. I could hear muffled laughter coming from the dressing rooms on either side of us. Poor twin-setters. They were probably having trouble finding dresses small enough.

"Let's not get bogged down by a number. Wedding dresses are made small. Most brides have to buy a size larger than they normally wear. That's why they make most samples in a size eight," Greta reassured me.

"How horrible. Imagine how all those poor size sixes must feel."

"How 'bout we try this one, first," she said, freeing a dress from its plastic bag. "I thought this one would suit you because of the sweetheart neckline—it will draw attention up to your face. And you have *such* a pretty face."

It was hideous. The exact antithesis of every wedding gown I'd clipped out, dreamed about. Instead of thin, elegant spaghetti straps there were puffy, stiff sleeves dotted with rhinestone-studded rosettes. Instead of a smooth, sleek bodice there was a wide trunk covered in the tackiest sort of lace-and-pearl appliqués. Instead of an elegant A-line skirt, there was a shiny satin tablecloth covering so many crinolines that it stuck out at right angles from the waist. And it was stark white, almost fluorescent (*Bridal Guide,* Fall: "Why Off-White Is Right-On").

Perfect. I'd show them. "Mom, I'd like to surprise you, if you don't mind. Let me try it on, and then we'll call you in."

She seemed to like that idea, and obligingly trotted out of the room. Alone with Greta, I took off my clothes and let her help me into the dress.

The first time you see yourself in a wedding gown is supposed to be an experience you never forget. We've all heard those stories about the brides who buy the first dress they try on because they can't get that heavenly, haunting first image of themselves out of their minds, and nothing else can compare. You're supposed to feel like a goddess, a virgin and a model all rolled into one. But what I saw in the mirror was beyond horrible, beyond my wildest nightmare—a blur of bulges and rhinestones and flounces and fabric. A pregnant white hippopotamus, with sausage links for arms and shiny balloons for breasts. In the mirror, I could see Greta's pointy face light up in a twisted yellow smile. She clasped her hands together and sucked in her breath.

"You see? I told you! I do have a knack for this!" she shrieked. "Mrs. Mays, Mrs. Mays! Come in and see!"

Mom pushed the door open and froze. Now she would see how wrong she was to make me do this, how evil Greta was, how horrid I looked, how ashamed I was.

"Oh, *Evelyn,*" she breathed, her bottom lip trembling. Tears welled up in her eyes. "You're beautiful."

At that moment, I made three very serious vows—to never go wedding dress shopping with my mother again, to lose *more* than forty pounds, and to go home and smack Bruce for making me go through all of this. If he hadn't proposed, I would never have been publicly humiliated in so many different ways in so little time.

A few days after her little tantrum, Bertie finally got over her selfishness and came through with the wedding plans. Through a grand concession of my own—agreeing to give up my dream of a June wedding—we were booked in for August 18 at the posh Fairfield Inn on the Connecticut shore. It was absolutely perfect—a grand, white, colonial-style mansion with an elegant ballroom and a newly renovated Bridal Suite (*Bridal Guide*, Winter: "Finding the Perfect Venue: Five Features You Can't Live Without"). Bertie's friend Cookie had two of her daughters' weddings there, so it passed the snob test, too. It had been reserved, of course, but by a brilliant stroke of luck, Bertie popped in on the very day when one Mrs. Pimbleton-Smythe called to cancel her daughter Sukey's wedding, due to the unfortunate suicide of the groom-to-be.

Even Bruce liked the place when we popped in for a look, and whistled when he saw the four-poster bed.

"So this is where it's all gonna happen," he whispered into my ear while Bertie discussed the merits of veal versus roast beef with the event manager. "After all these years, you'll finally be unable to resist my charms."

"Yeah right," I snorted. "I don't know *how* we've waited so long. Oh, wait—weren't those your charms I succumbed to on our first date?"

He snickered, and Bertie shot me a mean look. "Yes, Brucie dear," I said loudly. "This is where we'll spend the most romantic night of our lives. The only thing that could possibly make it any more perfect would be knowing that our guests had thoroughly enjoyed the milk-fed veal in the mushroom-cream sauce."

The event manager raised his eyebrows and nodded in agreement.

★ ★ ★

Despite a few minor glitches, Bertie and I were getting on remarkably well. Thanks to her years on the Palm Beach charity ball circuit, she's the type of person you really want on your side if you're planning something big—she acts fast, she has good taste and she won't take no for an answer (unlike Mom, whom I was very happy to leave out of the entire process). Bruce, on the other hand, wasn't dealing well with his mother at all—and we'd barely been engaged three weeks. He almost lost it when he heard she wanted to have 150 people at the engagement party (tentatively scheduled for January 20), and threatened not to show if she invited more than ninety.

Mercifully, Bruce and I were to be spared most of the remaining meetings with florists and photographers, although we felt it was important to step in and approve any final decision, in case we wanted to veto something. But I have to hand it to Bertie; she knows how to get things done. She indiscreetly prodded the event manager at the inn into telling her exactly who else Mrs. Pimbleton-Smythe had hired for her daughter's ill-fated nuptials, and then booked them immediately.

Although it was shaping up to be the event of the season, I have a feeling poor Sukey Pimbleton-Smythe would not have wanted to be a guest at our wedding. By all rights, it should have been hers, were it not for a few handfuls of Xanax and a very fine bottle of cognac.

5

The morning after Thanksgiving, I swore to Bruce that I didn't want to see our families in the same room again until the wedding. And quite possibly, not even then.

"Your mother was a shrew," I said, pouring myself a cup of coffee. "While you and your dad were watching football, she was lecturing my mom about the importance of buying a new dress for our engagement party. You didn't hear her. She was *cruel.* Christ! Did you use the last Sweet'n Low?"

"I've never tried that stuff in my life. Just use sugar. It won't kill you."

"Are you trying to sabotage me?" I growled as I jealously eyed Bruce's bagel.

"Evie, get a grip. It's not a reason to be upset. This is not a big deal."

"Oh, so you're saying it's okay for your mother to treat mine like she's an embarrassment? It's obvious she's worried what her friends will think if my mom wears a ratty old dress. Like she's the help, or something." For all his intellectual wisdom, Bruce has a surprisingly limited understanding of the subtleties of class politics.

"No, I'm saying it's okay to use sugar instead of aspartame for once in your life. And you're putting *cream* in your coffee, for God's sake. You think a teaspoon of sugar's going to make a difference?"

"If you'd bought milk like you were supposed to—"

"That's enough, Evie," he snapped, slamming his *Harry Potter* book down on the table. "I'm not going to sit here and be your punching bag. If you're upset about last night or your diet or whatever, we can talk about it, but I'm not going to let you insult me for no reason."

"First of all, I'm not on a diet. It's a lifestyle change. And as far as your mother's concerned, if you'd been there to hear what she was saying, you wouldn't have stood for it. I didn't know what to do. She knows my mom can't afford to buy fancy clothes and she was deliberately making her feel bad in front of everyone. Why do you think Claire came in to watch with you? You think she likes football? She probably had to leave the table before she said something horrible to your mother and ruined the entire dinner."

"Well, you did a pretty good job of that yourself when you asked Rosita to sit down and join us. You think that helps? All you did was make everyone uncomfortable as hell, especially Rosita!"

"It's just that dinner was already served, and there was nothing left for her to do, so I don't understand why she has to eat alone in the kitchen when there's plenty of room at the table for her. God, she's been living in your house for like twenty years!"

I could feel the tears welling up. Maybe everyone was right—I think I do freak out when I can't eat what I want to. Because I was honestly ready to fling myself into traffic, for absolutely no reason at all. And it had only been about eighteen hours since my last piece of cake.

Bruce sighed. "Evie, my mother just thought it would be nice to have a Thanksgiving with our families together. She's really making an effort." What a saint. "Both my parents want to get to know your mother and Claire better, so I don't think it's fair of you to try and make a big thing out of this. If she was snobby or bitchy or whatever it's just how she is and you're all going to have to accept it."

"All? *All?* So it's you against us, now, is it? The upstanding Fulbrights vs. the Italo-American Clampetts? And tell me, how should I comfort my mother? She looked like she wanted to die all night. *I* was the one who was embarrassed. And you should be, too." The tears were flowing now, and I was nearly hysterical, but Bruce wasn't biting. And why should he? I was being utterly ridiculous.

"*Puhlease!* You make it sound like your mother is some poor helpless soul who can't defend herself. She drives you crazy ninety-nine percent of the time and now she can do no wrong. And you expect me to feel like it's all my fault." He paused for effect. "I'm sorry if you were that embarrassed by my family, Evie. I had no idea you hated them all that much. But you know what? You're right. I *was* embarrassed—by YOU!"

He waited a few seconds for me to say something, but I just sat there and cried. Then he stormed out of the kitchen. He turned the stereo on loud in the living room. It wasn't supposed to be like this. Everyone was supposed to get along. Mom and Bertie should have been the best of friends by now, and Bruce and I should be picking out our china pattern. But all we were doing was fighting all the time. All of us.

Bruce's dad even got into the act last night when Bertie suggested he be the one to tell half of their friends why they wouldn't be invited to the engagement party.

"But Bruce doesn't want a lot of people there, Daddy," sister Wendy said sweetly.

"This is the first I'm hearing of this," he said with uncharacteristic irritation. "Do you actually expect me to tell James and Cookie that they won't be invited? We were invited to their grandson's christening just this summer!"

"No, not James and Cookie, dear," said Bertie, rolling her eyes. "They'll be invited. But I don't think there'll be room for Phyllis and Harvey or Judy and Norman."

Bruce Sr. was shaking his head. "I won't do it. I just won't. We've known them for twenty-five years. And what about Barry and Lynne?"

"Oh, there's definitely no room for any work friends, Daddy," said Brooke, looking up from her cuticles.

It was all a big nightmare. On the way home, after we dropped Mom off at her place, Claire started in with her usual advice.

"It's gonna get a lot worse from here on in, kids. If you want to keep your sanity, you're going to have to take hold of yourselves. Don't let other people's expectations get in the way. Engagement's supposed to be a happy time, an exciting time."

"But as you can see, Bruce's parents are nearly impossible," I pointed out between clenched teeth. Bruce sat silently in the back seat.

"Lillian's no treat herself," Claire said sharply. "Bruce, I'm just glad your mother had the foresight not to offer her another drink."

"She wasn't drunk," I protested. "She was just nervous."

Bruce snorted. I guess he finds it funny when I defend my mother, since I spend most of the time complaining about her. But just because she's a bit of a lush or maybe not as sophisticated as some doesn't give anyone else but me the right to judge her.

"Well," I said, "I guess I'd drink too if I knew certain people would be judging everything I said and did for six hours straight. And what the hell was all that about Bertie's charity work? And how she's so happy and grateful that she didn't have to work a real job, and how important it is to be there when your kids come home from school. What a witch!"

"Uh, Evie? I'm still here, remember?" Bruce grumbled as Claire pulled up in front of our place.

I suppose I was being a bit of a hypocrite about this—criticizing one's mother should be the domain of blood relatives alone. But in-laws must form some sort of exception, shouldn't they? Especially when they're so wicked.

"Come now, Evie. Take it down a notch," Claire said seriously.

"Sorry," I said. "But it's not like she doesn't know Mom worked when I was growing up. And that she still works. Like there's something wrong with working! She knows working isn't a choice for some women. Some women just have to work!"

"Your mother did the best she could, Evie. For the hundreth time, you know she never meant to leave you out on the stoop that day. She had no way of knowing Mrs. DeFazio wouldn't show up that aft—"

"I know that! I'm not talking about that!"

"Come, now—you're getting hysterical," Claire said, patting my hand.

"Would you mind if I come home with you tonight, Claire?" Bruce asked, managing to make me angrier than I already was.

She laughed loudly. "Brucie dear, you know there's always a bed for you at my place. You're a pleasure—a real pleasure. Evie, I wish I could say the same for you." Bruce snickered.

Claire wiped the corners of her eyes and sighed. "But I'm afraid you're on your own tonight, Bruce. You two go inside, talk it out. That's what separates the good marriages from the bad, you know—not the fighting, but the making up." She paused to think for a moment, then looked at me. "We had some doozies, your grandfather and I. And don't believe that crap about never going to bed angry. There's nothing wrong with going to bed angry. Nothing wrong with waking up angry, either, come to think of it. That's going to happen. So long as you can agree to disagree, you'll be fine. Respect each other's differences. That's the real truth of it," she smiled, and winked at Bruce.

I hugged her and we got out of the car. "'Bye, now!" she said cheerily as I closed the door. She turned the stereo up right away, and we could hear the muffled strains of James Taylor blaring from behind as we trudged up the steps to the front door. We turned and watched her old Lincoln float off down the street until it disappeared out of sight.

By Monday, I couldn't do up my pants. After a brief period of abstinence Friday morning, I'd spent the whole weekend in sweats, eating leftover turkey and, when that was all gone, cranberry sauce out of the tin. If I could have called in sick, I would have, but I'd just used up my last sick day of the year the week before when Morgan needed some hand-holding at the gynocologist's following three inconclusive home pregnancy tests. It was the second time this year she'd thought she was pregnant, but, mercifully, it was not to be. She suspects Billy's been poking holes in the condoms, although there's been no real evidence of any tampering.

"Maybe you should go on the Pill," I suggested.

"Yeah, right!" She cackled, tightening the lid on her cup of pee. "Me—on the Pill. I'd be pregnant *and* I'd have the clap."

"The clap? Are you kidding me? Do you really think Billy would sleep around? He doesn't seem like the type. I mean, you know him better, but I just thought he was really into you and only you, you know?"

She raised her eyebrows and looked at me like I should know better.

"Oh," I said, the light dawning. "Who?"

"Peter."

"Morgan, not again," I groaned. Peter is Morgan's boss. He's an absolute jerk—gorgeous, married, rich and heartless. Morgan adores him, or rather, adores being thrown down onto his big glass desk and ravaged every once in a while after everyone's gone home.

She shrugged her shoulders unapologetically. "After a few

months, the sexual tension just builds to the point where we have to release it or it'll become obvious to everyone."

"Couldn't you ask for a transfer or something?"

"Why would I want to do that?" she said, throwing her long red hair back over one shoulder. "I like Mergers and Acquisitions. Besides, I didn't spend all those years busting my ass in business school just to let a prick like Peter get in the way of what I want."

"Well, excuse the hell out of me, Madam Maneater," I said.

"Gimme a break, Evie. I've been working my way up there for three years and it's one of the top investment banks in the city. I'm not about to throw it all away!" She slammed her bottle of pee down on the desk in front of a frightened receptionist, and plopped down on a chair between two very unhappy women who appeared to be about ten months pregnant. What a piece of work.

I pictured poor Billy, sitting at home alone poking holes in condoms by candlelight, an uneaten dinner for two laid out on the table. Innocently believing Morgan was working late, as she often does. She probably just forgot to call, he assures himself.

I suppose love really is blind. Actually, in Billy's case, love is deaf, dumb *and* blind.

I wonder if Bruce would do something devious like that. The condom, I mean, not the cheating. Probably not, on both counts. The idea of having kids thrills him, I know that. Plus, the thought of condoms brings out his softer side, if you get my drift. In any case, birth control sabotage isn't his style. The only thing Bruce might consider poking a hole in would be the theory of relativity or something lame like that. Besides, he probably charts my cycle to know exactly when I'm ovulating, anyway.

I reached into the back of the closet and pulled out the black Anne Klein II Fat Suit (*Allure,* December: "Five Work Essentials To Suit Every Figure"). In a state of emergency such as this, I would never get on the scale. But judging from the snugness of never-fail Fat Suit—and the lines my underwear were leaving on my hips—things had gone from bad to worse. Better skip breakfast and break out the big guns. After work today, I'll stop by the drugstore. Annie told me that Nicole dropped ten pounds in four weeks on a combination of ginseng ampoules and chromium supplements. I haven't seen her, and I'm sure she still looks frumpy, but ten pounds, for her, that's something. I bet she probably took laxatives, too. There must be something at Walgreen's that'll work for me.

At work, I studied the calendar. *Let's see...today was Monday, November 27. That gives me about nine and a half months to go until the wedding. Or 265 days. Thank God it's a leap year—that's an extra day which might come in handy.*

I lost five pounds in a single day once, on the cabbage soup diet. But if I wanted to buy my dress soon, there was definitely no time to mess around. Besides, my metabolism ain't what it used to be. When I was twenty, I lost (and then gained) ten pounds six times in a single year. It was so easy—all I had to do was cut out French fries and chocolate. But I'd been doing that for two whole months, and I'd gained God knows how much. Maybe there was something wrong with me, like some sort of fat-creating disease or something. It was a hopeful thought.

Pruscilla wouldn't be back till Monday, so all week long, I devoted myself to researching that very question on the Internet. While Thelma flitted about nervously, preparing neat piles of color-coordinated folders on Pruscilla's desk, I diligently studied the facts. Unfortunately, the facts were as follows:

Fact #1: An underactive thyroid may be to blame. Symptoms may include weight gain, irregular periods, flaky skin, depression, weakness, constipation and a puffy face. *Eureka!* Maybe this was the miracle I'd been praying for all these years.

Fact #2: I do not have an underactive thyroid. Or type-two diabetes. Or undiagnosed edema of any kind. No systemic medical condition is to blame. An emergency lunchtime visit to my doctor on Wednesday confirmed these findings. Not at all worth the $120 fee to rush the results of the blood test.

Fact #3: Pregnancy causes weight gain.

Fact #4: I am not pregnant. That is, unless there has been an immaculate conception.

Fact #5: In 1991, doctors at Stanford University Medical Center removed a 303-pound tumor from the right ovary of an otherwise healthy thirty-four-year-old woman. She made a full recovery.

Fact #6: There is no such tumor in either of my ovaries, also confirmed by my doctor. I do not even have a small tumor.

Fact #7: Obsessing over one's weight can be a sign of anorexia. Might I be teetering on the brink of losing half my body weight?

Fact #8: After completing 14 self-diagnosis questionnaires, it appears the only eating disorder I might be afflicted with is something called binge-eating disorder. Symptoms include eating until feeling painfully full, eating alone due to embarrassment, eating when not hungry, and feeling disgusted and depressed after overeating. The prognosis? Weight gain and, eventually, obesity.

By Thursday afternoon, I had reluctantly drifted away from the hopeful expectations of the medical Web sites to the more familiar depression-inducing body mass index calculators of the diet sites. There, I was forced to concede that my symptoms, although severe, were not altogether uncommon. In fact, they were quite mundane. What I did learn is that my body has betrayed me in a way as cruel as any organic disease, as ferocious as any pathological malignancy. It seems the years of yo-yo dieting have taken their toll. The culprit? A wonky metabolism. The cure? None to speak of, although one thing has been known to help other sufferers—exercise. The time of desperation was nearly upon me; the only option, painfully clear.

I would have to join a gym.

What else could I do? If I'd learned anything from my research—aside from the fact that there were also downsides to thyroid problems and massive abdominal tumors—it was that I was verging on an unhealthy attitude regarding weight loss. I would have to accept that, despite all promises to the contrary, there is no quick fix, no magical ampoule full of ginseng that would make my ass fat morph into muscle. Only hard work and a healthy outlook could prevail.

As I stared at the daunting pile of color-coded folders Thelma had gradually been depositing in my In Box, I realized that I'd done nothing all week but pray for various horrible illnesses, research the best liposuction clinics in the five boroughs, and neglect my professional responsibilities. Pathetic. How could I expect to be promoted if I can't even bother returning an e-mail or two? Bruce was right—I *was* in danger of losing it. Well, not anymore.

On Friday afternoon I left early since I figured it would be my last chance for a while, with Pruscilla's return just one short weekend away. While I'd been embroiled in online research, Thelma had spent the better part of the week pulling her hair out in Pruscilla's office, which was by now a complete mess. The tension in the air was almost palpable, and it floated out of the office and hung over my cubby. I didn't envy her—she'd probably be in there all weekend. But it was hard to feel sorry for her. The simplest things seemed confusing for Thelma, even deciphering Pruscilla's handwriting proved nearly impossible for the poor woman. But it was no trouble for me. I'd gotten quite used to it, in fact, and almost looked forward to typing her long-winded reports and memos (Pruscilla's typing is slower than her writing), since it afforded me the rare opportunity to look busy while keeping my headspace completely free. I was getting quite good at drawing it out as long as possible.

The first week Pruscilla was gone, I didn't mind interpreting for Thelma all of the purple little Post-its Pruscilla had left stuck to everything. But then she started bothering me twenty-five times a day with questions about how Pruscilla does this and how Pruscilla does that, and since I wasn't put on this earth to save Thelma's ass (and neglect my work besides), I developed a set of avoidance techniques to divert her ceaseless calls for help. Mostly, that meant pleading ignorance. For example, Thelma has no idea that part of my job is to coordinate the printing of all promotional materials. Nor is she aware that I have input all of Pruscilla's notes and market-research data for all new product launches for the next 18 months. Best of all, she thinks most of my time is spent returning Pruscilla's e-mail. If she wants to be a good manager, she's going to have to learn a little bit about self-reliance.

As I got ready to leave, she yelled out, "Evie, Evie! Wait!" In her hurry to stop me, I could hear a flurry of papers swishing to the floor. But I pretended not to notice, and scooted down the hall to the elevators. If Thelma doesn't get it by now, then there's nothing anyone can do to help save her. Besides, if there's one thing I've learned working at Kendra White, professionally speaking, it's to form alliances with the right sorts of people, not to go down with a sinking ship. That, and never name a lipstick after a disgraced White House intern.

Although there are tons of gyms in Brooklyn near our place, I decided I'd be more likely to go if I joined one near work. Not *too* close to work, of course, in case somebody should see me, but close enough so that I can walk over during lunch if I want. Part of the Kendra White benefits package includes paying fifty percent of employees' gym memberships—not that KW is such a saintly place to work; judging by all the fat ladies who work there, paying for gyms was a pretty safe bet—which meant I could afford something pretty nice. I remembered a place I passed by once when the subway station was closed because of a bomb threat and I had to walk to the next line.

It was still there. Mid-Town Fitness. Inside, it was the archetypical New York City health club—iron and granite decor, with a three-storey-high, half-block-long plate-glass window facing the street. Half a dozen Wall-Street types hung off a climbing wall off to one side. A battalion of machines crossed the length of the room, ten rows deep. Scores of pony-tailed socialites wearing diamond earrings bigger than the earphones on their Discmans walked, ran and stepped off the calories from the salads they ate for lunch. Up above, weight machines on a mezzanine. I scanned the room for a fatso, but the only person I could find who didn't look like she'd been born there was the dumpy old woman spraying down treadmill consoles with a bottle of pink disinfectant. It was perfectly awful, but morbidly fascinating.

I was so enthralled by the moving sea of boobs and biceps that I hadn't noticed a young red-headed tart descend on me from behind the front desk.

"Hi, I'm Missy. Can I help you?" she asked sweetly.

"Um, no, I don't think so," I said, turning to leave.

"Would you like a tour?"

What I'd like is to get the hell out of here. "I don't think so."

"You don't sound so sure," she laughed. "Have you ever been a member of our facilities before?"

"What do you think?"

She tried not to look, but her eyes inadvertently traveled down to the waist of my bulging trench coat. A single vein throbbed at the center of her forehead. "I'm gonna guess…no?"

"That's right, Missy, the answer is no. No, I haven't been a member here before."

"Come on, it's not so bad. Let me give you a quick tour. You'd be surprised how friendly everyone is," she said, oblivious to my extreme discomfort, and started walking. "Let me show you the women-only section. If you're shy or uncomfortable about a co-ed workout, it's the perfect…" I reluctantly followed as she yammered on and on. The deeper we got into the bowels of the place, the uglier and heavier everyone became. I felt a little better. It seems the thin and the vain crowd the machines at the front by the window because they *enjoy* being gawked at like zoo animals by passersby.

"…and wait till you see our new eucalyptus and tea-tree-oil steam room! Have you heard about it? *New York Magazine* did a piece on it last month. Did you know that eucalyptus can clear your body of cancer-causing toxins? My hand to God! Our smokers really seem to enjoy it. Do you smoke? You can get a regular steam, too, if you prefer, but I don't see why anyone…"

"Can I see the weight room?" I asked. Muscle, I'd learned, burns more calories at rest than fat does, if you can imagine that. So my plan was to get ripped.

"Of course! Of course!" she said, and trotted toward the stairs. "Our weight room is equipped with the latest air-pressure machines, free weights…"

Missy droned on. At the top of the stairs, I leaned on a railing to catch my breath and look around. Abs as far as the eye could see. Mostly men up here, thank God. Struggling with these ridiculous machines in front of skinny little girls would be worse.

"…of course, if you're trying to lose weight, you'll need at *least* three days a week of strength training, so we'll customize a program just for you…."

Then I caught a glimpse of myself in one of the mirror-covered walls. My face was red as a beet, and I felt like how those guys lifting the huge barbells looked—like they were about to have an aneurysm. Could I really do this? I peered over the railing down at the floor below. Rows of well-conditioned ponytails swayed from side to side as their owners marched silently onward with fists clenched. Would I ever look like one of them?

"…so if you opt for the deluxe membership package, you have access to both the cardio and weight rooms, along with towel service, of course, and—"

"Wait a minute," I interrupted. "I don't know if I can do any of this. I don't know how."

"There are three personal trainers on the floor at all times whose job it is to show you exactly how everything works and to make sure you have the right form!" Missy looked around wildly. "Jade? Jade! Come on over here, would ya?"

The fellow in question jogged over from the old bald guy he was spotting.

"Hey, Missy. Is this lovely young lady a new member?"

"She's thinking about it. She's never been to a gym before."

"Hi! Jade Hollowell," he grinned, and stuck out his hand. "Nice to meet you." His eyes were so green and his teeth were so white, it was hard not to stare at his face.

I grabbed his hand and looked down at it. Veiny. "Hi. I'm Evelyn. Evie, actually. Evie Mays. Hi." *I am such an idiot.*

"Jade's one of our top trainers. He's been with us five years," Missy said slowly. She looked at me with knowing eyes. She'd brought out the big guns for the hard sell.

I looked down and realized I was still holding Jade's hand. Oh God. I pulled it away quickly. "Sorry," I mumbled. But he didn't seem to mind. He just smiled.

"If you like," Missy offered, "you can book private training sessions with Jade up to five times a week. Or with one of our other trainers." She was a lot smarter than she looked, that Missy.

"I don't know..."

"It's more expensive, of course, but you get what you pay for," she said. "People find they improve quicker when they have someone to answer to. Plus, he'll help you get the most out of your workouts."

"If you want to get serious, I'm your man," Jade said, staring into my soul. Those eyes. It was like they could see the skinny person buried inside me.

"He really is good," Missy assured me.

Jade shook his head modestly. "It's just that I love my job," he said. "I can't help it. This is a great place, Evie, really low-key. Everyone here is super friendly. I personally guarantee you that you'll love it."

"Come on." Missy reached out and grabbed my hand. "Give it a shot—you've got nothing to lose!"

"If that were true I wouldn't be here," I said, and Jade laughed. He actually laughed. At *my* joke.

"Working out is addictive, Evie, you'll see. At least it is for me. You know, if I wasn't here all the time, I'd probably be a much better actor," he said grinning, and winked right at me.

Missy giggled.

"Where do I sign?"

6

"Didn't you once tell me that gyms were the devil's playground?" Bruce asked.

"Yes, but…"

"And wasn't that you who told me that exercise was the dominion of the vain and the indulgence of the wicked?"

"Well, I might have…"

"Yet you feel that this is something you'd like to do?"

"Not that I need your approval, but yes."

"I'm just teasing you, Evie." Bruce put down the paper and took off his glasses. "I think it's amazing. It's a great way to work off stress, you know. Maybe I should join, too."

"No way," I said. What a horrible idea. I would never be able to work out in front of Bruce, and he'd hate it there anyway. This was definitely something I needed to do on my own. "You're a beanpole. You don't need to lose weight. *I'm* the fat and revolting one. And if I don't lose weight fast, I'm going to be miserable and disgusting on our wedding day, and I'll never be able to look at the pictures for as long as we both shall live."

"Maybe we can use that last bit as part of our wedding vows."

Annoyed though I was, I had to laugh.

He put his glasses back on and sighed. "I think you look wonderful the way you are."

Liar.

Morgan was far more supportive of my newfound initiative. She works out seven days a week, and has been on my case to do this for years. We even went shopping on Saturday and picked out all kinds of fun workout clothes. Spandex, it turns out, also has miraculous fat-taming abilities if you buy your items a size too small, and I even considered wearing my new shorts under my work clothes on Monday to help control my wayward gut. But I didn't plan to tell anyone else about the gym.

Unfortunately, we bumped into Kimby and Theo at Annie's café.

"Morgan, you look *fabulous,*" drooled Theo. "I wish you'd let me steal you away to my studio sometime. That you haven't been discovered yet…it's an affront. I could maybe start a portfolio for you and then we could see where it goes. I know some people. What do you think?"

Morgan tugged at her skirt and pinched the back of my arm. It was my duty to get her out of there before she embarrassed me. Morgan has the unfortunate habit of saying exactly what she thinks to people she doesn't like, and I was tired of having to apologize for her. "Uh, Annie? Can we get those lattes to go?" I asked.

"Oh hush up now, Theo. You're always bothering her, the poor girl," said Kimby. "Evie! How are you? Why the heck didn't you call me back last week?"

"Last week?"

"You didn't get my message? We went out for Nicole's birthday on Saturday."

"Sorry about that, I had a ton of work," I lied. I just hadn't felt up to it. "But I called her and wished her a happy birthday."

"Nic looks *fabulous,*" said Theo. "Much less…engorged? Is

that the word I'm looking for?" Kimby nodded in agreement. "But she could never hold a candle to you, Morgan," he added.

He grabbed the arm of a good-looking guy who happened to be walking by and pinched Morgan's cheek with his other hand. "Is she not *gorgeous?*" he asked loudly.

The guy nodded and smiled suggestively at Morgan. Uh-oh.

"Thank you very much, sir. I've been trying to immortalize this vixen on film for years, but she's far too coy, *far* too coy. Don't kid yourself, though—she knows she's a knockout and she'll break your heart. You can go now, sir, unless you'd like to stay and join us. Are you a model yourself? Your bone structure is simply magnificent."

Kimby shrieked hysterically as the poor fellow muttered an excuse and scampered away. "Theo, you're awful. Isn't he awful?" she asked, delighted.

"Actually, he is awful," Morgan said. "He's a prick, too, and probably a misogynist to boot. Kimby, my condolences. Evie, I'm leaving." She grabbed her latte from Annie and headed for the door.

"Was it something I said?" asked Theo in mock confusion.

"Isn't it always?" Kimby sighed. "She really hates you."

"Miss Morgan's miffed? At me? My, my, whatever shall I do?"

"Sorry, guys," I said and grabbed my coat. "You know how she is. I'll call you later, Kimby. 'Bye Annie."

"Don't forget your bag, shopgirl," Theo said and handed it to me, but not before peering inside. "What's this? Could it possibly be...Nikes? And—oh my God—a *sports bra?* What are you going to do with these, Evelyn Mays?"

"I joined a gym," I mumbled. Morgan looked at me from the doorway and rolled her eyes.

"You?" gasped Theo, bringing a hand to his chest. "But didn't you once tell me that exercise is what shallow people do to feel deep?"

"No, that's yoga," Kimby giggled. "I believe she said exercise is what mentally weak people do to feel strong."

Theo smacked his forehead dramatically. "Oh, yes. You're right, of course. Well, good luck with it, dear. Call me if you need to borrow my body-fat calipers."

Let them have their fun. Let them laugh at my expense. This time, I don't care. Because I am going to do this. I will find strength in adversity. For once, I know I'm going to get it right. It is finally my turn. My turn to be thin and happy and beautiful.

Annie called me in tears the next morning. Her boyfriend of five and half weeks, Dieter, had left in the middle of the night, without so much as leaving a note.

By the time I got to her place, she was nearly inconsolable. She was sitting on the floor in front of his side of the closet, which was empty save for a few wire hangers and an old pair of flip-flops.

"Why? *Why?*" she moaned, rocking back and forth. "Why did this have to happen to me? *Again?*"

I sat down beside her. "It's not you," I told her, and wiped the tears from her cheeks. "It's them—they're all assholes." Granted, it wasn't a particularly inspired insight, but it was the sort of platitude she needed to hear right now. This was the third time in as many years that Annie had been suddenly dumped by a live-in boyfriend.

"Why do they all hate me?"

I figured she wasn't so much heartbroken over Dieter as she was concerned about her track record. "They don't hate you, Annie, they just use you. And after they get what they need, they move on."

"You mean sex?" she sniffed.

"No, I mean a place to stay." Annie claims to meet her boyfriends at work, but I've had a sneaking suspicion that she hangs out at Penn station, and just picks up any good-looking actor or musician fresh off the bus from shitsville with a duffel bag and a dream. "Your heart's in the right place, you just haven't met the right guy yet."

"But Dieter loved me. He *said* so."

"He did? My God, then! We should call the police! Maybe he's been kidnapped!"

She looked at me skeptically and laughed through her tears. "Don't make fun. I'm in serious pain here."

"I know," I said, squeezing her hand. "It's just gonna take some time. You know the rule—a week of misery for every month you were together. So by next Tuesday, I expect to see you back in action!"

She shook her head and sighed. "I just didn't see it coming this time. I thought he was a good guy. He bought me chocolates with his last thirty dollars."

"Wow. Then I'm just as shocked as you are. You'd think that after thirty nine days, you really get to know someone...."

"Evie," she giggled, "come on! This isn't funny."

"I know it's not. It's very serious. Very serious. Now tell me, do you still have those chocolates?"

With that, she collapsed in laughter and fell back onto the floor. "I guess it is kinda funny."

"It's not, actually," I told her solemnly. "We should have a moment of silence now for Dieter, the best boyfriend ever."

"Yes, let's," she giggled. "And one moment also for his grandmother in Austria, who he called every night from my phone."

"Fine. But just be thankful we'll have more than your long-distance bill to remember him by," I said, and retrieved a giant green flip-flop from the closet floor and held it up for closer inspection. "Hmm...if the size of his feet are any indication, I can see what you've been so upset about."

"Actually," she confided, "you know what they say about big feet...big shoes!"

"Well, then, I'd say that's definitely something positive you can take away from all this. Next time, look for a man with small feet and a big heart."

"Thanks, Evie."

★ ★ ★

Monday turned out to be a classic Day From Hell. Pruscilla's office door was closed when I got there, but I knew she was in from the smell of her perfume. That, and the look of abject fear that had returned to the pale faces of the Marketing Drones who occupy the third-floor offices of Kendra White Cosmetics.

All morning long, she was holed up in there. I could hear her on the phone, yelling. Probably at Thelma. Poor Thelma. She tried her best. I just hope Pruscilla realizes she did everything she could in her limited capacity. I was just relieved I'd done pretty much everything *I* could to keep things running smoothly on my end.

As I was getting ready to leave for my first-ever super lunchtime workout, her door opened. "Evie, come in here," she bellowed. "And close the door behind you."

Figures. Another fitness saboteur to contend with. I grabbed my notepad, anticipating a long list of nasty memos to get down.

She was sitting with her hands folded neatly on her desk, which showed no trace of the towering stacks of folders Thelma had been grappling with for six weeks.

"Pruscilla!" I said warmly. "Welcome back! How are you?"

"Fine, thank you."

"How was your trip?"

"I didn't go on a trip."

"Oh. How was your…time?"

"Everything went as well as can be expected, I suppose." She stared blankly at the wall behind my head. She seemed different, somehow, but I couldn't place it. "But now it's back to normal and I can already see that we're going to have our work cut out for us. Do you mind if I eat while we talk?"

"Go right ahead," I said. Pruscilla's lunch. What a rare treat. Nobody here has ever seen her eat before. We suspect she's a closet binger, because her breath always smells like peanut butter. Andrea's theory is that she keeps a loaf of Wonder Bread and a jar of Skippy locked in her desk drawer, along with Twinkies and Mallomars and things like that, and that she's really just stuffing her face whenever she goes into her office to "take a call." She's here at least 12 hours a day, and she's got to eat sometime. How else could she maintain that weight?

Pruscilla pulled a cloth napkin out of a drawer and placed it down on the desk. "I've been going over things with Thelma all morning," she said. "She'd been bringing me up to speed."

I nodded sympathetically. "Thelma totally tried her best, you know. She worked her butt off, put in a lot of overtime." Why not put in a good word for her? It was the least I could do.

"She certainly has," Pruscilla agreed. She pulled a crumpled brown paper bag out of her briefcase. Was that a new pink cape she was wearing?

"You can't really expect everything to be perfect. Filling your shoes was no easy task, especially for someone like Thelma. She was just overwhelmed, I guess. But I don't think she knew what she was in for."

"Oh no, Evelyn, don't misunderstand me. I'm *delighted* with what Thelma has accomplished. To tell you the truth, I could hardly have done a better job myself. If I had known this place was in such capable hands, I would have spent a lot less time worrying. Maybe I wouldn't have come back so soon." She shifted uncomfortably in her chair. Was she serious?

"Great," I said weakly.

Then she looked me right in the eyes and said, "Well, what do you think, Evie? Is there some reason I should have been worried?"

Suddenly, I had the feeling I was standing at the edge of a very tall cliff, and the wind was just starting to come up behind me. I thought about my bottom desk drawer, stuffed full with paperwork and invoices Thelma had shoved my way. *Steady, Evie, steady.*

"Um, I think you're right. Thelma did a great job."

Pruscilla pulled a bottle of Evian and two soda crackers out of her lunch bag and placed them on the napkin.

"And how have you found it?" Was she setting me up?

"Fine, Pruscilla. Everything went great on my end, just like we talked about."

"Yes, well…before I left, we discussed how important it would be for you to handle more responsibility and take some initiative if you ever want to move out of that cubby and into an office here someday…."

She was going to promote me! And to think, I was actually worried that a dolt like Thelma was going to foil my plans for corporate domination.

"I remember what we talked about, and I've been keeping it in mind these last few weeks. In fact…" I hesitated. Pruscilla opened a small Tupperware container and spooned a teaspoon of tuna onto each cracker.

"What?" she asked.

"What are you doing?"

"Eating lunch."

"That's lunch?"

"I have grapes, too," she said defensively, pulling a sorry-looking bunch out of the bag. "In fact what, Evelyn?"

"Oh. Um, I've implemented a new filing system. Aren't you going to be hungry if that's all you eat for lunch?"

Pruscilla sighed and put down her cracker. "I suppose you're all going to find out sooner or later. I just don't want anyone making a big fuss about it."

"Fuss? Fuss about what? What happened?"

"The reason I went away was to do something for myself, something I've wanted to do for a long time."

Oh God, she's had a sex change. Pruscilla is a man. A gay man. I *knew* it. I knew she looked different. And this would explain the pink cape.

"I've had gastric bypass surgery, Evelyn. To lose weight."

"What?"

Pruscilla appeared decidedly hurt. Shit.

"Wow—it's just, uh, that's not what I thought you were

going to say. I'm just surprised, that's all. Really. But, uh...wow! Surprised, but totally happy for you, of course!"

"I know, it's pretty drastic," she said, relieved. "But it's really becoming quite a popular treatment for morbid obesity. Insurance paid for it completely because I weigh over twice what I should. Or rather, I *weighed* twice what I should. I've already lost forty-five pounds in six weeks!"

She grinned broadly. Insurance won't pay for the monthly massages I need for my bad back (*Mademoiselle,* March: "Shiatsu or Swedish? Marvellous Massages, Radical Results"), but they'll shell out twenty grand for Pruscilla's intestines to be rerouted. Was there any justice in this world?

"It's wonderful, really, Pruscilla. I'm *so* happy for you. You know, I could tell you looked different, but I couldn't place how." Butter her up for a big raise *before* she offers me the promotion.

"I know, I know," she said excitedly. "Everything I own's already big on me. And it's so easy—the pounds are just melting off! My stomach is the size of a shot glass, so I get totally full after a couple of bites. I have no choice!"

I have to admit, it sounded like a good deal. I wonder if I would qualify? The possibilities raced through my mind.

"How much did it hurt? How long will it take to lose all the weight? Can you still eat cheesecake? Do you have to be obese to have the operation? I mean, do you think it would work for me? Are there any—"

"Don't be ridiculous, Evelyn. This was major surgery. It's not something to be entered into lightly. Now I don't want to discuss it anymore."

Well if that's how she was going to be about it... "Okay, back to me then," I said, wishing immediately that I hadn't. Pruscilla pulled out a red folder marked EVELYN and glared at me.

"I'm going to cut to the chase here, Evelyn. I'm putting you on three-month probation."

Probation? Was that good?

"I asked Thelma to keep an eye on you while I was gone."

She opened up the folder and began to read. "Left before 5:30, eighteen times. Arrived after 8:30, twenty-three times. Days absent from work, five. Should I go on?"

The room began to spin wildly. I could feel my face flush red with anger, and more than a little shame. *How could I have been so stupid?*

"Thelma was spying on me?" That evil bitch. To think that I defended her.

"Is that all you have to say for yourself?"

"It's impossible, Pruscilla. Her office is across the floor. She can't even *see* if I'm at my desk from where she is. And…and…frankly, this is an invasion of my privacy!" I suppose it wasn't the best thing to say under the circumstances, but I was on the spot.

"You figured just because I was gone, you could do whatever you please? When the cat's away, so to speak? Well, Ms. Mays, that's not the way things work around here."

I sensed that she wasn't going to fall for a civil liberties defense. "I missed a lot of work, I know, but I've been getting really bad cramps and—"

"Please, just stop. Your abysmal attendance is the highlight of this report," she said, waving the red folder in my face. "You've done nothing, absolutely *nothing,* that you were supposed to do. We had a quarterly report due two weeks ago. Thelma told me she had to work up all the numbers herself. That's *your* job. But it won't be for long if you don't smarten up. Three months, Evelyn, three months. If I don't see a complete and total turnaround, you're gone. Do I make myself clear?"

"Yes," I managed to whisper through the tears.

I almost wished she'd just fired me on the spot. It would have been better than staying on in that hellhole and suffering the humiliation that was sure to come. Why does this crap always happen to me? I guess I deserved it this time, but still—why do I always get caught no matter what? For just once in my life, I'd love to actually get away with something.

* * *

Bruce, of course, was completely unsympathetic to my professional angst. So I decided, after much thought on the subway ride home, that if Kendra White can't appreciate the subtleties of what I have to offer the company—and especially if I get canned in three months—then maybe I would be better off somewhere else anyway. Karl Marx had it dead right when he said he wouldn't want to belong to any club that would have him as a member. He knew that sometimes, even the worst clubs, like the Communist party, can often overlook the genius in their midst. And I know where he's coming from because Kendra White is probably a lot like the Communist party was back in those days, only with more women and better money.

Bruce says that's not exactly what Marx meant, that he was putting himself down or making fun of exclusive clubs for accepting lame people or something, and that it was Groucho Marx and not Karl Marx who said it, besides. But I think that proves my point even more, because there's always a kernel of truth in humor.

In keeping with my new enlightened outlook on things, I felt that the most sensible course of action would be to buckle down at work and hopefully climb my way back up the few rungs I'd dropped on the proverbial corporate ladder. However, at the same time, just in case things didn't work out, I would also learn a new trade, something that would allow me to work independently *and* make a lot more money. Kendra White, whoever the hell she was, could kiss my size fourteen ass. I knew I was meant for bigger and better things than the third floor of that sweatshop anyway (*Cosmopolitan,* September: "Live Up To Your Professional Potential!").

But Bruce wasn't so sure. As if agreeing with Pruscilla regarding my work habits weren't bad enough, he said that a change of career now would be too stressful for me, what with the wedding coming up. Whatever happened to unconditional love and support?

"Just put in some overtime for the next few months and see what happens," Bruce said wearily as we waited for a table at the SoHo Grill on Friday night. "Impress the hell out of them."

"I'll have a Double Jack," I said to the bartender. "And he'll have a Shirley Temple."

Bruce just looked at me. A few months ago, he would have laughed at something like that.

"What I really need is a new job. No—a new *career.* Something less stressful, where I don't have to worry about people standing over my shoulder watching everything that I do. Where I can be rewarded for my hard work, instead of making some faceless board of directors rich."

"I see," said Bruce. "Did you have something in particular in mind?"

"Ideally, I'd want to do something that lets me use my education, like you. You have a Master's degree in education. And that's what you do—you educate. It makes sense. I mean, what's the point of having a degree if I never get to use it?"

"So, you're going to be a...philosopher?"

"Don't be smart."

"Enlighten me, then. And, um, I think that drink is meant to be sipped."

"Well," I snorted, slamming the rest of it back. "So sorry to have offended your hard-coreness."

"Not at all. Please continue."

"Thank you. I've been doing a bit of research, and I've come up with three. Three things I could do that *I* would be good at and nobody else. With nobody there to give me shit." I knew I was slurring, despite the fact that I was thinking quite clearly.

"Shoot."

"One: Jewelry maker."

"Ah, yes. The ultimate philosopher's day job, which begs the timeless question—how can we know if a bead is ever truly a bead, and not just the illusion of beadery?"

Ignoring Bruce is sometimes the only way to get through

an entire conversation. "Two: Advertising executive in charge of my own entire advertising company."

"I had no idea you were interested in advertising."

"You know, in the '80s, huge advertising agencies were tripping over each other to recruit philosophy majors to sit around tables and come up with things for their ad campaigns, really smart and clever things, and they paid them, like, $250,000 a year," I informed him.

"I think that's a myth former philosophy majors tell each other as they serve espressos to twenty-year-old dot-com millionaires."

"Barkeep? Another drink, please. But none for my friend here. He's obviously had enough. And thirdly, for my final career move, I would like to be a…what do you call it?…oh YES—an orintholodist!"

"You mean an ornithologist?"

"Thassit."

Bruce thought carefully for a moment. "While working with birds certainly would be a hoot, I'm not sure New York City is the best place for it, Evie, what with all the paltry poultry here." A blonde with Elvis Costello glasses sitting beside Bruce snickered. She'd obviously been trying to get his attention since we sat down.

"Birds?"

"Ornithologists work with birds."

"No, NO! They don't! I mean, I want to fix kids' teeth. I love kids."

"Shhhh. You're wasted, Evie," Bruce laughed.

Elvis laughed, too, and said, "I think you better take her home. That's one fowl chick."

"For your information," I snapped, leaning past Bruce to get right in her face, "I'm actually quite fly."

All of a sudden, the prospect of being a dentist didn't make as much sense as it had earlier. Rather, it evoked a stream of unpleasant memories of *being* at the dentist, or, more specifically, of the ginormous retainer Mom made me wear for three years, which she had to work overtime to pay for since she was fighting with Claire at the time and…well, at least I made it to the bathroom on time. Bruce was more amused than annoyed, I think, even though we had to skip dinner. But he got lucky later, so what did he care? If given the choice, all men would rather have sex than eat—it's a well-known fact.

Bruce later admitted he was wrong for letting me drink so much at such a vulnerable point in my life. And while I admit that I may have been a little out of control lately, the man had been sullen and difficult since Thanksgiving. We'd both been getting on each other's nerves a lot, and our Friday night dates certainly weren't as much fun as they used to be. I think it was all the forced togetherness. It's like scheduling sex—a good idea in theory, but when it comes right down to it, if you need your Daytimer to get laid, chances are you probably have better things to do with your time anyway.

With Christmas just around the corner, we decided that we should spend the holiday apart—him with his family and me with mine. Which was fine with me. The only thing worse than having to endure another Christmas listening to Mom and Claire debate the pros and cons of dating in widowhood would be watching the Fulbright sisters push uneaten pieces of Bertie's allegedly fabulous stuffed goose around their plates. Not that I could blame them—who the hell actually makes a Christmas goose, anyway?

7

To cheer myself up after a week of bickering with Bruce, kissing Pruscilla's ass, avoiding Thelma like the plague and not going to the gym even one single solitary time, I guilted Morgan into joining me on a very special shopping trip. Although Mom and I had shared a few special moments in Sternfeld's that day, when it comes to buying the most fabulous dress I'll ever wear, I felt my interests would be best served if I had someone there I could completely trust, and that's Morgan. She hates shopping, but she agreed to suffer through it after some very tricky negotiations.

I thought it best not to give her any time to get out of it, so I ambushed her with the invitation on Friday night.

"But I don't know anything about fashion, Evie. Don't make me come."

True, she doesn't have an eye for it like I do, but she still wears an awful lot of Michael Kors and Donna Karan for someone who feigns fashion ignorance.

"That doesn't matter. I still trust you to tell me what looks good and what doesn't. I know you'll at least be honest. That's what I need."

"No."

"But it's your right to be there for me in every way," I told her.

"My right? Please! You mean my duty," she complained.

"But that's part of being maid of honor," I pleaded.

"Maid my ass. What a ludicrous concept. I am *so* not a maid," she said, delighted by the irony. "I'm about as far from a maid as a girl can be, wouldn't you say? And if you throw honor in, well then you can absolutely forget it." She really thinks of herself as quite the slut.

"Well, you're honorable, for the most part. I suppose we could call you a *matron* of honor, if you prefer, but I think that implies that you're married, not just that your maidenhood is a distant memory. Or how about, 'Trollop of Ill Repute'?"

She mulled this over.

"Come with me, or I'll tell everybody you didn't lose your virginity until college."

"Shut up!" she shrieked. "You know I get extra points because he was my professor."

"I don't think so."

"You'd ruin my reputation over this?"

"Yes I would."

"Okay, I'll come. But on one condition—I get to wear black and not that horrid beige you've chosen for the bridesmaids. It would wash me out completely."

No color could possibly look bad on Morgan, and she knows it. She just wants to be different—the thought of blending in with a sea of frilly bridesmaids probably appals her. To be fair, I did choose that color with my wicked sisters-in-law-to-be in mind. You see, champagne serves the dual purpose of fitting in with my fabulously elegant white-on-white wedding (*Martha Stewart Weddings,* Winter: "Perfect Pale Palettes: From White to Cream and Everywhere in Between") *and* looking less than spectacular on all of Bruce's ash-faced sisters. It's horribly cruel, I know, but Annie, Kimby and Nicole will look great, and that's all that matters.

"Don't be ridiculous. It's a wedding, not a funeral." I hope.

"I think it might make a nice statement. Weren't you the one that told me black and white are really going to be in this spring?"

"Yes, but that's for purses and prints, Morgan, not weddings, for God's sake." Actually, the idea was starting to grow on me.

"Oh well. I've got laundry to do tomorrow anyway," she said.

"Fine, then, wear black. Be a scene stealer," I said. "But I think it's only fair that I get to help you choose your dress." I couldn't trust her not to show up in something Cher might have worn to the Academy Awards.

"Deal," she said. "What time will you pick me up?"

"Be downstairs at three. I'll be in a cab."

"Isn't that a bit late?"

"3:00 a.m., Morgan. There's going to be a long line."

"What the hell are you talking about?"

"You'll see."

She hung up on me, but I knew she'd be there.

Thankfully, there would be only one place to go in my quest for the ultimate gown. Before Pruscilla blocked my Internet access, I came across some very interesting information regarding a once-in-a-lifetime opportunity for the young and fashion-forward bride-to-be—the Vera Wang sale. In case you've been living under a rock for the past ten years, Vera Wang is *the* top name in bridal fashion. No self-respecting starlet or socialite would walk down the aisle in anything else, unless they were trying to make some sort of peculiar anti-Wang statement. You know, the type who would get married barefoot on the beach like Cindy Crawford or who would prefer to wear a hemp gown or something lame like that.

But once a year, in a New York City hotel whose name is kept quiet until the last possible minute, there's a gigantic Vera Wang blowout sale and all her dresses are marked down seventy or eighty percent. People come from all over the country and start lining up in the middle of the night to get first crack at the best gowns.

Sure enough, there was already a line when we got there, stretching halfway down the hall. Most of the girls had brought their mothers. Some strategy—these slow-witted, middle-aged mommies would be no match for us. Morgan was still a little drunk and obviously hadn't been to sleep, which was a good thing. I wanted her bitchy and on edge, in case she had to fight someone for a dress.

"Keep your eye out for anything you think would look good on me," I said as I eyed the crowd.

Morgan just yawned.

"I think we've got a good spot, here. The ones at the front of the line will either overshoot the good stuff or be trampled underfoot. There's one chick up there, though, she looks wily. She brought her own full-length mirror. Smart. Very smart. And her mother's wearing running shoes. Keep your eye on her, Morgan. And take a look at these...."

I handed her a stack of ads I'd ripped out of magazines. "I've already memorized them, and you'd do well to do the same. If you see any of these—and I mean *any* of these—grab 'em. I don't care if you have to rip a dress out of someone's cold, dead hand. Just do it. Grab 'em all and we'll sort them out later."

"You're demented, you know that?"

"I'm *determined*." Okay, and maybe just a touch sick. But this was my one and only chance to be able afford the dress of my dreams. Besides, there was no harm in it, was there? And it was all in good fun.

"Yes, I can see that."

"It's almost four now, and the doors don't open till eight. There's lots of time to familiarize yourself with the dresses."

But she just slumped down against the wall and closed her eyes.

By 8:00 a.m., I'd had four cups of coffee and almost missed the doors opening because I was stuck waiting in line at the bathroom. Morgan waved to me from the crowd and I fought my way forward just in time to make it in with the first group. We would have exactly one hour before they kicked us out and let the next group in.

Inside the room, rows and rows of dresses wrapped in plastic hung neatly on portable silver racks. But not for long. It was like watching an army of ants devour an entire picnic in fast forward. Plastic was flying every which way. Girls were stripping down to their underwear and frantically pulling dresses over their heads while friends or mothers looked on approvingly. Our strategy was to divide and conquer. Grab whatever looks good, and narrow down the field later.

I ran through the aisles wildly pulling out dresses and pushing plastic aside. There were so many to go through. But none of them seemed right. All I could find were rejects—last year's models, some were damaged, a few weren't even close to white. A wave of terror swelled up within my chest. The clock was ticking. I saw the girl from line jumping up and down in joy, holding a stunning gown to her chest, while her mother supported the mirror with one hand and wiped tears away with the other. *Dammit! Where was mine? Where was my dress?* I was starting to sweat. People were pushing me from every which way. It had already been almost forty-five minutes—all the good ones were sure to be gone! The room began to get dark. I looked up. The chandelier swayed like it was about to come crashing down onto my head....

I crawled out from the fray, sat down on the floor next to a security guard and put my head in my hands, trying to catch my breath. It was no use. My dream dress, it seemed, was exactly that—a dream. Worse than that, it was a cruel hoax, a false ideal concocted by misogynist male capitalists in order to coax impoverished young brides-to-be into maxing out their credit cards for a gown they'll wear for six hours, then leave to rot for two or three decades, only to be passed over by their ungrateful daughters in favor of what ultimately amounts to nothing more than yet another overpriced white tablecloth.

Then the sea of dresses parted and Morgan appeared from between the rows, my knight in shining armour. In her arms, she bore a single, precious gown.

When she saw me, she ran over. "Evie? Are you okay? What are you doing?"

I stood up and wiped my eyes. "Having a panic attack, I think."

"Are you okay?"

"I…I don't know," I answered. "If you're aware that you're losing your mind, does that mean you're not really losing it?"

"Okay, now you're scaring me."

"I'm scaring myself. But I'm okay. I think I just had too much coffee."

"You sure? Maybe we should call Bruce."

"No, I'm fine. I just need to eat something I think." I already felt a little better.

"Okay," she said. "Let's get out of here. But is this one of the ones from your pictures?" she asked innocently, holding the dress up for me to see.

"It is," I said calmly, because I could see that it was. If there was one Vera Wang dress that I could have chosen, this would be it. It was a simple, strapless A-line gown in glowing ivory duchesse satin, with delicate beading at the top and at the hem. It was so elegant, so understated, so breathtakingly perfect that it took my breath away. Grace Kelly would rise up from the dead and remarry if she knew this gown existed.

I pulled aside the plastic and touched it carefully. It was real, all right.

"Happy?" Morgan asked.

"Yes," I said, and hugged her.

"Good. So stop crying. Now are you ready for the bad news?"

"No."

"It's a size eight."

"Eight?" I gulped.

"Eight."

"All the dresses here size eight, ladies," interrupted the security guard. "Some even size six. This a sample sale. All the dresses the same size."

"Thank you very much," Morgan snapped, "but you should really mind your own business."

In light of this new information, I examined the dress again. For all its glory, it appeared to have been designed for half a Barbie doll.

"Maybe they're made big," Morgan offered. She had no way of knowing what Greta from Sternfeld's said about all wedding dresses being made small. "At least it's an eight—it could have been a six."

A feeling of calm and certainty washed over me. It didn't matter. Better than that, this was exactly what I needed.

"It's okay," I told Morgan. "I'm going to take it. This is it. This is The Dress."

"These dresses all non-refundable," the guard offered, looking me up and down skeptically.

"For your information," Morgan shrieked at him, "*this* is a Vera Wang gown that retails for $8000 on sale for $1800! *This* is my best friend Evelyn Mays, and *this—this* is the dress she'll be wearing on her wedding day! She'll go on a liquid diet if she has to, goddammit!"

Could you ask for a better friend than that?

I immediately brought the gown to Mom's place so that Bruce wouldn't see it. As soon I took it out of the bag, she had to give me credit.

"I didn't know they made wedding dresses like this," she said, examining it carefully. "It's *very* pretty."

"The only thing is, it's a little small." Best to state the obvious before she started in on me.

"Yes, I can see that."

"But I'm not worried. I can do it."

"Well if you say so, Evelyn. How much was it?"

"The real question is, how much did I save."

"No, the real question is, how much was it?"

"Eighteen hundred dollars."

"Well, that's not so bad." Well what do you know.

"How much did your wedding dress cost, Mom?"

"The crystal beading is absolutely lovely. It's almost like little drops of water…"

"Mom?" She could be such a scatterbrain.

"Yes?"

"Your dress. How much was your dress?"

"What? Oh. I don't remember."

"What did it look like?" There were no pictures of my parents' wedding. I assume it's because they eloped, and probably didn't have time to find a decent photographer.

"Don't worry about your dress, Evelyn, I'll pay for it."

"Oh, Mom, you don't have to—"

But she cut me off. "I want to. A girl shouldn't have to pay for her own wedding gown."

I could tell that this was important to her. "Thank you, Mom. This really means a lot to me."

She thought quietly for a second, then reached out and took my hand. "If your father were alive, it wouldn't even be a question. He was an exceedingly generous man. You know he'd have given you the world, Evelyn. If he could have."

"I know, Mom," I said, and hugged her.

She doesn't much talk about my father anymore. I suppose she never did, really. Apart from a few well-worn stories and a handful of old pictures, the impressions and images I have of my father came mostly from Claire. I didn't even know how he died until I was ten years old. Mom just never talked about it. When Claire found out I had no idea how it happened, she brought me to a tall building downtown and pointed. "He was working construction over the Christmas holidays, to earn a little extra cash. It was snowing, slippery. And he fell, but just like an angel, he flew up to heaven." Years later, it occurred to me that he must never have known Mom was pregnant. She didn't even know until after he was gone.

Later I went home and told Bruce what happened. He was really happy for me, glad I found my dress, and glad that my mother and I were getting along. Some days he's not so bad, really. Maybe he was even a little bit right about a few things. And maybe it would be nice to have Christmas together, just the Mays women, one last time. Pretty soon, I was going to be a Fulbright. There were worse things to be, I suppose. But for all their blondness and thin ankles and perfect posture, they can't hold a candle to us.

The Kendra White Christmas Party is mandatory. Some years, I guess when business is good, they do it at a nice big hotel. But this year, the third floor was being transformed into a nondenominational "Winter Holiday Wonderland" by Santa's little do-gooders from Health and Fitness. What fun.

Bruce was looking forward to it more than I was, probably because he was excited to see his little fan club. After he proposed, word of his romanticism spread through the offices like the plague. Now, even girls I don't know from the second and fourth floors ask me if it's true. The lame story in the monthly *Kendra White Chronicle* didn't help ("Third-Floor Marketing Assistant Evelyn Mays Says 'I WILL,'" which ran right next to a bit about the offices' thumbs-up from the asbestos inspector). So now I'm known as the Girl Whose Boyfriend Proposed. Needless to say, many people were quite pleased to hear that the famous Bruce would indeed be attending the party.

Although I haven't got around to filling out the forms yet, I've always been of the opinion that going on welfare might be an acceptable alternative to having to attend those work-related social functions. Potlucks for baby showers, potlucks for retirements, potlucks for breast reductions, for God's sake. The only thing lucky about any one of them is if you manage to get through it without dying of food poisoning first. I mean, really—the thought of eating a mystery casserole prepared by someone who you know doesn't wash her hands after she pees (or worse) is beyond frightening.

Although at first glance, the Christmas Party may seem preferable to the dreaded potluck (i.e. it's catered), it's not. Because the only thing worse than Vivian from Cosmetics' Turkey Tetrazzini with last year's mayo is watching your elderly coworkers get blitzed. When you throw alcohol into the mix, people you didn't respect to begin with somehow manage to go down a notch. The first year, it was entertaining, the second year it was embarrassing, and now it's just excruciating.

"They shouldn't make these things on Friday nights," I huffed as we climbed the stairs to the third floor (*Self,* January: "10 Little Things You Can Do To Burn Big Calories"). "It interferes with the employees' personal lives."

"Oh come on, it's just once a year," said Bruce.

"They should do it during the day, on company time. Is there lipstick on my teeth?"

"Yes."

"How do I look?"

"Great. How do I look?"

"Good." He was wearing a tie with bumblebees on it, but my mother gave it to him, so it was okay. Bruce always looks the same—skinny, cute, freckly.

"Do you like the new glasses?"

"I picked them, didn't I?"

"You sure did, honey," he smiled, and kissed me on the forehead. "I like you in high heels."

Bruce is six-one, and I'm only five-four. He must get sick of looking at the top of my head. "You wouldn't like them if you knew how much they hurt me," I pouted.

"Then why did you buy them?"

"They're Manolo Blahniks," I explained. I got them three

years ago at Neiman Marcus Last Call in Las Vegas. They're half a size too small, and they're a dreadful shade of puce, but they were only $199. I even bought a dress to go with them. But I wasn't wearing it tonight, since everyone already saw it at last year's party. You can do the same shoes two years in a row—who would possibly remember?—but not a dress, and especially not a sleeveless puce gown. Tonight I was wearing a basic black DKNY shirtdress. Casual chic, but the shoes dress it up.

Not that you can be underdressed for a party which involves moving collapsible cubicles out of the way to make a dance floor. There was the requisite DJ dressed like Santa Claus, and mistletoe hanging from the fluorescent lights. Everything was covered in silver tinsel. Here and there, a Hanukkah menorah floated overhead.

"They better put my cubby back exactly where they found it," I grumbled under my breath.

"Don't worry," said a girl I'd never seen before. "We copied down the floor plan before we moved everything. You're Evie Mays, aren't you? I'm Jessica, from Health and Fitness downstairs. Nice to meet you. Is *this* the famous Bruce? I told all my friends about what you did! It's just like in *Pretty Woman!* You *singlehandedly* resurrected our faith in romance."

Bruce grinned like an idiot. The Jessica person grinned like a slut.

"Well, not exactly like that," he said. "There was no limo involved, and Evie works in marketing, not...well...you know."

"And he's even seen *Pretty Woman,*" she sighed, placing her hand over her heart, or whatever dark void lay underneath.

"I'd like a drink now," I interrupted.

"Me, too. I'll have an eggnog," Bruce said.

"You're going to have to try a lot harder than that if you want to be funny," I said.

He shrugged his shoulders and gave Jessica a dramatic "What's with her?" look, and said, "Come on, Evie, I was just teasing. Let me get you ladies a drink. Jessica, what's your poison?"

"Never mind," I said, and went off to find the bar. If Bruce wants to make me jealous, he'd have to find someone a lot better-looking than that. Her teeth stuck out from her gums at right angles.

As I picked tinsel out of the bowl of eggnog with a plastic fork, Andrea sidled up beside me, clutching a gray-skinned man with no hair.

"Hi, Evie, this is Phil. Where's Bruce?"

"He's here somewhere," I said.

"How are things with you guys? How are the plans coming?" she asked. It was obvious that she'd heard we were having an engagement party in January, and expected to be invited. Since it was also obvious that she was dying to tell me something about her own life, and didn't really care about mine, I decided not to let her in on any of our plans.

"Couldn't be better," I said, trying to appear distracted by my own important personal thoughts.

"Guess what?" she asked, barely able to contain herself. She was hiding her left hand behind her back.

"Phil asked you to marry him?"

Her face contorted from an impossibly wide grin into a painful grimace. Phil closed his eyes and breathed out softly.

"No," she said, and shot Phil a dark look. "I was going to tell you that Pruscilla had her stomach stapled."

"I know!" I laughed. "Isn't that crazy?"

"Well if anyone could use it, it's her." She was still hiding her hand behind her back.

My curiosity got the better of me. "What's in your hand?"

"What?"

"Your left hand."

"It's a tampon, if you must know."

"Oh. Sorry." Not exactly an engagement ring. I guess I just had weddings on the brain. I'd have to stop assuming everyone else was getting married, too.

"Yes, well, whatever." She turned to go, then stopped and said loudly, "Nice shoes. I like them better with this dress than that gown from last year." Everyone within earshot looked at my feet. What a hag.

By the time I found Bruce, he was deeply immersed in conversation with Pruscilla. She looked pretty good. There was no denying it—she was a lot slimmer. You could see the bones in her face now, and her breasts stuck out farther than her stomach. If that's not inspiration, I don't know what is. The day Pruscilla Cockburn looks better than I do...I can't bear to think about it.

Bruce already had a drink in his hand, courtesy of Miss Health and Fitness, no doubt, so I finished mine quickly and started in on the one I'd brought for him.

"You look great, Pruscilla," I said. "Doesn't she, Bruce?"

Pruscilla flushed bright red.

"She sure does," Bruce agreed. "I told her I barely recognized her."

"I've lost almost fifty-five pounds!" she gushed.

"It really shows," I said. She seemed very susceptible to flattery these days, at least about this one thing. It certainly hadn't done me any good when I told her I thought her people skills made her the perfect candidate for the President of Marketing and Sales (West Coast) position I'd seen posted in the Newsletter.

"Everyone's been so supportive," she said. "Especially people who understand. Evie, you know how hard it is to struggle with your weight. But I finally feel like I've got it under control." Great, now we were sharing the most intimate secrets of our personal lives.

Bruce nodded, and said, "Evie joined a gym."

The rest of the soiree was equally bad, except for when a drunken Doris from Skin Care made a very public pass at Gregory from Fragrances, who is much, much younger than her, and was there with his boyfriend, besides. You can hardly blame her, though. The pickings are pretty slim at Kendra White.

While Bruce chatted with Pruscilla and made the rounds, I lurked in the corner and got tipsy with two girls from Skin Care. Ashley, one of the few people who I feel truly gets it at KW, called a play-by-play on Doris's clumsy attempts at seduction.

"Do you think it's possible she doesn't know?" Wendy asked incredulously as Gregory's boyfriend fondled his ear. But Doris just kept trying to pull him onto the dance floor.

"Oh, I know that she knows," Ashley assured her. "She just thinks she can turn him."

"If I were gay, it would take a lot more than the likes of Doris to convince me to switch sides," I said.

Wendy shook her head. "That's for sure. She looks like a thirteen-year-old Russian gymnast with all those barrettes in her hair."

"What is she, fifty?" I asked. There was a definite dichotomy at KW between the older women and the younger ones. We each tended to keep to ourselves.

"Oh, at least," said Ashley. "But I don't think she's ever even had a boyfriend."

"No wonder she's so desperate," I said. "But isn't she his boss?" We stared as Gregory reluctantly tangoed Doris across the floor.

Ashley nodded. "You're thinking sexual harassment? It's possible. I wouldn't put it past her. When I was her assistant, she once tried to get me to pick up her dry cleaning."

Wendy laughed. "Oh, yeah, that was something. She told Doris she'd be happy to—as soon as Human Resources added the term 'Spineless Lackey' to her job description."

"You did not," I said.

"I sure as hell did," she said as she tugged at her waist, then mumbled, "Fucking control-tops. Why do I even bother? It's not like there's anyone here to impress."

"And you got away with it?"

"Damn strait I did. All she did was laugh, like she'd been kidding about it or something. Some cover-up. But I wasn't about to pick up her god damn dry cleaning."

If only I had the guts, I thought wistfully. Somehow, though, what comes across as self-assuredness and confidence in Ashley would seem contrary and difficult in me if I tried to pull the same thing. "I wish I could tell Pruscilla off like that the next time she orders me to work through my lunch, but as you know I'm—"

"ON PROBATION!" They both yelled at the same time and gulped back their eggnogs.

At least that was the only Christmas party I'd have to deal with this year. The shindig at Bruce's school is an employees-only thing, thank God, which means I would be spared small talk about this little prodigy's knack for recombining DNA and that little virtuoso's stellar turn at Carnegie Hall.

When he came home from that, the following evening, he told me they were promoting him to a scout, or Parker School Representative, as they call it. Yes, they have talent scouts at these schools. Essentially, Bruce explained, he'll still be teaching, but starting in January, he'll also be traveling around the country once in a while to convince the parents of gifted kids to send their precious little bundles to his school. I think they should give him a commission for each one he brings in, but he balked at the idea of suggesting it. With tuition alone at over ten thousand dollars a year, I think it was the least they could do to thank him.

If anyone deserves a raise at that school, Bruce does. He loves those kids, even though they're irritating to most everyone but their parents. Plus, he has a Master's degree. If I had a Master's degree, I probably would have been promoted by now, too. Morgan has an MBA and she's been promoted countless times. Maybe if Bruce makes enough money, I could quit Kendra White and go back to school full-time in the fall. It was definitely something to think about. A Master's degree would make a marvelous Christmas present. If Bruce can't think of anything to get me this year, I just might suggest it.

8

The holidays passed pleasantly enough, partly because for once I didn't stuff myself to the gills with chocolate and pie. It's not that Mom doesn't cook well; she does (although the turkey was a little dry), it's just that I've had an epiphany of sorts. A real Christmas miracle.

According to the most recent literature on the subject, the key to getting rid of those unwanted pounds forever is not what you put in your mouth, it's about changing your perspective and using positive visualization (*Shape,* January: "See It, Be It: Get Fit in Your Mind First"). It was such a relief to hear that Mars bars have nothing to do with it. Instead of torturing myself over every delicious, forbidden morsel, all I have to do is actively imagine how fabulous I'll be when I've dropped forty-five pounds, and then the weight will magically melt away. You see, when the end result is more appetizing than what you can eat today, you just won't be as hungry. You will completely lose your desire to snack. Poor Pruscilla—if only she had known, she could have avoided unnecessary surgery.

Why hadn't anyone told me about this sooner? The information has already completely revolutionized my relationship with food. To think, I've spent all these years cursing calories, instead of just embracing them as the fuel my body needs to sustain energy. It was all so simple, really. Armed with this healthy new approach, I felt certain I'd be able to circumvent any unnecessary diet-related craziness on my part. Bruce would be thrilled.

Before the big Christmas dinner, as an appetite suppressant, I went into Mom's closet and peeked at The Dress. It was as stunning as ever. I imagined myself in it, walking down the aisle. "She's thin as a rail," guests would whisper to one another as I floated by. "How ever did she do it?" Even the minister would suck in his breath when he saw me. This visualization technique worked so well, in fact, that I didn't even have dessert.

It was all part of the master plan, which I'd hammered out very carefully during a particularly bad wave of nausea the morning after the KW Christmas Party. And wouldn't you know it? Pruscilla's rapidly emerging collarbones were enough to spur me on to the gym, too. I'd been going religiously three days a week, for one week so far, and it was going fantastically. I wouldn't want to counteract the effects of my new workout regime by forcing myself to eat dessert just because it happened to be Christmas.

Mom and Claire couldn't help but notice my resolve.

"No fruitcake, Evie?" asked Claire.

"Not tonight. I'm stuffed."

"But you love my fruitcake," Mom said, her brow furrowed.

That may have been true at one time. I've always felt that fruitcake got a bad rap. If you like Sara Lee pound cake, I used to say, and you like maraschino cherries, then what's the problem?

"I just don't feel like it, Mom."

"Leave her alone, Lillian. She doesn't want any." Claire, who has always been quite slim herself, understood these things.

"All right. Will you at least have some tea?"

"Yes, please. With milk."

And so it went.

It was actually quite a nice evening. Bruce even stopped by later on, after his dinner at Bertie's was finished. He showed up in a Santa beard and hat, which his school let him have a few years back after the kids proved to be more interested in sled aerodynamics and Amundsen's trip to the North Pole than Bruce's anorexic interpretation of Saint Nick.

"It was nice of you to come," I said, feeling festive. "How was your dinner?"

"Why, Santa has no time to eat dinner on Christmas Eve, little girl! It's my busiest night of the year!"

Claire rolled her eyes and Mom laughed. "Maybe I could make a nice plate for Santa?" she asked hopefully.

"Well," Bruce said, rubbing his nonexistent belly, "maybe just a small one. But go easy on me—I don't want to get stuck in a chimney!"

"Maybe Santa should take off his beard before he eats," I offered.

"Maybe you should have a seat on Santa's lap and tell him what you want for Christmas," he slurred. "More gravy, please Lilly."

Mom beamed, and loaded it on. Disgusting—there's enough fat in one spoonful of that stuff to put a girl over her limit for the day.

"No wonder the kids were afraid of you," I said.

"Santa will deal with you later, little girl," he said slyly, jiggling his belt buckle.

"Bruce!" Mom gasped.

"Don't be such a prude, Lillian," Claire laughed. "They've been living together since college. And I think Santa's been into the eggnog."

Defeated, Bruce pulled off his beard. "Can't a guy be in a good mood without being drunk?"

"Oh my God, it's Bruce," I said flatly.

"Ho, ho, ho," he said. "Where's your holiday spirit?"

Claire sighed. "Speaking of holiday romance, Lillian—"

"We were speaking of no such thing," Mom interrupted.

"Yes, well, anyway, I've been meaning to ask you something, and I thought since we're all in a such good mood...." Claire hesitated.

Mom's no fool. "Go on," she said suspiciously.

Bruce helped himself to a huge slab of fruitcake.

"He must be starving after that goose," I explained.

"I met a woman last week in my sculpture class. She's a very nice lady. Name's Francine. Well, we got to talking and it turns out she has a son. A widower. And he's only fifty-two, if you can imagine that."

"Oh, I can imagine that very well, Claire," Mom snapped, getting up to clear the table.

"I told her all about you, and she seemed very interested. I thought maybe this fellow could give you a call sometime. He's a contractor, and he's very handsome. I saw his picture."

"What does he look like?" I asked.

"He could look like Wayne Newton for all I care, but it makes no difference because I'm not interested," Mom yelled from the kitchen. "And the discussion is closed."

"Well, he seemed tall. He's got that, oh, whaddyacallit? Salt-and-pepper hair, that's it. And a very distinguished nose. Very Roman." Claire said loudly. What the hell was a Roman nose? "Maybe I'll just pass her number along anyway," she whispered to me and winked.

Mom came back in with a glass of wine and sat down.

Bruce, fortified by rum and fruitcake, had dispensed with his normal inhibitions. "Come on, Lilly! It can't hurt to talk to the guy, can it?"

"Yes, Bruce, it can," she said curtly, and shot Claire a nasty look. "You see? You see this? You and your nosy little friend should stay out of my personal life. Try and find some men of your own, why don't you."

Claire hooted like it was the funniest thing she'd ever heard. "That's exactly what *I* said! I told her that if you didn't want him, I'd be happy to take him off her hands! He lives at home with her, so he sounds like a bit of a mama's boy, if you ask me, but it's not so easy for an old lady like me to get a date. I can't afford to be picky!"

"Claire, really! You should be ashamed of yourself, carrying on like that. And, dare I ask, don't you already have a boyfriend?" Mom was quite happy to change the subject.

"Oh, Eddie left me for an older woman. She's seventy-six!" My crazy granny slapped the table so hard, some of Mom's wine sloshed out of the glass. But we all laughed anyway—even Mom, who tried hard not to.

Despite everyone's willingness to let her get away with being so difficult to talk to on this subject, I decided right then and there that one of my New Year's resolutions would be to find Mom a date for the wedding. It didn't seem fair. Here I was, marrying Bruce, on the verge of being thin, and deliriously happy at least once in a while, while Mom is all alone and miserable. The thought of going home to an empty house every night for, like, twenty-five years is the worst possible thing I could imagine.

I remember, vaguely, that she had a boyfriend at one time, when I was in middle school. I was probably only twelve or thirteen, and I don't remember his name or anything like that, but I do recall him coming over to our house for dinner once. Mom got all dressed up, put on her pearls and perfume. She made me wear my white confirmation dress, since it was the only nice dress I had. I hated it—all white and frilly and babyish—and I remember being self-conscious about my boobs. The guy had very bad breath and brought me a Barbie doll, even though I was far too old for them, so I pulled her head off and flushed it down the toilet. Then I screamed and cried until I threw up, and locked myself in Mom's bedroom. We never saw that jerk again. With losers like him on the circuit, no wonder she swore off dating.

Still, though, it's about time she tried again. I'll see if Claire has any ideas on how to trick her into a date. Maybe she has another friend with a son or an ex-boyfriend or something. But hopefully not one who still lives with his mother. I can definitely appreciate Mom's unwillingness to date a mama's boy. She's fifty-one years old, and the last thing she needs is some freak show who's never done his own laundry.

By the time we got home after dinner, Bruce was so tired he fell asleep in his beard. I couldn't help but be a little pissed off, because I had been seriously considering having sex with him. But he made up for it the next morning when we opened our presents. Although I never got around to telling him I wanted a Master's degree for Christmas, he did pretty well shopping on his own.

"Do you like it?" he asked sheepishly. As if I wouldn't like a diamond tennis bracelet.

"How could I not like it?" I held it up to the light. "Is it real?"

"Of course, Evie!" he laughed. "You think I'd slip you a fake?"

Sometimes I forget that Bruce comes from money. It really would never cross his mind that cubic zirconiums are actually an option. In fact, they can be quite pretty, as the entire contents of my jewelry box can attest (*Glamour,* May: "Diamonds Are Forever, But Paste Is Pretty, Too!").

"It must have cost a *fortune.* Have you been saving for this forever? Here—do it up for me."

Bruce beamed. "Since the summer. Granny Fulbright's ring was free, so I thought this year, I could get you something really special."

I jumped up and hugged him. "I really love it, Bruce. It's perfect. And it looks so good on my wrist. I'll wear it on our wedding day."

"I hope so," he said. "I really love my presents, too. Thanks, Evie."

I'd given him a ludicrously complicated calculator I knew he wanted, and a book about Quidditch, some sort of Harry Potter thing.

"I feel terrible. They don't even compare." Truth is, I'd almost screwed up big-time yesterday morning when I realized

I'd been at the gym for two hours and that the stores closed at noon. Thank God Jade remembered to remind me.

"Are you kidding? I'll have more fun with this stuff than you ever could with that useless bracelet. Believe me." Bruce always knows the right thing to say. "Although it does look pretty sexy on your wrist...."

He was right. I held out my arm to admire the bracelet from afar. Why, it could have been the wrist of Elizabeth Taylor, Ivana Trump or any such lucky lady. It even made my arm look skinnier. Come to think of it, the bracelet made Bruce look a whole lot sexier, too. Although I had the distinct feeling I was somehow being manipulated, we then tore off each other's flannel pj's and had quite a passionate romp on the floor next to the Christmas tree.

The only real low point of the holidays was New Year's Eve, which was lamer than normal. We usually do something fun with Morgan—last year we went to an S&M-themed dinner club in the meat-packing district—but this year we couldn't. She wanted us to go with her and Billy to a huge party at some bar, only I was having a body crisis and didn't feel up to achieving the required level of trendiness. As late as that afternoon, she was begging us to come.

"Don't be an idiot, Evie. You'll look fabulous, you know you will."

"Seriously, Evie, *please* come. Drinks are on Billy—all night!"

"I don't think so. But don't worry about us, we'll find something to do."

"You're going to miss a great party. And Bruce will miss looking at my tits. Peter bought me a leather bustier for Christmas." Morgan rarely misses a chance to tease Bruce about his wanting to sleep with her, which he probably does. I know she'd never bother with him, although she's turned making him blush into a sport.

"Won't Billy mind?" I asked.

"Mind what—Bruce checking me out, or Peter's leather fetish?"

"Um, both?"

"He doesn't care. Billy knows Bruce is too much of a puss to actually make a move on me—"

"How would he know that? They've never even met!"

"Well, I must have told him, then. And he has no clue Peter exists. Safer that way, don't you think? Back to what about you, though. Are you really not going to come to a great party just because of some lame body image crisis?"

"I don't think it's lame. In fact, out of respect for me, you probably shouldn't go there, either. I would never buy a Volvo, you know, out of respect for you." Morgan's parents split up when we were sophomores in high school after her mother caught her dad cheating with a Volvo salesgirl. "Safe cars, my ass!" Mrs. Russell used to say.

"You could buy a thousand Volvos for all I care. If it hadn't been for that little Swedish meatball, my mom wouldn't be with Marco today." After the divorce, which was quite ugly, her mom met Marco, a nice-guy carpenter who won slightly more than four million dollars in the New York State Lottery three days after they got married. "Luck of the Irish, my ass!" Mrs. Russell now says.

"I still wouldn't do it," I told her. "And I won't go to the party!"

"You suck," Morgan said, and hung up.

"And a happy New Year's to you, too," I said into the receiver, and slammed it down. "She can be such a bitch."

"You knew that when you married her," Bruce sighed.

"So what are we going to do?" I whined. Not having Morgan to automatically tag along with meant we were dangerously close to the dreaded New Year's Couples' Fight. It happens when you and your boyfriend can't agree on what to do, so you end up having a huge fight, doing different things and resenting each other the whole night, or else having a huge fight, doing nothing together and resenting each other the whole night.

"We could see if Chad and Mimi wouldn't mind us coming to their annual shindig," he suggested ignorantly.

"Or, we could just kill ourselves now." Did he really think I'd say yes to that?

If I've neglected to mention Bruce's friends thus far, it's because I hate them. A dinner party with private-school boys from Greenwich, Connecticut, and their twin-setted wives does not a wild New Year's make. The first and as it turned out final time I agreed to socialize with them was at Bruce's five-year high-school reunion. If you're wondering who the hell bothers with a five-year high-school reunion, the answer is people who are such overachievers that they can't wait ten years to shove their accomplishments in each other's faces. If I sound bitter, it's because Bruce went off with his football friends and left me stuck trying to make small talk for four hours with sorority types named Charity and 'Lizbeth, not to mention that I was the only fat girl there (and I wasn't even that fat five years ago). At least his college buddies are a little better, but most of them are pretty boring, too, albeit in a completely different way.

So with few options remaining and the clock ticking, we finally decided to hook up with Nicole, Kimby and Theo, who were on their way to a drag-queen party at some bar in the Village. Annie couldn't come because she was committed to a ridiculously small understudy part in an ABBA-themed musical production of *The Nutcracker Suite.* If I didn't know for a fact that it existed, I wouldn't have believed it myself. But it does, I assure, you, and good luck getting tickets—it's been sold out for months.

By the time we finally got dressed, got to the city and found the place, it was almost eleven. The bar, as promised, was packed to the rafters with cross-dressers and queens in various stages of undress. Theo, clothed rather conservatively in a zoot suit, chaps and a feather boa, was trying to convince some of his friends that Nicole was really a guy. It wasn't such a stretch. She was wearing the most dreadful sequined top and a miniskirt with go-go boots. And the ten pounds she'd lost in the fall seemed to have been sucked directly from her chest. Kimby, who nobody, no matter how wasted, could ever mistake for a man, was laughing hysterically, pointing at Nicole's crotch.

"If you squint and tilt your head this way, you can see it," Theo said to a cute guy he was obviously trying to impress.

When he noticed us, his eyes widened. At first I assumed it was because he could tell I'd lost some weight—six pounds since the office Christmas party two weeks ago!—but he was far too smashed to notice.

"Evie! Hi! This is Phillip. Phillip, this is Evie and her *fiancé* Bruce. Oh, how I wish *I* had a fiancé," he shouted above the music, and winked at Phillip, who rolled his eyes. "Bruce, you old dog, I can't believe you actually had the balls to show! You look like my father in that sweater vest, why don't you take it off?"

Bruce smiled and looked around nervously. "Be nice, Theo," I laughed. "It was hard enough to get him to come here at all and—"

But Theo was already trying to convince an obviously uncomfortable Nicole to enter the wet T-shirt contest.

"Just do it!" he said. "They'll love you, *I promise!* I'm sure you'll win. It's so ridiculous, how could you not?"

"Forget it! I won't!" Nicole whined, stirring her Bloody Mary.

Kimby, who's a surprisingly mean drunk, joined in eagerly. "Come on, Nic, don't be shy! Everybody will just think they're implants!"

"Or like he's been messing around with estrogen," Phillip added.

Nicole struggled visibly, trying to decide if that was a good thing or a bad thing.

"Oh, leave her alone," I told them. "Nicole, your tits look real.

They're just saying that because they're much perkier than they used to be." She looked at me thankfully while Kimby stifled a laugh. Poor Nicole.

"Yeah," she said. "But do I look like I'm in drag?"

"Of course not—it's just the shirt, that's all," I assured her. "Half the guys in here are wearing sequins, so it's kind of deceptive at first glance. But anyone who bothers looking will see that you're a hundred percent woman."

Theo, whose attention span was even shorter than his relationships, turned to me and asked, "Where's that slut Morgan?"

"Not here, obviously," I said, and gulped down the rest of my drink. Bruce just stared mutely at the floor, refusing to join in the conversation. I believe he was having even less fun than I was. But I was starting to feel bad for him.

"I'm *dying* to shoot her, Phillip, but she hates my guts. Seriously, though, she's the most *gorgeous* redhead I've ever seen. Come to think of it, she's the *only* gorgeous redhead I've ever seen. Freckles turn me off. What about you?"

After another few insufferable minutes, a waiter came to the table with a drink for Bruce, and pointed to the bar. A very tall woman with an Adam's apple smiled and waved. And that was it for our New Year's Eve in the Village. With unusual firmness of purpose, Bruce grabbed my elbow and silently steered us out into the street, without so much as a goodbye to anyone.

We rang in the New Year on the train, completely alone in the car.

"I guess even the bums and weirdos have better places to be tonight than here," Bruce sighed.

"I guess."

But I did think it was kind of romantic, with the city lights twinkling in the background.

9

This was to be the Year of Keeping New Year's Resolutions, I resolved. On the advice of Jade, and to appease Bruce, I turned convention on its ear and threw out my scale. The one at the gym is more accurate, Jade says, and weighing myself every day, or even several times a day, for that matter, is not going to help my focus, nor is it a good indication of my progress. Besides—I was taking on this whole exercise thing primarily for health reasons and to feel better about myself mentally. *Or at least that's what I would tell myself if I didn't lose any more weight.*

Still, I'd been making strides, so the thought of ditching my old friend didn't sit too well with me. But Bruce was utterly insistent, so we had a small scale-smashing ceremony in the bathroom one night, followed by rice cakes and Crystal Light. On the upside, when I saw what it looked like on the inside, all rusted and greasy from years of shower steam and tears, it was apparent that it had not been functioning properly anyway.

With the engagement party less than a month away, now was definitely the time to firm my resolve. After weeks of agonized deliberation for everyone involved, Bertie had finally whittled the list down to a hundred people, and we'd settled on January 20, a Saturday night. She hired a very good local caterer and a party planner—or *stylist,* as she likes to say—who was determined to turn her house into a winter wonderland for the occasion. The invitations had already gone out, and there was not a moment to waste if I expected to look halfway decent by January 20. I decided to up my gym schedule to four times a week. Jade was very impressed with my commitment.

"Most people start coming to the gym *after* New Year's," he said as he filled up my water bottle. The personal training sessions were expensive, but I needed the motivation. "You're the first client I've had who started the week before Christmas."

"I don't have the luxury of time," I panted. In just three weeks, I'd gone from fat to, well, less fat—eight whole pounds of me were gone forever.

"Why not?" he asked. "Back on the stepmaster. And don't lean on the railings—that's cheating."

I'd been very careful not to discuss my personal life at the gym. Morgan's been schooling me in exercise etiquette, so that I don't make an idiot out of myself. She says only pathetic, needy women turn their trainers into their shrinks, and quite frankly, I agree. It's completely unattractive, and irritating for other people who are just there for a good workout to have to listen to this one's problems with her philandering husband, and that one's panic over her four-year-old's overbite.

"Trust me, you don't want to know." *Oh please, please, ask me again.*

"Sure I do," he said, and looked me right in the eyes and smiled. God, was he gorgeous. Who knew sideburns could be so cute?

I'm the first one to admit that a small part of my newfound enthusiasm for the gym stems from the fact that looking at Jade makes the minutes fly by. And it doesn't hurt that I desperately want to please him, and would probably jump off the Brooklyn Bridge with rocks in my pockets if he ever thought ill of me. Granted, that probably isn't the most normal of motivations, but I never claimed to be normal.

"Well, you see…I'm…I'm…" It was getting harder to talk. "I'm…"

"Hold that thought, Evie. I'll be back for you in half an hour, then we'll do the weights," he said, and trotted off to help a young woman whose disproportionately large breasts were preventing her from making it up the climbing wall.

Better to keep it to myself anyway. Why would Jade care about my life? This is just a job for him. He's not interested in my engagement party, or my problems with my mother, or my distorted body image. He probably has his own things to worry about. He probably has his own relationship troubles. He's probably gay, for all I know. Well, if not probably, then possibly. Oh, who am I kidding—the guy oozes heterosexuality from every perfect pore. Still, though, why should he care about me?

By the time I finished and made it upstairs to the weight room, I was exhausted. Sticking to my rigid four-times-a-week schedule had been a lot easier when I was on vacation. After working a whole entire day (which now involves actually working, since Pruscilla's been watching me like a hawk), it takes just about everything I have to get my ass here and slap some spandex on it.

Jade rushed over with my chart. "Sorry about before. Giselle was in a bit of a rough spot. So, you ready to pump some iron?"

I smiled weakly. "I'm tired," I said.

"You're tired?" Jade looked at me in mock horror.

"Yes." I knew I was pouting, but I couldn't help it.

"What happened to not having the luxury of time?"

"I don't know."

"Do a few reps for me, and tell me why you're in such a rush."

Defeated, I settled into the machine. "I have an engagement party on January 20."

"Whose?"

"Mine."

"You're getting married?" He seemed surprised, but I couldn't tell if he really cared or not.

"Yup."

"You don't wear an engagement ring?" Funny question. Does that mean he was looking for one?

"I do, just not to work out."

"Well I hope you don't keep it in your locker here. There have been a few thefts lately, you know."

If I didn't know better, I'd say that he actually cared. "Thanks," I said. "I'll keep that in mind."

He stared at me for a second, then said. "You look so young to be getting married. How old are you, if you don't mind my asking."

"Not at all. I'm twenty-seven."

"Wow. You don't look twenty-seven."

"It's the fat—smooths out the wrinkles."

"Oh, Evie, come on, now. It's just that you just have a young face. Besides, I've never heard of a twenty-seven-year-old with wrinkles, no matter how thin. And you're *not* fat. You just need to tone up a little."

"Thanks. You lie very well. I can see why you're the most popular trainer here."

"And I always thought it was because of my boyish good looks," he grinned.

"That, too," I panted, struggling through my last set. Was I actually flirting?

Jade just smiled and ticked things off on his clipboard. "Three, two, one. Good job. Next stop—hamstrings."

We walked over to the next machine.

"Well, if my opinion counts for anything, you don't have to worry about looking good for your party, because you already do."

"Thanks, Jade." I'm glad my face was already beet-red, because I probably would have blushed like a schoolgirl.

Mental note: Ask Morgan if it's okay to tip your personal trainer for a job well done.

It's a good thing Christmas sales last until well after New Year's in New York, because I still had nothing to wear to the party. Of course, I didn't want to buy anything too soon, or else I'd have to have it taken in, and I was in no position to be spending frivolously on things like alterations. I planned to lose another three pounds before January 20, for an anticipated grand total of eleven pounds gone forever.

Morgan flat-out refused to ever come shopping with me again, using the whole wedding dress thing as an excuse, and Annie and Kimby were busy. Even Bruce was occupied, on some type of extra-credit field trip behind the scenes at the planetarium. I had no choice but to ask Nicole, even though shopping just wasn't our thing.

"Please, Nicole. I have nothing to wear, and I can't trust myself to go alone."

"I was planning to catch up on my reading," she said. "My thesis is due the end of August, you know, not that you ever ask me about it. I bet you don't even have a clue what my topic is."

"Of course I do," I lied. True, I'd been a little preoccupied lately, but it's not like she asks me much about my life either. Nicole and I aren't the sort of friends who spend hours chatting on the phone anyway, and she knows it.

"Okay. What is it, then?"

"What?"

"My topic!"

"Oh. Something about...infanticide in Burma?" I suggested hopefully.

"First of all, Evie, it's *Myanmar,* not Burma. It hasn't been called Burma in, like, fifteen years. And my thesis is on the mythology of gender and sexuality in New Guinean folklore. *God,* it's not like I haven't told you a thousand times."

I don't how she managed to do it, but I suddenly felt really guilty. The truth was, I guess I had been neglecting my friends a bit lately, what with all the time I was spending at the gym. Suddenly, I worried that I was becoming obsessed without realizing it. But wasn't trying to get healthy a full-time commitment? Surely, everyone would understand that my time was at a premium now. Still, I silently vowed to renew my commitment to the girls. I couldn't just expect them all to drop everything and run when I needed them if I didn't put out some kind of effort, even if that meant asking Nicole about Burmese lesbians once in a while.

"You're right, Nicole. I forgot. I am *so* sorry. I guess there's just something about Burmese lesbians that makes my mind completely shut down."

"Evie!"

"I'm kidding! I'm kidding. Jeez! It's Myanmar. I know."

"It's New Guinea," she said, even though she knew I was still kidding. "And lesbians have nothing to do with it."

"So, uh, how are they doing there? Gender-wise, I mean."

"Forget it, it doesn't matter."

"How can you *say* that? Have you no respect for their oral traditions?"

She giggled. "Give it a rest, Evie. I'll come shopping with you. But only if we go to Saks, because I could use a few things too and my sister gets a five-percent employee discount on regularly priced merchandise."

"Thanks a million, Nic! I owe you."

I knew she didn't feel like spending the day studying anyway. Who would?

We met in the cosmetics department, and wasted half an hour talking about eyeliner to her sister Cherie, who definitely got the looks in the family, if not the brains. Not that working at an Estée Lauder counter is something to be ashamed of, but if I was as pretty as she is, you can bet I'd have found some way not to work at all.

On our way up the escalator, Nicole asked, "Have you lost weight?" She'd had a good, long look at me from behind, and now there was no denying it. But I was delighted anyway—she was the first person to notice without me pointing it out first.

"Why, yes, I have—I don't know exactly how much, though," I lied. "I've been working out a lot, but I threw out my scale because my trainer says it's not a true measure of progress."

"You have a trainer?"

"Yup!"

"I've managed to keep my weight off, too, but I haven't lost anything in over a month," she said as we made our way to the designer dresses.

"Just stick with it. You've probably just hit a plateau. And you might want to try exercising—it's the only thing that's worked for me in almost five years."

"Really?"

"Yeah. It's because my metabolism is so screwed up from all those plans I've been on. And having a personal trainer is the best, and he's absolutely gorgeous, and I think he's even been flirting with me. Can you imagine?"

"Not really," she said. "Which gym do you go to?"

I *definitely* didn't want her there. (*O*, January: "Fitness Saboteurs: Sorting the Friends from the Foes?"). That would ruin everything. "Just some place near work. It's probably not worth it for you to join, though. It's pretty far from you."

Nicole rolled her eyes. "Don't worry, Evie, I won't crowd your little party."

"You make it sound like so much fun. It's not, believe me. He's making me work my ass off."

"Well, that's the idea, isn't it?" she smirked.

"Ha, ha. What do you think of this one?" I asked, pulling a microscopic red-and-pink Betsey Johnson off the rack and holding it up hopefully. "This is a large."

"Umm, I don't think that's going to work so well," she said

diplomatically. "How about that?" She pointed to a drab gray Saks Fifth Avenue suit on a mannequin.

"I don't want to look like I'm going to a lunch meeting. Think sexy and sophisticated."

"It's your party—you can look like a tramp if you want to," she said, shrugging her shoulders. "So tell me, does Bruce know about your crush?"

I almost choked on my Tic Tac. "Don't be an ass," I told her. "I don't have a *crush* on Jade. He's just my trainer. And he happens to be a little flirtatious. It's all in good fun."

"Oh, so it's *Jade,* now. Quite a fancy name."

"Make fun if you want, I couldn't care less. But it sounds to me like someone's a little bit jealous."

"Of what? An imaginary love affair between you and some ape? I think not," she said. But I think she must have been, because she dropped the subject.

After an hour of trying things on, I finally found a great dress. When I stepped out of the changing room, Nicole's jaw practically dropped.

I stood back to admire myself in the mirror. It was an ocelot-print D&G satin-stretch wraparound with a plunging neckline. It was also a size ten, and admittedly a little tight, but I still had two weeks to go before the party.

"Well—is it too much?"

"Depends," breathed Nicole, smiling broadly. "It's not too much if you're going for a Queen of the Jungle thing."

"Are you sure? Even with the cleavage?"

"The cleavage is actually quite elegant." Her envy was almost palpable.

"Are you sure I don't look like a fool?"

"You? Look like a fool? With all the fashion magazines you read? That's virtually impossible."

"I'm serious now, Nicole. Don't jerk me around. I really need you to tell me if I look like an idiot."

"What? You think I'd tell you it looked okay if it didn't?"

"With a pair of control-tops, it'll be fine, right?"

"Oh, definitely," she said.

It wasn't easy, but we also found shoes and a bag to match, all with Cherie's five-percent-off card, which amounted to quite a considerable savings. Although she's a touch defensive at times, Nicole can actually be a pretty good friend when the going gets tough. I even promised her that I would proofread her thesis when it was done, and we made plans to meet for lunch next week.

When I got home, I was so excited about the dress that I wanted to try it on and show Bruce right away. I could tell he was in a bad mood, and thought it might cheer him up.

"Are you sure you want me to see it?" he asked.

"It's not like the wedding dress," I said. "You can see me in it before the party."

I went into the bedroom and changed. Bruce probably hasn't given any thought whatsoever to what he's going to be wearing. He'll probably break out one of his tired old suits again. I'm sure they both needed to be dry-cleaned.

Unfortunately, I didn't get the grand reaction I was hoping for.

"So…what do you think?"

He seemed terribly confused. "Umm, it's…nice?"

One of the reasons I fell in love with Bruce is that he's honest. But the flip side of that is that he can't lie.

"You don't like it?"

"I didn't say that. It's just, a bit, you know, sexy."

"Sexy bad, or sexy good?"

"I'm not sure."

"Sexy, as in Auntie Prue will have another stroke, or sexy, you'll want to ravage me in the poolhouse?"

"Again, I'm not quite sure," he said, stifling a laugh.

"Sexy, the police will pick me up before I get to the party, or sexy—"

"Enough, Evie! I said I don't know."

I felt my face flushing red with embarrassment.

"I think it's a great dress, *and* it's a size ten. If it was too small, I wouldn't have bought it, but Nicole said it was flattering. And keep in mind I still have two weeks to lose a few more pounds."

"I think Nicole may have been having a bit of fun with you."

"What a horrible thing to say. I'll just pretend you said it's lovely and that I look wonderful." What did he know? I wasn't about to let a guy who wears shirts with button-down collars dictate my fashion sense. It's not like he even has the slightest clue how hot animal prints are this year (*Mademoiselle,* January: "Show Your Stripes: Leopards and Tigers and Zebras, Oh My!")

"Was it expensive?"

"Don't push me, Bruce," I warned him. "You're on thin ice as it is."

"Seriously."

"It was on sale," I said. Five percent counts.

"How much?"

"Two hundred and fifty dollars, but I don't have to justify that to you. I've been busting my ass at work lately. And I think I deserve at least something for being so good about going to the gym. This is the first item of clothing I've bought since, you know." How dare he tell me how to spend my money?

"First of all, you get paid the same no matter how hard you work, and secondly, haven't you only lost eight pounds?"

"You animal!" I shrieked at him. "Why don't you just punch me in the face!" Then I burst into tears. That usually works quite well at getting him to see my side of things, but he wouldn't have any of it today, for some reason.

"What about those shoes, Evie, and the matching bag? I'm happy that you've lost some weight, but in case you haven't noticed, we're a bit tight for money right now. Maybe it would be a good idea if you started cutting back on a few things."

"Like what?" I sniffed. "I didn't have a bag that matches, otherwise I wouldn't have bought it." Duh.

"So keep the damn bag, if it makes you so happy. But what about your personal trainer? You're spending seventy-five bucks a pop, Evie, plus the gym membership."

"Work pays for half, remember?" I sobbed.

"That's still almost two hundred dollars a week. We can't afford that right now."

"Who are you to say what we can or can't afford?" We had agreed, since we got engaged, to pool all our money together, since we were going to be married soon anyway.

"I take care of everything around here. When was the last time you paid a bill, or even looked at our bank balance? All you do is withdraw and charge, withdraw and charge. You have absolutely no idea how much money is coming in or out, and I do. *That's* what qualifies me!"

"Well...well..." I struggled to remember some sort of bad fiscal judgment on his part. "Well you're the one who went out and bought an expensive diamond bracelet, not me!" *Oops!* Didn't mean for that to come out. There was certainly no sense in shooting myself in the foot.

He looked at me like I was nuts.

"I mean, that was fine, because it was a once-in-a-while thing." I scrambled to undo the damage. "And that's what this is—a dress for our engagement party! Why don't you just say what you really mean—you make more money than I do! And you don't think it's fair that I get to spend it!"

"No, that's not what I think at all. What I think is that you never learned the value of a dollar, and that you can be a spoiled brat who takes everything for granted."

"Thanks, *Dad!*" I gasped, and ran into the bedroom and sobbed on the bed for a while. After about half an hour, when I had calmed down and was ready to forgive him, I heard the front door slam. Was it me? I don't know if I'd ever seen Bruce that mad, except maybe for the time I read his journal. But he never actually ran away.

Since Mom and I had been getting along so well since

Christmas, I thought maybe she could help me understand what was going on with him.

"Mom, Bruce just ran out on me."

"What?"

"No, not *left* me, left me, but ran out of the house. We had a big fight."

"What happened?" she said, as the waves of relief washed over her.

"I don't really know. One minute we were talking about my new dress, and the next, he was freaking out and yelling about money."

"Oh dear," she said, and thought about that for a while. "You must have done something to provoke him?"

"As usual, you know just what to say. Aren't you supposed to be on my side? You don't even know what *happened.*" I was crying again.

"Don't you screw this up, Evelyn," she said in what to her must have seemed like sympathy. "Bruce adores you, and he may very well be the best thing to happen to you in your whole life. Think about it from his perspective for once—he's probably going through some things, too, just the way you are."

"I'm not going through anything," I said. "I'm fine." How could she tell?

"You can be so foolish. Marriage is a blessed union, dear, but it's also a *partnership.* You have got to realize that it is not always going to be about Miss Evelyn Mays and *her* problems and who's done *her* wrong. When you and Bruce are husband and wife, it'll be up to you to make sure he's okay and that his needs are met. *Forever.* Understand?"

"So, I'm just supposed to completely subjugate my personality in order to make sure that Bruce's feelings aren't hurt. And we're not even married yet!"

"Exactly. Things are just going to get worse. So you let him worry about things like money."

"That's very progressive of you, Mom. Well, thanks for your

help. You've made me feel a whole lot better. I'm going to go put my head in the oven now."

"You have an electric oven, dear. You'd know that if you'd ever used it."

If Sylvia Plath's mother had been half the support mine is, she'd probably have been too broken down to even bother killing herself. But I did wonder if maybe I'd been a little hasty to get so pissed at Bruce. I did have a pretty ugly credit card bill every month—he was right about that. I guess I'd been counting on getting promoted for so long, that maybe I was living a little beyond our means.

When Bruce came home a few hours later, he went right to the computer and didn't say a word to me for the rest of the evening. I spent the whole night on the couch eating celery sticks and watching a *Biography* marathon on A&E. Between Pope John Paul II and the Marquis de Sade, I tried to extend the olive branch.

"I'll return the purse!" I called out from the living room.

Silence.

"I'll buy cheaper shoes!"

Still nothing.

If that's how he was going to be about it, then I might as well keep everything and order a matching bra and panties. I'd noticed an eye-catching cheetah-print set in the Victoria's Secret catalog the other day. If I did decide to buy it, I vowed never to let him see me in it. (*Cosmopolitan,* June: "What Lies Beneath: Sexy Lingerie Just for You.")

Bruce slept with his back to me the whole night. Sunday morning I went out and picked up some coffee and even some bagels, as a concession to him, but he didn't touch them. He just read the paper in silence. Whoever said the way to a man's heart is through his stomach wasn't dating a WASP.

"Can we please not be in a fight anymore?" I pleaded.

"Fine. We're not in a fight anymore."

"Can't we just agree to disagree?" That's a favorite line of mine, because if you agree to disagree, everybody saves face.

"Don't you want to be right?" he asked, still not looking up from the paper.

"I don't care anymore."

"Are you actually admitting that you're wrong?" It was so unlike him to hold a grudge like this.

"Whatever it takes. I'll return the dress." I liked it and all, but this just wasn't worth it.

"It's not the dress, Evie. You can dress however you like. I don't have to like it. It's the way you spend money that upsets me." He folded the paper and put it down.

"Aha!" I yelled, and jumped up. "So you admit that you don't like the dress!" Finally.

"You're really impossible, you know that?" he said sadly. "We have to work this out. I don't want to go into our marriage with this big thing hanging over our heads, and then fight about money for the rest of our lives. I am dead serious here. You have to learn how to take responsibility for your finances, and start paying down your credit cards. I'm a teacher, Evie, and I'll never make as much money as my dad. So if I want to give our kids all the things I had growing up, which I do, then we're going to have to do it the old-fashioned way."

"Inherit it?"

Bruce couldn't help but laugh. "No, you idiot, by saving and planning."

"Or maybe a little of all three?"

"Fine," he said. "You call Claire and tell her we've already got her coffin picked out."

"I will, if you agree to stand idly by for years while I slip trace amounts of arsenic into your mother's Metamucil."

"Deal."

10

The week before the party, Auntie Lucy called from England to say that she and her husband Roderick would in fact be attending. It was incredibly exciting—I hadn't seen her since Mom and I took that horrible mother-daughter trip to London three years ago, and she's never even met Bruce. Mom, on the other hand, was a bit worried. When she heard that Lucy and Roderick were staying with my grandfather instead of her, she was insulted, of course, and nervous that it would somehow lead to a fight of some sort. She was also suspicious—she couldn't understand why they were schlepping all the way here for the engagement party, when they were planning to come to the wedding in August anyway.

On Thursday night, we met them at a restaurant near Mom's.

"Evie!" Lucy shrieked when she saw us walk in. She jumped up from the table to greet us. I could see Mom gesturing to the waiter, probably apologizing for the outburst.

"Auntie Lucy!" I gave her a big hug. "I'm so happy you came!"

"It was no trouble, dear," she said, squeezing my hand. "We wouldn't miss your party for the world."

It was so good to see her. Although they're supposed to be

identical twins, Lucy looks much younger than my mother, probably because she's a lot heavier, and has enough sense to color her gray.

"Hello, Roderick," I said, extending my hand.

He shook it weakly. "Hello, Evelyn. Good to see you."

Bruce cleared his throat.

"Is this the groom-to-be?" Lucy asked, looking him up and down. "Handsome guy, Evie. Well done!"

"Ohmygod, sorry! Yes! This is Bruce."

"Hello," said Bruce cautiously, unsure what to make of this jolly, chubby version of my mom.

"Bruce, Bruce, *Bruce!*—I feel like I've known you forever. Come and give your old auntie Lucy a hug," she said, grabbing him and shaking him back and forth like a rag doll.

"Lucia, please, will you sit down," said Mom. "Roderick, how do you put up with her?"

Roderick shrugged his narrow shoulders. They're living proof that opposites do attract. He and Lucy met when Roderick was selling junk bonds in New York in the '80s. They had a few wild years, got married on a whim in Barbados, and have been blissfully happy ever since; well, at least we take Roderick's silence and general willingness to do whatever Lucy says for happiness. When the bottom fell out of the market, he and Lucy moved back to England (to escape some unhappy creditors, Mom says) and Roderick, a broken man, has been working at his father's sanitary napkin factory ever since.

It sounds horrible, but Lucy was more than happy to leave, since she spent a good deal of her time looking after my bitter old coot of a grandfather. Why he was willing to accept Roderick, as non-Italian as a fellow can be, and not my father is beyond me.

"Roderick doesn't seem well," my mother whispered to me, as Lucy listened raptly to Bruce's life story.

I looked over at him. Pale, wan, slouchy.

"He looks the same to me," I said.

"Something's not right… Mark my words," she said out of the corner of her mouth, still smiling at Bruce's perfect SAT score story.

It was only eight o'clock, and Roderick was nodding off a little, but, to be fair, he'd just been on a plane for six hours listening to Lucy's incessant chatter. It burns me that Mom always has to find the negative in everything. Here was her sister, whom she hasn't seen in years, and all she can do is have psychic fits about which illness Roderick is about to drop dead of. But Mom's never happy unless someone else is miserable. It gives her faith that she's not alone in her agony. She clips obituaries of anyone under fifty-five and puts them in alphabetical order in a folder beside her bed. When Bruce asked her why, she said she'll stop doing it as soon as she turns fifty-five.

"What about you, Lucy?" I asked.

"Same, same," she sighed. "Still working at the museum. A new exhibition's coming in next month—'French Dollhouses, From the Reformation Through the Revolution.' Unfortunately, it's not as interesting as it sounds, but that's a whole other story. I'd love to retire, to tell you the truth, but we're still saving up for the girls' college fund," she winked and nudged Bruce in the ribs. The "girls" are Shmoopie and Lulu, her two West Highland Terriers. They're ridiculous little white things, but she loves them as much as if she'd given birth to them herself.

I must admit, we did have a good time, despite Mom's knowing glances in my direction. What she thinks she knows, I cannot say for sure, but I was careful to ignore her for most of the evening. And because I spent three hours at the gym—I left work early for the first time since that whole Pruscilla thing broke—I treated myself to a cannoli, even though my final weigh-in before the party was tomorrow.

I took the day off work on Friday (unpaid, since I was still on probation), and went to the gym early.

"I had dessert last night," I confessed to Jade as I stepped on the scale. "But I haven't had so much as a sip of water today. And I'm PMS-ing. I'm so bloated, it's not my fault if I gained."

Jade shook his head. "You've lost three pounds."

"Really?" It couldn't be.

"Are you sure you've been eating?"

"Sporadically." I couldn't lie to him. A trainer is like a therapist—there's no sense in lying to them, because you'll only end up hurting yourself. "I think it's because my stomach's shrinking. I'm just not as hungry."

"You're down thirteen pounds in five weeks."

"It's a miracle!"

"Don't starve yourself, Evie."

"I'm not." Well, I wasn't—starvation was definitely an overstatement. Admittedly, I knew I wasn't exactly eating *well,* especially this past week. I'd had a latte for breakfast every day and an apple for lunch. Dinner I let myself go a little, and usually had one of those Lean Cuisine frozen meals. Sometimes I felt a bit woozy, sure, but then I'd just lie down for a bit. I didn't mind the hunger so much; the only thing nagging at me was that I could feel myself caring less and less whether I was being healthy or not—just as long as the pounds kept flying off. But maybe it wasn't so bad. I *was* taking a multivitamin. "Didn't you tell me that the weight comes off quickly at first?"

"Yes, but it's been over a month now. Slow down, be patient."

"It's working. I think it's because I've never exercised before and my body is finally learning how to reject the fat."

"That's a theory they never taught us in personal trainer school, but if that works for you, fine. Just take it easy, okay?" He was so concerned.

"Do they really have a personal trainer school?" I imagined a class full of Jades showering after a gruelling session.

"I was kidding."

"Oh. You think I should cut back my workouts? I'm coming five times a week."

"I didn't say that. You're motivated now. You're seeing results. That's good. You don't want to lose your momentum."

"Am I getting in shape faster than your other clients?" *I crave your approval. Please, please give it to me.*

"You sure are," he said, and finally smiled. "I knew I was good, but this is crazy. You're my *best* client, Evie."

The way he said *best* sent chills up my spine. "I couldn't have done any of it without you, Jade."

"You're welcome. Have a great time at your party. And promise me you'll eat something!"

"Of course!"

It was wonderful to put on my new dress and feel good in something for the first time in ages. As a concession to Bruce, I'd returned the matching bag and bought something a little cheaper, a nice black Kate Spade with leopard-print on the inside (*Vogue,* December: "Bargain Bags for Under $300). I sprayed some perfume on liberally, and asked Bruce to do up the clasp on my bracelet.

"How do I look?"

"Great."

"You see? The dress is good. You like it now, right?" I asked.

"Yup," he gagged. "But you're wearing too much perfume."

"I have to put a lot on or it'll wear off by the time we get there."

"Ah."

"You could have used a haircut," I said. "And maybe some new shoes." Bruce has no sense of fashion at all. If it weren't for me, he'd still be wearing the pink Polo shirt I found him in.

"I think we should both try not to drink too much tonight, Evie."

"Fine," I said. There was no time to fight, Claire was picking us up any minute.

"I'm serious. No drinking."

"*Okay,* already."

* * *

On the way there, Bruce warned me again to be on my best behavior.

"Do you not trust me or something?" I asked. "You think I'm going to make an idiot out of myself in front of your parents' friends?"

"No, I just want to make sure we all have a good time, so let's not let things get to us tonight."

"That's good advice, Bruce," Claire said.

"You know my mother's going to be very nervous," he continued. "She wants everything to be perfect."

"Perfect shmerfect," I said.

By the time we finally got there, I was the one who was nervous. Bruce looked a little green, too, but that was probably because of Claire's driving. My feet were already killing from my new shoes, and I'd only walked from the car to the front door. I rang the bell before we walked in, just to make Bertie think someone had arrived early.

She came running into the hallway in a panic.

"Oh thank God, it's just you. Hello, Claire, nice to see you again."

"You, too, Bertie," Claire said as we walked in.

"The house looks wonderful, Mom," said Bruce. "Very Narnia."

Her so-called "planner" had really gone to town. Little white lights twinkled everywhere, and fake trees covered in fake snow lined the hallways. Everything glittered. Even Bertie, who was wearing a light blue Chanel suit trimmed in white fur.

I took off my coat and handed it to Rosita. Bertie's face twisted into a painful grimace.

"Oh my God, Evelyn! What are you *wearing?*"

"Don't worry," I said. "It's not real ocelot."

"I can see that. Ocelots aren't made of polyester, dear," she said, unable to tear her eyes away. I'm sure she could tell that I'd lost a lot of weight, but it was clear that she was far too self-absorbed to bother complimenting me. She rushed off into the kitchen to make sure the caterer had started to warm the hors d'oeuvres.

Bertie hired a photographer for the night and we were planning to have formal pictures taken with the whole family, but Mom, Lucy and Roderick arrived late, of course, so there was no time for anything but hasty introductions. Roderick and Mr. Fulbright went off to see his new pool table, and Mom and Aunt Lucy tried to sustain a conversation with Brooke and Wendy. Apparently, Diana had some sort of zit and, in a fit of teenage angst, was refusing to come out of her room.

As the guests began to arrive, I had the distinct feeling that I was going to make quite a gracious hostess one day. I flitted from group to group, making polite conversation and offering witty observations. Bertie's friends all seemed to like me, thank God. I just wish Bruce had been around to notice. Predictably, he barely made an appearance, and was probably tucked away in his dad's game room playing pool, so I accepted the gifts and congratulatory wishes as best I could on my own.

Mom was being sullen, and hadn't moved from her spot on the couch. Every time a waitress would pass her with champagne, she took another glass. *She better not make a fool out of herself tonight in front of everybody.*

"Lucy, will you keep an eye on her, please?" I whispered when nobody was around.

"Love your dress, Evie. Don't worry about her. She's just a little upset that Daddy wouldn't lend us the car, so we had to take a cab."

"You took a cab here from *Brooklyn?*"

"It's okay, don't worry about it."

"Why wouldn't he lend you the car?"

"Because he said that he didn't want your mother in it."

"And you told her?"

"Are you nuts? She figured it out on her own."

"Oh God, Lucy. Please just make sure she doesn't puke on

anything," I said. "She's starting to look a little woozy." I saw her drop a stuffed mushroom cap on the white carpet. Like a blue bullet, Bertie darted over from the other side of the room and picked it up.

"Don't worry, Evie. She's all right."

Before dinner—a fantastic buffet of crab cakes and lamp chops and rosemary baby potatoes—Bruce's dad gave us a nice toast, and everybody clapped. People seemed to be having a good time. Especially Claire, who was whispering intimately in the corner with some old guy she met who knew Grandpa from when he was a lawyer. I was a little pissed at Morgan, who told me I looked like a call girl, but she was already drunk by the time she arrived, so I just chalked it up to alcohol.

There was no sign of any real trouble until I saw Diana running down the stairs crying and into the kitchen. She could be such a scene-stealer, the little brat, in her barely-there slip dress. And all this over a zit. There were so many people milling about, that hardly anybody even noticed her. *Serves her right.* Then I saw Roderick teetering at the top of the stairs, obviously wasted off his ass. His face was bright red, and he was talking to himself.

I looked around frantically for Bruce. He'd finally emerged from seclusion and was now trapped between two of his dad's co-workers. But he saw Roderick, too, and immediately flew up the stairs to pull him away before anyone else noticed. I followed Diana into the kitchen, where she was hugging Rosita and crying as waitresses swirled around her with silver trays.

"…and then…and then…he tried to touch my boob," she sobbed, "and…and…I said *no*…and…and…"

Rosita looked at me, obviously alarmed.

Shit. This can't be happening. I backed out of the kitchen, and scanned the room for Bertie. She was talking to some of her garden club friends, thank God. As long as Diana remained hysterical in the kitchen, there was still plenty of time to make everything right before anyone found out.

I put on my biggest and brightest smile (*Marie Claire,* June: "Be a Bleach Bunny: Get those Pearly Whites their Whitest") and discreetly made my way toward the staircase.

"Evelyn?" Mr. Fulbright's voice froze me in my tracks.

"Yeah?"

"Have you seen Bruce?"

"No."

"Well, see if you can find him—I want to introduce you to my cousin Freddy. He just came in from Seattle."

"Sure thing, sir," I said, and scrambled up the stairs.

"Bruce?" I whispered.

There were about twelve doors in the upstairs hallway, and each one was closed.

"Bruce!" I said loudly. "It's me. Where are you?"

The door to Diana's bedroom opened and Bruce popped his head out. "Over here," he said sternly. The look on his face told me things were pretty serious.

Inside, Roderick was sitting cross-legged on Diana's bed, his head hung over a little pink garbage pail. His fly was down.

"So sorry," he mumbled. "So sorry. I thought she wanted to play with me."

I couldn't help but laugh. Suddenly, it all seemed pretty funny.

"Evie, this is fucking serious," Bruce said, pacing the floor.

"I know," I managed. "It's not funny. It's not funny."

"She was wearing pigtails. She looked like a little runny babbit," Roderick slurred, gripping his bucket.

"Watch it, man," Bruce growled at him. "That's my sister you're talking about. She's only eighteen."

I didn't know what to say. Roderick had never displayed this type of behavior before. As far as we knew, he wasn't a pervert at all.

"What the hell happened?" I asked.

"I have no idea," Bruce said, "but I can guess. This isn't good, Evie. This isn't good. My mother's going to tear his heart out with a spoon. Where's Diana?"

"Calm down. She's in the kitchen with Rosita. Your mother has no idea—"

The door flew open and in walked a sobbing Diana, pulling her mother along by the arm. Bertie's normally pale face turned deep purple as she assessed the scene.

"See? *See?*" Diana cried. She really did have a huge zit on her forehead. "He just came into my room without even knocking. And then he got on my bed and...and...oh...it's just too awful...he...he...."

"Spit it out, Diana!" shrieked Bertie.

"He grabbed me!" she wailed, and ran into her bathroom and slammed the door. Yes, she has an ensuite bathroom.

"If I may say something in my own defense..." said Roderick, then heaved into the pail.

Bruce and his mother looked at me as if he were my responsibility. "What are we supposed to do with this disgusting animal?" Bertie spat.

"It's not my fault! I barely know him," I said.

"No one's saying it is, Evie," Bruce sighed. "Maybe we should get your mother and aunt up here to deal with him."

"Noo," I whined. "I don't want this to ruin the party."

"It's a little late for that," Bertie said curtly. "The guests are starting to leave anyway. I don't think they know what happened, and that's the important thing. So help me, if your father finds out, Bruce..."

Roderick hiccupped. "Don't blame poor Eve," he said. "'Snot her fault. The little rabbit wanted me to jump up and down with her on the bed."

"If you know what's good for you, you'll shut up," Bruce warned.

"Eve, you're more of a moose than a rabbit," Roderick said thoughtfully. "But you're still a good girl. She's a good girl, that girl Eve. Bastard that she is. Bastard."

"What the hell's that supposed to mean?" Bruce was really getting pissed off. I kind of liked it. In this day and age, a girl can't afford to take chivalry for granted, even in a terrible situation like this.

Roderick tried to put his finger up to his lips. "Ssshhh…issa secret. Her mommy never told her. Ssshhh…"

"Told me *what?*" I hissed.

"That she never married your daddy," he sang.

Bertie and Bruce stared at me. Roderick's eyes rolled back into his head and he fell forward, spilling the contents of his bucket all over Diana's white lace bedspread and then landing in it facedown. Nobody said a word.

My face felt like it was on fire.

"Evie?" Bruce reached over and grabbed my hand. "Evie?"

I couldn't say a word.

Bertie threw her hands up into the air and went into the bathroom after Diana.

"Maybe it's not true," Bruce said. "He obviously has no idea what he's saying."

Tears spilled down onto my cheeks.

"No… No…please don't cry," he said, and hugged me. "Don't cry."

But I just cried harder.

"I hate you!" I screamed at Roderick, who could have been dead for all I knew, and pulled away from Bruce. I ran into one of the guest rooms and flopped down onto the bed. Bruce came in and sat beside me. I guess I cried until I fell asleep.

When I woke up, Lucy was stroking my hair.

"Are you okay, hon?"

I turned away from her.

"I'm so sorry, Evie. You shouldn't have found out like this."

"So it's true, then," I said quietly.

"Yes, it's true, but it doesn't really matter."

"Easy for you to say. You're married."

"Believe me," Lucy sighed, "right now, I wish I wasn't."

"Why weren't they married?"

"It doesn't mean your dad loved your mom any less. Andrew adored her, and wanted to marry her very much. She was the one who was waiting."

"He never even knew I existed."

"He knows now, hon. He's always watching over you. I know you can feel it. And he would have loved you more than anything or anyone in the entire world. Don't doubt that for a second. He was a wonderful, kind, gentle man. A lot like Bruce," she said, wiping away a tear. "Oh, Evie, he would have been so happy for you, so proud of you."

"How come nobody told me?"

"When you were younger, your mom thought it was best not to, and then I guess she just never figured out the right way to tell you. Please don't be mad at her, Evie. She didn't want to hurt you."

"Yeah right."

"She wants to talk to you. Can I send her in?"

"No. Tell her to go home."

"You can tell her that yourself," Lucy said.

"Only if you stay, too."

"Sure thing."

I had so many questions, but I was too angry to ask her any of them. At least if she saw how miserable I was, she'd feel bad. And that would make me feel a bit better.

She came in and sat down on the bed, but I pretended to be asleep.

"Evelyn, I'm sorry."

I don't think she'd ever apologized to me before. Not seriously, anyway.

"You can stay mad at me for as long as you like, since you were probably going to be mad at me for one reason or another, anyway."

"Thanks. I will, then."

"I knew right away there was something wrong with Roderick," she said. "I could see it in his eyes."

"This isn't his fault, Mom, it's yours."

"He's not supposed to drink," Lucy explained. "He's on antidepressants."

"Where's Bruce? I want to go home."

"I'm here, Evie," he said from the doorway.

"Please can we go home?"

"Sure we can," he said.

It was almost three in the morning by the time we left. I was definitely mad at Claire, too, and didn't want her to drive us, so Bruce borrowed Diana's car. At home, I peeled off my tear-stained ocelot dress and crawled into bed. Bruce knew better than to try and comfort me. I was utterly inconsolable, and expected to remain so for quite some time.

11

I didn't talk to Mom for one month.

Claire called me almost every day to try and get me to see her side, as if she actually had a side. To be honest, I was almost as mad at her as I was at Mom.

"It's not about sides, Evie," Bruce huffed late one evening as we trekked to the corner store for some milk. Snow swirled up around our faces. It was already the third storm in as many weeks, and February was barely half over.

"Yes it is. It *is* about sides. Claire's always been the one to defend me to Mom. She's always seen things *my* way. Of everyone in the whole world, she was the only one who ever told it to me straight."

"What about me? You don't think I'm honest with you?" Bruce shook his head and stopped walking. "Well here's some honesty for you. You don't always want to hear it straight, Evie. You hear what you want to hear, or else you choose not to listen."

"Exactly. Which is why I thought I could count on her. And if you're going to be a jerk about it, then let's just drop it."

"Do you hear what you're saying? You're proving my point!" He was working himself up into a real state.

"Stop yelling. I can hear you. I understand what you're saying, but look at it like this—it's about hypocrisy. That's why I'm so pissed. Claire's always going on about the importance of being honest, and how people today can be such phonies. How she'd rather hurt someone's feelings than humor them. And I agree with her one hundred percent. It's far better to tell a person a truth that may be painful to hear in the hopes that it will do some good than it is to enable someone's self-serving fantasies for fear of bursting their bubble. I can respect that philosophy, and I respected Claire for it. But she's the real phony, lying to my face. I expect it from Mom, but not from her."

He just stared at me, confused. "Where do you get this stuff from? I've never heard her say anything remotely like that. Come to think of it, though, that sounds an awful lot like something your mother would say, if she were ever able to articulate the motivation behind her mean-spiritedness. But Claire would never willingly hurt someone's feelings."

"Well she has. Maybe it was before your time," I grumbled. He'd just insulted my mother, I think. At least that was something.

"Look. Claire deferred to your mother's judgment on this one. And frankly, I can understand why. It was her decision, not Claire's. How can you be mad at her for that? And why do you think they never told you, Evie? To be mean to you? To hurt you? To deliberately deceive you? Grow up, already. They weren't conspiring against you. God! I am so damn sick of this conversation. It's all we ever talk about."

I immediately burst into tears. "I'm a bastard! A *bastard!* And all you care about is how bored you are of listening to my problems. So much for romance, you jerk! Tomorrow's Valentine's Day and this is how you treat me? Thanks a lot!" I spun around on my heels and began trudging for home.

Typical. It was so like Bruce to twist everything around so that it was all about him. Really—pretending to act supportive when he was really just being manipulative. And at a time like this, yet. He was so whacked out lately, I had to wonder if he even knew he was doing it (*O*, February: "Toxic Relationships: Are You Getting Sucked In?").

"Evie!" Bruce yelled. "Evie!"

I wouldn't answer. In fact, I resolved never to answer him again. Not until he learned a few more things about love and respect for his partner.

"Evie!"

I felt a snowball pelt me in the back. Still, I refused to turn.

"I'm still getting the milk!" he bellowed. "And it's not going to be skim! You hear me? No skim! I like WHOLE milk and that's what I'm going to buy! Maybe I'll even get some cream! Put *that* in your coffee!"

By the time I got home, I was more sad than mad. What was happening to me, to us? Bruce was driving me nuts, and I knew it wasn't really his fault, but I could barely control myself anymore. Even the slightest bit of criticism was setting me off, and it wasn't just because I was hungry half the time. But shouldn't Bruce see that I'm on the verge of losing it and cut me some slack? For some reason, what should have been the best year of my life was turning into the most miserable one ever—especially now that the one thing I always had faith in, everything I once believed to be true, had turned out to be a lie.

If it hadn't been for Jade and the gym, I don't know how I would have made it through those weeks. Even Morgan seemed to be unavailable to listen to me bitch and moan, though I couldn't hold it against her. She'd finally been promoted to Vice President of Something or Other, which meant she'd be putting in sixteen-hour days for much of the foreseeable future.

She e-mailed me the good news the Tuesday after our party.

>>hi evie. guess what? my years of hard work have finally paid off! they offered me the promotion yesterday. your oldest and truest friend is now the youngest female vice president ever. but first i told them i'd have to think about it! that i was currently considering other offers. Peter advised me to make 'em sweat—get more money out of the old farts upstairs. this morning, they offered me a nice contract and i accepted. what do you think?

Morgan had always planned for a career instead of babies, so this was all shaping up quite nicely for her, and ahead of schedule, too.

I wrote back,

>>that's fantastic, morgan. you deserve it. and you thought you'd be 30 before you'd make any serious coin. good job. just one thing—by years of hard work, do you mean all those long nights you spent slaving over a hot boss?

>>funny, evie. if i had the time, I'd laugh. but I'm too busy counting my soon-to-be-hatched chickens—there are many details to be worked out, you know, such as having my hot young male assistant file the paperwork for my corporate platinum credit card, and deciding whether or not the desk should face the window in my ginormous new office. ahh, such are the perks of the corporate courtesan....

I had to hand it to her. She really knew how to get the most out of every situation.

>>poor peter. I suppose he'll have to find a new eager young associate to break in.

>>actually, he's a senior veep, so i will still have occasion to work under him from time to time. besides, I'm sure he will want to monitor the progress of his most recently promoted protegee.

Of course, Morgan was much smarter than that. She knew how to keep her eye on the prize.

>>you vamp—he's the one that needs protection! congrats, congrats!

>>thanks, dear. great party, by the way. were you too fabulous to say goodbye to your guests?

Of course, I'd been too humiliated to call and tell Morgan, or anyone for that matter, what had happened on Saturday. I think Bertie just told everyone I had a headache and was lying down. Thankfully, I later decided to impress anyone who eventually discovered my shameful secret with my cool and laid-back attitude toward the whole catastrophe. My ability to brush off even the most horrific of family tragedies would be legendary; publicly at least, I would soldier on, breaking through my checkered past to emerge triumphant on the other side. There was a lot of room for sympathy here, after all. For not only was I posthumously produced, but I was, technically speaking, a love child as well.

>>long story short—drunkle roderick spilled the beans on a most intimate family secret: turns out my daddy never actually married my mommy. illegitimately yours, evelyn mays.

It took her a few minutes to respond.

>>seriously?

>>seriously.

>>whoa, that's heavy shit, evelyn.

>>no big deal, really. I always knew my mother was a wh—

"Wow, Evie!" someone whispered incredulously from behind me.

I spun around in my chair. Andrea, that hag, was standing over my shoulder, her mouth agape.

"How *dare* you spy on my own private affairs?" I hissed as quietly as possible.

"Interesting choice of words. Seems you're not the only one with private affairs!" she giggled.

From somewhere within the dark recesses of my mind, Bruce's sensible voice called out, *You catch more flies with honey than with vinegar.*

"Andrea," I started. "Please..."

She put her hand on my shoulder. "Oh, don't worry. I won't breathe a word. We all have our crosses to bear, though for some of us those crosses are larger and more humiliating than others," she said simply, and skipped off.

Shit, shit, shit. Now she had something on me, and I knew she'd never let me forget it. I could hear Bruce's voice speaking to me once again, *only this time he was saying, What goes around comes around*. I guess I deserved it—Andrea had apparently caught a blast of crap from her boss about personal phone time the day I had her calls rerouted.

>>evie? you there? i'll try and call you later, but i'll be working late.

>>i hate this place morgan. do you need another assistant? please help—

"Evelyn!" Pruscilla shrieked from her office. "Come in here immediately."

I sighed and shut off the screen. What the hell did she want now?

Her face was purple with anger. "You call this a report? All you had to do was proof it and check the numbers. It's *full* of mistakes."

"I must have given you the wrong version," I mumbled. "Sorry about that." There was no satisfying this woman. I once thought her bitterness was a byproduct of her unfortunate physique. But now I could see that her still formidable (albeit shrinking) girth had absolutely nothing to do with her sour disposition. She was mean as a snake from the inside out.

"Do you have any idea how much heck I would have caught if it went out like this? Thanks heavens I had the sense to look it over. What an embarrassment. This is it, Evelyn. It's going to take more than just showing up on time. One more goof-up..." Her eyes glowed red.

Anger and courage swelled up uncontrollably from someplace deep within me. "Well, I certainly would hate for you to catch any *heck* on my account," I snapped. "You were obviously right not to trust me. I told you, it was a MISTAKE! We all make them."

She shook a chubby, fuschia-tipped finger at me. "Just so long as you understand that it was the second-to-last mistake you're ever going to make here, if you catch my drift. And I'll choose to ignore your tone because it's obvious you're not thinking clearly right now. Just have the right report on my desk within the hour."

My stomach churned. That *was* the right report. I had to get out of this place.

★★★

Working out was my salvation. One month after the party, I'd lost another eight pounds, for a grand total of twenty-one pounds gone forever. The only thing that sucked was that I was scared to tell Bruce—I knew he'd think I was losing too much, too fast. He was probably right, but I hadn't weighed under 150 pounds since high school, and seeing that thingy on the scale slide to the left instead of the right every week was undeniably intoxicating. It was easy, for the most part, since I was going to the gym almost every day. As a concession to Bruce and our financial situation, I did agree not to exceed three times a week with Jade.

But being the great guy he is, Jade always made sure to offer his support pro bono whenever I was there. When I broke the twenty-pound mark, I think he was almost as happy as I was.

"Amazing," he said as he marked my weight on my chart. "You should be our poster child. Maybe we'll put you in the brochure next year...like a 'before and after' shot, you know?"

"Well, you make me look forward to stepping on the scale, which is something I never thought I'd be able to say."

He smiled and I could swear I saw his cheeks turn pink. I instantly realized that I love a man who blushes.

"Well, you did it all by yourself. I can only take credit for opening your eyes to the joys of physical fitness. Actually coming here every day is up to you."

"And not eating like a pig, too," I reminded him.

He laughed. "And not eating like a pig. Just promise me you're not starving yourself."

"I'm not, I'm not."

The handful of Cheerios I'd had for lunch—sitting like a brick in my tummy—reminded me of that. So what if my stomach grumbled in protest on occasion? It would just be for a little while, until I could fit into The Dress. That would make it all worth it. Of course, Jade was so encouraging that it made me want to keep going, but if it weren't for the thought of that dress, wrapped in plastic in the back of Mom's closet, I'm not sure I'd have the will to go on. It was sick, actually, but I couldn't help it. Imagining myself fitting into that dress was more addictive than any drug could ever be, and far more enticing.

Jade was turning out to be the upside of my dark little obsession, and I admit that the short-term boost of seeing him was enough to get me back in there, day after day. Spending so many hours with a person in such an intimate way really lets you get to know them quickly, and I don't think it was a stretch to say that Jade and I were becoming quite close. We had plenty in common, so why not? I knew we could probably even be really good friends outside the gym, too, although Morgan thought that was absolutely ridiculous and that I really just had a whopping crush on him.

"You're getting married in six months, you're not talking to your mother, your job sucks and your trainer is gorgeous," she'd said. "Hmm...do you think it's true love?"

"I'm not that much of an imbecile," I reminded her. "And it's not love, because it's not even like. It's just that we seem to have a lot to talk about. And he thinks I'm funny."

"Sure he does," she said. "And it doesn't have anything to do with the fact that he makes a living off boosting the egos of chubby rich girls. I'm not saying he doesn't genuinely like you. Maybe he does. It's just that even if he didn't, he'd make sure you thought he did. Remind me, what did you say he did again? I mean, when he's not working you out?"

"He's an actor," I said defensively. "Where are you going with this?"

"Ah, an actor. And a good one, too, it seems."

"Oh, shut up, Morgan," I laughed. "You're just jealous."

"Of what? I've been there, Evie, and I've *done* that. You'll remember that I've had two of my trainers for lunch. On the whole, they're tasty, but not all that smart, unless you count an instinctual understanding of what a woman wants to hear."

Morgan believes that my overwhelming success at losing weight validates Jade's daily existence, so he can't help but become personally involved in my life, which is what accounts for anything beyond financially motivated pleasantness. It's not that what Morgan was saying had never occurred to me—it had. But I'm also a pretty good judge of character, and I know when I'm being taken for a ride. At the very least, Jade doesn't *despise* me or anything like that. I'd know it if he did. We never have a hard time making conversation, and he's told me all about his life and I've told him all about mine. But even if it's not real friendship, I'll take it, whatever it is—the anticipation of hanging out with a gorgeous, fantastic guy at the end of a hard day's work makes it all worthwhile.

"Evie?"

"Hi, Claire. If you're calling to bother me about Mom, I'm hanging up."

"Wait—give me a second. I want to say my piece."

"Fine," I said. "Go ahead."

"It's been over a month since the party, and I think that's more than enough time for you to have absorbed the information. This is no great tragedy, Evie, and I think you're old enough to understand that. Your mother is very upset, I'll have you know, and I think she's suffered plenty already."

"Actually, I'm still not quite sure about that." The thought of Mom being upset and guilt-ridden was an interesting reversal. I had to admit, it was strangely liberating.

"Forgiving someone is a gift you give yourself. It will lighten your heart, and I know you need that right now, Evelyn," Claire said quietly.

It wasn't like her to get all serious. "Are you going Christian on me, Claire?"

"Just call her, please. Put this nonsense to rest."

"I just don't know if I'm ready to speak to her yet," I said.

Bruce, who was reading in the bathtub—an irritating habit of his which had ruined countless perfectly good magazines and books—had been listening to the conversation, and called out, "Call her, already! You know you want to!"

"Shut up, please!" I yelled back.

But I suppose enough was enough. My curiosity was starting to get the better of me, anyway, and I had a lot of questions I needed resolved about the whole thing. "Fine, Claire," I said into the receiver. "I'll talk to her. But you call her and tell her. I'm not calling first."

"Hallelujah!" Bruce jumped up out of the tub and ran into the kitchen, stark naked and dripping wet, waving his hands in the air. "Hallelujah!" he yelled again. For some reason, he's always labored under the misconception that random nudity is good for a laugh.

We agreed to a meeting on neutral territory, in public, so that Mom wouldn't be able to make a scene. I still anticipated problems, though, so Bruce, whose fairness and objectivity no one could fault, agreed to come along as a mediator. Despite his earlier insistence on seeing things from their side, I was now pretty sure he was sympathetic to my position (*Cosmopolitan,* January: "Quiz of the Month: Do His Loyalties Lie with You?").

When we walked into the restaurant, they were already there. Mom smiled.

"Hello, Claire," I said coolly.

Bruce rolled his eyes and said to no one in particular, "It's gonna be a long night."

I took off my coat and sat down.

"Evelyn," Mom gasped. "You're so *thin.*"

Bruce looked at me hopefully as if to say, "See? She wants to make nice."

"Well, I've lost a few pounds," I conceded.

"Fifteen, to be exact!" Bruce added.

"More than that, I'd say," she said. "I don't remember the last time you looked this good."

"Oh, she looked beautiful before," Claire added, and turned

to me. "But I'm happy if you're happy. Maybe we could go shopping for some new things."

"I would like that very much," I said. Good of her to make a peace offering, too. After all, she was far from innocent in this whole debacle.

"Shall we order?" Bruce asked. He was always hungry. Sometimes I think he has a tapeworm of some sort.

"Let's have a drink first," Mom said, and ordered a Bloody Mary.

"I'll have one, too," I said to the waiter. "With extra celery."

"So?" I said.

"So," Mom said, and breathed out slowly.

Bruce tried to break the uncomfortable silence with small talk about his job and the New York Rangers, but for once, nobody was very interested in what he had to say. By the end of the meal, and a few drinks later, things loosened up a little.

"I was right, you know, about Lucia," Mom slurred.

"Right about what?" I asked.

"She didn't come here just for your party. She was here to help my father with some things. Business things," she said cryptically.

No one took the bait, so she added, "The city is threatening to take away his house because he hasn't paid his property taxes in four years."

"Well, well, well," I sighed. "Once again, Mom, you were right. And we know you just have to be right. God forbid my aunt should come to my engagement because she actually loves me, and was happy for me. So thanks for clearing things up."

"This isn't what we're here to talk about," Bruce interjected.

"Yes, forget about that, Lillian," Claire said. "Why don't you tell Evie what you wanted to tell her."

"What I wanted to tell her?" Mom asked, feigning confusion.

I turned to Bruce. "I don't know why I'm here. She's only going to make me crazy."

"Didn't you tell me you wanted to apologize?" Claire said gently.

Mom sighed, and thought for a minute.

"It's like pulling teeth," I muttered. "Why can't you just say it?"

"Don't you think I've suffered enough?" she said. "My own father hasn't spoken to me in twenty-seven years because of this."

It hadn't occurred to me—the real reason he hated her.

"I knew I was pregnant when your dad died," she continued. "But I never got the chance to tell him. I was waiting for Christmas morning. God, maybe he wouldn't have been up there that day if he knew. You think you have all the time in the world…." she stared into her glass for a bit, then continued. "Anyway, after he…the accident…I told my parents… My dad disowned me, said it was my fault Andrew died, that God was punishing me for being a tramp. He wouldn't even let my mother come to the funeral."

A lump throbbed bigger and bigger in my throat. "That's awful," I managed.

"It's true," said Claire.

Tears welled up in Mom's eyes. "So I *am* sorry," she blurted. "I'm sorry about everything. I'm sorry I didn't tell you earlier, about your father and me. I'm sorry I didn't marry him when I had the chance, when he asked me to. I'm sorry my father was right about everything. I'm sorry I spoiled you for so many years and always let you get your way. I'm sorry I wanted you to stay here with me and not go away to school. And I'm sorry you hate me so much, Evelyn. I'm most sorry about that. I'm sorry you hate me so much. But I'm *not* sorry that I want you to have what I missed out on, what was taken from me, from us. And I'm *not* sorry if I do everything in my power to make you realize that so you don't end up like me. No, I'm not sorry about that at all."

Stunned silence. We all just stared. Her chest heaved in and out as if she'd just run a marathon.

A waiter approached her from behind. "Would you like another drink, ma'am," he asked. Startled, she practically fell off her chair.

"Get away from her," I snapped.

Mom got up to leave the table.

"Don't go, Mom. Sit down," I said. Bruce grabbed her hand. She sat down. Never had I seen her so vulnerable, so pathetic. It was awful. What was the fun in kicking someone when they were down? That's not what we were about.

"I'm sorry, too," I said. "Not as sorry as you, though." I thought a little comic relief might do some good, but no one laughed. "I know you didn't mean to hurt me," I continued. Claire nodded at me. "And I know you thought you were protecting me. From what I don't know, but I do believe you tried to do the right thing. I was just mad because you were the one who was always so obsessed with me getting married, and then this, and I thought it was so hypocritical. But I can see that it wasn't."

She grabbed my hand. "Thank you, Evelyn."

I squeezed it back.

Bruce motioned to the waiter. "We're feeling much better here, and I think we're ready for some dessert. Mom, do you want some desert?"

Mom? Had he completely lost his senses? Granted, we were having a Hallmark moment, but *please*—calling your in-laws Mom and Dad went out with the baby boomers.

"I mean, would you mind if I call you Mom?"

She reached over and squeezed his cheeks between her hand. "Of course you can, Bruce. And I'd love some dessert. I'll have the tiramisu. Evelyn, you look like you could use some, too. And wipe that look off your face."

"Don't even joke about something like that, Mom, because it's not funny. Just bring me some herbal tea with sweetener, please."

"So long as you don't make a pig of yourself, dear," Claire said.

"I'll ignore that," I retorted. They make fun of me when I'm fat, they make fun of me when I'm not. I was beginning to think it had nothing to do with the way I looked.

"C'mon, have a cannoli, Evie," Bruce pleaded. "You love cannoli."

"No I don't," I said, and shot him my sharpest "shut your trap now while you're still ahead" look.

I still needed some closure on this. "Mom, before we're too far off topic, can I ask you something? Like does all this mean that I'm not really a Mays? Shouldn't I have your last name? And if you were never married, shouldn't *you* have your last name?"

"Don't worry, you're still a Mays. It's on your birth certificate. Technically, though, I suppose I'm still Lillian Valerio, even though I've gone by Mays for so many years. Nobody ever asked me to prove it."

"What about your wedding band?" asked Bruce.

"My father gave it to Lucia after my mother died, and then she gave it to me. So I'd have a piece of her, too. She was a wonderful lady, Evelyn. From another time. It's too bad you never got the chance to know her." She thought for a moment. "If you like, you can have it to wear as your ring when you get married. If that's all right with you, Bruce."

Her wedding band was lovely, an intricately woven band of gold and diamonds.

"It's fine with me," he said. "It's a beautiful ring."

"Thanks, Mom, I'd really like that."

"I suppose I don't really have much of a use for it anymore," she said with a smile.

12

Today was a milestone. No words could describe the moment I slid my absolutely gorgeous size-eight Vera Wang wedding dress over my hips for the first time. It almost ripped from the effort, and I couldn't zip it up, but I didn't really care. Last month, even with an industrial-strength pair of control-tops, it was hopeless. Now, standing here in Mom's bedroom, ten pounds lighter, I was wearing a size eight. A *small* size eight. The hunger, the fighting, the sweating, the agonizing descent into obsession and madness—it had all been worth it. The wedding was exactly five months away and I was right on track.

When I got home and told Bruce the good news, he was decidedly less enthusiastic.

"I think you have an eating disorder," he said dourly.

"I *wish!*" It was hard not to die laughing at the thought. "Me? With an eating disorder? That's a good one. Unless there's such a thing as a dyslexic anorexic!" I hadn't told him what I'd learned about binge eating, but I don't think it would have helped my case. Thank God I hardly saw him anymore—he'd probably tie me up and force feed me.

"I'm serious, Evie. Think about it."

Even though I knew he had a bit of a point, I also knew he'd never be able to understand that I was still mostly in control of things. And besides, it was only temporary—as soon as I was where I needed to be, I would start eating healthier and just maintain. But admitting that he was right, even a little bit, would have just made things worse. And I wasn't the only one with a problem. "You're the one who's in denial," I told him. "As soon as you realize that you *like* me fat, and that my weight problem served a purpose for you, then we'll talk. Until then, I can't trust a word you say on the topic."

He always seemed to forget that I minored in psychology. You see, some people use weight as a shield to protect themselves from painful emotional issues. My being fat probably allowed Bruce to hide from his feelings of failure at not living up to his overbearing mother's expectations that he find a woman who met her impossible standards.

He cracked his knuckles and breathed out deeply. "All right, I'll admit it once and for all: I like you fat. In fact, I *love* you fat. I love you no matter what you look like."

"Aha! You see? You see? You've been trying to sabotage me. All these years. You're *such* an asshole!" And I'd just thought I was big-boned.

"You know, Evie, I used to find the warped way in which you view the world endearing, but now I find it a little bit scary and a whole lot irritating. Do you hear what you're saying? Do you really think that you have a weight problem because I dig fat chicks?"

"*Had* a weight problem," I corrected him "But in a nutshell, yeah. That is what I think. I've been fat since you met me—that's probably why you liked me in the first place—but now that I'm getting thin you're pulling away from me. Do you know we haven't had sex in almost a month? You've become emotionally distant, Bruce. It's like you're somewhere else."

"I know EXACTLY how long it's been since we've had sex,

and the reason for that is because you come home from the gym every night at ten and you're too tired to even say good-night to me. And on the weekends, you're either shopping or running. So do NOT lay the whole sex thing on me."

"You're the one who's been cold and aloof."

"She said while filing her nails."

"Funny."

"And just for the record, what attracted me to you in the first place wasn't your body."

"Are you saying I wasn't attractive?" He could be so hurtful.

"EVIE! You can't have it both ways! God, you're so exasperating."

"Don't yell. Go on. Why did you like me, then?" There's always time for compliments, even when you're bickering.

"Well," he sighed, and thought about it for a little too long. "It's hard to remember these days, but I guess I loved your attitude. You were just so damn funny. And your utter ridiculousness. I'd never met anyone like you."

"Nobody ethnic, you mean."

"No, that's not what I mean."

I rolled my eyes, as if to say, "Yeah right."

"But now I'm just completely exhausted by you. You're changing, and I'm pretty sure I don't like it. And you can rest assured it has nothing to do with the way you look. It's how you're acting—you're completely obsessed. You're barely eating a thing. You look unhealthy, your skin is gray, your breath is bad, your hair is limp!"

Ohmygod. Bad breath? Had Jade noticed? "Are you serious?!" I asked, appalled.

"Evie, I just want things back the way they were. I want to spend time with you like we used to."

"You're making it sound like I'm wasting away into nothing. Don't forget that I'm still a cow. It just so happens that I'm somewhat of a smaller cow."

"You're not a cow. You're five foot four and 140 pounds. I'd say that puts you squarely in the camp of average. So be warned, Evie. I'm keeping my eye on you. You're not going to get away with anything—I won't let you."

Average. That had a nice ring to it.

People at work were far more impressed than Bruce was. They couldn't get over how much weight I'd lost.

"It's just thirty pounds," I told Andrea by the coffee cart one afternoon. "I have at least another twenty to go if I don't want to look like a total pig in my dress."

"Still, thirty pounds is a lot. Have you sworn off eating entirely?" she asked politely.

"Actually, I owe it all to exercise. I have an excellent trainer. I could give you his name if you like," I said, knowing she'd never take me up on it.

"No thanks, I'm fine the way I am. Chocolate?" she offered, holding out what looked like a peanut-butter cup. "It was my birthday this weekend, and there was an enormous box of them on my desk this morning from all the girls."

"No thanks. I'm still stuffed from lunch." I'd have to remind people not to do that for me this year—was there a subtle way to request a fruit basket instead? *Was I crazy?* My birthday wasn't until September, why was I worried about eating chocolate six months from now? Maybe Bruce was right. Maybe I really did have a touch of anorexia. Even worse, why did the possibility delight me so much? *It's just until the wedding. Then I'll be normal again. I swear.*

"Oh—sorry!" she giggled. "Of course you can't. But I didn't want to be rude."

Not that I really wanted one, but even if I had, I certainly wouldn't have given the little bitch the satisfaction. I was no stranger to these types of subversive diet-wrecking tactics. From Bruce's subtle attempts to trick me into ordering pizza for dinner, to Bertie's incessant yammering about the importance of sampling wedding cakes, I knew by now how to bow out gracefully from any manner of caloric situation.

Surprisingly, I think it was Pruscilla, who herself had lost more than eighty pounds since her surgery last October, who admired my resolve the most. Last week, during a departmental "lunch" meeting which lasted until 4:30, I managed to almost completely ignore the trays and trays of catered food spread out over the boardroom table. By sheer determination, I consumed only an olive which had fallen off someone's salad, two and half celery sticks and four cups of black coffee. Even Pruscilla, whose stomach was the size of a shot glass, couldn't resist a few bites of a ham-and-cheese croissant. Afterward, she whispered to me, "You must be ready to faint—you haven't eaten a *thing* all day," which I took to be quite a compliment, since it was obvious she was looking to me as an example of what and what not to eat.

Who would ever have imagined it? Me, Evelyn Mays, a model of self-restraint for the new millennium. It was as much of a surprise to me as anyone, but if I could inspire just one person to see the value of living a more calorically restrained lifestyle—and all the aesthetic benefits that come along with that—then it would all be worth it. So what if I was hungry and miserable on occasion, and completely consumed by thoughts of a stupid white dress hidden in the back of my mother's closet? Success tasted better than any chocolate peanut-butter cup ever could, from what I remembered.

The filthiest of the diet industry's dirty little secrets is not the inherent failure preprogrammed into the powders and pills and infomercial exercise equipment (*Shape,* March: "Weight-Loss Witchcraft: A Billion-Dollar Business"), as is the commonly held wisdom on the subject. I propose that the vendors of these products are far less cruel than they seem at first glance. They are simply attuned to the financial payoffs of human nature, which dictates that we're willingly deceived into deceiving ourselves.

It's eat now and pay later, but if you don't want to pay later, the easy way out is readily available—for a surcharge. Whatever guilt you may encounter from supersizing those fries is assuaged by the belief that tomorrow's herbal supplements will make it all okay; if, for some unfathomable reason, grape-seed extract is no match for those fifty or hundred or two hundred extra pounds, there's a doctor waiting in the wings who's willing to remove ninety percent of your stomach—and an insurance company delighted to pay for it all, based on a careful cost-benefit analysis.

No, it doesn't take a marketing genius to get an unhappy forty-five-year-old, four-hundred-pound woman from Hayseed, Arkansas, to believe she'll look like Kate Moss if she diligently takes her fat-metabolizing capsules. As far as I'm concerned, it's not particularly deceptive, either. She knows, at least subconsciously, that it won't work. But her desperation speaks louder than her doubts, and her common sense is stifled equally well by either a Twinkie or Suzanne Somers's New and Improved ThighMaster. She's no victim, at least not in that sense. So is it fair to curse the quacks for selling us exactly what we want? Probably not.

I believe we should put the blame where it really lies—squarely on the shoulders of the fashion industry. The greatest cruelty, the most contemptible scam, perpetrated against the overweight people of the world is that the clothier has orchestrated the entire charade for his own benefit.

It's a simple shell game, and one I know all too well: The more weight a woman loses, the more clothes she buys, discarding anything old and large that reminds her of her former self; conversely, the more weight she gains after her methods ultimately fail, the more new fat clothes she must purchase to cover her ever-expanding flesh. Herbal supplements are expensive, sure, but not as expensive as a new wardrobe two or three times a year. Yes, the fashion world is the real winner in this whole mess, pulling the strings from behind the scenes, with a complicit diet industry happy to turn a profit in its wake. I, for one, am outraged by the lack of accountability in this matter, and intend to expose the entire ruse. For it is one thing to bank on a woman's insecurities when she's feeling large and hopeless, but to bilk her when she's at her thinnest, transforming her vanity into corporate profits—that's just *monstrous.*

All this to say, I'd virtually maxed out both of my credit cards since the engagement party, and sincerely believed it wasn't my fault. Nobody ever told me how expensive it would be to lose weight. I'd budgeted for the sessions with Jade, of course—that expense was a necessary evil—but the shopping was completely unexpected. Had I known all of this beforehand, I'm not sure I would have even bothered at all.

"On the surface, it looks bad, I can admit that. But it's not like I'm being frivolous," I told Morgan one day. "These are all things I *need*. They really are. Can I help it if I'm the sort of person who likes to present a certain image of herself to the world, who must maintain a certain standard? You know what I'm talking about, in your line of work. Going around in saggy-assed jeans and oversized tops just doesn't make a good impression."

"It certainly doesn't," she concurred. "And what's the alternative? It's not like you have a *choice.* I mean, you can't go around naked, or barefoot for that matter. The new shoes were an absolute must. And while we're on the subject, if you don't mind my asking, exactly how much weight *have* your feet lost?"

"Well...none, I think, but I just don't like my fat shoes anymore. They don't look right with most of my new stuff."

"Don't say another word—I *completely* understand," she said.

It was sometimes hard to tell if she was humoring me or not.

"But as a concession to my creditors," I continued, "there is some room to play around with my gym-clothes budget. Since most of the stuff I'm buying is stretchy, anyway, there's no reason why it can't take me all the way through to one hundred and twenty pounds. And if my spandex shorts are baggy in a couple of months, then so be it."

"That's the spirit! You're already on your way to financial freedom."

"But it's hard, Morgan, it's *so* hard," I explained. "The shopping is murder. It's going to be the end of me. Bruce is freaking, he really is. I don't know what I'm going to do. You're the financial whiz. You've got to help me...."

"Have you considered cutting up your credit cards?"

"No." As if.

"Well, how about this. I knew this girl in college who went on a completely crazed spending spree one day that she knew she couldn't possibly pay for. Afterward, she was so disgusted with herself that she cut up her card. Of course, she instantly regretted it, and called Visa immediately to request a new one. It took them two weeks to send it to her. As soon as she got it, she went to the mall. At the end of the day, she cut the card in half, then called Visa again. It went on like that for years. She was smart—she limited her spending to just two days a month. Maybe you could try something like that."

I thought about it for a fraction of a second, and decided against it. There was no need to get completely hysterical just yet.

Morgan sensed my reluctance. "Maybe I'm not fully understanding your problem," she said. "Are you more worried about how you're going to pay for everything you've already bought, or that you won't be able to buy anything more? Because if it's that, then why don't you just get another card?"

"Get a new one?" That was interesting.

"...provided Bruce doesn't kill you."

"Oh." He would. What a jerk. "So what do I do? It's crucial that I have the buying power I need. Things come up, you know, and I deserve it, don't I? But I'm almost maxed out."

"Ahh," she said quietly. "Therein lies the paradox."

Morgan was no fool.

"Evie, you're my best friend, so I'm going to tell it to you like it is. You can either stop spending money, which sounds like it's not really an option for you, since your sense of entitlement is obviously more powerful than your sense of fiscal responsibility, or..." she paused for dramatic effect.

"Or what?"

"...or you can increase your income."

"Get a...a second job?" I stammered, aghast. Was she mad?

"No, you idiot—a raise. Get a raise."

"I don't know..." I said. "I'm not due for one until the fall, and even then..."

"Look, if they haven't already fired you by now, then chances are they want to keep you. So march right in there and ask. Now I gotta go—I have a lunch date with Billy. He's been waiting at the restaurant for over an hour."

It was actually a pretty good idea, provided I could catch Pruscilla in the right mood. Although the three-month mark of my probation had come and gone without a pink slip, I still got the sense she was suspicious of me, like she knew I was slacking off but just hadn't figured out how yet. It might be better to wait until she was once again ready to see me as a valuable asset to the company before I broached the topic of raises. But since I needed the money so desperately, I resolved to stay on the lookout for the perfect moment to bring it up. It's not like I'd be asking for a promotion, which I had definitely given up on, since my professional performance had been less than exemplary. I was willing to admit at least that. On the other hand, though, my extraordinary willpower had surely saved the insurance company the cost of a future gastric bypass, so I figured the least Kendra White could do was raise me a measly few thousand bucks. And aren't employee salaries tax-deductable anyway?

With this in mind, I popped into Barneys on my way to the gym. Call me a hypocrite, if you like, but being aware of the fashion industry's duplicity doesn't make me immune to its considerable charms. I was a victim in all this, too, remember. And Barneys was my new favorite place to succumb to the urges

(*Elle,* January: "Department-Store Psychology: NYC's Best Retail Therapy").

As I pored through the racks, it occurred to me how I was beginning to enjoy shopping by myself. Instead of dragging someone along with me to tell what made me look fat and what didn't, I found that lately I needed the peace and quiet that only comes from being alone with your thoughts in a retail environment. I no longer needed the constant reassuring of others—I could now trust the salesgirls to tell me the truth. Even if they were lying, I figured, how bad could I look? I was a perfect size ten, and things were looking brighter every day.

A now-familiar wave of exhilaration washed over me as I selected a few things to try on. The humiliation of the almost-plus sizes was behind me forever. Since most decent designers shy away from being associated with any item larger than a twelve, the pleasure of shopping freely in a place like Barneys is a high unlike any other. Best of all, I was free to experiment with styles and fabrics which were previously atrocious on me.

Until I got my raise, I reasoned that it would be best not to get too carried away, so I left with only a pair of baby-blue pleather pants (*Jane,* March: "Fabrics of the Future: This Ain't Your Grandmother's Vinyl!") and a sexy Ralph Lauren bra that was on sale for $19.99.

As grave as my personal financials were at the time, at least the wedding details were coming along nicely. I'd been trying my best to stay out of things, which was working quite well. Unfortunately for Bruce, though, the brunt of dealing with Bertie was falling to him most of the time. It was either that or I'd have to do it, which meant things would get ugly, and he knew it.

To give him proper credit, he handled the money end like a pro when we first got engaged, delicately telling his mother that our families would be splitting the cost of The Wedding proportionately according to number of guests. Bertie didn't like that. She thought my mom should pay for half, no matter what—"What happened to the days when the bride's family paid for everything? Do you think your Granny Fulbright dished out one red cent for *my* wedding?"—but I gently reminded him to tell her that it was my grandmother who'd be paying, not my mom, and that Claire was an old woman who lived on a fixed income.

"Fixed my ass!" I could hear her tinny voice coming through the receiver. "The only thing that's fixed about her income is the interest rate she gets on that pile of cash her husband left her." It was true, but Claire would never agree to pay for half of Bertie's friends at $250 a head. Especially since Claire's idea of the perfect wedding would be something more akin to *Barefoot in the Park (In Style Weddings,* Fall: "The Most Romantic Movie Weddings of All Time"). But it still gave me great satisfaction when Bruce told me, in the strictest confidence, that his dad had secretly called my grandmother at the outset of the negotiations and offered to pay for the entire thing, but Claire wouldn't hear of it. Bertie would have an aneurysm if she knew about that one.

By the end of March, everything was right on schedule. The appropriate deposits had been sent off to the inn, the photographer, the florist, the band, the video guy and the limo company. I'd settled on a fabric for the bridesmaids—a lovely satin-backed crepe in just the right shade of champagne—and all six girls were already scheduled for their first fittings. Bertie had even retained the second-hottest calligrapher in Connecticut to address the invitations.

All that remained to be done was booking the honeymoon. I had my heart set on Maui, but Bruce preferred Ireland.

"You're the one who's always complaining about how expensive everything is, and you want to go all the way to Ireland?" I asked.

"Ireland is closer *and* cheaper than Hawaii, Evie. We'd even have a place to stay for part of the time. My mom's cousins offered to let us use their place in Galway, remember?"

"Don't be absurd." What was he thinking? Maui was definitely the best place to honeymoon right now (*Modern Bride,* Spring: "This Year's Honeymoon Hot Spots"). And where the hell was Galway? "I refuse to spend my honeymoon wading through shit on some sheep farm," I explained.

Bruce picked a handful of bras up off the floor and whipped them into the laundry basket. "How about you go to Maui and I'll go to Ireland?" He snapped.

"How about you go to Ireland with your mother and I'll stay here alone with the lights out so we can save some cash."

"I have a better idea," he said. "How about you return your blue plastic pants and everything else you've bought lately and we'll go to Bali for a month or two and stay at the Four Seasons. We'd still have money left over for first-class tickets."

"I'll ignore that," I said, and followed him into the kitchen.

"Good, because I don't want to talk about this again," he barked.

"Don't be mad at me. It's not really my fault. I know I've spent a lot lately, but I think I deserve it. It's been years since I actually felt this good about myself, you know, so what's the harm in treating myself now and then? Not to mention the fact that I really, truly don't fit into any of my old clothes."

Silence.

"I owe some money—I know that. But I'm working on a plan. Not just to cut back on spending, which I already have, but to get a raise as well. And work pays for the gym, or at least some of it, remember? Even if we don't get it back till the end of the year. So you can't count the gym with all the other stuff, right?" Although Bruce might have been peeved with my spending habits, he couldn't fault me for that. "Right?"

He glared at me as if to say he could indeed fault me for that.

My patience was wearing thin. "It's an investment in my

health, Bruce. My *health.* Isn't that supposed to be the most important thing? If you can't accept at least that, then I don't know why I'd want to marry a person like you anyway."

With an angry scowl, he took his dinner out of the microwave and stomped off into the living room to watch the news.

13

The only respite I found from the storm swirling all around me were the few short hours a day I spent with Jade. Which was a good thing, because I was sorely lacking in male companionship.

I barely saw Bruce at all throughout most of April. Although we'd settled the whole honeymoon thing—we both agreed on Las Vegas, a subtle blend of sun and fun at a reasonable price, provided nobody goes overboard at the tables—I was pissed off at him for leaving me alone on Easter weekend. It was the third recruiting trip he'd taken in the last month, trying to reel in as many little nerds as possible before the summer registration deadline, I suppose. Since Claire was on some Eldertour of Spain and Portugal, I ended up spending the holiday alone with Mom, which was about as much fun as having my teeth pulled. All she did was nag me about losing too much weight ("I can tell already that you're going to look sallow in the wedding pictures;" "Your hair! Your hair! What's happening to your hair?"). And I was a little angry at Bruce's parents, too. The least they could have done, knowing we were alone, was invite us over for Easter Sunday. Not that we would have gone.

Jade, on the other hand, was my rock and support. Despite what Morgan said, our friendship was getting stronger with each passing day. One night, after an incredibly strenuous and emotional session during which I finally sustained a level ten on the stepmaster for forty-five minutes, Jade was obviously impressed.

"Nice job, Evie. That's about it for now, though. Tomorrow's abs and arms, so you better save your strength."

"I'll be...here...at six," I gasped, scooping up my towel and water bottle.

"Hey—you in any rush? Right now, I mean?" he asked.

"No, not really," I said. He probably wants to go over my chart with me, I thought. It had been a while since we added anything new to my routine, and I'd been noticing lately that we'd been neglecting my glutes.

"You feel like getting a drink?" he asked. He said it just like that. As if it were no big deal.

My heart leapt up into my throat. "With me?"

"Of course, with you."

"Sure," I giggled adorably. "Just give me a few minutes, and I'll slip into something a little more comfortable."

He wants to have a drink with me. The hottest, sexiest, most popular trainer in the entire gym, and possibly all of Manhattan, wants to have a drink with me! I sauntered off to the locker room and showered and dressed as quickly as possible. While blow-drying my hair, it occurred to me that maybe I shouldn't be as excited as I was. But at the same time, I was wishing I had something sexier to wear than my boring gray work suit.

A little décolleté wouldn't hurt, I figured, so I took off my blouse entirely and put the jacket back on. I stared at my reflection. Surprisingly good. If I leaned forward, he'd be able to see my bra, since the suit was a touch big, but that was fine. After all, this nice little Calvin Klein number in black lace was meant to be seen, and I didn't want to look like a frumpy old schoolmarm. He'd probably take me to some fantastically trendy actors' bar that most dull normals don't even know exists. I imagined walking in on Jade's arm…heads would turn…oh, the possibilities were endless. A little red lipstick, and voilà—from day to night in no time flat! One last look—I was actually sexy. There was no denying it.

I found Jade still in his sweats at the juice bar, chatting up the silicone-infected man trap who works behind the counter.

"What'll ya have, Evie?" he asked when he saw me standing there.

I am such an idiot.

Defeated, I slid onto the stool beside him. "The wheat germ and carrot special. No parsley."

"Sure thing," Juice Wench said. "The usual for you, Jade?"

"Yup," he smiled at her. "Thanks, Kirsten." She winked at him and jiggled off.

"You sure do get a lot of winks," I said.

"You noticed?" He turned and looked right into my eyes.

God, I hope I didn't sound jealous. Because I was.

Better divert the question. "Can I ask you something? Is Jade your real name?"

"What, you think I made it up?"

"Not to state the obvious, but I could think of worse names for a green-eyed actor," I said.

"Cute. Very cute. Well, I'm sorry to disappoint you, but Jade is my real name. My parents were living in Hong Kong when I was conceived, if that's any explanation."

"My, my, quite the world traveler," I said. "Did you live there long?"

"Alas," he sighed. "I was nothing more than a well-traveled fetus. We came back home to Staten Island before I was born. Lived in New York ever since. How about you?"

"Brooklyn, born and raised. When I was eighteen, I wanted to move out to California for school, UCLA, but it…didn't work out." Morgan says it's always best to be a little bit enigmatic when you're talking to a man you're trying to seduce—so I'd leave him wondering about what motivates the mysterious Evelyn Mays. Not that I was trying to seduce Jade. That would be ridiculous. I was just having a little fun.

"Why not?"

"It just didn't. I'm an only child."

"Ah, so your parents couldn't bear the thought of their precious little girl all alone on the other side of the country."

"Something like that. But my dad lives in L.A.," I heard myself saying. "My parents divorced when I was really young." What the hell was I thinking? So much for Morgan's air of intrigue—I had completely obliterated any hint of mystery and moved on to tell-all fiction.

"Are you close with your dad?" Jade asked.

"Not really. I mean, I speak to him every couple of months or so. I guess that's why I wanted to go out there, to get to know him a little better. Find out what he's like."

"What does he do?"

Jade opened the door; I couldn't resist walking through.

"He's a...casting director, actually. Funny you should ask. He works for some big production company." My tongue was not my own, and my heart was racing. Could he tell that I was lying? I didn't even know if casting directors work for production companies. And did I actually think he'd like me more if my dad could get him a job?

Yes I did. And I hoped he would.

But Jade didn't so much as flinch. "So the dutiful daughter stayed home with her mother instead."

"Oh, I wouldn't say I was dutiful," I said cheerily, glad to steer the conversation away from my evil delusions. I couldn't trust myself not to lie, and desperately wanted to avoid promising Jade the lead role in some movie that didn't exist. "It was more like laziness, among other things," I told him.

"No money?"

"No money," I sighed.

"Yeah, I know what that's like. I wanted to move to L.A., too. Try the whole acting thing out there for a while, you know? But cash was tight. And I figured I was better off staying here anyway, pay my dues, maybe do some theater. You know? Then break into TV or movies."

"How's it going?" I asked. With his looks, I found it hard to believe that he couldn't get anything. He must be a dreadful actor.

"Not so good. Problem is, I refuse to do anything that involves nudity. For now anyway. I've had a lot of offers from...let's see, how should I put this...less mainstream productions."

"You mean porn?" I asked, almost choking on my juice. He'd be *fantastic* in porn.

"Yeah, I guess you could call it that. It's tempting, with the money they throw at you, but it can ruin your career if you're not careful."

"I bet. But I'm sure plenty of girls would pay money to see you naked." I'd be the first in line.

"But why compromise my artistic integrity when plenty of girls pay money to see me fully clothed?" he grinned. He was so cute I could almost die.

"I wouldn't call what you wear fully clothed, dear. Spandex doesn't leave much to the imagination."

"Have you been imagining, Evie?"

God, I was definitely in trouble. A *lot* of trouble.

I cleared my throat. "Have you thought about modeling?"

"I model on occasion," he smiled. "Catalogue stuff, mostly. But I just do it for a little extra cash."

"Anything I might have seen?"

"Probably not."

"Did you do the Abercrombie and Fitch catalog for spring? I think I might have noticed you in that," I said hopefully. He was just the type—prep-school good looks, tousled hair hanging down into his eyes, teeth as white as Chiclets and abs you could wash clothes on.

"Wasn't me," he laughed, shaking his head. What a laugh. A laugh so unselfconscious and so utterly sexy that it made me suck in my breath and look around to make sure nobody else heard. Juice Wench did, and shot me a knowing glance.

"And you never wanted to pursue it?" I asked, flustered. This guy could have been in his underwear on a giant billboard in Times Square. Instead, he was here talking to me.

"Nah, it's not for me. I know a lot of models, girls mostly, and it's a pretty dreadful business. Besides, I'm twenty-seven. I'm too old for all that shit."

I nodded understandingly. The whole modeling thing could be a real bitch.

"What about you, Evie? You're a woman transformed. You might consider it now that you've dropped—what is it?—forty pounds?"

Thirty-eight, but who's counting. "Ha, ha. Very funny. If I didn't know any better, I'd say you were flirting with me."

"What makes you think you know better?" he said softly.

There was an uncomfortable pause for a second. Before I could figure out what to say, Juice Wench was back with the bill. Jade grabbed it. "I got it," he said.

"Are you sure?"

"Yeah, yeah, don't worry about it." And he was chivalrous, too. God, was there *anything* about him that wasn't absolutely perfect?

"Thank you," I said. "I'll get the next one."

"Sure. Well, I don't want to keep you," he said.

"Keep me?"

"You're all dressed up. I assume you're going out."

"Yeah," I lied. "I'm having drinks with a few friends." *I dressed up for you, you idiot.*

"So, I'll see you tomorrow," he said, and kissed me on the cheek.

I didn't know what to do, so I just said 'bye and left.

Yes, love was in the air. Maybe it was because springtime was just around the corner, or maybe the stars were conspiring in the heavens, or maybe it was all just coincidence, but it seemed like everybody was getting a piece. Claire had a new boyfriend, some guy she met on the Internet. Morgan and Peter were preparing for a romantic weekend tryst at her mother's summer house on the beach, and she'd penciled Billy in for the weekend after that. Even that hag Andrea from Fragrances had finally harangued her boyfriend into proposing. The only notable exception was Bruce, who walked around the house in a constant snit, brooding silently over God knows what.

The real proof came at Mom's one Saturday afternoon. I'd gone over to try on the dress. In what can only be described as a feat of near-impossible restraint on my part, it had been a month since I'd even looked at it. Not that I hadn't thought about it almost constantly during that time, imagining how perfectly it would fit, and how wonderful it would make my wedding day. I knew that if I tried it on every forty-eight hours like I wanted to, it would only make my progress less dramatic, so I held back. Now, with four weeks gone, I was anticipating great things.

"I hope it fits, Evelyn. It's too late to find another one." She gave me crap about losing too much weight, but secretly, she was ecstatic about it.

"I'm 132 pounds, Mom. It better fit."

She spread a sheet out onto the floor (*Martha Stewart Weddings,* Spring: "Avoiding Dress Disasters") and gently removed the dress from its bag. I stepped into the gown and pulled it up smoothly. No snagging on the hips, this time.

"Do it up! Do it up!" I said. This was it, I could feel it.

"Hold on a second," she said, fluffing out the skirt. "Are your boobs properly adjusted?"

"Come *on* already!"

"Okay, sweetie. Here goes..." And just like that, she zipped it up and stepped back.

"Oh my," she gasped. "*Evelyn*—you're breathtaking."

I turned to face the full-length mirror.

It didn't look at all like me. Was that little waist mine? And those collarbones? Where had my breasts gone? Instead of pride and relief, I felt the vague stirrings of panic and fear.

Mom was getting a little teary-eyed. "I can't believe you actually did it, dear. I didn't think you could, but you did," she said. "When I saw it in the bag, it didn't look like much, to be honest with you. Very plain. But you were right—it's much prettier than the one at Sternfeld's. Much more elegant. You look like a princess. And that's how a girl should feel on her wedding day."

How would she know?

"Are you sure it looks okay?" I asked shakily. Maybe it was because I was having a bad-hair day, but I didn't feel much like a bride. It felt more like Halloween. I looked good, thin; the mirror told me at least that. But I felt strange.

"Don't fish for compliments, Evelyn. It's not attractive. You know it looks more than just okay. You look like a model. Try on the shoes and the veil."

I put the shoes on. They were a little higher than what I normally wear—okay, a lot higher.

"Try walking," she said. "I'll call the seamstress and tell her we're ready to come for the alterations now. It's just the right size, so don't you dare lose a single pound more..."

The phone rang and she darted off into the kitchen. I strayed off the sheet and tried walking around the room a little. My feet were already killing me. I suddenly just wanted The Dress back in the closet where it belonged. I took it off and lay down on the bed and tried to imagine how Bruce would react when he saw me in it for the first time. Then I imagined what Jade would say if he saw me in it. Then I realized that was just plain wrong, so I went back to thinking about Bruce. Maybe he would be so overcome by emotion that he'd fall to his knees right then and there. Or maybe he wouldn't even notice. I could wear a potato sack, he'd still think I looked beautiful. I knew that was a good thing. No, a *great* thing—but for some reason, it still annoyed me at that moment.

A strange sound was coming from the kitchen, distracting me. It took a second or two for me to realize that it was Mom's muffled giggles. I ventured into the living room so that I could hear better.

"Oh, you really shouldn't say such things," she said.

Who the hell could she be talking to?

"Albert, I'm fifty-one. You can't say things like that to a fifty-one-year-old woman."

Albert?

"No—don't stop. I was only kidding. Of course I don't mind." More giggles. It was revolting. "Oh, Albert, *stop* it."

But the hilarious Albert would not be stopped, and Mom cackled like a hyena. Enough was enough. I snuck up behind her.

"Mom," I said loudly. "Who's that?"

She jumped up from the chair and slammed the receiver down.

"Oh dear," she said sadly, looking at it. "I didn't mean to do that."

"Who's Albert?"

"You heard?"

"Yes I heard, this apartment only has four rooms. Who's Albert?"

The phone rang. She looked at it.

"Pick it up," I said. "What's the matter with you?"

"Yes, yes. Fine. I'll pick it up," she said. I'd never seen her so frazzled. "Hello?"

Poor Albert. Probably thought she was really mad at him.

"Sorry about that, Albert. But I'll have to call you back, Evelyn's here. Fine, I'll see you then. 'Bye for now."

She looked at me guiltily. "Now, I don't want you to get upset about this…."

"Do you have a boyfriend? That wouldn't bother me. Why do you think that would bother me? I'd be happy for you." I said it and meant it, but it somehow felt a bit like a lie.

"Good," she said, and exhaled slowly. "Because I do. Ha! I have a boyfriend!"

One of my New Year's resolutions was to find Mom a date for the wedding, so this was very good news. Shocking, but good.

"So, who is he?" I asked, and sat down.

"He's divorced."

"That's all you can think to say about this guy? He must be very interesting."

"I don't mind that he's divorced. But I thought you should know."

"Thanks for telling me. It'll take some time for me to get used to the idea since you know how seriously I uphold the tenets of the Church."

"He's Italian," she explained.

"Thank God."

"His name is Albert Casella, and he sells computers."

At least he had a job. "Where did you meet him?"

"On the Internet."

"But you don't have a computer," I reminded her.

"I let Claire fix me up. It started off that I just wanted to get her off my back. She found him on a...what do you call that...a Web site? A Web site where Italian mothers fix up their children. She gave him my number. I was mad at first, and I just wanted to get rid of him and tell Claire that I'd tried so now she could leave me alone, but we got along so well. We had so much to talk about. Can you imagine? And he lives right here in Bensonhurst, just off 18th Avenue, and he knows Mary Manardi. Remember her? She was my old boss at the DMV before she retired. Can you believe what a small world it is? Anyway, we still keep in touch from time to time, so I called her right away and asked about this guy Albert, and she said he's been friends with her son Freddie for many years, and that he always seemed like a nice person. And she knows his mother, too, from church."

I don't think I'd ever heard Mom say so many words in a row without complaining. She was definitely giddy. "Well, at least that's a character reference," I offered.

"Exactly, so I called him back and told him that he checked

out fine, and so we went to a movie a couple of weeks ago and then out for dinner."

"A movie? But you never go to the movies." She hadn't been to a movie in years.

"Have you seen the new one with Brad Pitt? It's excellent."

"Mom, stop it. You're freaking me out."

"So we've been on three dates since then, and we're going out tomorrow night, too. He's taking me to see *Rent*."

I shook my head gravely. "How do you know he's not some freak that wants to swindle you out of your pension or sell you termite insurance?" There were plenty of debonair lunatics roaming the country, preying on needy old women (*Harper's Bazaar,* January: "The Socialite and the Bigamist: A Tawdry Tale of Lust, Lies and a Leveraged Buyout Scam").

"For heaven's sake, Evelyn. Give me a little credit. I'm not so vain that I can't see the forest for the trees. He's fifty-seven years old, and he's losing his hair. He's not some handsome young con artist like on one of those TV shows. I think he wants what I want—a little companionship, someone to have a good time with. That's all."

"Well, I'm happy for you, Mom," I told her. "You deserve it." What else was there to say?

The thought of Mom having a social life was bizarre. For days, I couldn't get the image of her and this Albert out of my head, which was frustrating because I had no idea what he looked like. With the right light, Mom was still a very attractive woman, and she deserved more than some fat, old, bald guy. Bruce and I would go and meet him, I resolved. I'm sure Mom wanted our approval anyway. She was probably scared to death that we wouldn't like him or something. But we'd have to keep an open mind. This was probably her last chance.

That weekend, I had the overwhelming urge to clean out my closet for the first time in two years. It was stuffed with hideous and large things I would never be wearing again, which only served to remind me of my formerly enormous self and which were taking valuable space away from items which deserved to be there.

"What are you doing?" Bruce asked as I sat on the floor, surrounded by shoe boxes and old purses.

"What does it look like?"

"Cleaning?"

"Give the man a prize," I said.

"So the pack rat admits defeat," he smiled.

"I'm making a fresh start. Out with the old and in with the new," I told him.

"That's great. Hey—can I have that boa? The drama department could use it for the spring play. We're doing *Cage Aux Folles.*"

"No. I'm saving it for Halloween. Isn't that production a little risque for ten-year-olds?"

"Not really. They see it more as a mildly amusing contemporary farce. And it lets them show off their French. Besides, it could've been worse—they're deconstructing the relationship between homosexuality, violence and religious ritual within the plays of Jean Genet in their Language Arts class, so *Cage Aux Folles* is really a much safer choice, all things considered."

"Of course it is." Whatever.

I reached far into the depths of the closet and began pulling out anything I hadn't worn in two months. "Pass me that garbage bag, please," I said.

"You're getting rid of all that? You used to love that pinstripe suit. You said it was the only thing that made you look skinny."

"It's a size *twelve,*" I spat, and shoved it deep into the bottom of the bag.

He flopped down on the bed and made himself comfortable. "And what about those jeans? You don't want those anymore?"

"They have an elastic waist, Bruce. Would you mind leaving me alone?"

"It's just that I find this sad. I don't know why. Don't you? Even a little bit?"

"I find it exhilarating. If I never see any of these things again, it'll be too soon. Big and stretchy are now officially banished from my wardrobe. If you have a problem with that, why don't you put on a few pounds and see what it feels like."

"Well, don't throw anything out," he said, getting up. "We'll bring it all to the goodwill bin tomorrow."

Why bother? I thought. *People poor enough to wear some stranger's old clothes aren't supposed to be fat.* But I knew better than to say something like that out loud in front of Bruce. If it were Morgan or Theo, maybe. But not Bruce. "Why bother?" I said instead. "These clothes are so disgusting, nobody would want them. I'd rather see them on fire in the city dump. Or at least let homeless people burn them in those metal garbage cans to keep warm. That's what we should do. Donate them as fuel for the homeless this winter."

"Ah," Bruce said, his hand over his heart. "The spirit of charity is alive and well in our very own Evelyn Mays."

After he left the room, I pulled out the pinstripe suit. I did use to love it—a charcoal-gray Ralph Lauren that I got for practically nothing at a great sample sale two years ago. On days when I felt like a real cow, it was the only thing that made feel remotely human again. Maybe I could keep it and turn it into a lampshade or a pillowcase or something.

Yeah right.

I shoved it back into the bag. There was really no sense in hanging on to it—I would never wear it again. But like an old friend, it was still sad to see it go.

14

The perfect moment I'd been waiting for to ask Pruscilla about my raise never came, so I figured I'd have to take whatever chance I could get. Of course, I knew that the chances of her saying yes, even under the best of circumstances, would be slim to none, but it couldn't hurt to ask. After a few days of chickening out, I finally approached her. Not coincidentally, it was also the same morning I got my first-ever threatening letter from a collection agency, reminding me that I had not remitted my minimum Visa payment in three months, and that if I didn't fork over some cash soon, they were going to break my legs. Thank God Bruce didn't see it—he was on a trip to Pittsburgh to talk to some kid who knew pi to the 2500th decimal, whatever that means.

Pruscilla, ungodly freak that she is, is always happiest on Monday mornings, so I figured the timing couldn't be better. Not surprisingly, she was already buried under a pile of paperwork. She'd probably been in since five.

"Do you have a minute?" I asked her sweetly. It was 8:26, according to my watch—I was early, and that had to be good for a few brownie points.

"Sure, Evie. Come on in. Did you have a nice weekend?" Hmm…friendly. So far, my plan was working.

"Actually, no. Bruce was out of town and I spent the weekend trying to fix our overflowing toilet." It was an absolute lie, but a lie for the greater good.

"That doesn't sound like much fun," she mumbled, already disinterested.

"It wasn't. But we can't afford a plumber. Which brings me to the reason I wanted to talk to you." No sense in beating around the bush.

She looked up from her papers.

"I know I went through a rough spot in the fall when you were away, and there's really no excuse. Suffice it to say that you were right about being newly engaged and how hard it would be for me to concentrate."

"I don't remember saying that."

"Anyway, I think I've really turned things around since then. And call me crazy, but I think you've noticed. Haven't you? I also think you know by now how much I treasure working here, and how much I love the people I work with. This job means a lot to me." I was careful not to lay it on too thick.

I gave her a moment to respond, but she didn't say anything. So I continued.

"I wanted to take a moment to thank you, both for giving me a second chance, and for being my mentor. If you knew how many times a day I ask myself, 'how would Pruscilla do this?'…well, I don't want to embarrass you."

If that wasn't good for a spontaneous offer, then I don't know what was.

"To be honest, I'd rather not have to ask you this outright, because I'm like you in the sense that I think talking about money is crass and should be avoided whenever possible…"

"I don't mind talking about money," she said, shaking her head. I could sense she wasn't taking the bait. "But there's a time and place for it. The problem comes when people don't respect that."

An inauspicious beginning, perhaps, but when she heard the reason why I needed the raise so desperately, I hoped she would see things my way. Besides—the risk was definitely worth the reward. A raise would be a whole lot simpler than cutting back on shopping. "Well, I'll just come out and say it, then. I'd like a raise. I know I had one less than a year ago, but that was only $1800 more…"

"Your raise was in exact accordance with the KW pay scale for all employees of your position and level of experience," she interrupted. "Anything more than that has to be earned."

"I know, and since I figured I came through my probation period with flying colors…"

"I wouldn't say flying colors. It's more like you squeaked by without making any grievous errors."

"That, too, and I also tried really hard to improve my whole attitude. I take my job much more seriously now, thanks to you, and I give it my all. It's just that if you knew what's going on in my life right now…."

"Evelyn, employees are raised once a year, after their evaluations," she said shrilly. "The only exception to this would be if a manager feels that someone has gone above and beyond what is expected of her, and has displayed outstanding initiative and personal involvement. That type of commitment is usually rewarded with a promotion, which, in turn, leads to more money. Do you understand?"

For a split second, I thought she might mean she wanted to promote me. But then I came to my senses.

"In your case," she continued, "showing up five or ten minutes late compared to thirty or forty minutes late is not what I'd call outstanding initiative. Nor is figuring out new ways to make paper-clip sculptures, romancing yourself in the bathroom mirror every half hour, or delegating absolutely everything you do to the interns."

"Aren't they here to learn?"

"Heaven help us if they learn anything from you," she said, as if I weren't even in the room.

"I have no choice but to assume you're saying no, then?" I asked, all hope fading.

She slammed her palms down on the desk and stood up. "Not only am I saying no, I'm considering rolling back your salary to what it was when you started here. You certainly haven't accepted any more responsibility since then, and some of your mistakes have cost the company a lot of money."

"I've never made a mistake like that," I pointed out.

"Every time you screw up it costs us time. Time for me or you or someone else to fix things. And if you think I've forgotten about all that confusion last May regarding the egregious overpayment of your friend the photographer, whose dreadful overexposures virtually ruined our fall flyers... Oh, Evelyn, the prospect of remembering every one of your accidents and misunderstandings and 'but-it-wasn't-my-fault-Pruscillas' makes me wonder what's wrong with *me* that I've put up with it for so long. The fact that you could come in here and have the *gall* to ask for a raise right now shows me that you put your own interests above Kendra White's and that the only reason you show up every day is for the paycheck," she finished triumphantly.

Remorse and embarrassment churned in my stomach. It's a good thing my self-esteem isn't founded in my job, or else I probably would have tried to jump out the window right then and there. But what was I thinking, asking for a raise? Pruscilla was right—I was, for the most part, a professional failure. She didn't have to be such a bitch about it, though. That was for sure. I wanted to walk out the door and never come back.

Do you think people actually show up here every day because they're delighted by figuring out new ways to bilk bored housewives out of their husbands' hard-earned money? Do you think anyone with any sense of right and wrong would actually consider buying American-made, mail-order makeup in bulk? Do you think anything we do here makes one bloody bit of difference in the long run? Well, I don't need you! I can do better than this. Because I'm destined for greater things than being your lackey. Take this stinking job and shove it up your ass, you petulant cow!

Well, that's what I thought, and if I had any courage at all, I would have said it, too. I may not be the best little worker bee in the hive, but I surely didn't deserve to be humiliated either. And was I really the only one with the problem? If I was still incompetent after working here for so long, then surely Kendra White and Pruscilla should share some of the blame for their complete failure to motivate or inspire me. Well, there was no way I was going to let Pruscilla and her personal attacks make me feel lucky to have this shitty job. At the very least, I should have told her that nobody, no matter how incompetent, ever deserved to feel violated and abused in their own workplace, and that I wouldn't stand it for another second.

Instead, I mumbled "Fine. Sorry for asking," and skulked out.

"Mom, Bruce and I want to meet Albert." It had been a couple of weeks since she told me about him, and I was getting a little impatient.

"We've only been seeing each other for a month, Evie. Isn't that too soon to meet each other's kids?" She sounded very concerned. "Maybe I just don't know how things are done nowadays. But it seems soon. And he hasn't introduced me to his kids yet. I don't want to be the first. Why should I be the first?"

His kids? Suddenly, I had the distinct and unpleasant feeling my life was about to change. A montage of Christmas dinners at Albert's house and baby showers for evil step-siblings flashed before my eyes. I had to nip this thing in the bud and fast.

"It'll be casual, Mom. We'll just come over for dinner."

"We're taking things slowly," she said. "We agreed not to rush into anything."

"Don't get hysterical. Meeting me and Bruce doesn't mean he'll have to marry you. I promise."

"Don't talk like that Evelyn. You shouldn't joke about such things."

"I'm not joking. But I really think this is important."

"Fine, fine. We'll talk about it later."

"You can count on it," I said.

"Ahhh..." she sighed dramatically.

"What now?" I asked.

"It's nothing."

"Fine, then I'll speak to you later."

"Well, I don't want to trouble you, but there something else I've been meaning to ask you. Could you maybe ask Bertie to stop calling me?"

"She's calling you?"

"All the time. I wouldn't mind, but she's dropping a lot of hints that I should be paying for things. Wedding things. And I don't know what to tell her."

That bitch. "Don't worry, Mom. She won't call you again."

"Don't be rude to her, Evelyn. She's going to be your mother-in-law. Just please maybe have Bruce explain our financial situation to her."

I was outraged. It was obvious Bruce wasn't living up to his end of the bargain. And if he couldn't keep his mother in control, then I certainly would. I didn't care if it made things tense. I was so sick and tired of everybody pussyfooting around her for fear of setting her off. She needed to be put in her place once and for all. Why? Because *nobody* has the right to humiliate my mother except for me. It was the final straw.

After I got off the phone with Mom, I called Bertie and left a message on her machine.

"I just wanted to let you know that I don't appreciate the horrible things you've been saying to my mother. She's very sensitive, and you've made her feel terrible about not being able to contribute more. I think you owe her an apology as soon as possible. So if you have a problem with money, call my grandmother or me, but do not call my mother again. I hope you're happy that you've taken some of the joy out of this experience for her. To be frank, since you're always so concerned about doing the right thing and not insulting people, I'm surprised that I have to call and tell you this. You really should know better. That's it for now."

"Nice, Evie," Bruce said. I didn't know he'd been listening.

Saturday afternoon after the gym, I met Kimby, Annie and Nicole for lunch. Although my time was at a definite premium lately, these were my bridesmaids, after all, and they deserved my full attention (*Today's Bride,* Fall/Winter: "Keep It Cool: How To Stay Yourself Through All the Fuss").

"Did you bring the pictures?" I asked them. They were supposed to have snapshots taken in their dresses at the fittings so I could approve the final looks.

"Why does Morgan get to wear black and we have to wear champagne?" Nicole whined. I don't think she really had a problem with the color, she was just trying to find a way to vent her jealousy. Since the engagement party, I'd only seen her once, at Theo's birthday dinner in February, so I think she was pretty shocked to see how much I'd lost since then.

"She's the maid of honor," I explained. "She's allowed to look different. You're one of six bridesmaids, so you're not. Just for the record, I think I deserve some thanks for choosing only the fabric for your dresses and not the style—some bridesmaids get stuck wearing the exact same thing. But I didn't think that would be fair, since we all have very different body types."

Nicole rolled her eyes and exchanged a knowing glance with Annie and Kimby.

"What?" I asked. "What is it?"

"Tell me you don't really expect us to thank you for that," Nicole said. "Like we should be grateful we don't have to wear burlap sacks or something."

"No, Nicole," I snapped defensively. "It's just a figure of speech. My point was that it could be a lot worse for you."

Nicole threw her hands up in exasperation and shook her head. "I know you, Evie—I know what you're thinking. You're thinking the worse we look, the better you'll look. Gee, what fun!"

"Quit it, Nicole," Kimby said. "Evie, maybe you should think about this a little more from our perspective. This whole bridesmaid thing was supposed to be fun for us, remember? And for you, too!"

I could feel myself getting huffy. "Well I'm sorry if this has been such a miserable experience for you so far, not that anyone's actually done anything yet."

"I'm having fun," Annie assured me quietly.

"Yeah, but weren't you kind of pissed when Evie stiffed you the day you were supposed to go to the seamstress together?" Nicole reminded her.

"A last-minute thing came up with the caterer and I had to go with Bertie and sort it out. Annie, you didn't mind going alone, did you?" I asked her.

"No," she said thoughtfully, "but we could have rescheduled and gone together. It would have been nice."

"Well, I'm sorry," I told her. "You should have said something." But I knew it wasn't really her responsibility. I should have gone with her. We'd had the whole day planned.

"Yeah, well, it's a little late for that," Nicole said.

"Frankly, Nicole, it's none of your business, so keep it to yourself."

"C'mon, guys, stop it," Annie pleaded. "It's fine."

"Oh, she's just crabby because of her diet," Kimby said.

"Which one, Nicole or Evie?" Annie said with more wit than usual.

Kimby laughed. "I meant Evie, but come to think of it..."

Poor Nicole. She'd gained back almost all of the weight she'd lost before Christmas. Of course she was reluctant to go out and have a dress made—she probably felt like crap. And I wasn't helping things by being unavailable.

"Look, guys, I'm sorry," I said. "I have been a little preoccupied lately, I can admit that. I promise I'm going to try and stay in the loop a little better. And if anyone wants to back out, I'll totally understand."

"Just try and keep it together, okay?" Nicole said. "Or we just might."

"Okay. So you reserve the right to mutiny. Fair enough. Now let's see the picture. I'm sure it's not that bad."

Nicole made a "yeah, right" face and reluctantly slipped a Polaroid out of her purse and slid it across the table.

It was pretty bad. She looked like a toasted marshmallow wearing a belt.

"I told you," she moaned.

"Are you crazy?" I said. "It looks amazing."

"You look gorgeous, Nic," Annie agreed, squinting at the picture. "It's a really cool dress. It's just not finished yet."

"It's really not that bad at all," Kimby agreed. "I was there for the second fitting and I thought it was very flattering."

"You're just saying that because you both look beautiful in yours," she said, eyeing their pictures. "A skinny blonde and a skinny redhead. I don't want to stand next to them, Evie. Or Bruce's sisters. Any of them. Please don't make me. *Please!*"

"Oh God, Nicole," Kimby sighed. "Are you PMS-ing or something?"

She was near hysterics, and the last thing I needed was an uneven number of groomsmen and bridesmaids (Bruce had five groomsmen—assorted friends and cousins, plus Theo). (*Martha Stewart Weddings,* Spring: "Symmetry and the Art of the Perfect Processional.")

"Don't worry, Nic," I said in my most comforting voice. "You're going to look fantastic. Now I know we may have our differences sometimes, but you're a really good friend and it means a ton to me and Bruce that you'll be walking down the aisle for us. And I am not lying when I say that I think this dress looks really good on you already. But you don't even have to worry about it yet. It's only the end of April—there's still three and a half months to go, so if you lose a few pounds before the wedding, they can take it in."

Appeased, Nicole ordered a burger and fries. Really, what the hell did she expect, eating crap like that? It was hard to feel sorry for her sometimes.

After lunch, the three of them ordered dessert and I lit up a cigarette.

"What are you doing? You don't smoke," laughed Kimby.

Aside from a few years in college, it's true I was never much of a smoker. But it was a habit I was trying to take up temporarily in order to drop the last few pounds (*Cosmopolitan,* April: "The 10 Worst Ways To Lose Weight").

Annie coughed and waved the smoke away from her face with her hands.

"I have to sing tonight, Evelyn. Would you mind putting that out?" she said.

"Sorry," I mumbled. "I guess it's not the best habit."

"And what does the infamous Jade have to say about you smoking?" asked Kimby.

"Oh, he has no idea—he'd *kill* me if he ever found out."

"Good," said Annie. "It's disgusting." No wonder she didn't get called back for *The Vagina Monologues.* She was such a priss.

"Who cares about him, what about Bruce? *He's* your fiancé, remember?" Nicole pointed out.

"Obviously, he doesn't know either," I said.

"Don't you ever kiss him?" she asked.

"I try not to. He's been a huge pain in the ass lately. But today's his birthday, so I've got to be nice to him."

Annie's eyes nearly popped out of her skull. "It's his birthday? Why aren't you with him?"

"I had plans with you guys, remember? Come on, don't worry about him—he went to have lunch at his parents'. He's happy as a pig in shit right now. They're probably all sitting around making fun of my mother. I'll tell you one thing that pisses me off, though. Instead of just hopping into one of the four cars sitting on their driveway and coming to see him, his parents make him take the train all the way there and back and waste three hours of his birthday. I swear, I think Bertie's afraid to come into the city. She stays holed up in her Connecticut compound like Martha Stewart."

"Only she can't cook," added Nicole.

"I feel sorry for Bruce," Kimby sighed.

"Don't," I told her. "We're going to have a grand old time tonight. We're going to Luna."

"Ooh, your special place," said Annie. "How romantic."

"I meant because he's turning twenty-nine," Kimby said. "That's, like, only *one* year away from thirty. I'll probably have a nervous breakdown."

"I'm twenty-nine," Nicole grumbled.

"Sorry to break this up, girls, but I gotta get back to work," said Annie.

"It's fine, actually. I have to go, too," I told her. "I haven't even thought about what to get Bruce for his birthday."

The three of them looked at me as if to say, you bitch. You horrible bitch.

Thankfully, there was one of those Discovery Channel shops just up the street from the restaurant. As a notorious last-minute shopper, these stores have saved my ass more than once; I recommend them highly to anyone who's either in a hurry or simply uncreative. Nothing appears you've given a birthday gift more thought than something like an executive magic kit or a telescope. And Bruce loves all that gadgety sciency stuff.

It didn't take long to find him the perfect thing—night vision goggles. It was either that or the robotic dog. But since Bruce is allergic to real dogs, which is a major point of contention in our relationship, I decided the goggles would be a less confrontational choice. Plus, they were in the final sale bin, but only because there was no box, the salesgirl told me. And since Bruce was so uptight about our spending, there was no reason to feel like a cheapskate just because I'd only spent $12.99. If it's something you think someone will like, it's okay to spend a little less than you normally would have (*Glamour,* February: "Love on a Budget: Valentine's Gifts for Your Man That Won't Leave You Broke"). You see, *not* getting something simply because it's on sale is the height of snobbery. Bruce would kill me if I ever did anything like that.

I was mulling this over when a deep voice from behind asked, "Are you going to take that?"

I spun around and saw a very handsome man, maybe forty years old or so, standing there in an expensive suit, probably Hugo Boss. There was nobody else around.

"Are you talking to me?"

He laughed. "Yes. I'm sorry, but I wanted to know if you're going to take those."

"Uh, yes. Sorry," I told him, and squeezed by him toward the counter.

"Too bad—they're a great gift. For your little brother?"

"No—my fiancé," I said.

He sighed. "Too bad. I guess the pretty ones are all spoken for."

"Pretty goggles?" I asked. What the hell was this guy's damage? He probably had some sort of weird eyewear fetish. If he thought I was going to let him have the goggles, he had another think coming.

"No," he said quietly and leaned in close to my cheek. "I meant all the pretty women." He smelled faintly of soap and D&G cologne.

I couldn't help but grin. He was trying to pick me up! A stranger was trying to get into my pants. And he didn't seem like a loser or a pervert, either. I couldn't remember the last time something like this had happened—probably never, to be honest—and I admit it felt pretty good.

"Sorry," I said, flashing him my most demure smile. "You're too late."

"That's the story of my life," he said, turning to leave, then added, "Your boyfriend's a very lucky man."

At that moment, it struck me that this sort of thing probably happens to Bruce all the time. In a city swarming with single, young women, a cute guy like Bruce probably can't go into a public place without being accosted at least once or twice. I wondered what he said to them, if he blushed, or flirted with them before letting them down easy. Maybe he was so scared that he didn't say anything at all.

Another reason not to feel bad about Bruce's gift, I reasoned, was that part of his birthday present was my agreeing to go for Italian food (*Shape,* May: "10 New Reasons To Cut Those Carbs!"). We hadn't been to Luna all year, and tonight was just the right occasion. It didn't take a marriage counselor to notice that we desperately needed to reconnect on an emotional level.

"My mother wants to send the invitations out in two weeks," Bruce said in between mouthfuls of lasagna.

"In the middle of May? That's *absurd*. Two months before the wedding is plenty early. Tell her not to send them out a day before June 18. People will lose the invitations if they're delivered that soon," (*Martha Stewart Weddings,* Fall: "The Only Wedding Timeline You'll Ever Need").

"But they're ready and they're just sitting there. She says eight weeks isn't enough time to give people. A lot of her friends and my dad's colleagues go away in August, and she wants to give them enough warning so that they can plan their summers properly."

"So they'll either rearrange their golf games or they won't come," I said, pushing my linguini around the plate. "And it's not like your mother hasn't told every single person on her list exactly when and where it is a thousand times. Now can we talk about something else besides the wedding please?"

"Sure, Evie. Whatever you want. What's on your mind." He said it like he was doing me a favor.

"If you must know, I'm worried about Mom and this Albert guy. I think maybe he's after her money."

"She doesn't have any money, Evie."

"But he doesn't know that."

"I'm sure he does." Bruce poured himself another glass of wine. "Don't you think he's ever been to her apartment?"

"What's wrong with her apartment?" The thought of some strange man in Mom's apartment made my stomach turn.

"Nothing, but it's obviously not the Ritz. I can see where this is going, Evie, and I don't think it's fair of you to make things hard on her. Remember, this is what you've wanted for a very long time, that your mom would have someone, but now that's it's happened, you're freaking out. It's normal, and I understand it's weird for you—"

"But there's something not right about this guy," I interrupted. "I can feel it."

"Claire said he's really nice, and I trust her, so let's not make a big deal out of this," he said.

"But you didn't hear her when I said that we wanted to meet him. She was making all kinds of excuses."

"She's just shy, Evie. And nervous."

"Do you think she's embarrassed? Maybe he's an ugly freak. Maybe he's got a trunk growing out of his face like the Elephant Man. Maybe he's four feet tall…" The grim possibilities crowded my brain.

"Maybe she's embarrassed of *you,*" Bruce said. "Didn't you throw up on her last boyfriend?"

"*No,* I did not throw up on anyone. I've never done that."

"Maybe not. But you threw up when I proposed," he said matter-of-factly.

"*Did I?* Did I Bruce? Thanks for reminding me. I'd almost forgotten."

He rolled his eyes. "I just meant that you have a nervous stomach."

"Any excuse to bring it up. You're never going to let me live it down, are you? Yes, I threw up. I threw up at the thought of marrying you, Bruce. There. I said it. If you like, I'll admit it to you every day for the next fifty years, if we make it that far."

Bruce threw his fork down and pushed back from the table. "I'm tired, Evie. And I'm tired of this," he said. "Can we just go home, please?" His big brown eyes stared right through me. *Now you've done it.* My big mouth had ruined yet another perfect evening. You'd think I'd know better by now, but once I start I just can't seem to stop.

"But it's your birthday," I told him, and grabbed his hand. "It's been such a long time since we've hung out around here."

"Nah, I don't think so."

"Don't you want to walk around? Hold hands? Get some gelato or something?" I was desperate. This was supposed to be a night to relish in our coupledom, to get back to the way we were. Luna and Mulberry Street had worked their magic on us before. "I'm sorry," I said.

"*Sorry* isn't just a word, Evie. If you don't mind, I'd really rather just go home."

15

Albert turned out to be a very big loser, though not exactly in the way I'd expected. He didn't have boils all over his face or overly long arms or missing teeth. His looks really weren't that bad at all, unless you consider a man with white socks to be undatable (for the record, I do, but I'd have to cut Mom some slack—after all, she still wears acid-washed jeans). No, Bruce and I both agreed that Albert's flaws were purely character-driven in nature. Which is better in one sense and worse in another, I suppose.

At least if a man is ugly, you know he's going to try hard to compensate for his looks in other ways. Plenty of girls I know have dated guys they would have spat on in high school simply because there are no cute ones left in New York who aren't married, dead or gay, although Theo complains bitterly that all the hot gay ones are taken, too. Even Morgan dated a fairly ugly guy once, and he wasn't even rich. He was three inches shorter than her and had an orange beard, but he truly was the sweetest thing (*Elle,* October: "The Myth of the Male Model: Why Real Guys Are Better in Bed"). In the end, she realized she was only with him to get back at Tom, whom she'd dumped for staring at himself in the mirror constantly and stating publicly what a gorgeous couple they made. In the end, she did the right thing and sent Redbeard on his way—revenge is not a reason to date anyone for longer than three or four weeks.

There were plenty of reasons I could see not to date Albert aside from his fashion sense, not the least of which was his annoying habit of saying exactly everything that came into his head. Plus, he ate the entire meal with a toothpick in his mouth. I was thankful we'd decided to meet at Mom's for dinner and not in public somewhere.

As soon as we walked in the door, Albert came right up to me and put his hand on my shoulder. "You must be Evie," he said, looking me up and down, then shouted, "Hey, Lilly, she's not fat!"

Mom scuttled in from the kitchen, frantically wiping her hands on her apron. "Now, Albert, you must have misunderstood me. I never said *that*—I mentioned that Evie's *lost* some weight recently," she sang nervously.

"Well you look fine to me, honey," he said to me, then tucked his arm around Mom's waist and pulled her close. "In fact, you're the spitting image of your mother, and it's no secret what a fine-looking woman she is."

He didn't go so far as slapping her on the ass, but I could tell that he wanted to. Was this a joke? My stomach rumbled disagreeably.

Instead of running to the bathroom and throwing up like I wanted to, I just shot Mom a dark look and said, "This is Bruce."

"Nice to meet you," Bruce smiled.

"I've heard lots of good things about you, son," Albert said and shook Bruce's hand vigorously.

"That's some grip you've got there, sir," Bruce said when he got his hand back. A vein in his forehead throbbed angrily.

"A firm grip is my trademark. A weak handshake signals a weak constitution."

"Shall we have drinks?" Mom asked, ushering us into the living room.

I certainly needed one. Liquid courage was the only way I'd be able to handle a boor like Albert for an entire evening without completely losing it.

"I'll have a scotch, Lilly," he said, and Mom dutifully trotted back to the kitchen. He spoke to her as if they'd been married for twenty years.

Aside from the toothpick thing, which was really quite impressive once you got past how gross it was, Albert distinguished himself with a string of insightful observations over dinner, including, "Bruce, a smart guy like you should be in the computer business—let me see what I can do" and "Lilly, this meat loaf is enough to make a man curse his own mother's cooking." He also told me that he thought I'd look much better without so much makeup on (as if). Mom flipped her hair about a thousand times, and made a complete idiot out of herself.

By the time Albert downed his third after-dinner drink, things started to get a little too friendly for my taste.

"As long as we're being honest here with each other, and I think we are, I was a little afraid to meet the two of you," he confided. "Lilly worried it was too soon. Don't get me wrong—I knew *you'd* like *me*...but what if *I* didn't like *you!*" He laughed loudly and slapped Bruce on the side of the knee.

"Stop it, Albert!" Mom giggled from the kitchen.

"Mom, why don't you leave the dishes for later and come in here and sit with us," Bruce called in to her. He knew that if she was close at hand, I'd be less likely to blow my top.

"No, no, I'm kidding. You two are nice kids," Albert went on. "Maybe we can have a barbecue over at my son's place. The whole family."

Before I could come up with a reason not to, Mom came in with a tray of coffee and biscotti and sat down next to Albert. He put his hand on her thigh.

"Why don't you tell the kids a little more about what you

do," Mom said to him. Was she completely oblivious to what a fool she was making of herself, allowing this cad to paw at her like some horny teenager? It took all my self-control not to slap the filthy old bastard across the face. Instead, I kept telling myself that I was supposed to be happy for Mom.

"Like I told you already, I sell computers. Not much more to it than that. If you're wondering how an old man like me got into the computer game, then all's I can say is—my son's the boss!"

We laughed politely, but Mom roared.

"Casella Computers—ever heard of it? We've got eleven stores now, all over the five boroughs. There's one near NYU, Evie. We sell to all the students. I manage the one in Queens. I been telling your mother she ought to get one—a computer, that is, not a store!" More laughter from Mom. "Then she'd be able to e-mail that sister of hers out in London. Maybe for Christmas, eh?"

"Oh, Al. You're too generous," she said. "You're too good for me—"

"I wouldn't say that, Mom," I interrupted.

Bruce pinched me hard, sensing danger.

"What?" I said to him. "She could use a computer."

But Mom hadn't even heard what I'd said. She was batting her eyelashes at Al.

It was all I could do not to throw up on the both of them.

By the end of May, I had a problem of an altogether unanticipated kind—my dress was too big on me. Too *big* on me! Somehow, I was still losing a pound or two a week. Jade was amazed, and I was confused. Elated, but confused. The numbers on the scale seemed vaguely unreal—123 sounded more like an address on Sesame Street than what I, Evelyn Mays, lifelong fat chick, actually weighed. My formerly too-big boobs had gone from a small D to a big B, so the dress was gaping in the chest a little. The seamstress told me that I'd better not lose another pound, or else she couldn't be held responsible. Music to my ears.

The rest of my wardrobe was similarly baggy. Thankfully, I

did have the foresight to apply for a Saks Card (Barneys turned me down) before most of my credit problems made their way onto the radar. Since it technically wasn't a regular credit card, and didn't have that high of a limit, there was no reason to feel guilty. But it was shiny and new and desperately in need of attention. So with forty-seven pounds gone in less than six months and only three pounds to go before I could stop, I treated myself to a small shopping spree. Luckily, Bruce was out of town until Monday, so I wouldn't be forced to justify all the bags.

Since part of taking responsibility for one's finances involves tracking how much money one spends and on what (*Cosmopolitan,* April: "Five Steps to Financial Freedom"), here's my list:

1 pair Theory stretch capri pants, hot pink (size 4!)
1 pair original low-rise Earl jeans (size 6)
1 Earl jean jacket, indigo (small)
1 Moschino Jeans rhinestone stretch denim skirt (size 6)
2 DKNY square-neck T-shirts, chartreuse and magenta (medium)
1 ABS miniskirt, pumpkin (size 4)
1 D&G silk shantung tie-front shirt, watermelon (medium)
1 DKNY geometric print halter top, blue and white (medium)
2 D&G jersey bustiers with built-in bra, black and white (medium)
1 Tse classic cashmere sweater set, on sale, rose blush (small)
1 Frankie B low-waisted denim shirtdress (size 6)
1 Betsey Johnson ruffled gingham sundress, pink (size 6)
2 Ralph Lauren bra-and-panties sets, lime and lemon (34 B)

1 Saks Fifth Avenue fitted 3/4-length jersey, purple horizontal pinstripes (small)
1 pair fake Gucci sunglasses with orange lenses
1 pair Miu Miu open-toe faux-alligator platform pumps, caramel and red

I'm not sure if it was a good thing or a bad thing, but that one little trip maxed out the card instantaneously. There was no more damage to be done. Of course, by that point, I was obviously already completely insane, and cared not one bit for the consequences of any of my actions.

Morgan came over on Friday after work to see me model all my new stuff. Actually, she didn't really care about my purchases, but she did want to show me the dress she'd bought for the wedding. It was gorgeous on her, black and slinky, but with good coverage. Morgan was smart like that—she knew enough not to steal my thunder. Not that she really could anyway, since everyone knows that a bride is always the most beautiful woman in the room. To be fair, though, wedding day or not, Morgan will always have better bone structure than me. But I have thicker hair.

"The best part about all this is that I finally figured out a way to pay for everything all on my own!" I told her.

"I think I saw a hooker wearing those shoes down in the Bowery," she said. "They make you look like you're trying too hard to be tall. You're five foot four—you can't wear four-inch heels."

She doesn't know the first thing about fashion so I let it go. "For months, the solution was staring me right in the face, Morgan, but I never saw it—*the money we're going to get for our wedding!* Bruce's parents have tons of rich friends, and they're all invited." It was shocking that it had never occurred to me sooner (*Bridal Guide,* May: "Retirement Planning vs. Your First Home: What To Do with Your Wedding Money").

Morgan sighed skeptically. "What if you don't get as much as you think you will?"

"Trust me—I know these people. Not appearing cheap in front of their friends means a hell of a lot more to them than a measly few hundred bucks. When you add it all up, we're looking at tens of thousands of dollars!"

"You're an idiot, Evie. You don't actually think Bruce will go for this, do you?"

"That's the beauty of it, Morgan—this is exactly what the money's there for, to help us get set up and start our new lives together on the right foot. Bruce won't mind because he hates the idea of being in debt. He'll be delighted to wipe the slate clean and start fresh. Then, when I finally get a raise, or find a better job, I'll be able to get ahead of the game."

And that's exactly how I would present it to him. Even if he didn't agree, which he surely wouldn't at first, at least I'd be able to say that I had a sincere plan. Anyway, resistance was futile by that point: I was powerless against the shopping, powerless against that damn dress, powerless against my personal trainer. There was nothing to do but succumb to the forces that were acting upon me and indulge in all that was wrong and evil in the world.

"If you say so, Evie," she laughed. "You've really worked this out."

"Yes I have. Which is why I can't imagine a better way to celebrate my new, fat-free life than indulging in a few choice items such as these."

It was wildly liberating to realize that things weren't necessarily as bad as I thought they were. For a while there, I wasn't sure what was going to happen with all that money stuff. But finally, after years of hard work and heartache, I now had the body and the bucks (sort of) to explore my true fashion sense. And nothing was going to stop me. Especially not knowing better.

Morgan took in the bags and tags and clothes strewn all over the bed and floor, and said, "Evie, I'll go you one further—you need more than new clothes. I'd say you deserve an entirely new look."

"My new clothes are my new look," I said.

"No, I mean a real new look—a makeover, like the one you gave me before I went to Berkeley. I'll never forget it. You said, 'Never underestimate the power of highlights, Morgan.' And you were right."

My God, she spoke the truth. For months, I'd been so consumed by getting rid of my fat ass, that I hadn't given so much as a thought to the rest of me.

Morgan's whole life changed after that makeover. It gave her the confidence to go from a skinny, unpopular strawberry-blond geek to a fiery redhead who knew what she wanted and exactly how to get it. She completely reinvented herself on the other side of the country, and that makeover was the starting point. Truthfully, I considered it to be one of my greatest accomplishments.

Maybe a new look would do the same for me. I could definitely use the boost. Because no matter how many pounds I lost, I still felt somehow incomplete. I guess I just needed a few finishing touches, a clean break from the old me. Maybe then I would feel like I actually belonged in that dress instead of some kid trying on a Halloween costume. Morgan, despite her stylistic nihilism, had hit the nail on the head.

"And you never would have got layers, either, if I hadn't suggested it," I reminded her. "Who knows where you'd be today?"

"Exactly. So what are you waiting for? Beautician, layer thyself! I'll call my mother—she can get you in to her place tomorrow."

Morgan knew I was impressed that her mother went to Louis Licari. "But you need to book six months in advance," I practically shouted. "He's colorist to the stars!"

"She let her guy use her beach house last weekend. He owes her."

That left me only a few hours to consult the literature. Thankfully, I knew exactly where to look (*In Style,* May: "From Meg to Madonna, From Julia to J. Lo: Today's Hottest Celebrity Hair").

Even an untrained eye like Morgan could see that new hair would be the most crucial aspect of my makeover. Makeup was the easy part—I just went to Saks, where the Lancome counter gives customers free lessons in makeup application and color selection with any purchase over $175. But my coif needed more than a department-store freebie.

I'd never really bothered much with my hair; I was used to it long and plain and boring, with the usual trim and blow-dry every six weeks and a plain-Jane single-color rinse every two months. No matter what, it was always drab brown, with varying degrees of reddishness. And the only time I'd ever cut it short was on a regrettable whim senior year. Bruce and I had only been dating for a few months, and he mentioned that he thought I'd look good with short hair like Winona Ryder. Like an idiot, I went out and chopped it off. In theory, it should have worked, because I have delicate features, too, but I didn't account for the fat factor. Instead of irresistibly cute and waif-like, the pixie do left me disproportionally pear-shaped, with nothing on top to balance out my big butt below. It took two years to grow out, and I'm never making that mistake again. Besides, long hair is in again (*Vogue,* April: "Extend Yourself: Autumn Runways Fall for Long Hair").

This time, there would be nothing to worry about. I knew they'd do right by me at Louis Licari. At three hundred and fifty bucks for a cut and color, they'd better.

The salon itself was an oasis of calm. Razor-thin, black-clad stylists and colorists drifted from room to room, tending to clients and pushing around carts. Although I didn't recognize anyone in particular, the place oozed with fame and entitlement. It was all incredibly impressive, and I made a mental note to send Morgan's mom some flowers or something to thank her. The receptionist ushered me into a chair for my consultation. After about forty-five minutes, a team of two hairdressers and three color technicians decided on a shaggy shoulder-length cut with face-framing layers; for color, it would be a warm copper base with lots of chunky golden highlights over top.

Three and a half hours later, I stepped out into the warm sunshine on Fifth Avenue. Walking to the subway entrance, I caught a quick glimpse of myself in a mirrored window—a thin, blond stranger with fabulous shoes just going about her daily routine. It was shocking, sure, but it was also fantastic. Three guys turned to check me out as I passed by, and more than a few others stared openly at my chest.

I was gorgeous. Finally.

Jade whistled when he saw me walk into the gym Monday after work. He could barely take his eyes off me.

"Love the new look, Evie! It really suits you," he said as he adjusted the scale. "Surprise, surprise, down another pound. You're at the perfect healthy weight for your height. In fact, I'd say you were even on the low end. So that's it, Evie. You're done."

"Good—my seamstress will murder me if I lose any more."

"She won't be the only one," he said. "But don't get cocky. The really hard part's just beginning. Now you have to learn how to maintain. I'm gonna book you in with Giselle, the nutritionist. I suggest that all my clients go to see her when they reach their goal weight, if they haven't already."

The thought of not being on a diet was more than a little scary. What if I gained it all back? If I allowed myself to eat dessert, just once, it could be the beginning of the end. I knew what could happen—all my hard work would be down the drain. I didn't want to go to that cow Giselle. She'd be able to see right through me. And I certainly didn't want to hear her bullshit about everything being good in moderation, or making sure to get thirty percent of my calories from fat. I wasn't going to give this up. Not for anyone or anything....

Jade interrupted my reverie. "How's Bruce dealing with all this?"

"All what?"

"Your hot new bod, the hair, you know."

"Oh, well he hasn't seen the hair 'cause he's been out of town, but he's not so happy about the rest of it, to tell you the truth." By now, I was perfectly comfortable discussing all the intimate details of my personal life with Jade. Well, most of them anyway—we never talked about sex or anything like that.

"That's too bad. You've worked really hard for this, and you deserve to be appreciated. God, you've been virtually reborn. I mean, look at you!"

Jade had a flair for the dramatic, but I wasn't complaining. He was an actor, after all. "That's exactly what I've been thinking," I said. "But no matter how many times I try to explain it to Bruce, how important it is for me to finally be healthy, he just shuts down. He thinks if I don't eat a gallon of ice cream every day, that I'm anorexic."

He shook his head sympathetically.

"If you only knew how many times he tried to sabotage me," I continued. "You'd be shocked that I didn't *gain* weight this year."

"You're in the best shape of your life and you feel good about yourself, and you want to share that with him. But he just doesn't get it."

"Exactly." It was uncanny, how well he understood me.

He came up a little closer and said, "Not that I can blame the guy. He probably wants to keep you all to himself now that you're looking so good. If you want, maybe we could talk about it later, if you're not doing anything, that is."

"Um..."

"Over a real drink this time, none of that carrot and parsley crap," he added with a wink.

There was no denying it: The man was asking me out on a date. Was he mad? He knew I was engaged. I'm sure he could tell that I wanted to accept—after all we were very good friends and he could probably read me like a book by now—but did he actually think I would? More importantly, did I want to?

I sighed deeply. *There is nothing in this world or the next I'd rather do than go out for a drink, just the two of us.* Instead, I said, "I'd love to, but I really have to get home afterward. Bruce is probably already there, and I haven't seen him in days."

There was nothing wrong with a little innocent flirtation, as long as I didn't let it get out of hand. I'm certain that Bruce flirted endlessly with women all the time, I just wasn't there to witness it. So what was the difference?

"Maybe another time, then?" he asked, tucking an unruly strand of hair behind his ear.

"I think...uh, maybe..." I stammered. "But, I'd have to give it some thought. You understand..."

I was suddenly aware that nobody could really see us because we were in the back corner of the room where the scales are. He ran his forefinger lightly up my arm. The hairs on the back of my neck stood up. "Of course I understand," he said. "But there's not a lot of time left, is there?"

I was paralyzed.

A pasty teenager in white spandex and a pink thong walked up to us and began tapping her foot impatiently. She cleared her throat. "I think you're neglecting your other clients," I blurted, glad for the excuse to stop staring into those ungodly green eyes.

He spun around and said curtly, "Marla, I told you I might not have time for you tonight. Just do your regular workout and come see me tomorrow."

Marla stormed off to the treadmills in a snit.

"Sorry about that," he said and picked up my chart. "Shall we get started, Evie?"

"Sure, Jade."

Just saying his name made me feel incredibly guilty. Guilty because for a second, I'd actually considered his offer. Or at least, what I thought he was offering.

16

Bruce's jaw dropped when I walked through the door.

"What the..."

"I did my hair! Don't you love it?"

He stared at me for a long time, shaking his head.

"I go away for two days and this...*this* is what I come back to? A stranger in my fiancée's body? Oh, excuse me—it's not even your body anymore! What have you *done,* Evie?"

"It's just a dye job, Bruce. It's not like I had plastic surgery," I moaned, trying my hardest to shrug off this latest attempt to undermine my individuality. If Jade were here, he'd be outraged.

"Look at yourself. Is that what you wore to work today?"

"Yes, Bruce," I said, exasperated. "I wore a skirt and a shirt to work today. I'm such a slut."

"It's practically *underwear,* and that's not a shirt, it looks more like...like...a bathing suit or something."

"It's a camisole. It goes under a jacket."

"So where's the jacket?!"

"I left it at work."

"What are those shoes? Is all that new? *Did you go shopping again?*" He was absolutely mortified, and he wasn't even trying to hide it.

"Yes I did. I got a few things. But listen—I reached my goal weight! Can you believe it? Jade says I shouldn't lose another pound. I'm actually where I want to be. For the first time in my life! So I don't really have to buy anything else until the fall...."

"Are you serious?"

"Stop it with that voice! You're overreacting!" I shrieked.

"*Me?* You've been overreacting for six months straight! I think I have the right to be freaked out when you come home with blond hair and looking like you just stepped off the pages of *Seventeen* magazine!"

"I do not!"

"Yes you do! You're not a teenager. You can't wear...what are those? Clogs? Green clogs?"

"They're platform sandals, jerk. And what the hell do you know about it? You wear plaid shirts with button-down collars."

"Who cares?"

"I do, thank God! You think I want to go around with some guy who looks like he's about to go yachting?" If it weren't for me, he'd still be wearing yellow sweaters. "What's wrong with taking a little pride in your appearance?" I asked him.

"Nothing's wrong with taking a *little* pride in anything. But you're taking way too much pride in everything! It's offensive, and it's ridiculous. You're still the same person you were before you lost all this weight, you know—Evelyn Mays, plain and simple. Fancy hair and tight clothes don't fool anyone."

"Plain and simple? Is that what you think of me?"

"I used to, and I liked it."

"Well, then, you've just proved my point. Remaking myself into the person I've always felt like I was on the inside has been the greatest success of my life. The *only* success of my life. And if you don't like it...then...then you're obviously not man enough to accept the real me."

The tears were flowing now, and I was powerless to stop them. This had been building up for a long time, and I had to let it out. "You talk about how looks don't matter, and how you liked me so much better before. But how do you think that makes me feel? You might think I like hearing about how you didn't care that I was fat, that you liked me for who I was, but you're a liar... You're a liar, because all you talk about now is how I look, and how stupid I am, and how you hate everything about the new me. And that tells me looks do matter to you, Bruce, and that you care more about what I'm like on the outside than who I am on the inside."

He sat down on the couch and put his head in his hands. "When your life became all about how skinny you could get, you stopped caring about everything else, especially me. You've made it abundantly clear that you're more interested in pursuing *your* goals rather than *our* goals. I was okay with that at first, because you wanted it so much. But when your entire world revolves around how you look...that's where I draw the line. I can't pretend that I want my life to be about your new clothes and what you weigh. How can you expect that from me? And when was the last time you asked about what *I* want or how *my* job is or what *my* plans are? I go out of town and I come home and all you say when I walk in the door is, 'Bruce, your mother's been driving me crazy,' or 'Bruce, they're all out to get me at work.' You've never, *not once,* asked me about how my trip was, or if I had a good time. You're so damn preoccupied with your own life that you don't even know what city I'm in."

"Oh, believe me, I notice what city you're in!" I shouted. "I know when you're out of town because I don't get crap about not eating dessert and I don't get crap about how much money I spend and I don't get crap about..."

He threw his hands up in the air. "Don't bother, Evie. This is exactly what I'm talking about. You're so bloody self-involved that you can't put yourself in my shoes for a single minute, let alone for long enough to realize you're not the only one with problems and complaints. Why don't you acknowledge what I'm saying sometime instead of just defending yourself?"

Was he right? Did I really never ask him about his trips? Impossible—I knew far too many boring details.

"I know all about your trips," I sniffed.

"Of course you do, because I tell you about them. But not because you ask."

"That's not fair."

"That's exactly what I've been thinking."

"You know that's not what I meant," I said between clenched teeth.

"But, oh, how I wish it were."

What the hell did he want from me? "It's like you wait for me to fail. I bet every time you come home, you're just waiting for me not to ask you how your day was...."

"That's extremely paranoid thinking," he said, massaging his temples. "Could this be yet another charming character trait of the New-And-Improved Evie I can look forward to living with for the rest of my life?"

"...you wait for me to fail, you hold me up to your impossible standards, then when I don't come through, instead of talking to me about it, you pull away!"

"If I'm pulling away, it's because I'm being pushed."

"No—that's it," I said. It was suddenly all very clear. "And the more you pull away, the more I think you don't want me the way I am. If you expect me to turn into some demented Stepford wife like your mother or your sisters or your high-school girlfriend and spend my life in a twin set and pearls, cooking and cleaning and diapering your babies, you can forget it."

"Don't lay that shit on me. Although I can barely remember it now, it seems to me the reason I fell in love with you in the first place was because you were definitely *not* that person. You know I don't want that! But I *do* want someone who knows her own mind, and someone who's comfortable being herself, which you're obviously not anymore. And you can slam my mother as much as you want...God knows you love nothing more than reminding me how much you hate her guts...but the truth is that since we got engaged, you've become more and more like her every day."

"Liar! *Liar!*" I screamed. He crossed the line. He finally crossed the line. I could handle being told I was turning into *my* mother—that would be bad enough. But his?

I stomped into the bedroom and pulled the covers over my head to cry in private. But he followed me in and kept on at it.

"It's true—you're exactly like everybody you used to despise most in this world. Remember when you used to make fun of all the lollipop girls and fashionistas? But now you're the one not eating and you care more about what strangers think of you than the people who love you."

"Why don't you just kill me with your bare hands and put me out of my misery," I sobbed. "I can tell you don't love me anymore. You don't even *like* me anymore..."

"*You're* the one who doesn't like you anymore," he interrupted.

But I ignored him and went on. "...and it's really obvious you don't..." *Dare I say it?* "...you...you don't want to marry me."

"Unless you get a hold of yourself immediately and cut all this shit out, you're right. I don't want to marry you." I couldn't see him, because my face was under the pillow, but I felt him sit down on the bed. His voice started to crack, just a little bit. "Why can't you just be the way you were before? Why can't you just stop all this?"

"Me?" I said, sitting up. "You're the one freaking out." I'd never seen him this close to tears.

"Yeah, I suppose I am."

I reached over for his hand. "All my dreams are coming true, Bruce. It's everything I've ever wanted. Why can't you just be happy for me?"

"Be careful what you wish for, Evie," he sighed. "You just might get it."

"But it doesn't have to be a bad thing," I pleaded.

"Maybe not for you, but it certainly is for me. It's been a nightmare."

"I had no idea you were really this upset."

"Well maybe if you'd asked me once in a while, you'd know. Although you probably wouldn't have listened to the answer, anyway."

I wasn't going to let him get all aggressive on me again. It was out of character for him, and very irritating. Besides, hadn't I given Bruce more than enough opportunities to discuss things openly with me? There were plenty of examples to choose from, but I decided it was enough for tonight.

"So how was Boston?"

"Fuck Boston. I can't take this anymore," he said simply, and left.

I was afraid to go to the gym the next day. And the day after that. And the day after that. Until a week had passed. Not that I didn't trust myself, but I thought a little distance right now between me and Jade might be a good thing, just to be on the safe side. Plus, I couldn't bear the thought of telling him all about my big fight with Bruce. It was so humiliating.

Over an emergency lunch meeting, Morgan agreed.

"I've told you, never dump your problems on your trainer. Even if you're sleeping with him, it's very inelegant."

"But he's more than my trainer—he's my friend."

"Sure he is, Evie. But he also wants to get you into bed."

"I know," I said, still reeling at the thought of it. "Isn't it amazing?"

Morgan stared incredulously.

"Amazing-flattering, not amazing-good," I explained, but she still seemed suspicious.

"Either way. Listen, you have to decide if you want this," she said tentatively.

"Want to get married?"

"Of course you still want to get married, you idiot. I won't tell you that Bruce is the best thing that's ever happened to you. No man is that to any woman. But you two do work well together. You complement each other, and that's the secret to all great relationships, or so I've been told. So of course you still want to be with Bruce. What I meant was, do you want this thing with Jade?"

"What do you mean? Of course not."

"Are you sure?"

"Yes. No. I mean, yes I *want* to. He's gorgeous and he smells so good. But I could never actually..."

"Maybe you just need to listen to what your heart is telling you."

"Didn't you just say that I should stay with Bruce?"

"Yeeees..." she sang, waiting for me to get what she was trying to tell me. "But maybe there's another option..."

"You mean *sleep* with Jade?" I whispered.

She grinned broadly. "You've just had what I believe Oprah would call a Lightbulb Moment."

"That's ridiculous, Morgan. Thank you for your advice, but I think I'll take it from here." Was she crazy?

"Evie, you know I would never suggest you do something you don't want to do, but I would try to open your eyes to the potential benefits of doing something you *do* want to do. And you *do* want to..."

"But that's cheating."

"Oh, that *word*. That horrible word. Put it out of your mind. You're about to get married to the man you love. In this sad, lonely, random world, you and Bruce have found each other and want to make the biggest commitment of all...."

"If you're trying to get me to not feel guilty, you're doing a crappy job," I told her.

"Hear me out. But on the other hand, you've also experienced an awakening—physical, sexual, spiritual, whatever you want to call it, right?"

"I guess so."

"I know so. Losing fifty pounds is enough to make any woman take a good long look at herself. Evie, since it seems like nobody's ever told you this, then let me be the first: You're entitled to feel attractive, and you're entitled to enjoy a little attention from the opposite sex. You're a gorgeous, vibrant twenty-seven-year-old woman. There's nothing to be ashamed of."

"Then why do I feel guilty?"

"Because your mother did a number on you, and because you think you know how to avoid hurting Bruce. I bet you probably think monogamy is part of being a decent human being!"

"Hello? Am I missing something here?"

"Yes. You'll never be a good wife if you're not a good Evie first. And to be a good Evie, you have to be faithful to yourself above all others. If you go into your marriage wondering what might have been, or wishing you'd taken a chance just once, then you'll end up resenting Bruce—unfairly I might add—and it'll ruin your relationship."

"It's almost ruined now."

Morgan threw her hands up into the air and shook her head. "So what do you have to lose? Maybe you need to indulge your urges to finally be free of them. If that sounds crazy to you then whatever, but it's worked wonders for me. You think I sit around all day torturing myself over what I want or don't want or what I should or shouldn't do? As if. My advice in all this is don't be afraid of Jade. Go back to the gym and talk to him. See how you feel. If you want to have a fling—*a single solitary fling over the course of your entire life*—then this is the time to do it. The world won't end. You might even find it empowering. Then you can go forward with everything else. Evie, we all have a right to experience the joys in life, *and* to keep it to ourselves if we want to."

"It's frightening how wrong you are, and how sick that reasoning is," I snapped. "You're not enlightened, you're demented. And an amoral bitch, too. You know that?"

She laughed. "I'm so sorry if I've offended your delicate sensibilities, Miss Mays. I suppose I was kind of wondering if you were actually considering actually doing it...you know, before it's too late. And I guess I have my answer."

Morgan's tirade did inspire me to go back to the gym. I wanted to test my feelings, to see how strong they really were. I had to trust myself, that was the key. Of course, I would never actually *do* anything with Jade, but some of what Morgan said did make sense. And since playing with fire was something I'd never really done before, I had a right to know what it felt like. That could be empowering, too, without having to go all the way, of course.

Jade's face lit up when he saw me.

"I was beginning to wonder if I'd ever see you again," he said.

"I'm sorry. I didn't feel like coming."

"That doesn't sound like you, Evie. Everything okay?"

"Bruce and I had a big fight." I honestly didn't mean to tell him. It just came out.

"What happened?"

I guess I really needed to vent, because over the next couple of hours, I told him the entire story, sparing no details, from beginning to end. To my growing delight, he nodded sympathetically at all the right places, and even touched my shoulder twice to show support (*Mademoiselle,* March: "10 Ways To Tell if He Likes You"). I didn't feel guilty, like I thought I would, sharing Bruce's words with Jade. All I felt was relief.

By the time we were finished, I should have been emotionally and physically exhausted. Instead, I was unbelievably energized.

After I changed and showered, Jade caught up with me at the front door.

"I'm done for the night," he said. "Getting out early, for once."

"This is early?"

"Yup—my 8:30 cancelled. She finally went into labor. You walking this way?"

"Yeah," I said. "So what are you up to tonight?"

"I think I feel like going out. Whaddya say?" he nudged me in the ribs with his elbow.

There was no harm in it, I reasoned. I was really enjoying his company, in a purely non-sexual way. "Sure. Why not," I smiled. "Bruce is gone for the night, anyway."

"Again? He sure goes out of town a lot," Jade said.

"This is the last time. School's finished next week, and then he's off until September. Well, sort of. He teaches summer school in the mornings. Can you believe that? Those little geeks go to school in the summer for fun."

Jade didn't say anything, and we walked in silence for a minute or two. I was such an idiot—he obviously didn't want to hear about my fiancé's summer plans.

"So where do you want to go?" I asked.

"You sure you want to?"

"Yes," I said. "It's no big deal. Just two people with nothing else to do hanging out for a couple of hours. What's wrong with that?"

"Nothing, if you ask me. But just so you know, it's not that I don't have anything else to do tonight. I *want* to be with you."

Now it was I who said nothing. As long as we were skirting the issue and flirting harmlessly, there was no trouble making conversation. It was when Jade got serious with me that I seemed to freeze up.

He sensed my discomfort. "Umm, let me think…well there's a quiet little place just around the corner from my house. They make a mean apple martini. How's that?"

"Sounds perfect," I said quickly.

We took a cab to the bar, which was probably a really trendy place on the weekends, but since it was Tuesday night, it was pretty dead. We sipped our martinis and made small talk, mostly about our likes and dislikes, favorite movies, stuff like that. It reminded me of when Bruce and I first started dating, and the exhilaration of getting to know each other. Jade seemed genuinely interested in everything about me. He even asked me a few questions about my dad, which I skillfully avoided.

"So, did you ever think you'd end up sitting here with me having drinks?" he finally asked.

"You mean when I first saw you? I'd have to say definitely not. I thought you were just a dumb jock who flirted shamelessly to reel in customers."

He laughed. The bartender looked over and drooled.

"Nobody could accuse you of mincing words, Evie," he said. "So now what do you think of me?"

"Well, you're not as dumb as I thought, but you're an even bigger flirt than I imagined."

"I think you're the one who's flirting," he grinned.

"Easy, boy," I said. I hadn't eaten dinner, and the martini was going to my head in a wonderful way. I had this guy wrapped around my finger. Morgan was right—it was empowering.

"Easy yourself. You want another drink?"

"Sure. Couldn't hurt. But two's my limit on a school night."

I don't know whether or not it was my subconscious intention to get completely blitzed, but that's exactly what I did. Maybe it was because I was hungry, and the martinis came with little slivers of apple in them. Or maybe it was because I was just so sick and tired of thinking all the time, and being drunk was like giving my brain a much-needed holiday. Whatever the case, an hour and a half and four drinks later, Jade and I were strolling arm-in-arm down the street. The plan was to walk me to the subway, but we ended up at his front door.

"Don't ask me if I want to come in," I sighed. "Because I really don't."

"Then I won't ask you," he said, turning the key in the lock and leading me up the stairs. "The place is a mess, so you probably wouldn't want to see it anyway."

"No, I certainly wouldn't," I agreed as I stepped through the doorway. Despite my drunkenness, I was thinking clearly and felt quite wonderful.

"Then you definitely wouldn't want a tour, then," he said.

"No thanks."

"Good," Jade said as we walked through his apartment. "Because this isn't the bedroom."

I looked around the room. It was actually pretty tidy. The bed was made and there were lots of little white candles everywhere. Very unusual for a guy.

"I bet you bring all your clients here," I said, then added, "This room looks like a set from a bad porno."

"I told you I don't do that," he said as he fluffed the pillows. "And I hate to disappoint you, but you're the first one."

"You're a *virgin?*"

"No! I mean you're the first woman I've ever brought here from work." He lit a candle beside the bed.

"How many drinks did you have?" I asked him.

"Does it matter?"

"You're not drunk, are you?" I asked.

"No," he said. "Are you?"

"Of course not."

"Good," he said, and sat down on the bed. "Well, as long as you're in control of your faculties, why don't you come over here? I want to show you my condom collection."

"That's very funny, but I'm fine where I am, thank you."

"You're fine wherever you are," he smiled.

I couldn't help but laugh. "You think I'm going to fall for that?"

"Yes."

Jade stood up and walked toward me. The room was spinning, and I knew things were about to get heavy. I exhaled slowly. There was nothing to do but let it all happen.

He grabbed my waist and gently pulled me close to him.

"Evie," he whispered.

"Yes?"

"I'm sorry," he said.

"About what?"

"About this," he said, and kissed me.

It was a long one, very slow and deliberate. The best kiss I'd ever had. I knew that before it was over. He pulled away and looked into my eyes. My legs were shaking like the floor was made of Jell-O.

"Is this okay?" he asked softly. "If you don't—"

But it was definitely too late for that. I put my hand on the back of his neck, closed my eyes and kissed him again. It was just as good. Better, even. He tasted like heaven, like vodka and cinnamon gum.

Soon, we were on the bed, then under the sheets. My shirt was on the floor. He fumbled with my bra. I fumbled with his belt buckle. *Evie, Evie, what are you doing?* He let out a little moan. Slowly, the rest of the world disappeared.

It was almost impossibly surreal, like one of those out-of-body experiences you hear about on the talk shows where some old lady's heart stops beating during surgery and she sees herself lying on the operating table below. Only this time it was happening to me. Most miraculously of all, every time I opened my eyes, Jade was still there. Gorgeous. Breathtakingly gorgeous. And at that moment, he wanted *me,* Evelyn Mays, more than anything else. I knew there was no going back, even if I wanted to. Which I didn't.

Maybe if that first kiss was bad, I would have stopped right there and ran home to our shabby little apartment in Brooklyn. But it wasn't, and I didn't. And as good as that kiss was, the rest was even better.

17

Wednesday morning, it didn't take long for me to reach new heights of self-loathing. Of course, things didn't start out that way. When I snuck out of Jade's bedroom, it was with the intention of appearing kind of mysterious and elusive and fabulously noncommittal about the whole thing. Like a guy. Walking down the street, I imagined everyone could tell that I'd just spent the night with the most gorgeous creature in all of New York. Understandably, they were incredibly jealous. But when I got to the subway and opened my purse to get a token, there were my underwear, staring back out. On the train, it was almost as if I could hear them in there, mocking me. By the time I got home, those panties were no longer just the innocently sexy but otherwise innocuous Calvin Klein thong I'd bought on sale at Macy's only last week. Small though they were, they had somehow taken on tremendous proportions. They were sinister. Evil, almost.

The second I got home, I stripped off my clothes and stuffed them in a plastic bag at the back of my closet. I buried the thong in the trash, and was seriously tempted to throw out everything I was wearing, but the everything in question was a new navy-blue DKNY suit that looked fabulous on me (*In Style,* May: Seven Sexy Suits for Spring"). Definitely one of my better outfits, and worth salvaging. I vowed to bring it in that afternoon (if anything good came out of the whole Monica Lewinsky thing, it was that cheaters everywhere learned the importance of timely dry-cleaning). I took a very hot shower and collapsed on the bed. I only woke up when Bruce came home.

"Are you okay, Evie?"

"What time is it?" I asked.

"It's one o'clock."

"In the morning?"

"In the afternoon. I just got in now. My plane was delayed. Are you sick or something? I called you three times last night, but no one answered."

I turned over and buried my face in the pillow. It smelled like Bruce. "Yeah, I have a headache."

"I'll let you sleep. I'm going in to school, and I'll probably stay late. I'll call later to check up on you."

I didn't want him to leave. "How was Baltimore?"

"Buffalo. But thanks for asking." He shut the lights and I fell back asleep.

The phone rang and rang and I drifted in and out of consciousness until I had to pee so badly that I had no choice but to get up. It was almost five and the apartment was sweltering. I checked the machine—there were two messages from Bruce and a nasty one from Pruscilla, who was pretending to sound worried but who was probably really pissed off. I took another shower and went back to bed. But I couldn't sleep. All I could do was replay the events of last night over and over again in my mind, and wondered if it was really as good as I thought it was. There were fuzzy patches, of course, but for the most part, I think it was an earth-shattering experience. And the real trouble was, the better I remembered it being, the worse I felt.

Bruce came home and ordered a pizza. I pretended to be asleep. He brought me two Tylenol and then went to watch TV.

When my alarm went off, I could barely move, even though I'd slept about twenty of the last twenty-four hours. Bruce had already left for school, and I was all alone again. The thought of going in to work was too much, so I called and left Pruscilla a message saying that I needed a few personal days. Thank God she wasn't there, or I'm sure she would have given me crap for not calling in yesterday.

I also phoned Morgan before she left for work.

"Morgan, I need you," I whimpered, and promptly burst into tears.

"Ohmygod, you did it, didn't you?" She always had a way of knowing.

I nodded into the phone and sobbed.

"Don't worry, I'm coming over," she said.

"But...but...you..."

"Calm down, Evie. It's okay. I'm going to take the morning off. I'll be there in an hour."

It only took her forty-five minutes. I must have looked pathetic, because she hugged me as soon as she saw me, and Morgan's not much of a hugger. "Here," she said, handing me a bag of bagels. "You need to eat."

I hadn't eaten a thing since the apple martinis, and those weren't much of a meal. By the time the coffee was ready, I'd inhaled two bagels with cream cheese and some pizza from last night.

"So?" Morgan said, when she sensed I was ready.

"Well, I took your advice...."

"Whoa...wait a second. Advice is too strong a word. I was merely presenting an option, one of many."

"Fine, Morgan. Whatever. I did what you said."

She sucked in her breath. "I can't believe you really did it. I *really* didn't think you would."

"I'm touched that you're so impressed. But what I need right now is for you to tell me what to do. I'm just so screwed up, I don't know what's wrong with me. I can't even think straight. God, I'm such a piece of crap. I can't believe it. I just can't believe it." I put my head in my hands. "My thong hates me. I don't know what to do."

"Evie, it's okay. I promise. You're going to be fine. We'll figure it out.... Except for that thong thing. But I'm sure there's some sort of medication for that. Now tell me what happened."

I took a deep breath. "Oh, you know, we went out, got drunk. I guess I didn't think it was actually going to happen, you know? Like we were just going out as friends. But I didn't account for how much cuter he got when I was tipsy. I just didn't think it was possible. And the more I drank, the more impossible he was to resist...and I drank a *lot*."

"You slut! Did you even enjoy it? Were you so wasted that you can't remember it?" She was on the edge of her seat.

"I wish! Then I wouldn't be torturing myself so effectively." I was sobbing and laughing at the same time. "It was...*fantastic.*"

Morgan's eyes widened. "Give me details. I need details!"

"I don't even know where to begin." I paused for dramatic effect. "That man is like, I don't know, like a god or something. He was perfect. Everything was perfect. And I was good, too. No—I was great. With him, I was *great*. It was magical. It was passionate."

She waited for more.

"It was the best I've ever had."

"You're fucked," she said decisively.

It wasn't quite the reaction I'd hoped for. A wave of panic washed over me. "But you said if I gave in to my urges, they'd disappear! That it would be empowering!"

"What—you don't feel empowered?" she asked. "This type of liberating sexual experience is *exactly* what the feminists had in mind back in the '70s. If you don't like it, or you feel weird or whatever, it's just because you're not used to it. But I can assure you that what you're going through is normal, so there's no need to get hysterical. You think I wasn't weirded out the first time I slept with a married man? Or the first time I had a threesome? There's more to loving than what they told you in church, Evie. Physical, emotional, marital—it's all sort of the same thing when you see it without the spin. You just got your first glimpse of it, that's all."

"I don't know...."

"Look. If you don't want to freak yourself out for the next fifty years, just train your mind to sustain the way you felt last night. Something inside you allowed you to go through with it. And it felt good. So how wrong can it be? Knowing that it's okay, *that's* what's empowering. Who knows? The memory might end up being something you treasure forever," she finished triumphantly.

It was a compelling argument. "I guess," I said. "Yesterday morning I felt good about it, for a while anyway. But the more I think about it, the worse I feel, because you can't deny that this would really hurt Bruce." Understatement of the century. "But with Jade, you're right—I felt amazing. Not like me, but amazing. The problem is, now that I'm back in the real world again, it's way different. Like I know it's wrong, but I also know maybe it isn't. I can't stop thinking about him, Morgan. And the more I think about him, the sicker I feel, and the sicker I feel, the more I miss Bruce. I don't know. It was just so good. But maybe once was enough to get it out of my system. But if Jade were here right now, I don't know what I'd do. I don't know how I'd feel."

"How did you leave it with him?" she asked.

"Well, when I woke up he was still sleeping. I had to throw up, so I went to the bathroom. Have you ever had an apple martini? They're pretty damn good on the way down. I didn't feel sick at all until I woke up."

Morgan stared blankly at the wall. "Once, I told Billy I loved him after five apple martinis...they're killer."

No wonder the poor guy was still hanging around.

"Jade was still sleeping when I got back to bed."

"Did you wake him up and have fabulous morning sex?"

"No, but he looked truly gorgeous, just lying there. I guess I didn't want to ruin the moment, so I left."

"You just left? Just like that?"

"I pulled a Morgan!"

"I don't do that," she said. "Not to a guy I like."

"Well, I don't want him to think that I like him."

"God, Evie, you've evolved into quite the heartbreaker." Morgan thought *I* was being cold? It was an all-time first.

It occurred to me that on some level, I might have slept with Jade to impress her. Her approval did mean a lot to me. I knew she wouldn't ever want me to do something that I wasn't comfortable with, but she also didn't quite understand that she and I were different in a lot of ways. Very different. Especially when it came to men and relationships. Maybe that was why this whole cheating thing was so hard for me—no matter how much sense she made, and no matter how much I agreed with most of what she had to say on the subject, at least technically, I couldn't change the fact that I *felt* differently. It wasn't just about me, like she'd said. It was about me *and* Bruce. I knew at least that. I would never be able to see my infidelity as an intellectual exercise in some deranged form of feminism, the way she could.

Damn it. Why hadn't I realized this before all this shit happened? There was no sense in blaming her, though. I was the one who'd been so desperate to believe her.

"You know, I did sense that he was more into me than I was into him," I told her.

"Yeah, right!" she shrieked.

"Why not? You don't think I have him head over heels? Remember, *he* seduced *me.*"

"And I'm sure that was the biggest challenge of his life," she laughed, and then let out a big sigh. "Oh, I've got to come clean with you…"

"What?"

"You're probably going to kill me, but I've just got to tell you—I saw him! I saw Jade!"

"What are you talking about? When?"

"I couldn't resist. I was just so curious. So I went to your gym one day when you weren't there, since I knew you'd never bring me. I have to admit, Evie, he's much hotter than I imagined. You weren't lying. And you bagged him…! Oh, I can't believe it. I just can't. It's too much." She couldn't stop laughing.

"Thanks a lot."

"Sorry, but he's a bit out of your league. He's out of *my* league, for chrissake."

"Vain *and* humble, your mother must be so proud…."

"Well, if you're going to be like that about it, Jade and I are very much in the same league. I was just trying to boost your ego."

"I think I've had enough of an ego boost on this one to last me the rest of my life," I told her. But now that I knew how good it felt, would that one little taste really be enough to last forever?

"Well that was the whole idea, wasn't it?"

"I don't think so. Maybe at first…"

"So why did you do it?" she asked.

"I was drunk?"

"No, that's just *how* it happened. I mean, what were you trying to get from this?"

"Maybe I just wanted some excitement."

"Maybe." She didn't seem convinced.

"Or maybe I just had an itch and I wanted it scratched."

"Evie, I may not know the true workings of your mind, but I do know enough to say that this was about a lot more than just sex for you."

Of course, she was right. But my immediate concerns were far more urgent. "But what do I do now? What about Bruce? What about our wedding? Morgan, I seriously don't know if I can do this…."

"You mean get married?"

"No. I don't know. I think I mean lying to him."

"But you lie all the time. If Bruce knew how many credit cards you really have..."

"Yeah, but not about something like this. This is different. You know, it's not easy to lie to Bruce, even about little things. He has a way of believing everything I tell him that makes me feel like a total bitch. But this guilt is off the charts. I couldn't even look at him yesterday. I just kept thinking about the bag of clothes in the closet..."

"What?"

"My Clothes of Shame. What I wore Tuesday night."

"Stop being such a drama queen."

"Whatever. But I hate the idea of Bruce not knowing something this big about me. Like he's at work right now, happily going about his business, completely oblivious to...oh, God..."

"Stop torturing yourself! You'll go mental if you don't quit this shit right now. There's no use. You think I sit around making myself sick every time I'm with Peter? What's the fun in doing something if you can't enjoy it?"

"I know, but I'm not like you, Morgan."

"Well, you better get like me, or you're done for. What you do, have done, will do, whatever, is 100-percent your own life. You don't owe anybody access to your memories. Not even Bruce."

I wish I believed what she was saying, but I didn't.

On Friday morning, Bruce made an appointment for me with his doctor. Since I had no choice but to play up the whole headache thing, and it had been three years since I'd had a checkup, I was backed into a corner. Of course, Bruce decided to tag along, probably to make sure that I actually went.

"I'd feel a lot better if you just left me alone," I whispered in his ear as we waited.

"When you have a blinding pain behind your left eye for four days, it's probably a good idea to see someone," he intoned seriously.

"Please be quiet. It hurts less when you're quiet."

"I'm worried about you."

It was the longest conversation we'd had since he came home from Baltimore…no, Buffalo? I'm sure he knew something was up.

When I got home there was a message from Pruscilla to call her immediately. Normally, if I wasn't feeling well, I wouldn't have bothered, but since she probably really was starting to worry, I called her back. My plan was to return to work Monday, provided I was up to it.

"Pruscilla?"

"Who's this?"

"It's Evie. Hi."

"Oh. Hold on."

After about five minutes on hold, I hung up. Two minutes, fine, but five? Rudeness of that caliber is unacceptable, even when it's coming from your boss (*Cosmopolitan,* July: "The Dos and Don'ts of Office Etiquette"). About an hour later, she called me back. I was in the middle of a nap, and barely picked up on time.

"Hello?"

"Evelyn, I'm going to keep this short—"

"Thanks for calling, Pruscilla, but you really don't have to worry," I reassured her. "I'm fine. I just had a bit of a personal crisis this week, but I'm dealing with it now and hope to be back on Monday," I said. I glanced over at the closet. The Clothes of Shame were still in there, waiting for me. I hadn't been able to deal with them yet. "Ummm…let's say Monday afternoon, just to be safe," I added.

"Monday afternoon is fine, and remember to please bring a box. You'll be clearing out your desk."

Oh God.

"What did you say?"

"You heard me. We're letting you go, Evelyn."

"B-b-but *why?*" I stammered idiotically. "What did I do?"

"What *haven't* you done is more like it. For starters, you haven't shown up. And since that was an essential part of your job, Evelyn, we're terminating you."

This wasn't happening. "But didn't you get my message? I told you I needed a few personal days." Maybe the voice mail was down or something. She couldn't fire me for technical problems, could she? That wouldn't be fair.

"I got your message. You already used up all your personal days."

"So why can't you just dock my pay?"

"If you prefer to look at it that way, fine. From now on, we'll be docking your pay. Every day for the rest of your life. So don't bother coming in anymore."

Since I felt the tears coming on anyway, I figured I might as well try using them to my advantage. "I thought we were friends, Pruscilla," I wept. "After what we've been through together this year, with your surgery and our weight loss and my engagement. I thought we were finally connecting."

"That's not going to work, so give it a rest. We haven't connected and you know it. I don't know why, but you don't like me, Evelyn. You never did. It's no secret."

A woman like her, who could probably count all the friends she'd ever had in her entire life on one hand…was she really rejecting my olive branch?

"That's not true," I said.

"You know, I saw something in you, Evelyn. That's why I hired you. You have a creative spirit, but you haven't done a thing with it. It's best we all just go our separate ways. If you think about it, I'm sure you'll agree."

"But I want to stay," I whimpered. "I haven't done anything wrong this time, at least not professionally speaking."

"What's that supposed to mean? And in case you've forgotten, you were on probation…."

"Yes, but only until the beginning of March," I reminded her.

"No. Permanently. Until I was satisfied that you were committed to changing. And since that certainly never happened..."

"But I *was* sick." Sick in my heart.

"You can't change your story now. If you were legitimately ill, then you'll have to produce a doctor's note to that effect. If you can, then you'll receive your salary for those days you missed. If you can't, then your final paycheck will reflect your absence."

It was a good thing I told Bruce I had a headache—now I'd be able to get a note from that doctor. But it was dawning on me that what I really needed was a lawyer. Or rather, the threat of one. Maybe they'd reconsider if they thought I was going to sue.

"If you think I'm going to take this lying down..." I began tentatively.

"Evelyn, please," she sighed. "Be gracious. For once, just be gracious and accept what I'm telling you."

"But..."

"But nothing. You don't think we have grounds for this? It's not just your most recent sabbatical, you know, though that was the proverbial straw that broke the camel's back. We've been tracking your Internet usage, too, since you got it back. You spend at least two hours a day on personal matters that obviously have nothing to do with work. Unless..." I could hear papers rustling in the background. "...unless you're going to try and tell me that online mah-jongg and...what's this? Oh! And the message board at Oprah.com have something to do with cosmetics marketing research."

"I'm *outraged!* This is a *complete* invasion of privacy. No. It's worse—it's a deliberate smear campaign. And entrapment! It's entrapment, too! They can't do that!"

"Don't flatter yourself. It's a new company policy that's been in effect since January. KW now randomly spot-checks employees' Internet usage and e-mail correspondence. Apparently, there have been some problems with corporate espionage."

E-mails, too? God, she'd probably read all the horrible things I'd written about her to Morgan. I'd be mortified. Pruscilla was never really as bad as I made her seem, she was just anal about work stuff, and I found it entertaining to dislike her. Half the time I felt more sorry for her than anything, so the last thing I wanted was for her to see what a backstabber I'd been after she'd given me, like, fifty chances to shape up. It was all just too awful. How would I ever be able to face her again after this?

Well, enough was enough. The embarrassment wasn't worth it. At one point, you have to ask yourself, what's worse: losing your job or losing your self-respect? The answer for me was clear. And I certainly wasn't going to beg to keep a job I never really liked in the first place at a fascist corporate conglomerate like Kendra White. Especially since it obviously wasn't working out.

"You know what, Pruscilla? I'm not coming in on Monday. You can keep whatever's in my desk. Because I never want to see that horrible place again!" I yelled into the receiver, and slammed it down.

The silence in the bedroom was deafening. I sat there, stunned, and tried to figure things out. What was I supposed to do now? Without a job, the collection agencies would tear me to shreds within a few months. Bruce was going to kill me. My mother was going to kill me. Hell, *I* even felt like killing me. Because who was I kidding? I knew I deserved it. I deserved to lose my job.

Suddenly, I remembered the box of Turtles sitting in the back of the pantry. Bruce's dad had given them to me for Easter. He was pretty much oblivious to everything going on around him, so he probably hadn't noticed I wasn't eating chocolates anymore, let alone gooey, caramel-smothered, pecan-filled ones. It was sweet of him, though, since the old me really did have a thing for them.

At the time, I was irritated that Bruce wouldn't just let me toss them in the trash. Now, in my hour of need, I prayed that they were still there. I ran into the kitchen, certain that Bruce had found them at some point and devoured them. But there they were—hiding behind the cans of fat-free soup. I ripped through the cellophane and tore open the box. Twenty-four perfect little milk-chocolate blobs stared back out.

I ate every one.

18

And then there was the whole matter with Jade.

I was afraid to go to the gym, not that I really felt like it anyway, and also afraid not to. At first, I was dying to know where Jade was at in all this, what he thought about everything. But the more I thought about it, the less I cared what he wanted. Even though I'd be horribly insulted, I was praying he'd changed his mind about me. The worse thing would be if he hadn't. Should I bother letting him down gently? Or maybe the best thing to do would be to never, ever see or talk to him again. Not that I didn't trust myself around him. It was just that I knew if I saw him, it would remind me that I was the most horrible slut on the face of the planet.

My only moments of peace came when I told myself that it had never really happened, that I'd imagined it all, like some sort of extended TV dream sequence. But at least on *Dallas,* everybody woke up and resumed their normal lives. I seemed to be stuck in the nightmare indefinitely. The days passed by in a blur of sleep and tears.

There wasn't even anybody I could call for support—I hadn't

told anyone but Morgan, and she was out of town again with Billy. On the upside, the agony of it all was enough to make me not care so much that I'd lost my job and was teetering on the brink of financial ruin. All I could do was lie in bed and cry. Of course, Bruce didn't have the faintest idea what was going on.

But I could tell his patience was wearing thin, and he clearly didn't believe the whole headache thing anymore. Most of the time, he pretty much just left me alone, and I was happy with that, because it was all I could do not to break down and tell him everything.

On Saturday night, he went over to his parents' for sister Wendy's graduation party. Personally, I think graduating from an all-girls college is something one wouldn't necessarily want to draw attention to, but whatever. It's her life. At least I got out of it. Come to think of it, Bruce didn't even ask me if I wanted to go.

When he came home, he crawled into bed and woke me up.

"Evie, my mother's sending out the invitations on Monday. I can't hold her off any longer."

"So?" I mumbled from under the sheets.

"So...what should I do?"

"What do you mean?"

"Should I let her do it?"

"Are you trying to tell me something?" I asked him.

He turned on the light. "I think maybe you should start seeing someone," he said.

I rolled over and squinted at him. Did he know? Was he trying to trap me into telling him about Jade? "What do you mean, 'I should start seeing someone'?" I asked him in a panic. "You think we should have an open relationship?"

He stared at me as if I were mad and shook his head. "A *psychologist,* Evie. I think you need to see a psychologist."

"I don't need a shrink," I snapped. "I'm just having normal pre-wedding jitters." It wasn't a total lie—a lot of my current problems could, in fact, be chalked up to nerves (*Bride,* April: "Are You a Runaway-Bride-To-Be?").

"This stuff has gone way beyond that. And not that I'm complaining, but you haven't even been to the gym. In fact, you've barely gotten out of bed since Wednesday. You're obviously not yourself."

Ohmygod. Was he getting suspicious?

"If you don't agree right now to let me make an appointment for you," he continued, "then I'm going to tell my mother not to send them out."

"I'm not crazy, Bruce," I said, trying to sound like I believed it.

"Maybe not. But you're well on your way."

An immediate concession was required.

"I got fired."

"What?" he sat up.

I nodded. "That's why I'm freaking out."

"Oh, Evie, no. This is bad... This is *really* bad."

"I know that, Bruce," I sniffled.

"When?"

"Yesterday, when I got home from the doctor. Pruscilla called...." I said, then instantly regretted it. Why didn't I tell him I got fired on Tuesday? That would have explained my weirdness all week.

"Shit. What are you going to do?"

"You mean, what are *we* going to do..." I corrected him.

"Evie, you have to find another job. Right away," he said. "You'll start looking tomorrow."

"I *can't,* Bruce! I can't go out and find a job just like that! It takes time. And I don't know where to look..." I coughed through the tears. "I can't...I can't.... I don't know what I want to *do* with my life...."

He breathed out deeply. "Okay, okay...forget the job for now. Maybe you need a little more time. But Monday morning, I'm making an appointment for you. You're going to see someone. And that's that."

"Fine," I cried.

In the morning, Bruce went out to get us some breakfast, and I pounced on the chance to empty the closet. It was only a matter of time before he saw that losing my job had nothing to do with losing my mind, and then he might start to wonder. And I didn't need any shrink to tell me that getting those clothes out of this apartment would be therapeutic.

After a quick shower (I hadn't had one in three days), I was ready. I opened the bag and pulled out the suit. Although it was crumpled up in a ball and smelled like smoke, it still looked pretty good. The thought of actually wearing it, however, made my stomach churn. Even though it was the only summer-weight wool suit I had in a dark color besides black, I was beginning to sense that no amount of dry-cleaning would ever get it clean enough. I stuffed the suit back in the bag.

Enough was enough. I would throw it out. Throw the suit out and start my life fresh. Bruce and I could never be happy with this suit hanging in my closet. I grabbed a big black garbage bag from the kitchen and tossed in a couple sections of the paper and an empty milk carton, for a realistic effect. I brought it into the bedroom and shoved the suit bag into the bottom. Although in the past weeks I'd probably cried enough tears to fill the East River, I squeezed out a few more and vowed they'd be my last.

"What are you doing?"

Bruce was standing right behind me.

I spun around, wiping my eyes.

"What's that?" he asked again. He was holding a bag of bagels from our favorite place and two big coffees. "Why are you crying?"

"I...I didn't hear you." My heart pounded deafeningly in my ears.

"So?"

"How long have you been standing there?" I asked, and tried to laugh.

He put the stuff down on the dresser and looked into the bag.

"I was just about to clean out my closet."

I guess he didn't believe me, because he reached down into the bottom and removed the bag. He opened it, and looked at me.

"You see? I was cleaning out my closet. Just doing a little cleaning! Ha, ha!"

"What's wrong with this?" He took the jacket out and looked at it. "It smells like smoke."

"That's why I'm getting rid of it. It reeks," I said, making a face. "And I know how much you hate smoke...."

He must have felt something in the pocket because he reached in and pulled out the demon thong. And the bra that matched.

"Why are these in here?"

"I don't know?" I offered.

"WHAT THE HELL IS THIS SHIT DOING IN YOUR POCKET?"

It was too much. I broke down. I sobbed hysterically. Bruce stood there stiffly, waiting for me to compose myself.

After what felt like an eternity, I took a deep breath and said, "It's...what you're thinking."

"It better not be," he whispered.

I stared at my fingers.

"Who?"

How could I tell him? I shook my head.

"WHO?" he screamed, and slammed his fist on the dresser. The coffees tumbled over onto the floor.

I couldn't say his name. "My trainer."

He kicked the wall three times, hard, and stormed out of the room. Seconds later, the front door slammed.

I crawled back into the bed, vowing never to leave it again.

★ ★ ★

When I woke up, I heard Bruce on the phone in the living room, yelling.

"I told you, the wedding's off!"

Silence.

"No! I don't want to talk about it. You think this is embarrassing? Just be thankful you didn't send the invitations out. I'm hanging up now!"

More silence.

"Thanks. I know. I'm sorry. No. No! I'll be fine. But you're going to have to back off on this for now, okay? And could you tell Dad?"

Fine? How could he even anticipate being fine?

He stomped into the bedroom and turned on the lights.

"Pack a bag and get out. I don't care where you go."

"Bruce—" I sobbed. "Bruce. Don't..."

"Just get out," he said, and left.

What else could I do? I put Granny Fulbright's engagement ring on the bedside table, packed a bag and got the hell out of Dodge. I called Morgan from the cab and left a message telling her I was on my way. Going to Mom's wasn't an option. And maybe I'd somehow be able to fix everything before she found out. Maybe Bruce wasn't serious. He was just angry. Furious. And rightfully so. Calling off the wedding was a perfectly natural reaction for a man who just found out his fiancée had slept with someone else. Wasn't it? He'd probably cool down in a few days. Or maybe not.

I waited for three hours in the lobby of Morgan's building. The doorman took pity on me, and let me sit inside because it was pouring. Happy young couples came and went, chatting amiably about where to go for dinner. Wasn't anybody in this city single? I wished upon every smug one of them the misery I was now experiencing.

Finally, just when I thought I'd have to seriously consider getting a hotel room, Morgan and Billy swept in with their suitcases.

"Evie?"

I ran up and hugged her.

"What are you doing here?" she asked. "What happened to your hair?"

"I tried to call, but your cell wasn't on. Did you get my message?"

She shook her head and looked lovingly at Billy. "We just got back from Atlantic City."

"Oh yeah," I said.

"Hey, Evie. How's it going?" Billy said.

"Fine, I guess." I really hadn't anticipated this. Having a nervous breakdown in front of Billy was not what I'd envisioned.

"Come, come upstairs. Billy, take this," she said, handing him my bag.

"Thanks," I said weakly.

"So what's going on?" she asked as we rode up the elevator to her rent-controlled two-bedroom on the twelfth floor. For her twenty-fifth birthday, Morgan's mother had bribed a Realtor to get her into the building. "Is Bruce out of town again? Do you want to stay with me? I thought he was finished with all that for the summer."

"I just wanted to see you," I said, hoping she'd know immediately that I was lying.

She squeezed my hand. "I'm glad you're here. I've got something to tell you."

It was already past eleven, but she put on some coffee anyway. Billy went into the bedroom to change.

"You'll never guess what happened," she began excitedly.

"What?" I couldn't have been less interested. Why wasn't she asking me about me?

"I won at roulette! Over $5200! I put $150 down on black 13, Billy's birthday. And it came up!"

"Wow. That's great."

"I know," she gushed. "Can you believe it?"

"Good luck must run in your family."

"Yeah right. My mom's husband's the one who won the lottery. But I have another theory—our *men* are lucky. Without Billy, I never would have picked 13!"

"Imagine that," I said. "Listen, Morgan…"

Billy emerged from the bedroom wearing boxers and a T-shirt. He was pretty built. I'd never noticed before. No wonder Morgan was having such a hard time cutting him loose.

"Did you tell her?" he asked, sitting down at the kitchen table.

"Yeah," I said flatly. "Pretty amazing. Lucky 13."

"No," he laughed. "Not that."

"I was waiting for you," Morgan smiled at him.

Billy grabbed her hand and kissed it.

"Evie…there's something I have to ask you. Something important…"

"Spit it out, Morgan."

"Okay, okay!" She took a deep breath. "Will you be my maid of honor?"

The air conditioner hummed. They stared at me.

"Did you hear me? Billy asked me to marry him, and I said yes!" She held up her left hand to show me the ring.

"Uh… Oh, God! I'm…I'm so *happy* for you," I squeaked, and started crying. Sobbing, actually. There was no pretending these were tears of joy.

Billy looked at Morgan nervously. She motioned for him to leave and he dutifully obeyed.

"What's going on?" she asked.

"I got fired…."

Morgan rolled her eyes. "Well that sucks, but can't you at least be happy for me right now? I don't mean to be a bitch, but—"

"…and Bruce found out about You-Know-Who. He called off the wedding."

Her eyes widened in horror. "Oh, shit! I'm *so* sorry, Evie. I didn't mean…"

"It's okay, it's okay," I sighed, waving off her apology. "But he kicked me out. And I don't want to stay with my mom. I haven't even told her. So would it be okay if I..."

"Of *course.* You can stay here as long as you need. Wow. I'm really sorry, Evie. I can't believe it."

Billy popped his head into the kitchen. "Um...sorry, but I'm going to go down and get a paper and some milk for tomorrow." He probably wanted to get as far away from this conversation as possible.

"Okay," Morgan said, and blew him a kiss.

"God, I'm sorry. I don't mean to be such a downer," I told her. "I'm happy for you, Morgan. I really am. Billy's a great guy."

"Yeah, I know. Tell me what happened, Evie. I'm just so...in shock, I guess. Are you okay?"

"You know what? I don't feel like talking about it right now. I'm completely drained. It's been the worst weekend of my life. Make that the worst week. I'm sick of crying and I'm sick of talking. So I want to hear about you now."

"Are you sure?"

"Yes."

"Whenever you feel ready to talk about it, you just tell me."

"Fine. So how did he propose?"

"Well," she began cautiously, "when we got there, the suite was filled with flowers. White, red and pink roses..."

"Where were you staying?"

"The Taj Mahal."

"Okay. Go on."

"So, yeah, the flowers. They were everywhere. Tons of them. I didn't really think anything of it, I guess, because he does that sort of thing all the time. Then he drew me a bath. There was a bucket of champagne waiting on ice..."

"God, are you serious?" It sounded pretty cheesy to me.

"Uh-huh. I got into the tub. He joined me. I thought we were just going to fool around, but then he pulled a little plastic box out from under the bubbles."

Despite my misery, I couldn't help but laugh. "Plastic? He thought of everything."

"He must have hidden it between his cheeks because I totally didn't notice it. Anyway, there it was. He said something like, 'I adore you, blah blah blah, you mean the world to me, blah blah blah,' I don't really remember exactly what, and then I opened the box and said yes! Simple as that—it didn't hurt at all!"

"Wow."

"He's a true romantic," she sighed.

"Okay, now you're freaking me out."

"I am?"

"Come on, Morgan! Don't pretend this isn't weird. I feel like I'm in an episode of *The Twilight Zone.* I don't mean to be blunt, but…what the hell happened? I mean, last month you barely wanted to commit to *breakfast* with the guy, let alone the rest of your life."

"That's a very valid point," she laughed. "But a lot can change in a month."

"Tell me about it," I mumbled.

She looked at me with the saddest eyes. "Well, I don't know if this will make you feel better or worse, but I have you to thank, actually. Talking to you about the possibility of you sleeping with Jade got me thinking that marriage might not be a bad thing, provided you go into it with the right attitude. I've been thinking about it a lot…. Look at Peter, for example. He's got a great wife he loves and this whole family life thing going on, and then he's got me on the side for a little excitement and good sex. It works great for him. And with you…well, not anymore, maybe, but before it was like, Bruce and you were perfect for each other, but you could also have this little fling just for yourself, and otherwise share your life with a wonderful person who adores you and cares about you."

It was a bit much to hear, and I gulped back some more tears.

"Sorry," she said. "But that's where I'm at right now. I was giving you all this advice that I should really have been taking myself. So I did. You think I want to go from one noncommittal relationship to the next for the rest of my life? I want to be more than just the Other Woman. *I* want to be the one who has it all. *I* want to be the one with somebody on the side."

I was starting to get annoyed. "But you do have somebody on the side," I reminded her.

"Yeah, but it doesn't really count unless you're the one who's married. That's when you make a real commitment, so breaking it becomes all the more exciting. Before this, I was just Billy's sometimes girlfriend and your average homewrecker...well, above-average, actually. But I want more. I want more than just a life as a tramp or a boring old housewife. So I'm creating another option for myself."

"That's pretty dark, Morgan. Getting married because it makes the cheating better probably isn't the best idea. In fact, you're making me sick just saying something like that." Here I was, my heart and my life ripped in two because I had done exactly that, and she was actually going to seek it out. Morgan thought it was just about getting a thrill here and there, to keep things interesting, but she didn't realize how serious it was. I don't even think I did until that very moment. How could I have expected anything good to come out of something that would hurt Bruce?

"Don't judge me just yet, Evie. That's not the only reason. The more I thought about it, the more I realized I was running out of excuses not to fall in love with Billy. And then as soon as I allowed myself to feel something for him, it happened really fast. He's sexy, smart. And he makes a shitload of money."

"And he worships you."

"We had a talk about that. He agreed to take it down a notch. He knows I find it unattractive."

"What about kids?"

"Oh, we'd make beautiful kids."

"I know, but have you told him you don't want any?"

"Yup, and he agreed."

"And how did he find out about your little change of heart?"

"I told him. I guess he bought the ring the next day."

"Before you could change your mind, probably."

"Exactly," she laughed.

There was no point in trying to get her to see things differently. I think it was Oprah or Ghandi or someone like that who said that it's the way we deal with our mistakes, not our successes, which define us as human beings. Like me, Morgan had a long road ahead of her.

"Okay, then, I approve," I told her. "It sounds like you've thought of everything."

"If not, there's always divorce," she grinned. "And I think Billy would make a fabulous first husband."

I laughed and hugged her. "You go on toying with people's lives, sweetie. It's what you do best," I said, getting up. "I think I'm going to crash. I'm completely exhausted. Tell Billy I said good-night, okay?"

"Okay," she said. "I'm so sorry, Evie. About what happened."

"I know. Thanks."

I stayed in bed for precisely four days, venturing out only at lunch and dinner to answer the door for the delivery guys. Bruce must have known where I was, but he didn't call once. And I was far too afraid to call him. Same thing went for Mom. I checked our messages at home every morning, but nothing—although you'd think she would have called me once over the course of a week, just to say hi, but she didn't. Unless Bruce had answered, and told her I was out or something. But I was almost sure he wouldn't be answering the phone at all. He was probably too depressed to speak to anyone.

On the fifth day, Morgan threatened to kick me out if I didn't do something productive with my time. Since I couldn't bear the thought of looking for a job yet, I decided to just sit in Central Park for a few days and think about my miserable life. I must have eaten at fifteen different hot-dog carts. I didn't care if I got fat. What did it matter? There was no dress to fit into, no trainer to impress. Once, I thought I saw Bruce, which wouldn't have been so weird because his school was only a few blocks away, so I followed him all the way to the zoo. But it turned out to be someone else.

I'd been living out of the same bag for two weeks because I was afraid to go home in case Bruce was there. Seeing him was out of the question. Not until I was ready. Or until he asked. In any case, it was pretty clear there would be no quick reconciliation, so I was forced to give up on that fantasy. I assumed people were starting to notice that they hadn't received our invitations yet, although I didn't get a single call from anyone asking why. Not Kimby, not Annie, not even Nicole, who'd probably be delighted to hear that she wouldn't have to be a fat, ugly bridesmaid after all.

When I finally got a message, it was from Jade. Hearing his voice practically gave me a heart attack.

"Uh, hi. This is Jade. Evie's…trainer. I, uh, wanted to know if you're going to come back to the club. Your membership fees are, uh, due, because that last post-dated check was returned NSF. So call me…or whoever. 'Bye."

I erased it immediately, thankful that Bruce hadn't heard it yet.

So Jade actually caved in and called me first. That felt pretty good. I wasn't sure if he would, although he must have been wondering what the hell had happened to me. But with everything else going on, I hadn't bothered dealing with him. I just couldn't. Now that he was obviously interested in what was up with me—assuming that whole check thing was a cover-up to make sure Bruce didn't get suspicious—I figured I'd better call him and get it over with.

I phoned the gym and they paged him. After what felt like an hour, he finally picked up.

"Hello."

"Jade?" The pastrami sandwich and fries I had for lunch rumbled disagreeably. "It's Evie."

"Evie," he whispered. "What's going on? Where have you been?"

He cared. He really did. I don't know what I expected. I guess in all the craziness I forgot that we really shared something special, no matter how wrong it was or how much I regretted it now. Still, his concern made me a little uneasy. And so did the fact that I liked that he still cared. I didn't think I would, since the mere thought of Jade had made me sick to my stomach three times in the last two weeks.

"There's been so much going on, I just didn't know..."

"What are you talking about?"

Although I'd decided not to tell him what had happened, and just give him some line about how it would be better if we didn't see each other anymore, I decided to fill him in.

"Bruce knows."

"About what?"

"About you and me."

"Oh. Shit. How?"

"It's not important. Suffice it to say that he's very clever and has a way of finding things out."

"Well, does he want to kick my ass or something? 'Cause I don't want to have anything to do with—"

"No, no. He doesn't even know your name."

"Good."

"But he called off the wedding."

"Yikes. You okay?"

"Yeah, yeah," I said, being brave and tough. "It's for the best." My mental state was definitely none of his business anymore.

"So what are you going to do?" he asked.

"I'm not sure. Maybe travel for a while." I don't know where I got this stuff.

"What about your job?"

"Oh. I quit."

"Nice! That's good news, at least."

"Yeah, tell me about it," I said. Why was I bothering to lie to him? I should have just hung up. To hell with him.

"So where are you going to go?" he asked

"I don't know."

"Why don't you head out to California? Visit your dad. Hey! You know what? Maybe I could come with you. We could both use a vacation."

"I don't know if that's such a good idea." The image of us frolicking naked in a suite at the Beverly Hills Hotel then sharing a romantic dinner at some trendy beachside bistro in Malibu forced its way into my head. Maybe I wasn't as over him as I thought I was. Or maybe I was just afraid that it really was over with Bruce. And even if it was, did I actually want Jade in my life anymore?

"I miss you, you know," he said, lowering his voice. "That night was pretty hot. I'd like it if maybe we could do it again. Imagine what an entire week in L.A. would be like…"

It was a bit much. At the very least, I knew I couldn't trust myself to make any important decisions right now. "I'll let you know," I said.

"Sure," he said. "You've got a lot going on right now. I understand. Take some time. But promise me you'll give it some serious thought. You've got my number, right?"

"Yeah."

"So call me."

"All right," I said.

"Oh…and your check really did bounce. Can you bring in another?"

19

"Why haven't you called me, Mom? It's been over two weeks since I spoke to you. I could be dead in the gutter for all you know."

"Why should I be worried about you?" she asked.

That hurt. "Just because you have a boyfriend now doesn't mean you can put everything else in your life on hold and ignore your family," I informed her.

"I don't care for your tone, Evelyn. If you're accusing me of having a good time with Albert, then fine—I admit it. We've been enjoying each other's company quite a bit lately, which you'd know if *you* ever called *me*."

"Whatever."

"And if you must know, I did call you. Last week. I spoke to Bruce. He didn't give you the message?"

"No." It wouldn't have killed him to call me and tell me, although it sounded like at least he was being discreet. But at least he knew better than to broadcast our private business to anyone who called.

"Really?" she said. "I doubt that. But I accept your apology, Evelyn. You can see that I haven't been neglecting you."

"I didn't apologize," I pointed out, but she ignored me.

"Claire told me she hasn't spoken to you in over a month. Why haven't you called her? Forget about me, but are you so busy you can't even make time to call your own grandmother? Really. Your selfishness amazes me, Evelyn. Sometimes, it's hard to believe you're my own flesh and blood."

"But—"

"Why am I bickering with you about this? I have better things to do," she said, and hung up.

I called her back immediately.

"Aren't you wondering why you didn't get your invitation yet?"

"I hadn't noticed. But I didn't think I needed an invitation to attend my own daughter's wedding. Are you trying to tell me something? Is this your way of saying you don't want Albert to come? I'm not stupid, you know. I can tell you don't like him. You've made that pretty clear. What has he ever done to you? He's been nothing but kind to you and Bruce...."

"That's *not* why!" I yelled. "The wedding's off!"

"What? What are you talking about? What is it now? Oh, I knew this was too good to be true."

"He dumped me."

"Now why would he go and do a thing like that? Evelyn, I have no time for this. We've all had just about enough of your dramatics, I can tell you. But this really takes the cake. There are far better ways to get attention, you know, if that's what you're looking for, although you certainly get enough of it already, if you ask me...."

As she droned on and on, the only way I could think of to show her I was serious was the truth. To spare her the horror of what I'd done—and since I was already bearing the burden of enough shame over this for the both of us—I'd planned to lie to her about the whole thing and say that Bruce and I jus couldn't make it work, and that we wanted to postpone the wedding for a year, but I could see now that she'd never let it go at that.

"Mom...Mom! Listen to me for a second. I'm going to tell you why. But I don't want you to freak out," I said. This admission would have to be carefully framed so as not to elicit a nervous breakdown. On either of our parts.

"I'm listening Evelyn, but hurry up, because I have to pack. Albert's taking me to the Catskills and he's picking me up in one hour."

"I had an affair."

"What? What kind of affair? A party? And you didn't invite me?"

"No, Mom. Not *that* kind of affair! The grown-up kind. I had sex with my personal trainer! Wild, passionate sex! And Bruce found out about it and he kicked me out! *That's* why we're not getting married."

"AGGGGHHHHHH!"

"Listen Mom...Mom?" She was moaning. "I'm staying with Morgan now. If you need to reach me, she's in the book. Have a good time with Albert," I said, and hung up. That'd show her.

Telling Mom made it feel official, so I thought I'd better go home and pack a bag or two. I didn't even have any makeup with me, for God's sake, and only three pairs of underwear.

The Fourth of July would be a perfect time to sneak in and out with a few things, since I assumed Bruce would be at his mother's for her annual barbecue, an event nauseating enough on its own without the creamy coleslaw and potato salad sitting out in the sun. But when I walked though the door, there he was, sitting on the couch with a book.

"Hi," he said, without looking up.

"Oh. Sorry. I didn't think you'd be here. I, uh, just came to get a few things. If you want, I can come back another day." I had every right to be there, since more often than not I did pay half the rent, but I didn't want to make him feel uncomfortable. And it's not like *I* could have kicked him out. He hadn't done anything wrong.

"It's fine. I'll be in the kitchen. Take your time."

I grabbed a big suitcase from the storage room and filled it up quickly. Being there made my heart ache, and seeing Bruce again made me want to cry. His face was so familiar, yet I had the sinking feeling that I hardly knew him anymore. It suddenly occurred to me that I hated not knowing what was going on with him, how he was feeling or what he was thinking. And it had been that way for more than just the past two weeks. I hadn't been there for him in months, maybe even years.

As I stuffed lipsticks into my makeup bag, I thought about what it was like when we first started dating, before he became just Bruce. I was so intrigued by him, this completely straight, WASPy guy from Connecticut who'd gone to all the best schools and hung out with all the right people. As I got to know him, I realized how quirky he was beneath the surface. But I loved how different he was from me, how he seemed to be living in his own world, and how much I wanted to be a part of it. Everything he said amazed me. *When had I stopped listening?*

"I'm leaving," I called out.

"Wait," he said, coming to the door. "Here's your mail." He handed me a stack of envelopes.

I looked through them quickly. Except for one with a return address from Kendra White (hopefully my last paycheck), they were all from credit card companies and collection agencies.

"They've been calling, too," Bruce said. "What should I tell them?"

"Tell them the truth—that I've moved out, and you don't know where I am."

"I know where you are, Evie," he said. "You're at Morgan's."

"How do you know?"

"Where else would you go?" he asked, then clearly regretted it. The look on his face told me he'd never considered the other possibility.

"I'm not with him, you know," I said quietly, heat rising to my cheeks.

"It's fine. You can do whatever you want now."

"No I can't," I said, because I didn't want that to be true. Not because I was afraid to be alone, but because I wanted to be with Bruce. At that moment, I knew I wanted him back more than anything, *anything,* I'd ever wanted before. And I knew that I had messed it all up. *Me.*

"Yes, you can."

"But I don't want things to change," I said, dropping the bag and sliding down the wall onto the floor. Maybe he was feeling it, too, that this was all just a big mistake that we could somehow work through like everything else. But would he ever be able to forgive me? I had to find out. "I want to come back home," I told him.

"Well you can't."

His words cut through me like a blade, and I covered my face with my hands. "But why?" I whispered, not wanting to hear the answer.

"Because...because I don't know who you are," he said, fiddling with the lock on the door.

"Oh. Okay." I was numb.

"Yeah, well..."

"I guess I'll go."

"Maybe you'd better."

I picked myself up off the floor and stepped outside. "Are you okay?" I asked. It was sweltering-hot, and it didn't feel right just leaving him there all alone.

"Yes," he said, and shut the door behind me.

Morgan came home late that night to find me in bed with a pint of cherry-vanilla Häagen-Dazs and an empty pizza box.

"He's never going to take me back," I wept.

"I didn't know you wanted him back," she said. "Pass me that spoon."

"Of course I did. He's the best thing that ever happened to me."

"Don't sell yourself short. Maybe you're the best thing that ever happened to him. Did you ever think of that? If Bruce can't see that, then maybe you're better off without him."

She was only trying to make me feel better, but what I really needed was for someone to tell it to me straight. I'd been deluding myself for long enough, and I wanted to hear the truth for a change. "I don't think so, Morgan. I'm the one who fucked this up."

She shrugged and took a bite of ice cream.

"Maybe I should start getting my life back on track," I continued, although I had no idea where to start. Just because I knew the right thing didn't mean I could do it.

"Amen to that," she said, slapping my thigh. It jiggled ominously.

Even if her advice wasn't always the most constructive, Morgan had been a truly good friend, providing unconditional support at all hours of the day and night. Billy also loaned a sympathetic ear from time to time, and he always invited me to join them for dinner. Mostly, though, I just ate by myself, although I did appreciate the offers. I thought about what a shame it was that Bruce and I never really hung out with them. After getting to know Billy a little better, I'm sure that Bruce would actually have liked him quite a bit. But the idea of the four of us hanging out made me feel lonelier than ever.

"Where should I start?" I asked her. "How can I put my life back together?"

"You could try going out on a date," she suggested.

"I was thinking something more along the lines of a pottery class," I informed her. "I'm definitely not ready to date someone new. Unless…"

"Oh no. Don't even think it."

"Maybe You-Know-Who would be the best thing for me right now," I said, although I knew better. "I could use the distraction. And he makes me completely hate myself, which I deserve, so it would be a great way to make myself even more miserable for a while."

Morgan shook her head. "Oh, no you don't. You *cannot* have a relationship with that man. Punishing yourself is not the answer. He is *not* relationship material. Trust me."

"How would you know?" I was just curious.

"Evie, he's just not. I could see it in his eyes. And you can't turn a fling into a real thing. From the looks of you these days, I'd say you're barely even ready for a rebound guy. So just forget it."

"I guess. But the sex…"

"Don't make me laugh. That was definitely a one-shot deal. Nothing good can come out of it anymore, considering the baggage attached to that guy now. And do you really think dragging things out with Jade will make losing Bruce worth it? Believe me. It won't."

"I know that, Morgan. I'm not really considering it. I was just thinking out loud. But we did have real chemistry, you know. You of all people should be able to understand at least—"

"Chemistry is what happens in a lab," she quipped. "In the real world, you make your own sparks."

"But it was so thrilling. Different than being with Bruce."

"You know, you say that all the time, but I think you might be overlooking what was in your own backyard," she said sternly. "I can tell you right now that Bruce is fantastic in bed. And I usually have a pretty good instinct for these things."

A surge of jealousy swelled up into my throat. I sensed that Bruce was always sort of afraid of Morgan. He called her the Maneater, but he probably just wanted her to take a bite out of him. It had never occurred to me until now that it might have gone both ways.

"Bruce *is* good in bed," I said defensively. "And so am I. But maybe we're just not that great *together,*" I explained.

She shook her head. "Of course the sex is going to suffer if you have all these crazy issues hanging over your head. That's probably what happened with Bruce—you let it slide. You have to work on it, you know. And what you had with Jade, by the way, was just circumstance. Like me and Peter. You think we'd still be hot for each other if it wasn't so completely wrong for both of us? No way." Maybe she was right. If there was one thing the girl knew about, it was sex.

"Are you saying that me and You-Know-Who could just have casual sex as long as there was no relationship to get in the way, and it would still be good?"

"No. Look at you—you can't even say his name! You're way too involved. Besides, you've never done that sort of thing before, and while I condone the practice wholeheartedly, you're just not ready for the forced emotional distance it requires."

"I have so done it before. Remember Pierre?"

She rolled her eyes. "It doesn't count if he's a foreign exchange student who was only here for three months. And he was your first, for God's sake. Evie, you're twenty-seven years old and you've only been with three guys, including Jade, and you were with Bruce for like seven years. You're definitely lacking in experience."

"Some people would say three guys is a lot, you know."

"Who? Your mother? Just please trust me. You don't want to be starting anything with this guy."

I knew there was no potential for anything serious between me and Jade. Even if there had been, I certainly wouldn't have wanted any part of it. Not now, anyway. The more I thought about it, the less I believed our little tryst was about the sex or the circumstances or the excitement, and the more I saw it for what it was—a way for me to completely ruin my life while taking as little responsibility for it as possible. Kind of like a self-imposed nervous breakdown. Things had been out of control for too long, at work, with Bruce, with Mom. Sleeping with Jade made that all go away. And getting caught just sealed the deal. There was nothing to go back to after that. And miserable though it might be, at least my life was my own again.

But I still felt like I had to come clean with Jade for some reason, just to get some closure on that part of my life. Maybe I wanted him to know that I'd been the one using him, and not the other way around, the way Morgan obviously saw it. But Jade had been nothing but a perfect gentleman with me from day one, and as my friend he deserved the truth. No more lies. No more dishonesty. I was turning over a new leaf and putting it all behind me.

Friday night, Morgan went to the opening of a gallery designed by Billy's firm. They invited me to come, but I declined. I had a stiff drink, then called Jade at home.

"I've been thinking about what you said," I told him.

"Excellent. I've been thinking a lot about you, too."

"I want to come clean."

"Sure thing."

"Well," I said, bracing myself. "I haven't been honest."

"What do you mean?"

"I didn't quit my job. I got fired." Best to start with an easy one.

He laughed. "That's okay. There's nothing to be embarrassed about. You know how many times I've been fired? Once, in college, I was working as a night watchman for this huge electronics store, and my friends came by one night and—"

"Jade, let me finish. I can't go away with you. I don't think it would be a good idea. Any of it. You and me, I mean. We had some fun, but..."

"You sure you don't want to go to L.A.? Come on! Live a little!"

"Jade, my dad doesn't live in L.A. He's not a casting director." I took a deep breath. "He's...well...uh, he's dead."

He let it sink in for a bit, then said, "That's fine. I understand."

"I don't know why I lied. I guess I wanted you to like me. Isn't that ridiculous?"

He didn't answer.

"Wow. I'm *so* relieved," I continued. "I definitely didn't want you to think I was some kind of pathological liar or something, since I was thinking about coming back to the gym soon and, I don't know, if you ever went to L.A. or something and you thought my dad could get you a job, you know?"

"You're right. I'm glad you told me," he said finally. I knew it was the right thing to do. "And since we're being totally honest," he added. "I did lie to you, too. Once."

Uh-oh. "When?"

"That night, at my place. You asked me if you were the only client I'd ever brought home...."

"And you said no," I reminded him.

"But that wasn't entirely true."

"Oh."

"I've been there with clients before," he said.

"Like, one or two?" I asked cautiously.

"Well...less than a dozen."

"Oh."

"Yeah, well..."

"So I guess I'll talk to you soon?" I asked, sensing something not altogether good had just happened.

"Sure. Talk to you soon," he said, and hung up.

I tossed and turned all night. It was no good. Was he mad at me? *I* was the one who had a right to be mad. My lie was harmless. His lie was, well, deceptive. The only thing I knew for certain was that I was suddenly very glad I'd insisted we use a condom (make that condoms) even though he hadn't wanted to. I was also pretty sure that I had to go and see him in person and say my piece.

★ ★ ★

There was a new girl working behind the desk when I walked into the gym the following afternoon. I realized I hadn't been there in a month. Pushing thoughts of my impending obesity out of my mind, I flashed her my membership card and went straight to the cardio room to look for Jade. At first, I didn't see him. As I made my way toward the stairs that led up to the weights, I saw him. In the back corner, near the scales. He was talking very intimately with a girl, a chubby girl. He stroked her arm.

My God. He has an M.O.

I watched, disgusted, as he whispered something in her ear and she threw her head back and laughed. She looked ridiculous. It was too much to bear—I stormed over to the corner and waited for him to notice me.

Chubby cleared her throat and Jade turned around.

"Hey! Evie!" he smiled, in a masterful attempt to distract me from his guilt. "Long time no see."

"Hello," I said coolly.

Sensing my impending attack, he turned back to Chubby and said, "Why don't you go and start on your abs, Cecile. I'll be right up." She glared at me and left.

"You look different..." Jade said as soon as she was out of earshot. "Bloated, maybe?"

The nerve. "I'm not *bloated,*" I said. "And I'm not PMS-ing or hysterical or anything else, if that's what you're thinking."

"Calm down," he hissed, looking around to make sure no one had heard. "Don't go getting all weird on me. What's wrong with you?"

"Was that one of the clients you never brought home?" I wasn't exactly jealous, but I was a little mad—at myself. Why hadn't I been able to see through this guy?

"Actually, yes. I mean no."

"Well which is it?"

"Yes, she's a client, and no, I've never brought her home." His eyes were as hypnotically green as ever. It was tempting to take him at his word. "But we are sleeping together," he added.

Filthy cad!

"What did you say?" I gasped, shocked. This was not the gentlemanly Jade I'd fallen for. "Evie, I am *so* sorry if you somehow got the impression that we were exclusive," he said, putting his hand on my shoulder. "But I never said..."

"What the hell are you talking about? I dumped you, remember?" I smacked his hand away.

"When?" he laughed.

"Last night on the phone."

"Did you think I was waiting around for you or something?"

"No, that's not what I thought. But you—you lied to me. If I'd known you were sleeping with twenty-eight different people, I never would have..."

"It wasn't twenty-eight. Not even close to that many," he said, thinking carefully. "And weren't you sleeping with someone else, too?" he asked.

"Bruce doesn't count."

"Why not?"

"Because you knew about him," I said.

"So?"

"I didn't know about that...Cecilia, or whatever her name is."

"Actually," he said dreamily, "Cecile and I only had sex for the first time this morning."

"Ohh!" I moaned, putting my hands over my ears. *I was such an idiot.*

"Hey—you have no right to be pissed off. You never asked me if I was screwing anybody else!" He was beginning to get a little hot under the collar himself.

"But I *did*. When we were in the bar, before we'd even had a drink! I explicitly asked you if you were involved with anyone, and you said no."

"Well, I wasn't involved with anyone. But that doesn't mean I wasn't getting any."

Morgan was right. He really was a piece of shit. I don't know what disturbed me more—that I would never be able to trust my own judgment again or the fact that I was so easily flattered into this guy's bed. At least now I knew the vulnerability of my own ego.

"To think that I actually came here because I wanted to make sure things were okay between us, because I thought we were friends. But you know what? You make me sick!" I all but yelled. "You're like…like some sort of sex-crazed Dr. Frankenstein, creating worshipful adorers in your own image and then casting them aside once you've had your way with them…"

"Shhh," he said, and grabbed my wrist. "You might not have to show your face here anymore, but I work here every day."

But there was no stopping me. I twisted free of his grip. "And what was all that about wanting to go to L.A.? Was it just because you thought my dad could get you a job?"

He tapped his foot impatiently. "Whatever, Evie. I have to get back to work, so can we wrap this up?"

My face flushed hot with anger, then embarrassment. I would not cry. I would not cry for this loser.

"What am I even doing here?" I asked myself aloud.

"C'mon, lighten up," he said. "It doesn't have to end like this."

"If it wasn't ending badly, then it wouldn't be ending at all," I said. I remembered reading that somewhere, but it only now just made sense.

"Suit yourself," he conceded, shrugging. "Maybe once you've cleared your head a little, we can still be friends. I meant what I said the other day about having a good time with you."

"I don't think so."

"Well, at least think about it," he said, backing away. "And hey—if you're ever in my neck of the woods, give me a buzz."

I glared at him skeptically.

"Aw, don't look at me like that. You're breaking my heart! Seriously, Evie, call me—I thought we were pretty good together, didn't you? And now that you know what a good lay I am…" He winked at me, then bounded up the stairs, two at a time.

★★★

"Just don't say I told you so," I moaned to Morgan when I got home. I flopped down on the couch with a bag of chips.

"I told you so," she said.

"I can't believe what a prick he is."

"Most of them are," she confirmed. "Think of it as a life lesson."

"I'm trying to," I told her. "It just isn't fair. And no wonder he was so good in bed—he's been with *thousands* of women." (*Mademoiselle,* March: "Does Your Man Love Women *Too* Much? 10 Ways To Tell.")

"That has nothing to do with it. They're either born with it or they're not. Bruce was probably born with it, too, you just never noticed."

I was in no mood for her to be extolling the virtues of Saint Bruce.

"Maybe now would be a good time for you to take note that the whole 'somebody on the side' thing doesn't always work out, Morgan. It ruined my marriage before it even started. You might want to think about that."

"Oh, I have. I've called it off with Peter until after the wedding."

"That's very noble of you. Confusing, but noble."

"I know. And although I hate to point out the obvious, I think I'll be able to make it work just a little better than you did. You aren't very good at keeping a secret. I mean, please—it's like you wanted to get caught."

"That seems a little sadomasochistic, even for me. But you might have a point," I admitted. I did minor in psychology after all, and I knew that the mind has funny ways of revealing itself. My life was so out of control for so long, that maybe I just couldn't take it anymore, and so I sabotaged myself in order to bring everything to a crashing halt.

Morgan nodded. "You never did well with change, Evie. It was probably all just too much for you to handle."

"Well, in my case that may be. But sometimes accidents happen, lipstick ends up on a collar or whatever, and even the cleverest of cheaters gets caught. Did you ever stop to think about what would happen if Peter's wife found out about you?"

"I think she already knows."

"You don't know that. You just tell yourself she does so you can pretend it wouldn't bother her. We don't live in France, Morgan—wives here don't just ignore their husbands' affairs. I bet if she knew she'd kick Peter out in a second. And then his kids would have no father, and they'd be miserable forever and it would all be your fault."

"No, Evie," she said sharply. "It would be Peter's fault for messing around in the first place."

"Like if it wasn't you, it would be somebody else anyway, right? That's a lame excuse. And what if Billy found out and it totally devastated him and he divorced you and moved to a monastery in the Alps or something?"

"God, what a loss that would be to women everywhere," she said wryly. "He's incredibly well-hung, you know."

"Seriously."

She sighed deeply. "Well, then that would be my fault, I guess."

"When you get married, you can't just think about yourself anymore."

"I know that." She was getting huffy, but I didn't care—she needed to hear it.

"I'm just trying to spare you the pain and the shit I've been going through, and spare Billy, too."

"Well isn't this the pot calling the kettle black," she said.

"Maybe. But for once, I'm the one with the experience here," I said. "Why can't you see that Billy deserves to be treated as well as he treats you? You owe him that."

"What's all this about? Do you have a crush on my fiancé or something?" She glared at me accusingly.

"Don't be ridiculous," I snapped. "Listen to me. You obviously don't know what you're doing. You were all for my cheating on Bruce, and look how that turned out."

"Evie, the only reason you're in this mess right now is because you *didn't* listen to me, not because you did."

"I'm not saying it's your fault, Morgan, but you're the one who put the possibility of actually doing it in my head in the first place. You said it was okay...no, you said it would be *good* for me to have a fling!"

"No. What I said was, go for it, but only if you could handle it and avoid hurting Bruce, which you obviously couldn't. *You're* the one who did all the hurting here, not me! I haven't hurt anyone! So screw you!" she said, slamming the door on her way out.

She'd barely been gone for five minutes when the phone rang. The caller ID said Evelyn Mays. I picked it up.

"Hello?"

"Hi." It was Bruce. "Um, last week, I forgot to tell you that Claire called."

"She did?"

"Yeah."

"What did you tell her?"

"I spoke to her for a long time."

"What did she say?"

"She knows what happened. I guess your mom told her. She's worried about you, so maybe you should give her a call."

I'd been far too ashamed to talk to Claire about any of this. She's the only one in the family who seems to have any real moral standards (Mom's don't count, since they all come from the Church). Although I was embarrassed, I was also relieved. I was glad I wouldn't have to be the one to tell her. But I still didn't want to call her.

"Okay," I told him.

"And there's something else," he said. "If you want, I could still make that appointment for you. With the therapist. You seemed pretty down."

"So did you," I said.

"Well, of course…"

"Maybe we could see someone together," I asked hopefully.

"I don't think so."

Too much, too soon. But I wasn't going to let the opportunity slip away. "I understand. Maybe it would be good for me, though, like you said. Will you call me with the information?"

"Okay," he said agreeably.

Pretty much everyone I know has been in therapy or at least on Prozac or Paxil at one time or another, so there was really no shame in it. And if going to some shrink would help me get Bruce back, then that's what I'd have to do.

20

The next morning, I apologized to Morgan. I knew that what happened with Bruce wasn't her fault, technically speaking. She graciously accepted, and to celebrate we went out for brunch. Since most people seem to work six days a week in New York, Sunday brunch in the city requires a lot of patience, because there are about eight million people who had the exact same idea you did.

"I've been on edge," I told her as we waited in line at the hottest new diner in SoHo.

"No. Really?"

"And I'm beginning to feel a bit like an intruder at your place."

"Why would you say that?" she asked. "If I needed to crash at your place, would you mind?"

"No," I admitted. "But you just got engaged, and you and Billy hardly get to see each other as it is, so when I'm there all the time…I don't know, it must suck."

"I see Billy plenty," she said. "He sleeps over plenty. And we're not exactly the most codependent couple."

What I didn't mention was that when Billy did sleep over, I spent half the night awake listening to them have sex. At first I was grossed out (and a little impressed—the guy could literally go all night), but now I was just annoyed. I needed my own place. We were too old to be roommates.

"Still, you deserve your privacy. And I'd like to give you some rent, too," I told her.

"Forget it."

"Thank God. I barely have enough money to pay for lunch," I half joked. "But I figured I should at least offer."

Morgan shrugged it off. "If it weren't for my big mouth, you probably wouldn't be living with me, anyway."

"Please, let's not get into that again," I said. "But I'm serious. Is there anything I can do to help out? It would make me feel better."

"How about you pay for the cleaning lady this week."

"Okay," I said, happy to be able to contribute in some way.

Since there wasn't much left of that last paycheck after I paid off all the minimum balances on the cards, I was in deep trouble. Of course, I had no savings whatsoever, except for a meager $1100 in a 401k that I'd put aside in a fit of responsibility three years ago (*Glamour,* February: "Retirement Planning: A Little Now Means a Lot Later!"). But once I had a job, everything would be fine, I reasoned. And how hard could it be to find something, especially since I was willing to take anything, no matter how horrid, and consider it temporary.

A hostess finally led us to a booth. No sooner than I'd tucked into my eggs Benedict, I noticed a familiar face in the crowd. It was Theo. With Kimby, Nicole, Annie and a guy I didn't know. I thought I saw Nicole make a face when she recognized me. I considered making a break for it.

"Evie!" Annie said as the hostess led them past our table. There were like 18,000 restaurants in the city. What were the odds of them coming here?

Kimby seemed surprised to see me. "Hey, look who it is,"

she said coolly. "How are you?" They all stopped to revel in my misery.

"Hello, Mooorgan," Theo cooed, then whispered something into the ear of the guy he was with. They both giggled.

"Stop being so rude," Kimby said to them. "Evie, what's going on? I called you at work a couple of weeks ago and they said you'd left."

"And I heard the wedding was off," Nicole piped in. "My step-cousin went to school with Bruce's sister, remember?"

"But we didn't think it was true," Annie added, shooting Nicole a dark glare. "I figured you'd call if something had happened."

They waited for me to say that everything was fine, but I couldn't.

"She's had a lot going on," Morgan told them.

Nicole's eyes widened. "So it's *true?*" she gasped. "I can't *believe* it."

"That seems to be the standard reaction," I said.

Annie slid onto the bench beside me and put her arm around my waist. "I'm *so* sorry, Evie. I can't believe it." Annie was sweet. I knew she really meant it, and I suddenly felt awful for not telling her. She was, after all, supposed to be one of my best friends.

"Does that mean Bruce is available?" Theo snickered, and Kimby elbowed him. "What? Can't a guy ask?"

"I'm sorry I didn't call," I said. "I guess I didn't really feel like dealing with everyone, you know?"

"Of course, honey," Annie said. "You don't owe us anything."

"But I still should've called," I told her.

"Yeah, well I was starting to get a bit aggravated," Kimby admitted. "I thought maybe you'd forgotten about us. Nobody's spoken to you in weeks, and you never approved the final fittings."

"I was wondering why I didn't get an invitation," Nicole added curtly. She was probably disappointed that she no longer had a reason to be mad at me. "What are we supposed to do with our dresses, now? I was really starting to like mine." Maybe not.

"My food's getting cold," Morgan said loudly. Subtlety was never her strong suit, and I loved her dearly for it.

"Seriously," Theo said, ignoring her. "I was incredibly hot in that tux… And I was *sooo* looking forward to fulfilling my duties as a groomsman at the bachelor party…."

"All of you, shush!" Annie snapped. "You're being cruel. What happened, Evie? Are you okay?"

I couldn't talk.

"Things just didn't work out," Morgan said, sensing I was about to lose it.

"That's it?" Nicole said. "Something must have happened."

"Would you mind if I filled you in later?" I said. "I don't really feel up to this right now. Not here, anyway."

"Of course," Kimby said, eager to change the subject. "Give me a call this week. It's Annie's birthday on Saturday and we're going to this great new club on Avenue B."

Theo nodded. "Definitely. You've got to get back on that horse, dear—now's the time to snag another man! *Before* you get fat again."

I managed a weak laugh. "Thanks." He meant well.

"Don't listen to him," Nicole said, eyeing the greasy home fries on my plate. "I'm sure you'll keep the weight off." She was trying to jinx me. And I didn't even have the strength to resent it, even though my wardrobe was become progressively tighter by the day. I could hardly do up my pants.

"'Bye," I said, and hugged Annie. "I'll call you later this week."

After they left, Morgan said. "Well that sucked."

"They're not so bad. It was crappy of me not to call anyone. No wonder they're pissed."

"Still. You're the one they should feel sorry for, not themselves. You don't have to make excuses—a terrible thing happened to you and they should understand 100 percent. God, it's like they were actually *enjoying* it. Especially that fat one. How can you not want to kill her?"

"In case you haven't noticed," I said weakly, "I don't have many friends. If it weren't for them, you'd be the only one."

After an entire week of job-hunting, I only managed to land two interviews—one with a telemarketing company that sold gems in bulk, and one for a part-time position as an assistant basketball coach for a girls' high school in the Bronx. There was no point in going to either of them, since there was no chance in hell I'd take the first job (working on commission was out of the question), and I'd out-and-out lied to get the second. Since I'd clearly run out of choices, bankruptcy seemed the only way to go (*Cosmopolitan,* December: "Life After Chapter 7: Fight Your Way Back from Financial Ruin!"). I called and left a message for Bruce so that he could tell the collection agencies to stop harassing him.

He called me back almost immediately.

"Declaring bankruptcy is definitely *not* a good idea," he pleaded with me. "It'll take you *years* to build up a decent credit rating again." Like that was such a bad thing. No matter how angry he was, I knew that Bruce wouldn't be able to resist trying to prevent me from making what he thought was an asinine decision.

"What choice do I have? At least this way, they'll stop hassling you," I told him.

"Save the martyr act, Evie," he said. He sounded mildly amused. It was a start. "Call Claire. Tell her what's going on. That's my advice."

"I still have my pride, you know." Just barely.

"You won't if you go bankrupt."

"We'll see."

"You really have no clue what you're doing, do you?" he mused. "And that reminds me. I wasn't sure if you were serious, but I made an appointment for you with Dr. Shloff. Next Monday at nine."

"Nine a.m.? Bruce, that's a little early to be dissecting my issues with my father with a complete stranger, don't you think?"

"Just tell me if you're not going to go because I'll cancel it. Someone at school did me a really big favor to get the appointment. Dr. Shloff's practice is pretty much closed and she's very hard to get in to see. But I still think it would be a really good idea for you—she's supposed to be wonderful."

"I said I'd go!"

"Good. So that's July 23, okay? At nine."

"I know, Bruce. You told me."

"And promise me you won't do anything stupid until you speak to Claire. It could ruin your life."

My life already was ruined, but at least he still cared.

It didn't take a genius to see that Bruce was probably right about the bankruptcy thing. I did a little research, and found out that if I filed, it could be ages before anyone would give me a credit card again. The thought of that was enough to scare me straight. No doubt about it—family was the way to go in times like these. It was the least of all possible evils. I'd definitely ask Claire, though. Even if Mom could help me out for a while, which she probably couldn't, the protracted torment of her I-told-you-sos and witless lectures on fiscal responsibility would surely make declaring bankruptcy seem like winning the lottery.

Instead of calling and asking over the phone, I stopped by Claire's apartment on Sunday night when I knew she'd be home.

Her wrinkled face lit up when she opened the door.

"Evie, is that you?" She rubbed her eyes.

"You know it's me."

"I wasn't sure. I barely recognized you."

"Ha, ha."

"Come in. I'm sorry, dear. You should know that I've talked to Bruce, and your mother, and I already know about everything," she said before I could even sit down.

"I know. I should have called, but I was too embarrassed."

"There's nothing to be embarrassed about—you're my own flesh and blood," she said as she put some hot water on. Claire thought the answers to all the world's problems could be solved over a pot of tea.

"Yeah, but what I did…"

"What you did was a mistake, plain and simple," she said without skipping a beat. "And it sounds like you already know that."

"I do. I really do."

"Of course you do," she said. I suddenly remembered why I spent most of my teenage years at her place. Just being in the presence of unconditional love has a way of making even the most insurmountable problem seem like a cakewalk. "The only question now," she continued, "is what are you going to do about it?"

I told her absolutely everything, including my intentions to make it up to Bruce and win him back. She spoke to him all the time, so maybe she'd put in a good word for me when the time was right, or at the very least, let him know I was on the right track. For the first time in a long while, after I'd poured out my entire heart and soul, I really believed that everything was going to be okay.

Before I left, she took out her checkbook, signed three and handed them to me.

"Take whatever you need. No granddaughter of mine is filing for bankruptcy," she said, more to herself than anyone. "But it's a loan, not a gift. When you're back on your feet and you've found a job, we'll come to an arrangement about your paying me back."

"Thanks, Grandma," I said and kissed her cheek. "You're saving my life."

She stared at me, shocked. "So that's all it took to get you to start calling me Grandma? I should have done this years ago!" she said.

"I'm so sorry about everything."

"Evie, just promise me you'll be good to yourself from now on. Take some time to think about things, grab hold of your life again. And cut up your credit cards!"

"I already have!" It was true—sort of. Technically, Morgan had done the dirty deed for me.

"Everybody deserves a second chance, sweetheart. Just try to make the most of it."

With the weight of the world lifted from my shoulders, I vowed to take advantage of my fresh start. And that meant getting Bruce to see the new, responsible me was a top priority. All that remained to be done was find a job, see that shrink and keep from doing anything completely idiotic.

But why was it always so much easier than it sounded?

Despite a few days of relative calm, things got ugly again the next weekend. I was still calling in for my messages every day, since I had applications pending at four or five potential employers (including Iberian Airlines, who I'd heard were desperate for flight attendants—good thing I had those two years of high-school Spanish under my belt!). There was no sense in giving out Morgan's number because I didn't know exactly how long I'd be there, and Bruce didn't seem to mind me giving out my old number. Actually, he probably had no idea I was doing it.

And then there it was, clear as a bell, the following Friday morning—a woman's voice on the machine.

"Hi, Bruce. Um, I guess you're still at school, but I just wanted to confirm for tonight. Six o'clock at the Boathouse in Prospect Park, right? I'll bring the wine. So…I guess I'll see you there, then. Oh [giggle giggle]—it's Daphne, but I guess you already knew that! Yeah, well…I think I'd better hang up know. 'Bye!"

Daphne? I knew that name. She worked with Bruce—I think she was a teacher's aide or a janitor or something like that. I immediately dialed the school.

"May I speak with Daphne?" I asked.

"Sorry, she's off Fridays during the summer. Can I put you through to her voice mail?"

I hung up. My head was spinning. Bruce had a date? A *date?* It couldn't be. We'd hardly been broken up for a month, and he was dating? It didn't make any sense. But why else would he be meeting her there? Unless it was a work thing. There was a zoo in Prospect Park… Maybe they were planning to take the kids on a field trip there in the fall and they were scouting locations. But those kids wouldn't be interested in some lame old zoo. And why would she be bringing wine? *Oh God, this can't be real. I cannot let this happen.*

My first instinct was to erase the message. Bruce probably hadn't heard it yet, otherwise he would have erased it himself. But even if I did get rid of it, what difference would it make? Bruce would never forget about a date, and I'm sure he knew exactly when and where it was.

After several long hours spent teetering on the brink of emotional collapse—especially after I called to listen to the message for the seventeenth time only to discover that it was gone—I vowed to do what Claire had advised, and take control of my life. As much as I may have wanted to, I didn't call Morgan, who'd probably try and deter me from my plan. I would go to the park and see for myself what was going on. Bruce would never know. He'd never see me.

I arrived at 5:30, just in case either of them were early. That left me with plenty of time to relax and wonder about why Bruce had never asked me on a date to the Boathouse in Prospect Park. I sat down on the grass behind a twisted old elm, the perfect vantage point from which to view the happy couple. It was a beautiful day, and the sunlight was just beginning to fade. The reflection of the Boathouse's white columns and arched windows shimmered on the water. Worse still, tiny white flower petals rained down from the trees. It was alarmingly romantic, straight out of *The Age of Innocence* or something like that.

She arrived first. I knew it was her because she looked like someone I wouldn't like and I could see the top of a wine bottle sticking out of her backpack—and who the hell wears a backpack, anyway? (*Marie Claire,* September: "Grow Up! 12

Trends You're Probably Too Old For.") From where I was sitting, I could almost make out her features, which were nothing to write home about, and I could have sworn that she also had some sort of hideous scar. Her hair was ash-blond (an immediate strike against her), and she was wearing a prissy Laura-Ashley-type dress with flat sandals. I couldn't entirely tell how fat she was, because her dress was so billowy, but I could say with some degree of certainly that she was heavier than I was, even now. She paced back and forth from one end of the building to the next, waiting for my Bruce.

Maybe he'd changed his mind, I thought. Maybe he wouldn't show. That would teach her to steal another woman's man. But he wasn't my man, at least not anymore, I reminded myself. He was his own man, and he had every right to date whomever he pleased. What I had done more than released him from any obligation to me. And now it seemed I was the only one who retained any sense of loyalty, and that barely counted since it was obviously too little too late to earn me any points. I glanced at my watch. It was almost six. Then five past, seven past....

Just as the first hints of relief began to wash over me, he appeared from behind the Boathouse carrying a picnic basket. Instead of being furious with his tardiness and leaving him right there on the spot, she smiled broadly. He kissed her on the cheek. The bile rose in my throat and I had to sit back for a moment and catch my breath. By the time I was ready to look again, I almost couldn't find them. But there they were, walking hand-in-hand toward a clearing in the trees.

I followed them down the path until they'd picked their spot. She opened her backpack and laid out a big blanket. Bruce began pulling things out of the basket. I couldn't hear what they were saying to each other, but it didn't seem like they were fighting.

How could he?

This was all wrong—this was not how things were supposed to turn out. Before I knew it, I was walking toward them.

Maybe I could pretend that it was just a coincidence. It was a lovely day, and why wouldn't I be out taking a walk in the park? If he was embarrassed, then he should have known better than to parade his little tramp in public for everyone to see.

When Bruce saw me, the color washed out of his face. He jumped to his feet. Daphne was still smiling. She had no idea who I was.

"What...what are you doing here?" he asked, stunned.

Daphne stared at him in confusion. He smiled uneasily at her.

"I believe *I'm* the one with questions, Bruce," I said. Tears were streaming down my face. I could taste them.

"I'm sorry, Daphne," Bruce snarled between clenched teeth. "This is Evelyn, and she's a little bit confused right now. Would you mind excusing us for a few moments?"

She nodded. "Sure. Nice to meet you, Evelyn." *Nice to meet me?* Didn't she know who I was? Had Bruce not mentioned me at all?

He grabbed me by the elbow and quickly led me away.

"What the hell's the matter with you?" he asked. "No—you know what? It doesn't matter. I don't care. I want you to leave. Now."

"But, Bruce," I wailed. "I heard her message, and...and...I couldn't help it. I had to know what was going on...and I...I...you..."

"It's none of your business anymore, Evie. And I'm changing the password, so you can forget about any more stunts like this."

"You mean you're going to see her *again?*" I gasped. "What about me? What am I supposed to do? Don't you care about me anymore?" I was pathetic, I knew it, and I couldn't help it—the words were just flying out of my mouth. For all my intentions, I couldn't be cool about this. I was desperately jealous. Needy and jealous.

He sighed. "Look. I'm not angry, but will you please just go. I don't want you to make any more of a scene than you already have. It's not fair, Evie."

How could he say that? What was the matter with him? It *was* fair—why should he get to go on with his life if I couldn't? Just because I was the one who made all the mistakes didn't mean he got to stop hurting so quickly. "Is that all you care about? Me making a scene in front of your girlfriend?" Daphne, having doubtlessly been very ill-raised, stared at us indiscreetly.

"I'll give you something to look at!" I yelled at her, then slapped Bruce across the face. Or, I tried to, anyway. He pulled back at the last second, but I did make contact with the corner of his glasses, and sent them flying into the air. Instead of smashing dramatically into a thousand pieces, they landed softly on a mossy rock. He shook his head, laughed and then picked them up.

"I'm glad you're so amused, Bruce," I sobbed. "Well, congratulations for being the first to move on with your life. From now on, you won't have to worry about me. I promise. I'm calling a mover on Monday to go pick up all my stuff."

"Um, you don't really have anything there, unless you count the stacks of old magazines and stuffed animals. The furniture's all mine."

"But we bought everything *together,*" I cried.

"Yes, but, um...let's see...how can I put this? Oh yes—I *paid* for it all."

Pointing out something like that was the height of rudeness, especially in front of her. "I won't stand here and be humiliated."

"Fine. Goodbye, then," he said.

"But before I go," I said, turning to Daphne, "there's something I want to say to you...."

They both eyed me nervously.

I planned to explode into a rant about what a tramp she was, and how she didn't deserve Bruce, and how she better keep away from him if she knew what was good for her, but the words just wouldn't come. Probably because I barely believed it myself. All of my anger just melted into sadness. Bruce deserved to stop hurting, even if I was destined to suffer on forever. And Daphne was cute—there was no trace of the scar I thought I'd seen earlier—and she seemed nice. Why the hell would Bruce want to be with someone like me when here was Daphne, doting on his every word? Daphne, who wanted to go on picnics with him. Daphne who hadn't broken his heart.

"...take good care of him."

I walked away slowly, careful not to kick over their bottle of wine, although I wanted to very much.

21

The famous Dr. Shloff stared at me from across her big wooden desk. She was about a hundred years old, and I didn't trust her. Not for one second. How could anyone trust a woman who wears a tie? Especially when it comes to your love life.

"Evelyn—"

"It's Evie, actually," I told her.

"Sorry. Evie, then. Since this is our first session, let's take things slowly. I want you to tell me a bit about yourself and why you're here, and what you hope to accomplish from our sessions together."

"Sessions? I don't know that I need *sessions,* exactly. I thought maybe this could be like a one-time thing. Just to get me through this rough patch."

She glared at me through oversized glasses. On the editor of *Vogue,* they might have worked. But not on her.

"Therapy involves a serious commitment. It takes months, sometimes years to make real progress and see the effects in your everyday life."

Sounded like the only effect she was interested in was *my*

money on *her* life. "I'll think about it, but I'm pretty sure this will be a one-shot deal," I explained.

"Fine. Let's start with today, and see how it goes," she said.

"So…where do I start?"

"Start at the beginning."

"Okay." I took a sip of water and undid the top button of my shorts so I could breathe a little better. "There's not much to say. I guess I was pretty much doomed from birth…."

"Why do you say that?"

"I just was. I used to think it was my mother's fault, but now I'm not so sure."

Dr. Shloff sighed and took off her glasses, a ponderous task. "Maybe we could start with something a little less…deep-seated, especially since we only have forty-five minutes left and you don't plan on coming back."

"All right."

"I understand you've had some changes in your life recently, something that precipitated your coming to see me. What was that?"

"I was engaged. But we broke it off."

"Who did?"

"Bruce."

"Ah," she said and scribbled on her pad.

She was taking his side already. It seemed I couldn't even *buy* a whiff of sympathy in this town. "But it was the right decision. I know that. At least, for him it was."

"And why is that?"

I thought about it for a bit, then said, "I guess because if I were him I would have done the same thing. I cheated on him. Just once. And he found out."

"You told him?"

"No, he caught me."

"In the act?" She looked up from her pad.

"Sorry to disappoint you, but no. He walked in on me trying to dispose of the evidence. It's a long story."

"Did you consider your relationship to be a good one, before this happened?"

"We'd been together since college. He annoyed me sometimes, but he was my best friend."

"That sounds good."

"It was." I shifted uncomfortably. The last thing I needed was for her to tell me what I already knew.

"So why did you have an affair?"

"You're not very subtle, you know," I told her. "Aren't you supposed to beat around the bush a little here?"

"Tick-tock..."

"If you're trying to get me to promise to come back, it's not going to work."

"I don't care if you come back or not," she said. "It makes no difference to me." Sure it didn't. "But may I ask why you came here at all if you weren't planning to return?"

"Because Bruce wanted me to. He's worried about me."

"He still cares...."

"Yes," I said definitively.

"And you want to please him."

"You make it sound sick. I feel bad. I hurt him."

"How does he feel about everything that's happened between you?"

"Well, not very good. He dumped me, remember? He's mad. And incredibly depressed." I couldn't bring myself to tell her about Daphne. Sometimes, in my darkest moments, I thought I'd be happier if Bruce really was depressed. At least that would prove that he still cared.

"So you're trying to make it up to him."

"Yes," I said.

"That's a pretty tall order, don't you think?"

"I don't know." It probably was. And his new girlfriend definitely wasn't a good sign (*Mademoiselle,* July: "Will He Forgive You or Forget You? Five Ways To Tell").

"This man you had an affair with—"

"Why do you assume it was a man?"

"Was it?" she asked, without looking up this time.

"Yes."

"So this man, do you still see him?"

"No," I said. "He's a complete and total loser."

"Did you know that at the time?"

"No. Why would I have slept with him if I knew he was an asshole?" It sounded like Dr. Shloff needed some help in the romance department herself.

"Were you emotionally involved with him as well?"

"At one point, I thought he was really into me, but I was just attracted to him physically. Then, after... you know...I realized I was probably just using him, and that it wasn't going to work out. And even the thought of him was making me sick. It was a constant reminder of what I did to Bruce," I said. Summing it all up made everything sound a whole lot simpler than it really was. Or maybe not.

"What were you using him for?"

"At first, validation, I guess. He made me feel attractive again for the first time in years." I didn't want to tell her the rest of it, that it had been the surest way to shut down everything else that was going on in my life. If she was a good shrink, she'd be able to figure that out on her own.

"Did you and your fiancé enjoy a good sex life?"

"That's a little personal, if you don't mind."

"Everything we say in here is personal," she said. "On the off chance you do decide to come back and work with me, which I can already tell you would be a good idea, then I'd like you to understand that sharing emotional intimacy and sexual intimacy are two sides of the same coin. Being honest counts for a lot here. Filtering what you tell me won't speed up your progress."

"Would you prefer I save us both a lot of time and tell you when this crap really started? It all started with that damn dress!" Where the hell did that come from?

"Dress?"

"My wedding dress."

"Ah. Everything was fine before you bought the dress?"

"I think so. At least, it was all stuff I could handle—just nerves."

"So tell me about the dress." She was practically foaming at the mouth. It was like I'd just told her I was dreaming about big, fat cigars.

"It's beautiful. It's a Vera Wang. You know Vera Wang?"

Dr. Shloff shook her head. She had a practice on the Upper West Side and she didn't know about Vera Wang. The woman probably made her living off rich and jittery young brides, yet she'd never bothered to ask any of them about their dresses? It didn't sound like she was doing her job very well.

"Anyway," I continued, "It's my dream dress, or at least I thought it was. Now it's more like a nightmare—a two-thousand-dollar nightmare sitting in my mother's closet wrapped in plastic. It'll probably never see the light of day. Not that I care, because I never want to see it again. Maybe I should sell it…" I mused. "Or burn it!"

"Let's stay on track," Dr. Shloff interjected.

"Yeah, well, this is what happened. I bought the dress in…I guess it was December. But it was a size eight because it was a sample sale and they were all size eights. So I had to lose weight in order to fit into it. Fifty pounds. I never thought I could do it, but I did."

The doctor's eyes widened. "You lost fifty pounds since December?"

"Pretty much," I said nonchalantly. "Except that I've gained some of it back. At least ten pounds, maybe fifteen. I'm not exactly sure, because Morgan, who I've been staying with, doesn't have a scale. I just can't seem to stop eating. But that's a normal part of depression, isn't it?" I was looking for any excuse other than run-of-the-mill gluttony.

"That's quite a bit to lose," Dr. Shloff said. "How did you do it?"

"Bruce thought I had an eating disorder. Don't get excited—

I didn't. The truth is, I did it the old-fashioned way—exercise and semi-starvation. And positive visualization. When you have a goal that's important enough to you, anything's possible."

Or, almost anything. Losing a few pounds was one thing, but I seriously doubted that positive visualization would be enough to get Bruce to take me back. After seeing him with Daphne, I knew things were never going to be the same. Even me coming to see Dr. Shloff wouldn't be enough to make him forget what I'd done to him, or convince him that I'd changed. The only reason he wanted me to come here was for my own good, so that I'd feel better. But that was Bruce—always thinking about my well-being, even when I didn't deserve it.

He had his own life to live now, and whether or not he forgave me was probably irrelevant at this point, although it would be nice. So there was no point in obsessing over it—the most important thing now was getting a life back. Not my old one though, a better one. One in which maybe I could even be a little happy again one day. That's why I was here. Bruce thought that seeing this kook would help, and I secretly hoped he was right.

Dr. Shloff cleared her throat. "And your goal was fitting into that dress."

"By August 18. That was supposed to be our wedding day." I couldn't believe it was coming up so quickly. I made a mental note to get the hell out of the city that day and find something interesting to do, because if I sat around and thought about it, I'd probably lose my mind.

"Maintaining good eating habits is important when you're feeling down, so don't be too hard on yourself if you put on a few pounds," she said. "And exercise is a great stress-reliever. Do you still work out?"

"No. I couldn't keep up my gym membership after I got fired. They paid for most of it."

"You were fired recently, too?" she asked.

"Yeah. But it was a shitty job. I'm totally over it." My fault or not, Kendra White was finally behind me. At least that was a good thing. I definitely needed a fresh start, career-wise. "You're right about the exercising thing, though," I told her. "It clears your head. Unfortunately, it also really has a lot of negative associations for me now."

"Why is that?"

"Because my trainer was the one I slept with."

"Ah!" she said, and almost fell out of her leather chair. "Your trainer!" It was a therapist's dream. She couldn't have been more excited if she'd struck gold.

I looked at my watch. "So what do you think?" I asked her. "The hour's almost up."

She put her pen down and leaned back.

"I'm sure you know that I can't give you all the answers, Evie. You have to find those for yourself. All I can do is help steer you in the right direction."

"Yeah, yeah. Save the touchy-feely crap and give it to me straight, Doc."

"You're a rare bird, Miss Mays," Dr. Shloff declared, greatly amused. "All right. Here's what I think. I think maybe you bought a dress you hoped you'd never be able to wear. And I think maybe you panicked when you found out one day that it fit you perfectly."

"You mean, I never wanted to get married at all?"

"You tell me. Next week."

Morgan decided that six weeks was plenty long to be in mourning for a seven-year relationship, so, despite my protests, she fixed me up with a friend of Billy's, some guy he knew from work.

"Do you want Bruce to be the only one on the rebound?" she asked.

"Yes," I said. "I don't want a boyfriend."

"Everyone wants a boyfriend, Evie. Whether they admit it or not."

"But this is the first time I've been single since college," I protested.

"And look how much fun you're having. Trust me. This guy's great—a hell of a lot more interesting than most of Billy's friends. If I were single, I'd snap him up in a second."

"But I don't have anything to wear." I'd thrown out everything that was too big on me months ago. I never imagined my thin days would be so shortly numbered.

"You've got plenty of clothes," she said, eyeing the mess that had taken over her second bedroom. "Just wear anything. Tight is sexy. Preston will like that. Billy said his last girlfriend was a scuba instructor and that he liked it when she wore her wetsuit in the sack."

"That's ridiculous," I said.

"Maybe, but it does make for some interesting possibilities...." Morgan said thoughtfully.

I couldn't think of a single one.

"Will you at least come with us? Please?" I begged. "If you're going to ambush me with this, then it's the least you can do!" She'd already told Preston all about me and he'd agreed to a date tonight, so there wasn't much I could do to stop it now. If I didn't go, I knew Morgan would hold it against me forever. It would be easier just to suffer through it.

"No. We're not in high school anymore. Just go out and have a good time, get your mind off things. He's picking you up at eight, so be ready. I'm trusting you."

"I don't want to," I objected weakly. "It's not right." Even thinking about another guy right now felt like cheating on Bruce again.

"I can tell what you're thinking, Evie, and you better stop it right now. I bet Bruce would be jealous if he found out. Maybe it would even be a good thing."

"I don't think Bruce feels jealousy. He thinks jealousy is for couples who don't trust each other. And since we're not even a couple..."

"Well, he's right. But that doesn't mean you're not going," she said on her way out the door. "Don't worry…it won't be so bad. I promise. Besides—blondes have more fun!"

I threw a pillow at her.

At precisely 8:45, the buzzer rang from downstairs.

"Eve?" a voice crackled over the intercom system.

"Yeah?"

"It's Preston. I'm here."

"Only forty-five minutes late."

"Sorry. Traffic in the tunnel."

I waited for a better explanation.

"Hello?" he said. "You there?"

I pushed the button. "I'm coming down."

When the elevator doors opened, he was standing right there. Not holding flowers, I should point out. He obviously wasn't a romantic—Bruce had given me flowers on our first three or four dates. And after that, he brought me food.

"You must be Eve," he said, licking his lips. He moved in to kiss me on the cheek.

"Nice to meet you," I said, extending a hand instead. "And it's Evie."

"Whoa! So formal! Billy said you knew how to have a good time—I hope he was right!"

I grinned feebly.

"Let's get going…my car's out front and I hate the thought of her being all alone. No need to worry, though—I slipped the doorman a few bucks to watch her for me."

"Good thinking," I said.

He ran ahead of me through the lobby when he noticed that the doorman was inside on the phone instead. I seriously considered getting back into the elevator that second, but I figured it might make an interesting anecdote for my memoirs (*Cos-*

mopolitan, August: "10 Great Careers You Can Have from Home").

"Let me get that for you," he said when I finally made my way outside. "The handle can be a little tricky on this side."

"Don't worry, I won't touch it," I told him.

"So, Eve, you ever been in a Porsche before?" he asked as we headed for FDR Drive.

"Is that what this is?" I asked as disinterestedly as I could. "Where are we going?"

"I thought you might like to see how she handles on the highway. If there's no traffic, I'll open 'er up—you won't believe the ride!"

"Don't you find it pointless having a car in the city?"

"Naw—this baby makes it all worth it. But you've got to be willing to make sacrifices. I don't even wanna tell you how much I pay for parking every month…$450! Can you believe that! What a racket. Well, nobody can say I'm not a devoted daddy!"

"That's sick." What a vile creature. Morgan was really going to get it. Preston wasn't even remotely cute—there was more hair on his knuckles than on his head, and I could only assume he'd gotten dressed in the dark. Not only that, but he drove like an asshole. "Uh, could you slow down, please? You cut that guy off," I said, looking back. "I think he might have hit the wall."

"That shitbox? It shouldn't even be allowed on the road. So, where you wanna go for dinner?"

"Didn't you make reservations somewhere?"

"Nah. I just figured we'd see where the night takes us…." He stared at my legs.

"Hey—eyes on the road," I said.

"Well, I'll be honest with you, Eve. I thought if you were a real dog, we'd just grab a quick drink at some hotel bar. But Billy was right—you're not bad. So dinner it is! You got any ideas?"

"Um, maybe we could just get that drink. I guess Morgan forgot to tell you, but I've already got plans for later."

"Oh. Okay," he said as we slowed for traffic on the exit ramp, but he was distracted by some sort of roadblock up ahead.

"I think it's just one of those spot-checks," I said. "They're doing them a lot on the weekends now. You know, to check for drunk drivers."

He checked the rearview mirror nervously, as if he were contemplating backing up the ramp. A car pulled up behind us and he slammed his palms against the steering wheel in frustration.

"You're not *wasted,* are you?" I asked. That would be rich.

"No. But hold on." He threw the gear shift into Second and squealed around the car in front of us.

"What are you doing?" I screamed.

"I'm blowing it!" he shouted as he made for a spot between two parked police cars. Fortunately, there wasn't even close to enough room for us to pass through, and the cop standing there slapped his light stick down on the windshield. Preston lowered the window.

"What's the problem here, officer?" he snapped.

"Turn off the engine. You in some kind of hurry, buddy?" The cop asked. "You can't wait your turn?"

"Ha! You see, my girlfriend here isn't feeling well. I'm bringing her to the hospital."

I smiled and waved.

"She looks fine to me. License and registration."

Preston made a face and handed them over. The cop walked slowly back to his cruiser.

"What the hell's the matter with you?" I shouted. "Are you brain damaged?"

"Calm down, calm down. When he gets back, just tell him you're really sick. We'll say...what'll we say...help me out here if you have any ideas... Got it! We'll say you're pregnant and that you think you're losing the baby! Yeah! Just bend over and moan or something...they'll have to let us through right away."

Before I could tell him that I would be doing no such thing, the cop came back and said, "Mr. Betancourt, it seems your driver's permit was suspended three months ago for $1400 in unpaid speeding fines and failure to appear. Please step out of the vehicle, sir."

"There must be some kind of mistake. I *paid* those tickets!"

"Sir, please step out now. We're impounding your vehicle." Preston turned white as a sheet. I guess he didn't see the poetry in it. "Unless…" the cop continued, "*she* has a valid license," he said, motioning towards me with his pen.

"No! No! She can't drive my car!" Poor guy. He was in a real snit. "She doesn't drive standard!"

"Yes I do, officer. And I have a valid license."

"Either she drives," the cop said, "or we impound the vehicle. What'll it be?" Preston reluctantly stepped out and came around to the passenger's side. I slipped behind the wheel and turned the key.

The cop handed Preston two tickets. "Driving without a valid permit, that's $350, and driving without a seat belt, $50. You're lucky I don't put down attempting to blow a roadblock, too—that's a criminal offense. I could arrest you for that."

It had been a while since I drove stick. A few years ago, when Bruce was driving his dad's old Caddy, he gave me lessons in the parking lot of the high school around the corner from our place. At the time, I didn't see the importance of it, especially since I was never really any good. But now, I was delighted to be able to help.

"Here goes!" I said, grinding the gearshift into what I thought was First. I eased off the clutch and onto the gas. The car lurched backward. Cops scattered out of the way.

"That's reverse!" he yelled, clutching at his chest.

I laughed. "Whoops!" Slowly, we inched forward, gathering speed. I popped it into Second. The engine purred agreeably. "This is fun! Let's take 'er out on the highway!" Preston stared at me in abject horror.

As soon as we were safely out of view, he made me get out so he could drive.

"Take me home immediately," I demanded.

"What about our drink?"

"I've had enough fun for tonight."

"I had a blast!" I told Morgan and Billy when they walked in the door an hour later.

They looked at each other in surprise.

"Really? I didn't think you'd actually have fun," she admitted.

"Well that shows how much you know," I said. "I got to drive a Porsche!"

"He let you drive his car?" Billy gasped.

I nodded.

"That doesn't make sense...." he mumbled to himself.

"Why not?" I asked him. I wanted them both to admit they'd set me up with a complete psycho.

"Why are you home so early?" Morgan asked, her suspicion growing.

"I was having too much fun—I thought we'd save some for our next date."

"What happened, Evie..."

"Oh, you know, the usual. He tried to blow a police roadblock and almost got us shot and killed."

Morgan rolled her eyes and slapped Billy on the arm. "You said he wasn't a loser," she yelled at him.

"Wait. I *never* said that. All I said was that he's a fun guy. And he is. Happy hour with Preston is a blast. Once, he got the waitress at MacDougall's to give us free pitchers all night because he convinced her we were beer critics from the *Times*..." Billy laughed to himself and shook his head..

"I thought *you* knew him, Morgan!" I shouted.

She tried not to laugh, too. "I'm *so* sorry, Evie. Technically, I never met him. But I screened him on the phone for you, and he sounded fine. Was he at least cute?"

"Nope. Not even close."

She slapped Billy again. "What?" he said. "How am I supposed to know if a guy's cute or not. He seems okay to me."

"It's fine. Don't worry about it. This merely confirms what I've suspected for weeks—that Bruce was the only man for me and that I'm destined to die miserable and alone, having blown my one true shot at happiness. Good night to the both of you," I said curtly and went off to my room.

Since neediness is one of the surest ways to lose a man's interest (*Allure,* March: "Are You Scaring Him Away?"), I waited until after my third session with Dr. Shloff to call Bruce and apologize about the incident in the park. This way, I reasoned, he'd be dazzled by my newfound insightfulness and unable to resist me. Or at least resist hanging up on me.

We had a pretty good conversation—very open and honest, although we avoided the subject of Daphne for the most part. Not only did I not want to know, but I didn't want to make him uncomfortable. He seemed glad that I was still going to Dr. Shloff, and he agreed with me that I'd had a bit of a breakthrough about the whole wedding dress thing.

"It doesn't make me feel very good to think you might not have wanted to marry me, but at least you're making progress," he said.

"The beauty of the theory is that it's not all my fault—the having doubts part, I mean, not that, uh, other stuff. I was motivated by subconscious fears and issues!"

"Maybe I was pushing you into all of it," he said. "You weren't ready."

"Bruce, you can't blame yourself."

"I'm not."

"Oh. Good."

"But maybe I should have waited until we'd talked openly about getting engaged instead of steamrolling ahead. I just wanted it to be romantic, you know?"

"It was," I assured him.

"Until you puked."

"Until I puked," I said, then giggled as adorably as I could.

Things were going so well that I even told him about my ill-fated date (including the fact that Morgan had forced me into it, just for good measure). He laughed at all the right places, and asked if I planned on going out with Preston again. I knew he was joking, but still—it definitely denoted interest on some level. We didn't make plans to see each other or anything, but he did say I could stop by and pick up my mail anytime.

I'd barely hung up the phone when it rang again. I figured it was Bruce, impulsively calling back to ask me out, but it was Mom.

"I have to keep the line free, Bruce is calling me back."

"Why? Is there something I don't know?" She'd probably be happier over a reconciliation than I would be.

"We're finally starting to be on good terms again and I don't want to miss his call," I said. "Seriously, I have to go."

"That's good, Evelyn. That's very good. Do you really think there's a chance he'll take you back, after what you did?"

"*Mom,* I'm hanging up," I said, and almost did.

"Wait! I have to tell you something. Are you sitting down?"

Please, don't let her and Albert be getting married. I couldn't take another surprise engagement. I was far too fragile for this right now.

"What is it?"

"Well, I'm not sure exactly how you're going to feel about this, but your grandfather died."

"Oh."

"Apparently, he'd been in the hospital for quite some time. Even Lucia didn't know. He had lung cancer," she sighed. "My father never smoked a day in his life."

I'd never even met my grandfather, so I didn't feel too weird about it, but for Mom, it was a different story. I knew she'd always secretly hoped he'd forgive her one day. "Are you okay?" I asked.

"I'm fine," she said. "When it's your time to go, it's your time to go. I should know that better than anyone. Death is going to take every one of us, Evelyn, even you, so there's no sense in getting all worked up about it now. The man lived a long life." Mom could be very pragmatic when it came to things like this. Still, there was no need to remind me that I'd be worm food one day. "To die alone, though," she continued thoughtfully, "…well, I suppose that was his own choice."

"Do you want me to come over?"

"Thank you, Evelyn, but you stay there. Albert is here, and I'm really fine. I promise. And Lucia's on her way. But the funeral's the day after tomorrow. There won't be any visitation or a mass or anything like that—his priest will say a few words at the cemetery and that's about it. If you want to come…"

"Of course."

22

The only people who came to Ray Valerio's funeral were me, Bruce, Claire, Mom, Albert, Auntie Lucy and some old woman who'd apparently fed his cats while he was in the hospital. If he had any friends, they didn't bother to show. Or maybe they had no idea that he'd even died. There was nobody to call and tell them.

When I phoned Bruce to tell him what had happened, he immediately insisted on coming, out of respect for Mom. Secretly, I hoped that he was looking for an excuse to see me, but since he still spoke to both Mom and Claire on a regular basis—probably more often than I did—it was most likely a combination of both. It was nice of him, and I was glad to have him there. I'd told Morgan not to bother coming, although she'd also offered. It wasn't that big a deal. I never knew the man, after all.

The worst part of it all for me was that I didn't have a thing to wear. The only item I still had that fit me was that stretchy ocelot dress from the engagement party, which I hadn't thrown out because it looked even better after I'd lost more weight. Unfortunately, it was almost surely inappropriate for a funeral. I ended up buying a cheap summer dress for $29.99 at K-Mart that doesn't bear description. To add a much-needed touch of class, I also wore the diamond tennis bracelet Bruce gave me for Christmas.

The only other funeral I'd ever been to was Claire's sister, who died about ten years ago. This one was much quicker. The priest struggled painfully to find a few nice things to say, Lucy cried when they lowered the casket into the earth, and then we all went to Mom's to eat. Except, thank God, for Albert, who had to go back to work.

"Bruce, how's your mother doing?" Mom asked as she filled his plate with lasagna and salad. It wasn't weird at all, having Bruce around. It felt familiar and comfortable, except that he was still having a hard time looking me in the eye.

"She's fine. Still a little upset about all those nonrefundable deposits, I think. But she's doing okay."

Claire laughed.

"Maybe Evelyn should offer to help pay for those," Mom said matter-of-factly.

"Mom! *Please.*" It was humiliating enough that the entire family plus Albert knew about my little indiscretion. I didn't need to be publicly reminded of it every time we sat down to dinner, too.

"Uh, I don't think that's necessary," Bruce offered. "Evie's got enough financial responsibilities for the time being."

"You're too good to her, Bruce," Mom said.

I grinned weakly at him.

"Isn't this a time when we should be talking about Dad?" Lucy asked. She hadn't said much since we got back from the cemetery.

Mom rolled her eyes. "Fine, Lucia. Is there anything you'd like to say?"

"He had his good points, you know. Don't tell me you don't remember. He was an okay father back in the day. Strict as hell, but fair. And he absolutely adored Mom. Did you know that when she was sick, he brought her fresh flowers every day?

Every day for six months, just to brighten her room." Mom glared at her skeptically. "I'm not saying he was right, Lilly, how he treated you, but he wasn't all bad, either. Evie deserves to know that."

"I was his only grandkid, and he never wanted to meet me," I told her.

"Oh, I bet he did. Probably more than anything. But that would have meant him admitting he was wrong, and that was a little more than he could handle," she said. "He was so stubborn. It was ridiculous. And look what he missed out on! We could all learn a little something from him in that respect." At least now I knew where I got it from.

"Yes, yes, Lucia, that's fine," Mom said impatiently.

Lucy ignored her. "You know, Evie, I never really noticed, but you have his eyes. You definitely have his eyes."

I did? There was nothing particularly special about my eyes. Boring brown, although I'd flirted with green contacts for a while (*Glamour,* October: "Grabbing What Mother Nature Never Gave You").

"She also inherited his financial irresponsibility," Mom said. "Which brings me to something I wanted to discuss with you, Evie, and now's as good a time as any. Bruce, you're a part of the family...well, you were anyway," she corrected herself, and shot me a dark look. "...so I'm sure nobody will mind if you hear this, too."

Lucy nodded in agreement.

"It seems that your grandfather has willed his house to you."

"What?"

"Hey, Evie, that's great!" Bruce said.

"But what does that mean?" I asked.

"That means it's yours," Lucy said.

Surely there was a catch. Why would he give it to me? He hated me. "Why didn't you get it, Lucy? Because you live in London?"

"No, because I guess he wanted you to have it. He loved that house very much. Your mom and I grew up there."

"I know it's in Carroll Gardens somewhere, but I've never actually seen it," I told them.

"It's an old brownstone," Mom said. "Probably needs renovations."

"At least it's in a good neighborhood. I bet it's not that far from our place," I said.

"You mean *my* place," Bruce added.

"Sorry, Bruce. *Your* place."

"A house is a very big responsibility, Evie," Mom cautioned shrilly. "It's not something to be taken lightly."

"I know, I know."

"I'm sure you have absolutely no idea," she said.

"Leave her alone, Lilly. Don't spoil it," Lucy said, and smiled at me. "I've known for a few years that Dad was planning to do this, you know. And boy am I glad I never told Roderick. When we were here in January, he paid all the back taxes on the place. It was either that or put Dad into a home, which would have been a lot more expensive."

"What a loving gesture," I said.

Lucy laughed loudly. "Dad told him to consider the tax bill my dowry. Man, was he pissed when I told him the house was going to Evie."

Mom snorted in delight.

"I thought Roderick didn't come because he was too embarrassed to see us," I said. "After that whole thing with Diana."

Lucy shrugged. "I don't know, but I'm sure that's part of it. Don't worry, though, he's not mad at you, Evie. He'll get over this...he always does. Poor, dear Roderick," she sighed.

"Oh, he does it to himself," Mom snapped.

"He's constantly humiliated over one thing or another. You know, I'm beginning to wonder if I should be, too, by association. Ahhh, I suppose he's just my cross to bear," Lucy giggled. What she saw in him was anyone's guess.

"Well, I think it's wonderful," Claire said, raising her wineglass. "Congratulations, Evie."

* * *

We left Mom's as soon as Albert showed up after work. Sensing I was a little frazzled, Bruce took pity on me and asked me over for some coffee.

"Thanks," I told him as he poured me a cup. "We need to talk."

"Uh-oh. Maybe we could just watch TV instead."

"Seriously, Bruce. I feel really bad. About a lot of stuff. Like what you said about your mom. Is she really mad? This must have cost your parents a fortune." In all my self-absorption these last couple of months, I hadn't really thought about what calling off the wedding would mean for them.

"Don't worry about it—it wasn't that much. A few thousand bucks. To tell you the truth, I think she's actually pretty relieved about the whole thing. I heard her telling one of her friends that you'd always been unstable, so she wasn't surprised."

"That makes me feel a whole lot better."

"Hey, I'm just being honest."

"Well, I was going to say I should call her and apologize, but now I think I'll stick to my earlier plan."

"That it would be a cold day in hell before you apologize to my mother for anything?"

"Exactly." This felt good—just like old times.

"Yeah, I think that would be best. Although my dad might like to hear from you. Just to say hi or something."

He was right—I should have called him. "Okay. If you think he wouldn't mind hearing from me. Do, uh, they know why we....called it off?"

"Not my mom. But my dad does."

"You *told* him."

"Yeah."

"God, I'm so embarrassed."

He shifted uncomfortably in his chair. "Well, maybe you don't have to be."

"Why not?"

He made a face, and said, "I wasn't going to tell you this, and I only will if you promise not to tell anyone, okay? Especially your mother."

"Okay," I said.

"Well," he said, taking a deep breath, "my dad told me that the same kind of thing happened to them once."

"Your mother had an affair?" Ha! I had a feeling Bertie was harboring some sort of dark secret, and this finally confirmed my suspicions. I'd always figured she was probably a repressed lesbian or something. But this would do.

"No," Bruce said. "My dad."

"Get *out!*" I yelled.

"I'm not kidding. I still can't believe he told me," he said, shaking his head.

"With who?" I couldn't imagine Bruce's dad with anyone except his mom. And even then, it was a stretch.

"He didn't really give me details, which is good because I definitely didn't want any. But it was a long time ago, before the girls were born. He was out of town, speaking at some sort of preserves conference."

"A sticky situation…"

"Ha, ha. It was a one-time thing. But when he got home, he told my mother right away."

"And she forgave him?"

"Maybe she didn't feel like she had much of a choice. I was just a baby."

This explained a lot. "And I suppose he's been trying to make it up to her ever since."

"I don't know. Probably."

"Why do you think he told you?"

"Because I told him about us, I guess. Or maybe he just needed to get it off his chest. But it was kind of weird. When we were talking, he sounded okay with it, like he didn't really regret it very much or something. Maybe because it was so long ago. I don't know."

This was my big chance.

"*I* regret it, Bruce," I said.

He'd been playing with the sugar, but now he looked me square in the eyes. "I know," he said. "But I still can't believe you actually did that. I thought I knew you."

"Imagine how I feel, knowing all this shit is my fault."

"Sorry, Evie, but I feel a little worse for myself here."

"Of course. Sorry," I mumbled. I wished he could read my mind. Then he'd be able to see how much I regretted everything. "I want you to know that I would never ask or expect you to forgive me for this. What I did was unforgivable."

"It was," he agreed.

"And I don't deserve anything from you. I don't even know why you're sitting with me here right now. You don't owe me a thing."

"I don't," he said.

"And I wish…I wish more than anything that I could take your hurt away," I said. "And put it on myself."

"For a while, I wished that, too. Along with some other things. Worse things."

"But now…" I said hopefully.

"Now nothing. I'm still thinking up new ways to torture you."

"Very funny." I said. A joke. That was okay. "Have you come up with anything interesting?"

"I thought an old-fashioned tar-and-feathering would do. Or maybe just tossing you off the Brooklyn Bridge."

"I've considered that myself…"

"Don't joke about that," he said seriously.

"What would you care?" A cheap and manipulative tactic, I admit, but more often than not, this sort of thing worked.

"Of course I'd care. I'd care a lot." See?

"I wouldn't blame you if you didn't," I said.

"If you think I'm going to tell you not to be so hard on yourself, I can't."

"That's okay, I'm not looking for absolution," I said. "Feeling miserable is the only thing that makes me feel better, if you can believe that. Torturing myself helps the guilt go away."

"*Absolution*... That's a heavy word, Evie. Have you been talking to your mother?"

"Yes. She told me that if I said about three million Hail Marys, all would be forgotten."

"Sounds like a start," he said.

"Actually, I think I've finally accepted that there is no easy way out of this. I'm going to have to live with my mistakes for the rest of my life."

"We all do."

"There's an upside, though. My mistakes are so huge and catastrophic that they dwarf everything else in my life, so I can't help but learn something from them."

"Have you really learned anything, aside from trying not to get caught when you cheat on your fiancé?"

"That's a very dark way to look at this. And by the way, I know that getting caught wasn't the mistake. But part of it was letting it come to that in the first place. I should have talked to you more, Bruce. I don't think I really knew then why I was feeling everything that I was feeling, or why I was behaving the way I was, but maybe if I'd given you the benefit of the doubt, we could have talked it through before it was too late."

"So why didn't you?"

"I guess because I didn't think you understood how important it was for me to be skinny, and I resented you for that. And then it all just got more and more out of control, and I felt completely alone, and even when I knew I was getting into trouble with it, and at work, and all that, I didn't want to disappoint you. Or give you the satisfaction of being right. Or hurt you."

"It sounds like Dr. Shloff is earning her fee."

I got up and poured myself another cup of coffee, and topped it off with lots of cream. Getting this stuff off my chest was good, but I also wanted to know where he was at.

"What do you want from me, Bruce?" I asked. It was a fair question.

"Nothing."

"Then why am I here?"

"You can go if you like," he said. *Whoops!*

"I'm serious," I said. "Dr. Shloff thinks you should be confronting your feelings about me."

"Does she?" he laughed. "That's great. Tell her I've been doing that every waking minute for the last two months."

"You have?"

"Of course. But I still haven't figured any of it out. And I guess the reason you're here is simply because I asked you."

"You mean you want to be friends?"

"No, no, no. We absolutely cannot be friends."

"Oh." This was a bit confusing. "What then?"

He thought carefully for a moment or two, then said, "For today, how about lovers? If you're up for it."

"Are you asking me to…to…"

"Sure. Why not? Just this once, though."

This was very unlike Bruce. Very blunt. Reckless, almost. I liked it.

"It is *so* not us to do something like this."

"Exactly," he said, getting up from the table and extending his hand for me to take.

"Now?" I asked, half panicked. I was wearing horrible cotton granny underwear.

"Now," he said.

We didn't do it right there on the kitchen floor, or anything like that. And we made it to the bedroom without tearing each other's clothes off. That wasn't what it was about. Kissing him was familiar and sweet, but it was also strange and exciting, like we both knew it was probably a better idea not to. And for the first time in years, it was truly amazing. Really wild. And totally intense.

Afterward, we talked like it was no big deal. In situations such as these, most girls know that mature, post-coital banter is essential in order to offset any accidental impressions of neediness.

"What was *that* about?" I asked, fanning my face with my hand. All guys like being complimented after sex, and he definitely deserved it this time (*Cosmopolitan,* March: "5 Politically Incorrect Ways to a Man's Heart").

"You complaining?" He still seemed a bit bewildered.

"No! God, no. But you're like a new man!"

"No I'm not, Evie."

"Say what you want, but I'm telling you, that was something else."

"I know. I was here, remember?"

"I'll never forget it."

"Stop it. You're being an idiot. What am I going to do with you?"

I fluffed my pillow and snuggled back down under the covers. "Just ignore me," I said.

"That's not so easy. You always seem to be around."

"You can tease me as much as you like. I don't care. And I may not know exactly how you feel about me these days, but one thing's for sure—you're still pretty hung up on my family. You can't get enough of us. Admit it."

He pushed me away. "Well, your mother's a much better cook than you ever were."

"Too bad you lost out on all that when you dumped me. A lifetime of lasagna, and you gave it all up…"

He shook his head. "I don't think so—she brings me food every Sunday!"

"She does not!" I gasped.

"Go look in the freezer. There's turkey for Monday, cannelloni for Tuesday, meatballs for Wednesday…"

"Unbelievable. She's unbelievable."

"Don't you dare tell her to stop! I'll never forgive you," he said.

"It isn't fair, Bruce. You're giving her false hope." I was hoping he'd say something like, "No, I'm not—there's still a chance for us, Evie. Can't you feel it?" But he didn't.

"I probably should try to back off a bit," he agreed instead. *Damn.* "But all the cooking aside, they've both been great to me, Claire and your mom. Claire, especially. Really supportive. How can I tell her I don't want to talk to her anymore? She's my pal."

"She's always adored you," I said. All of Bruce's grandparents were dead, so he'd sort of adopted Claire in that sense.

"You know, I don't really mind the blond so much," he said, tucking a stray hair behind my ear. "It suits you in a weird way. And it kind of makes me feel like I'm lying here with a stranger."

"I'm changing it back. I just haven't bothered yet."

"Really?" he sounded surprised. "But what about the new you?"

I sighed. "The new me got old."

"Yeah, I figured that might happen," he said, moving a bit closer. "So I guess I better take advantage of you now, Blondie, before the Old Evie shows up again."

"I'm starting to hope they're both gone for good," I said.

"You *didn't,*" Morgan said.

"It's no big deal," I told her.

"Were you overwhelmed with grief or something? Was he comforting you?"

"No, it wasn't like that."

She shook her head. "But Bruce so always does the right thing, and that was definitely the wrong thing. He's too level-headed for ex-sex."

"Ex-sex?"

"You know—well, I guess you don't, actually. It happens when you've forgotten all the reasons you broke up in the first place, or pretend you don't care, just to indulge in one last romp in the hay to get it out of your system."

"I don't think it was like that for us."

"Of course it was. Think of it as a much nicer way to say

goodbye than all the horrible things you probably said to each other when you broke up. If I've done it once I've done it a thousand times. Well…not that many exactly, but you get my point." She lowered her voice and said, "Two weeks after I told Peter that I couldn't see him anymore, we did it once, just for old times' sake."

I rolled my eyes. "You're hopeless."

"What? Just because I'm toying with the idea of monogamy doesn't mean I can't fall off the wagon once or twice. And I haven't touched him since." She paused thoughtfully. "But he's been in Singapore for a month."

"But you and Peter were just about sex," I reminded her. "Mine and Bruce's relationship had nothing to do with sex. Wait… That's not what I meant.…What I mean is, for me, not being with him is like saying goodbye to the biggest part of my life. And I'm ready to deal with that. If that's the way it has to be, then I can learn to handle it," I said, hoping that saying it out loud would somehow make it true. "Only now, I can't help but think it's sort of the same way for him, too."

"Evie, it's different for guys," she pleaded. "He probably wasn't thinking about all that. He just wanted to get laid. Ex-sex. You see?"

"You don't get it. He's far too cerebral not to consider the consequences of his actions, regardless of what's going on in his pants. I know this doesn't mean we're getting back together tomorrow or anything like that, it's just that I know he'd be super-careful about making sure he didn't give me the wrong impression. And he speaks to my mother all the time. She still cooks for him, for God's sake! He's not exactly cutting all ties—"

"But he's been getting on with things, with that chick," she interrupted.

"This has nothing to do with Daphne. It has to do with us. Me and him. That's it… But if you must know, he did mention that he and Daphne are just good friends for now. And no, I didn't ask him if he slept with her, because I'm trying to avoid that whole psycho ex-girlfriend thing, but I'm almost a hundred percent positive he didn't."

Morgan made an If-You-Believe-That-Then-You're-Even-More-Deluded-Than-I-Thought face. But she didn't know Bruce the way I did.

"Look, ex-sex or not, I know it was weird of him to initiate it, but I think he just wanted to be in control for a change. And all I'm saying is that if we were drawn to each other and we both let it happen, then isn't it possible that there might be some sort of future for us someday?"

"No way! It's about nostalgia, plain and simple."

An emotional Popsicle like Morgan might never have the capacity to understand a thing as complicated and delicate as my relationship with Bruce.

Since I feared that hounding Bruce after our little tryst might scare him off, I resolved not to call him until I had something new to say. Which is why I was so relieved when I finally found a job a couple of weeks later. Not a very good one, but one that'll get me through until I find something respectable. So as of next Monday—instead of enjoying the first day of my honeymoon as originally planned—I would officially begin my tenure as the new In-House Director of Marketing and Communications at...oh, God...Casella Computers. Technically, I'm the only one in the department, but the title works for me.

It was all I could get without a reference, since I obviously couldn't give out Pruscilla's name. And although they don't pay for employees' gym memberships, the insurance package, which kicks in after three months, will reimburse me for up to eighty percent of my therapy costs. Which is a good thing, since it looks like Dr. Shloff and I will be getting to know each other pretty well.

Bruce was very happy for me when I filled him in on things, although Mom had probably told him everything already. Still, he listened politely to all the details, and even said that he'd like to take me out to celebrate. Instead of sounding too eager and pressuring him into setting a date, I casually told him to give me a call when he had a free evening. It was brilliant.

But Morgan was somewhat less receptive. She thought it was a terrible idea for me to get a job through Albert, although I thought I heard a hint of relief in her voice.

"I'll be out of your hair before you know it!"

"Yeah, that's great, Evie. But don't take a shitty job on my account—I don't care if you stay for another six years."

"I can just see it…you, me and Billy, living happily ever after."

"Joke all you want, I know you'd love that—you'd get to see him in his boxers all the time, you'd accidentally walk in on him in the shower in the mornings…."

"Shut up!" I shrieked. She was still convinced that I wanted him. But I had no interest in another woman's man. Except maybe Daphne's.

"Methinks the lady doth protest too much…." she laughed. "Don't worry, Evie. Billy and I aren't setting a date any time soon—we plan to have a really long engagement. I think that's enough for now."

"That's absurd. What's the point if you don't plan to get married?" I said, wishing I'd thought of that last year.

"We're still working out all the kinks," she explained.

"I know, my bedroom is right next to yours…."

"You're a pig. I could leave the door open, if you want to steal a peek."

"No thanks."

"Just let me know if you change your mind," she said, and I think she meant it. "So, not that I want you to leave, but when can I tell Billy we'll be putting the whips and chains back in your bedroom?" she asked. "He's missed them so."

"After a paycheck or two."

"I hope you know what you're doing. I can't imagine working for my mother's husband."

"That's because he's a carpenter. Or he used to be, anyway. Look, Morgan, it's not like I have much of a choice—I can't be dependent on Claire forever. I'm almost twenty-eight, for God's sake. And I won't be working for Albert, by the way. His son was the one who hired me."

"As a favor to Albert," she added.

"You make it sound awful, but it isn't. They were looking for someone anyway. It's a growing company. There are lots of flyers to coordinate. And a catalog, too."

Morgan yawned. I guess it did sound a little drab.

"At least I won't ever have to see Albert," I said. "When I told Mom she could set up the interview for me, I only agreed to it on that condition. He's in Queens. I'll be at the Manhattan branch—the flagship store!"

"Oooh. The *flagship* store! Sounds fantastic," she said. "Can you do my toes for me?"

"Give it a rest, will you? There are some decent perks, like it's not far from your office. So we'll be able to have lots of extra-long lunches! And since I came clean about the fact that I don't know a thing about computers, they already know not to expect great things. Not right away, at least."

"Sounds like you've thought of everything," she said grumpily.

"Why do you care so much?"

"I think you can do better."

"Morgan, I can't find anything better right now, unless you want to hire me."

"Are you kidding? I'd *never* hire you. You're far too much of a slacker. And judging from your track record, you're not good with numbers either, especially those with a dollar sign in front of them."

"You see? Plus, I don't have any references. I'd be better off telling people I've been in jail for the last three years than giving out Pruscilla's number."

"I guess. Now will you do my toes?"

"Sure. Get me the polish."

She jumped up excitedly and returned with a bottle of blood-red Chanel. "You do them almost as well as my girl," she said. "Maybe you should go to pedicure school or something. That would be a good career for you."

"Your toes are one thing," I said. "But touching a complete stranger's feet? I don't think so. I'm okay with this job, Morgan. Don't worry about it."

"If you say so. But promise me you'll quit if it sucks."

"Of course I will. Do you think I'd do something I hate?"

She glared at me.

"Kendra White was different," I explained. "I was personally involved."

"You hated it from the beginning," she said.

"Well I won't hate this. It'll be great...sort of like being my own boss! And if it doesn't work out, I can always get a job dancing topless or something. I don't think you need references for that."

"Oh, I assure you, you do," Morgan said.

"The only problem with this job is that I don't have a single decent outfit to wear, now that I've completely let myself go...."

"Tell me you're not serious," she moaned. "Maybe we should give the nude dancing some more thought. *Please.* NO more shopping."

"What? I think it's a good thing. Better than starving myself to fit into the clothes I already have. It'll be fine—it's not like I have any credit cards anymore, and I won't use any of Claire's money for this. I'll wait till I get my first paycheck and just pick up a few things."

Dr. Shloff thinks my spending habits are far less troubling than my weight issues, and I agree. Provided I don't get too out of control, we feel it's in my psychological interest to spend a few bucks on clothes rather than succumb to that whole crash-and-burn diet and exercise cycle again. She's assured me that as soon as I learn to feed my emotional needs in other ways—a breakthrough which might be just around the corner—then I'll stop gaining weight.

"I'm going to look at this as a sign of my progress," I told her.

"How so?"

"Well, that I'm ready to shop…it must mean I'm feeling like myself again."

"God help us all," she said.

EPILOGUE

The first thing I needed to buy for my new house was a scale. It wasn't funny. No less than three months after sleeping with my personal trainer, I was nineteen pounds heavier…and hopefully, a little bit wiser. The truth was, it didn't even bother me as much as I thought it would—the extra pounds made me feel a little more like me again, which was a good thing. I guess I just wasn't destined to be thin. But I did plan on starting a daily walking program sometime soon, as a way to keep my head clear (and to keep from gaining too much more). There were worse things to be than chubby, I suppose. Like single at twenty-eight, with a dead-end job and no romantic prospects whatsoever except for a stubborn ex-fiancé who hadn't called in over a month.

But all that was fine. For now.

Luckily, the house was enough of a distraction to keep me from going out and joining another gym or doing something crazy like that. The first time I walked in, I was crushed to discover that it would definitely not be the devastatingly stylish urban retreat I'd hoped for, at least not without a truckload of money. It wasn't even country-in-the-city quaint—the tomato plants and flowers Grandpa grew out on the back patio were long-dead by the time I got there. In fact, it could barely pass for shabby chic. The entire place smelled musty and old, and most of the windows had been painted shut for years. Geriatric contemporary was more like it.

I figured I'd just sell the place. It seemed like a lot more trouble than it was worth, and it was far too big to live in alone. Besides, what the hell did I know about taking care of a house? I could barely do my own laundry. But then I spoke to Claire's new boyfriend, who's in real estate, and he advised me to wait, since property values are on the rise. He said that even though it isn't in the trendiest neighborhood right now, I'd probably be able to get quite a bit more for it in a few years. Still, I was ready to take the money and run, but Morgan convinced me it would be better to move in.

"It looks pretty good from the outside," she said as we stood and stared at it from across the tree-lined street. "Why sell it?"

"It's gross. A weird old man lived there alone for, like, twenty years. There's canned food in the pantry that expired in 1989."

"So, you clean that up. Get your mother to help—she likes throwing things out."

"There's more to it than that. It needs work."

"How bad can it be?"

"Come and see for yourself, but don't say I didn't warn you." I led her through the three floors of creaky hallways, toothpaste-colored bedrooms and dank closets. Even the attic rooms, which must have been spectacular a hundred years ago, weren't much to look at anymore, with their windows blacked out. And I couldn't even bring myself to take her into the basement, which was packed solid with two lifetimes' worth of broken furniture and jam jars, and probably at least one dead body.

But she seemed more convinced than ever that I should move in.

"You could really do a lot with it, Evie. It's so exciting! God, I wish I had a place like this. Do you realize how lucky you are?"

Morgan wanted something that I had? Now *this* was a first. "But I can't live here alone," I said. "It's too creepy."

"You'd prefer a studio in Bensonhurst? Because with your salary, you'll be lucky if you could afford even that."

She had a point. Why look a gift house in the mouth? And somehow, selling the place wouldn't feel right, especially if I just used the money to pay back Claire and subsidize my rent and shop like a fiend for a decade or two. Because good intentions or not, who was I kidding?—that's exactly what would happen. And besides, Grandpa wanted me to have it. Even if he was a jerk to Mom, if I'd learned anything from years of watching *The Young and the Restless,* it was that the enemy of your enemy is your friend.

Aside from the generations of renovations ahead, the biggest obstacle would be dealing with Mom. She thought I should sell the house, of course, and put the money into a 401k and whatever else life threw at me over the next fifty years. I took that to mean she wanted me to subsidize her retirement. Although the thought of putting her in an old-age home as soon as possible was appealing, I certainly didn't want to be the one paying for it. So I decided to keep the house.

It was like pulling teeth to get her to come see the place. I think she half expected her father to be sitting there when she walked in. After I accused her of being afraid of ghosts, she finally agreed.

"In all these years, they never changed a single thing," she mused, opening a kitchen cupboard and running her finger along the tattered shelf paper with disdain. "What a catastrophe. This is going to take more than a coat of paint, Evelyn. I hope you know what you're in for."

"I'm going to do it all myself. I bought a book."

She turned the hot-water faucet. A shuddering wail erupted from the pipes, followed by a trickle of brown liquid. "Hmm. I hope there's a section in there on plumbing."

"Thanks for your support, Mom. You better watch it, or I won't let you live here when you're old."

After a few days of harping on me about how roofs sometimes unexpectedly cave in and sharing her memories of the basement flooding, she finally warmed to the idea and took charge in classic domineering fashion. Not that I'm complaining, because I wouldn't have had a clue what to do or where to start. The week before I began work, she and I did our best to clean out the clutter, most of which was crap. We put all of the clothes into garbage bags and brought them to the church. And instead of throwing everything out, we had a big yard sale. People actually bought some of the stuff, including the cats, which I had the brilliant idea to sell for $2.50 each, including their dishes, collars and ear-mite medication.

A few antique dealers came by at dawn, hoping for the first crack at any hidden treasures. They didn't seem too thrilled by any of it, although one slunk away happily with Grandma's entire collection of porcelain clowns for thirty dollars. We knew there wasn't anything much of value. Lucy had gone through the house before she left and packed up a few boxes of good stuff to have shipped back to London. And Mom didn't give a crap about any of it, except for her mother's jewelry box.

To mark the occasion of my transition from renter to owner, I hosted a combination housewarming-birthday party, although I didn't actually turn twenty-eight until September 12, the following week. As a present to myself, I hired a professional housecleaning service, which helped get rid of some of the smell and all of the stains in the bathtub.

Because I only have a few close friends, the guest list was small and intimate. Billy came with Morgan, who agreed to tolerate the usual suspects on the condition that she be allowed to leave whenever she wanted. Although it would have been a good excuse to call him, I didn't invite Bruce—there would be enough tongues wagging as it was with my growing backside on display.

"Evie, this place is *amazing,*" Annie said. She looked around as if she couldn't believe her eyes. "Is it really all yours?"

Kimby and Theo echoed her sentiments. "It's got a *ton* of potential," Theo said. "With the right touch, it could be fabulous. I just don't know if you have the right touch," he added skeptically.

But I didn't care. Even though I hadn't done anything to earn it, being a homeowner gave me a real sense of accomplishment. Finally, here was something that was all mine, that I could be proud of. And for the first time, I was actually looking forward to being financially responsible. Not that I had a mortgage to pay, or anything quite so scary, but there were still going to be plenty of bills and taxes, and that would be enough to start. Dr. Shloff thought the house would help give me some confidence in my ability to take care of myself, and I hoped she was right. Bruce had always taken care of all that sort of stuff before, so it was all going to be new for me. New and exciting.

"Well, I can assure you I do have the right touch," I informed Theo. "I have great plans for the place. The first thing I'm going to do as soon as I save up a few bucks is redo the floors and get rid of the wallpaper." Refreshing the basics always goes a long way toward creating a more inviting living space (*Better Homes and Gardens,* October: "From Chintz to Prints: A Decorating Primer").

Theo raised an eyebrow. "Yes," he said, motioning grandly to the living room walls. "This fruit motif has got to go."

"Is there any more wine?" Nicole asked. She was always bored unless the conversation revolved around her or, failing that, someone else's misery.

"I'd also recommend sanding the paint off the doors and mantles and restoring it all back to the original wood, if it's not too badly damaged," Billy said, picking at a door frame. "You know, it's the details that really make these old places come to life. Then maybe I'd put in some sconces, here and here, and possibly even an antique bannister…"

"*This* is the man who finally melted the Ice Queen's heart?" Theo shrieked. "But he's one of us!"

"He's an architect, you idiot," Kimby said. "Not a fag!"

Morgan laughed. "Poor Theo, foiled again."

"Wench," he spat.

"I've been thinking about maybe turning it into a B and B once it's all done," I said. "Wouldn't that be fantastic? Can't you totally see me doing that?" Urban pieds-à-terre can be a very profitable and rewarding business, provided they're run properly (*Martha Stewart Living,* September: "The New Cottage Industry: Do You Have What It Takes To Run an Inn?").

"An old spinster, renting out rooms in her boardinghouse. It's perfect for you," Theo said.

"I'm sure people would love to stay here. It's a really great neighborhood," Annie said. "How can you not adore Carroll Gardens? Ever since *Moonstruck* with Cher." She belted out a few verses of "That's Amore."

"It is pretty amazing," I told them. "Except that there's an Italian bakery on virtually every corner. And the takeout is sick. It's hard not to lose control completely around here."

"Why bother?" Nicole said. "Just enjoy it."

Theo snorted. "Easy for you to say, you're obviously off the wagon."

"Shut up," Annie said. "Don't listen to him, Nic, he's just being a jerk."

"Why is he always with us?" Nicole asked Kimby. "Can't you ever just leave him at home?"

"I probably should," she said. "But he has separation anxiety and eats my slippers."

"Watch it, or I'll piss on the couch," he said. "And as for you, Nicole, you're the one we should be leaving behind."

"Shut up, Theo! Or else!" Nicole warned.

"Or else what? You'll bop me on the head with one of those Twinkies in your purse?"

Morgan laughed. This was by far the most fun she'd ever had with my friends. No doubt about it—I was a fabulous hostess. All these years and I'd never even known it. What a shame. From now on, I vowed to have legendary dinner parties on a regular basis.

"I'm having a Halloween party," I announced. "The First Annual Evelyn Mays Costume Ball."

"I'll only come if Theo isn't invited," Nicole said.

"And I won't come unless Morgan does," Theo added.

"Neither will I," said Billy.

Morgan shook her head in disbelief. "What a bunch of idiots."

"It'll be great," I said. "But I won't let you in if you're not dressed up. And the costumes have to be good. No sheets with eyeholes cut out or anything like that."

"Are there going to be more people than tonight?" Theo asked, looking around.

"Invite whoever you want. But make sure they wear costumes."

"We should all wear our bridesmaid dresses," Kimby said. "And put fake blood on them and stuff."

"Oh! And Evie should wear her wedding gown!" someone added.

"Yes," I said. "What fun that would be. And if any of you actually show up here in those dresses, I can assure you there will be real blood on them instead of just ketchup…."

"Evie!" Annie said nervously. "Why don't you tell us about your new job?" Always the peacemaker. The girl really knew how to bring down a room.

"Oh, it sucks." It only took me about forty-five minutes to discover that writing dreary blurbs about printer ink and producing a lame company newsletter known as "Bits and Bytes" would be a grave misuse of my talents.

"I'm sure it does," Theo said. "Catalogue work is tantamount to professional suicide."

"Well, I'm keeping my eye out for other prospects." I did have applications pending at several of the larger publishing companies and television studios, but none had called. Until they did, I would have to make the most of being an In-House Director of Marketing and Communications. For now, I was in no position to be picky—a paycheck was a paycheck. Maybe Mom would dump Albert, and then, if I found something better, I could dump the job without having to hear about it for the next three decades.

"Oh, you'll find something," Kimby said.

Nicole, bored again, went into the kitchen to get more dip.

"She's so moody," Theo complained. "I don't get it."

"Maybe it's because we're all incredibly self-absorbed and nobody ever asks her what's going on in her life. We just sit around and make fun of her instead," I suggested.

"That could be it," Theo concurred. "I do enjoy the sound of my own voice."

"We all do. Sometimes too much, I think," I said.

When she came back, I asked her about her thesis. Her face lit up.

"Well, it's *finally* finished, but the hard part's coming up in November when I have to defend it."

"Well, then, I think that deserves a toast," I said. "To Nicole and the Guyanese lesbian freedom fighters! May they be successfully defended!"

"I'll drink to that," she giggled, and everyone clinked paper cups.

I had no alternative but to admit to myself once and for all that Bruce was uninterested in resuming our relationship. It wouldn't have been my choice for the perfect happy ending, but it was an ending nonetheless, and I knew that making peace with it and accepting it was the only way I'd ever be able to get on with my life. He did call to wish me a happy birthday, though. We made pleasantries, caught up a bit on each other's lives, and left it at that. The thrill of speaking to him lasted a day or two, then I returned to the drudgery of my daily existence, which alternated between scrubbing tile grout with a toothbrush and proofreading coupons for pricing errors. Still, for the first time in as long as I could remember, I was content and—dare I say it?—almost happy.

And then, about a month later, he called again.

"I realized that I never took you out to celebrate your new job," he said.

"Or my birthday, or my new house," I pointed out.

"So, you busy tomorrow night?"

"Saturday? Nope. I was just going to sit around and clean out one of Grandpa's scary closets. You wouldn't believe the stuff I've found around here. There was a pile of newspapers from 1973, and Dodgers tickets for a 1955 World Series game at Ebbets Field just sitting in a desk drawer."

"The Brooklyn Dodgers? My God! That was the year they won the pennant! You could probably get a fortune for those on e-Bay!"

"I threw them out. I didn't know."

"*What?* Evie—you have to be careful about stuff like that. Forget dinner. We'll order in and I'll help you clean out the closets. Finders keepers, right?"

"I could cook, if you want. I think I've been getting better, and I might even take a class with Annie, since we're both totally hopeless in the kitchen."

"Uh, let's order in for now."

"Okay."

"See you at around seven?"

"Great."

I struggled to get the house perfect, which was hard since I'd only been living there for a couple of months, and it still smelled a bit musty. Drinking wine out of paper cups with my friends was one thing, but I wanted Bruce to be impressed. I sprayed lots of perfume, and turned off most of the lights except for a few lamps in the living room which made the shabby wallpaper seem warm and inviting.

When Bruce showed up, he handed me a bottle of red and a bag with a bow. Inside, there was some sort of scary doll.

"It's a birthday-housewarming gift."

"Er…what is it?"

"It's a kitchen witch. It's supposed to bring you luck in the kitchen. You'll need it."

"Thanks, Bruce. That's incredibly…sweet of you. I think."

"So, do I get the grand tour?"

I led him through the house. Downstairs, there's a big kitchen, a living room with a fireplace, a dining room, a bathroom and a tiny bedroom off the kitchen.

Bruce liked the little room. "Wow. This is the smallest bedroom I've ever seen. Are you sure it's not a closet?"

"Mom said it was designed to be a maid's room. All these old places have them. She remembers an elderly aunt or someone living in it for a while when she was a kid."

"Creepy. They probably buried her in the garden. So what are you going to do with it?" he asked.

"What am I going to do with any of these rooms? I have no idea. But wait till you see the master bedroom—it's got a real fireplace. Maybe you can show me how to work it. And there's two other bedrooms on the second floor but I'm going to make one into a den."

"I haven't even been here for half an hour and already you're trying to lure me into your boudoir? Have you no shame?"

"You'll find out soon enough," I said, playing along as I led him down the hallway. "But let's have a glass of wine first. Shall we adjourn to the parlor, monsieur?"

"That would be lovely," he said, and made a big show of flicking some crumbs off the couch.

"That's an antique," I told him. "Don't break it."

"Ah, yes. I can see that. A vintage 1980s reproduction of a 1950s copy of a mid-eighteenth-century Chippendale, if I'm not mistaken. Magnificent craftsmanship. Is that the original plastic covering?"

"Give me a break. I'm just glad this place came with furniture, or else we'd be sitting on the floor right now. Until I put a bit of money aside, everything's staying as is. The only thing I bought was a new mattress. The thought of sleeping on Grandpa's old one…yuk."

"I can understand that."

I brought out some wineglasses and put them down on the coffee table. "If I'm going to seduce you, it'll be a lot easier if you're drunk, so please go ahead."

"A toast, first, if you don't mind." He raised his glass. "To the *New* New-and-Improved Evelyn Mays. May you have health, wealth, happiness—and the time to enjoy them all."

"Thanks, Bruce. That's very sweet," I said. "Bottoms up." We both took a good, long drink. There was still some tension between us. I couldn't tell if it was good, bad or sexual, but it was definitely there. It made me realize that we probably never could be friends, and I wondered why he was even here. Seeing each other from time to time wasn't going to do either of us any good.

After dinner, we went out to explore the neighborhood. It was a relief to get out of the house.

We walked a long way in silence, kicking through the fallen leaves, and gazing into store windows and up at the immaculate Victorian brownstones in the nearby historic district. Something about the air reminded me of last year, when Bruce proposed.

"We've come a long way, baby," he said finally, as if he were thinking the exact same thing. "Feels a bit weird, doesn't it? Being together?"

"It feels different," I said simply. "Things have changed." This was my grand finale, and I knew it. We either went forward from here, or we called it quits for good. But there was definitely no point in beating around the bush anymore. I knew Bruce. Flirtatious banter aside, he wasn't into games. And since I was playing to win, not playing games was the biggest trick I could muster. "Say something, will you?"

He stopped in front of a bench and sat down. I sat next to him. We watched the people walking by for a bit. Then he said, "There are days when I'm happy, there are days when I miss you, and then there are the days when I'm still mad as hell."

"That's okay," I told him.

"I know it's okay, but I can't get past it."

"Do you want to?" I asked hesitantly.

He thought for a minute. "I'm not sure. But maybe I should be walking through the doors that are open, not banging on the ones that are closed."

What did he mean? "My door's always open," I said, and hoped it made sense. I still loved him. No matter what had happened—or what was to come—I knew that intentionally cutting Bruce out of my life would never be an option. I'd have to leave that up to him.

He took off his glasses and looked at me.

"I can't help myself, but for some reason I only want good things for you. What…what I'm trying to say, I guess, is that no matter where life takes us, I sincerely hope that you can forgive yourself."

After all I'd put him through, how could he still be so good to me?

"I'm getting there," I told him. "Or I'm trying, at least. I don't think I hate myself anymore, but I'll always hate what I did. To both of us."

He nodded.

"What about you?" I asked tentatively. "Do you think you would ever be able to forgive me?"

"Forgive, maybe. But not forget."

My heart thumped wildly, and my eyes burned with tears. "I can live with that."

Bruce stood up and walked over to a big tree a few feet away. There was a paper stapled to it advertising a nearby apartment for rent. He pulled it off. "How do I know you're serious? That you won't pull an Evie again."

"Pull an Evie?"

"Losing it whenever you get exactly what you think you want."

I knew I had to answer very carefully. "I only lost it when I got what I *didn't* want. So I guess the key is knowing my own mind."

"That's a start, I suppose. Do you know what you want now?"

"I think so," I said. "I don't want to get married anytime soon, that's for sure."

"I think we've already established that," he said with a smile. "What else?"

"Well, I don't want to be skinny anymore."

"Ha! Do you actually expect me to believe that? It's me, here. Remember who you're talking to."

"It's *true.* I'd be happy to stay the way I am. I don't want to lose any weight."

He laughed, and so did I—that sounded so ridiculous, coming out of my mouth.

"Okay," I sighed. "So maybe a pound or two wouldn't hurt..."

"There you go!"

"What? I can admit it. At least I know now that my problem area isn't really my thighs—it's in between my ears. That's a big thing for me!"

"Evie, I've been telling you that for years."

"Yeah, but Dr. Shloff got me to believe it. I never trusted you on this, Bruce—you had ulterior motives."

"Like what?"

"For starters, you can admit that you have a thing for fat chicks."

"So sue me—I like having something to hold on to." He sat back down beside me. "Seriously, though. How do I know you're not going to go nuts every time something changes?"

"Well, this last year was the only time, really..."

"No, it wasn't. Even the littlest things can turn you into a complete freak."

"That's ridiculous," I said.

"Remember after college when you were temping at that PR firm?"

"My first real job," I sighed.

"Well, all you wanted was to go on that cruise, remember?"

"I finally had a bit of cash. I thought it would be a fun trip for us."

"Well, I didn't want to go. I knew you wouldn't like it. But you wouldn't shut up about it. And what happened when we finally went?"

"Is it my fault I'm prone to seasickness? I had no way of knowing…."

"You puked the entire time. Even when the boat was in port. And you cried every day."

"How could you *not* have felt it? God! It was like the Cyclone at Coney Island, only you couldn't get off for seven days. Who could think that was fun?"

"Classic," he sighed, and kissed me on the forehead.

"Look, I guess I can't promise that I won't ever freak out over anything ever again. I am who I am. But at least I'm trying now."

"I suppose…"

"Oh, come on—you love every minute of it," I said. "You can't get enough of the crap I put myself through."

"You mean the crap you put us *both* through. I haven't had a good night's sleep since that whole Buddhism thing last year. Those statues, my God. Just last week I dreamed that my mother had ten arms and a bun."

"You're Dr. Shloff's wet dream, you know. Do you want me to see if I can get you an appointment?"

"That's not funny. And if you don't need that altar stuff anymore, I'm throwing it out. It's taking up too much space in the storage room."

"I was at a spiritual crossroads in my life," I laughed, and slipped my arm through his. "How can you fault me for that?" In my defense, Buddhism was pretty big at the time (*In Style,* April: "Can Hollywood Really Free Tibet?").

"And what about the tattoo?" he laughed, shaking his head as if he still couldn't believe it. "You were so afraid of the pain, and you agonized for months over what you wanted and where to put it, and then when you finally decided to go through with it, you regretted it instantly."

I smacked him playfully on the arm. "Jerk!"

What else could I say? I did have half a yin-yang on my ass.

Engaging Men
Lynda Curnyn

RED
DRESS
INK
TM